Evil Blooms

M. K. Sherlock

Cover Art by Dana E. Coplin

www.danaecoplin@yahoo.com

DEDICATION

To the people who have always been there and I love:
    Valton
    Travis
    Elizabeth
    Ray
    Cheryl
    Dana

My siblings whom are all very special to me:
    Doris (a wonderful critic)
    Larry (A Coast Guard career man)
        Spouse, Nickie (one-armed bandits stand up and sing for
her)
    Benjamin (an ultimate caregiver)
    Martha (my avid believer)
        Spouse, Bill (a man of God)
    Homer (young of heart)
    Phyllis (ultimate sense of humor)
    Richard (forever in our hearts)

Special thanks to Janice Ernest, a friend and fellow author, whose unwaivering faith in my work brought this novel to fruition.

EVIL BLOOMS

CHAPTER 1

Year: 1402

Laughing Doe slipped from the doorway of the crude hut and held the flap in place to conceal the interior from prying eyes. Few actions went unnoticed in the small village, and her show at secrecy turned several heads. Smiling inwardly, she stood motionless to allow her neighbors to stew in curiosity. Her rapidly beating heart threatened at any moment to burst from sheer exhilaration. No longer able to contain her excitement, she pivoted, and with an exaggerated flourish, swept aside the flap. Wind Who Warms stepped into the opening. Swathed in heavy furs and somewhat bowed by their weight, she staggered through the low doorway.

Spirited cries erupted from the onlookers.

Laughing Doe beamed. Sucking in a deep breath, she raised her head, squared her shoulders, and with her back arrow-straight, escorted Wind Who Warms into the heart of the village. The approaching figures were greeted with an ever-growing chorus of enthusiastic shouts and ear-piercing whoops. Dogs barked. Heads appeared from doorways. Clay cooking pots were jerked from fires, sopping laundry tossed on drying rocks and infants pressed into the arms of men or older siblings as women rushed to fall in step with the mother and daughter. Laughter and good-natured bantering filled the air.

"Ah, Wind Who Warms, so you finally bleed—"

"Soon you will warm Standing Bear's bed—"

"You are lucky, little one. Such a hunter—"

"And such a warrior—"

Wind Who Warms found the cumbersome furs stifling in the late afternoon heat. Stinging rivulets of sweat streamed down her back and damp hair clung to her neck and forehead. She gasped mouthfuls of heavy air. Despite the discomfort, she was elated to at last wear the ceremonial robes that declared her passage into womanhood.

A chill snaked up her spine as the bantering group neared the

Hut of Women. She would soon endure the Chosen One's ritual of purity. The sight of the ancient medicine woman emerging from the hut brought her to a dead stop. The Chosen One, ancient beyond imagination and steeped in an aura of mystery would decide Wind Who Warms's fate in the next few minutes. If found impure, she would not be allowed to marry Standing Bear and would be delegated for the rest of her life to the lowliest work in the village.

The old woman beckoned her inside with a flick of a bony finger.

Her legs too shaky and weak for support, Wind Who Warms relied on her mother to all but carry her into the hut. The women, now silent, filed in behind and crowded about the walls.

Directed by the Chosen One, Wind Who Warms disrobed and stretched out on a fur blanket positioned in the center of the hut.

The old woman unfolded a soft leather bundle revealing a highly polished strip of wood that had been tapered to a keen point. She picked it up and held it high for all to see. With little fanfare, she knelt and spread Wind Who Warms's legs. The tool arced downward, and as the sharp point pierced Wind Who Warms's womanhood, she swallowed a scream against the fiery pain. Hot blood gushed from her.

Silence hung in the stuffy room for what seemed an eternity, and then the Chosen One grinned and nodded her approval.

Sounds of laughter and jubilation spilled from the hut and alerted the men of good news. With a joyous, gratifying laugh, Wind Who Warms laid aside her pain and joined in the jubilation.

Caught up in a high-spirited air of merriment, the tittering women exited the hut to begin preparations for the young virgin's forthcoming marriage to Standing Bear.

On day five, Wind Who Warms, clothed in velvety soft suede, her olive skin aglow with perfumed oils and raven hair entwined with a myriad of wild flowers, stepped gracefully from the Hut of Women. Her beauty, enhanced by an aura of innocence, stole the breath from more than one man who looked upon her. A number of young warriors turned envious eyes on Standing Bear. Several chuckled at the sight of him. With his mouth agape, he stood lost in a moment of undisguised yearning, his hands positioned to cover the result of his lust.

"Ayee, a snake," a prankster shouted. "A big snake in Standing Bear's loin cloth."

A chorus of boisterous laughter and good-natured backslapping initiated the wedding celebration.

Bare weeks passed before the Spirit of Life smiled on the young couple, and in Wind Who Warms's belly a child began its journey toward life. Wind Who Warms was yet to realize that thirteen was a young age to lay aside one's childhood.

Standing Bear sat cross-legged before his fire with his back bowed as if the weight of the world lay on his shoulders. Turbulent wind screeched and howled in fury at its inability to penetrate the thick hides protecting the crude dwelling. Sleet and snow battered the hut like feral beasts intent on gaining entry. He tightened his robe, and stoked the fiery coals to coax a bit of additional heat.

For two days and two nights Wind Who Warms had been in labor with their firstborn. As hard as he tried, the faces of four squaws who had died during childbirth could not be forced from his mind. A picture of his wife's pale corpse stretched out on a burial shroud flickered through his head. The image was more painful than an enemy-driven spear to his heart. A single unmanly tear spilled down his right cheek. He could not remember a time when he did not love her.

Anemic light crowning the horizon, the Chosen One left the Hut of Women and summoned the tribe to assemble. In frigid gray dawn, people bundled in thick furs spilled from the warmth of huts and formed a tight circle around her. Bone-weary, Standing Bear stood frozen under her piercing gaze. Fear roiled his belly like a tangle of poisonous vipers.

And then a miracle happened. The old medicine woman smiled cutting a swath through the mass of wrinkles that made up her face and exposing a few jagged teeth. Standing Bear realized that today her words would hold no sorrow.

"It is a man-child," she said. "Robust and strong." She reached out and grasped Standing Bear's shoulders with surprising strength. "Wind Who Warms lives. You are blessed, my son."

The people cheered. Rejoiced. Sounds of celebration and laughter reverberated through the forest setting wildlife on the alert.

Standing Bear returned to his hut. Within minutes Wind Who Warms stepped through the doorway, a bundle pressed to her breasts. His heart grew heavy at the sight of her ashen skin and pinched features. Unsteady on her feet, she placed the bundle in his arms. "Your firstborn son."

He smiled. "You have done well."

As she collapsed to her sleeping blanket, he unfolded the layers of fur. He sucked in deep at the sight of his son. "Your name is Running Wolf," he whispered. He then hefted the infant high above his head. "Running Wolf, look upon your mother who gave you life."

Wind Who Warms smiled with pleasure.

"I'm sorry, I must take him to the Counsel Hut for the ritual of induction into the tribe. I will send your mother to care for you until I return."

"No, please, I only want to sleep. Now go."

With a nod, he turned and left the hut.

A chilling wind swept into the hut, dancing embers about the small room before Standing Bear dropped the flap over the doorway. She sat up and tightened a fur robe about her shoulders. She cradled her milk-heavy breasts and rocked in misery. Her throbbing body cried for relief. She fingered a pouch of herbs the old medicine woman had given her.

When you are ready for sleep, boil a pinch in water, she had told her. *The medicine will help you rest. A pinch only, too much would be dangerous.*

Wind Who Warms filled a stone bowl with water, placed it on the fire and added a single pinch of herbs. Mere flecks floated about. She added more of the crushed leaves. Still the amount looked sparse. She turned up the pouch and shook the entire contents into the bowl. A heavy layer of herbs floated on the surface.

"Too much," She murmured. "A swallow now, the rest for later."

As soon as the brew bubbled, she removed it from the fire and set it aside. Her eyes locked on the potion, willing it to cool. Unable to endure another minute of agony she gulped a mouthful and grimaced at the bitter taste as it burned its way down her throat.

She laid back and waited for the potion to perform its magic. A jolt of abdominal pain forced her upright. Down went another large gulp of the potion. A scathing wave of pain coiled her into a tight ball. "Holy One, please make it go away." Dismissing the old woman's warning—*too much would be dangerous*—she turned up the bowl and swallowed the remaining content.

Numbness crawled down her throat and through her body. Her head lolled and the room spun. She floated in a dense gray fog, adrift and weightless as a leaf on a gentle breeze. A patchwork of shimmery particles appeared in the mist and began to crystallize. A man materialized before her. His shrewd black eyes studied her intently.

"You know me, Wind Who Warms?"

"No."

"I attempted to visit you. More than once I tried. Your pain drove me away."

Yes, she did recall the man's strange face hovering above her during labor. And those piercing eyes—how could she ever forget them.

"I am the Spirit of Truth, and this time, I will not be driven away."

The spirit took her back to the time when Running Wolf entered her body to begin his journey toward life. The presence caused her to see herself gagging and vomiting. The sounds of retching continued long after her stomach was empty. The air reeked.

"Your child poisoned you."

She was conveyed forward in time to look upon her puffy face and greasy lifeless hair. Angry lesions marked her distended belly.

"He made you ugly."

She saw Standing Bear sleeping soundly as she tossed and turned or paced about the small room.

"Your son robbed you of sleep, took you from your husband's bed."

The presence showed Standing Bear taking meals at his parent's hearth while she lay too ill to prepare his food. She burned with shame.

She found herself in the men's Council Hut. Horrified to have invaded the forbidden quarters, she attempted to explain, but no one responded. No one could see or hear her.

"You have embarrassed and dishonored your husband," the spirit said. "Listen and you will know."

Standing Bear spoke of her weaknesses. Young and old alike laughed and murmured in agreement. No one supported her. Not her father. Not her brothers. The humiliation was unbearable.

"Please take me from here."

"The women are talking of you also."

It was true. Now in the Hut of Women she could hear their voices. "Wind Who Warms turns her back on her duties," the Chosen One was saying. "Standing Bear has been neglected far too long. I say it's time for a second mate." With a cackle, she nodded at Moon who stood to her right. "How about you, my pretty one? Share a fine brave's bed?"

A chorus of laughter cut into Wind Who Warms's heart like a sharp knife.

Her mother spit out, "She did give him a strong son."

"Strong? For how long?" the Chosen One retorted. "What makes you think that lazy girl will be any more attentive to her child than to her husband? She's weak, too weak to bear more children. Standing Bear deserves better. A second mate. No more words, I have spoken."

Standing Bear returned to the hut to find his wife staring into the fire. He placed Running Wolf into her arms. "He is hungry."

Almost as if guided by unseen hands, she bared a breast, and the infant began to suckle.

Content with the world, Standing Bear sank to his sleeping fur, laid back and sighed. He descended into a state bordering on unconsciousness.

The sun appeared as no more than a pale haze against the leaden winter sky. Frigid air, refusing to be ignored, coaxed Standing Bear—layer by layer—from deep sleep. He sat up sluggishly, and stared in confusion at the lifeless coals in the fire hole.

As the last fragments of sleep faded, uneasiness descended on him. The uneasiness expanded to fear as a quick search determined neither his wife nor son were in the village.

Skilled hunters gathered and spread out beyond the village where they soon spotted Wind Who Warms's trail. Confident of an easy sighting, they forged ahead. Their confidence began to diminish as they traveled for miles without catching up to a mere squaw.

Sitting huddled before a campfire, his fur robe pulled tight against the cold, Standing Bear relived the past five days of the grueling trek. The food and water supplies had run low. No game had been encountered and dry creek beds were the only evidence the desolate land had ever tasted water. Sharp rocks had inflicted deep cuts on the soles of two of the warriors. Intent on staying up with the group, the two men limped along, pain written across their features.

He was certain that only corpses awaited them. So far they had been lucky. No one had been seriously injured. Foolish to chance sacrificing lives for a lost cause. The women, children and old ones in the village needed every able-bodied warrior to replenish meat and provide protection against enemies.

His companions balked when he ordered them to return to the village while adequate supplies remained to carry them home. Even their most persuasive arguments failed to dissuade him; he would continue the search alone.

At dawn, the warriors began the long trek home while Standing Bear walked deeper into the desolate wilderness. He picked up Wind Who Warms's trail, and continued on what felt like an endless and fruitless mission. Within an hour's time, he detected a faint stench of decay on the breeze. The heavy sweetness told him the carcass was some days old, and therefore, could not be the remains of his family. Accustomed to death and nature's efficient means of disposal, he gave the unpleasant odor little attention. The stench gradually intensified, blanketing him like a dense cloud. He covered his face, leaving only his eyes exposed, but even that failed to lessen the foulness that had settled in his nostrils, wormed its way down his throat and seeped into his pores. The odor brought to mind disemboweled buffalo carcasses left to putrefy under a fiery sun. He lost his meager breakfast. He rinsed his mouth, but even the water had been tainted by the unclean air.

TURN BACK, an inner voice insisted.

His need to find his wife and child, alive or dead, refused to let him entertain the thought for more than a second or two. Swallowing against waves of nausea and his vision blurred by a constant stream of tears, he trudged on.

In the distance he detected splashes of green and red. As he neared, the colors began to take form and soon emerged as lush bushes with spectacular bloodred blooms.

Impossible, he told himself.

Without the warmth of the sun and water, nothing could grow.

But they were here, and thriving in this frigid and arid climate.

He brought one of the breathtaking blooms to his nose and immediately reeled away, gagging. His stomach lurched.

"Holy Great One."

The stink was worse than a carcass that had ripened for days under a hot sun.

His nose pinched and mouth covered, he followed his wife's trail into the greenery. The scene he stumbled upon failed to register for several seconds. On her knees, Wind Who Warms gazed at a blossom cupped in her hands. Before her lay the marble-white corpse of Running Wolf, his throat slashed. A stone knife, dark with blood, lay near.

Standing Bear dropped to his knees and gently drew his son to his chest. Back and forth he rocked as if comforting the lifeless body. A knot of anguish formed in his stomach, spiraled into his heart and spread to his lungs. The aching pressure escaped his lungs in a loud wail that reverberated for miles.

He spread his robe and placed the tiny corpse on its downy softness. After a reverent kiss on the forehead, he turned his attention to Wind Who Warms. She succumbed docilely to the poking and prodding of a close examination. He found deep abrasions and extensive bruises, but nothing life-threatening.

He lifted her chin with a gentle finger. "Why? Why did you do this unspeakable thing?"

He may as well have addressed the wind, she stared straight through him without so much as a blink.

He jerked her to her feet and slapped her. Her head jerked backwards, and she would have fallen if not for his firm hold on her arm. A pulsing red handprint bloomed on her left cheek. Her lids fluttered and recognition settled in her eyes. She smiled serenely. "See the flowers, my husband. Beautiful . . . and smell so wonderful."

"You slaughtered our son, and you talk of flowers. What is wrong with you?" He shook her violently.

"Stop it," she said, wrenching free.

"Answer me."

"I will tell you why. The child was evil."

His mouth dropped. "Evil?"

Chin jutted and shoulders squared, she placed her hands on her hips. "The Spirit of Truth showed me the boy's vileness, and led me to this place. I did what I must." She swept her arms. "What better than the blood of an evil child to give these wonderful flowers life?"

Blood? Red flowers? Blood? Where had he heard this before?

As if once again a child perched on his grandfather's knee listening to the old man's spellbinding narration, a story unfolded in his mind. Everything fell into place. He understood why the flowers carried such a stench for him and not his wife. He understood why his son had been slaughtered. They were not alone in this wretched field. They were in the company of the Evil One, the ruler of the nether world and collector of souls.

Since the Great One breathed life into humans, this unclean spirit has walked the earth in search of victims, seeking the afflicted, the weak of mind or body and the amoral. Weakened by her difficult pregnancy, Wind Who Warms had been easy prey for this deceiver of man.

As his grandfather had told it, the beautiful flowers were one of the Evil One's most formidable weapons. When nourished by human blood, diabolical plants sprang to life. The blooms' potent scent repelled the just and drew the weak into the demon's clutches.

Erupting with purpose, he wrenched the plant nearest him from the soil, tossed it aside and reached for another.

Wind Who Warms's features drew into an ugly grimace. When a second plant was twisted from the earth, her face darkened with rage. Foamy spittle oozed from the corners of her mouth and her eyes bulged with unadulterated hate. Her fingers coiled into menacing talons as she advanced on her husband.

"Noooooo!"

Sharp nails cut deep swaths down his face as her teeth sank into his arm gnawing at his flesh like a wild animal.

His elbow slammed into her face, shattering bone and driving splinters into her brain. In the frenzy of a man gone mad, he continued tearing at the plants. When the last one had been unearthed, he bundled Wind Who Warms and his son in his fur robe and secured it with strips of rawhide. Their remains must be taken to the cave of the dead where their spirits will walk with the ancestors.

He gathered red seeds scattered about the corpses of the bushes and placed them in his empty water pouch. When satisfied that not one seed had been missed, he mulled on how to destroy them. No kindling or sticks lay about to spark a fire for burning. Pounding a seed again and again with a large stone failed to damage it.

Take them back to the village, played through his head. *Many fires there . . . one at every hearth. Your only choice.*

His neck hair stiffened, and he threw the bulging pouch to the ground. The Evil One had touched his mind, attempted to trick him.

He buried the pouch deep beneath a large boulder and covered the site with heavy rocks.

With the bundle containing his family's remains over his shoulder, he began the long journey home.

CHAPTER 2

Time: Present Day

In the pleasant glow of early morning light, John Wilkerson stepped off the porch and headed at a brisk pace toward the barn. He massaged his uncomfortably full belly. A deep belch provided relief from his overindulgence at breakfast.

A lifetime of exposure to the elements had given his face the look of creased leather. Age spots competed for space on his craggy features. His stooped posture brought to mind the gangly oaks that dotted the large farm. Like the trees, John had spent his entire life eking his sustenance from the land.

At the sound of John's footsteps, Ditcher raised his head and brought his ears to attention. His tail thumped a spirited beat on the ground. He stretched—his haunches in the air and enormous chest lingering inches from the ground. A wide yawn exposed a mouthful of sharp canines. He bounded off to meet his master.

John saw the dog racing toward him, and braced for the impact of the large animal's ritual greeting. He struggled to maintain his balance against paws that slapped down on his shoulders. He attempted to dodge the long supple tongue.

"Okay, okay, I'm glad to see you, too." He shoved the dog to the ground. Ditcher's nose disappeared into the folds of his pocket.

He rumpled the animal's muscular neck. "Didn't think I'd forget you, did you, boy?" he reached into his pocket and pulled out a greasy, balled up paper towel.

Ditcher wiggled as two country-sized pieces of sausage materialized. In one gulp, he bolted down the offered treats and then nosed the paper towel for more.

"Sorry, fella, that's all I brought. Maybe sneak another treat at lunch."

John opened the cumbersome barn door and stepped into the dank interior. He grasped the wheel of an ancient Ford tractor and pulled himself into the seat. A groan spilled from his mouth as his aged joints tweaked him with sharp pain. The outmoded machine was a picture of rust, dents, cracked tires and faded, oil-blackened red paint. Attached to the relic was an antiquated plow.

"Okay, Henry Ford, gonna do some plowing today or be contrary and spend the whole damnable day in the barn?"

He pressed the starter. A weak grind with no promise of potency emitted from the tired motor.

"Damn."

He pumped the accelerator. The engine coughed, sputtered and emitted a rumble. As it caught and roared to life, a bang like the sound of an exploding grenade and a crack like the pop of a bullwhip pierced the air. Rusted remains of the tail pipe expelled a belch of soot and black smoke. Eye-burning vapors plumed through the room. The walls vibrated.

He chuckled. "Ain't gotta trade you in for one of those Deere-boys after all."

Several startled cats jumped from their resting places and made beelines for the door. A few of the more seasoned felines gave this almost daily routine little notice and simply twitched an ear or made it an opportunity to stretch and find a more comfortable position. Drawn by plentiful rodents and snakes, and tantalized by the comfort and safety of the large shelter, feral cats had made a permanent residence of the old barn. The large kindhearted dog had appointed himself master and protector of the continuously exploding population.

John forced the stubborn shift into low. The tractor lurched forward, and he guided it out of the barn and toward a parcel of land bordered by large fertile cotton fields. A glimpse of Myrtie through the kitchen window brought a smile. His mind drifted to their early years of marriage. Warmed by a glow of contentment and pleasant memories, he steered the slow-moving tractor through a lazy path.

Some fifty-odd years ago, John brought his lovely bride home to his parents and the large family farm. In his eyes, seventeen-year-old Myrtie was more beautiful than any actress who ever graced the silver screen. Thick blond hair the texture of corn silk cascaded to a waist so tiny that he could encircle it with his large calloused hands. Her smile, figuratively speaking, could charm birds right out of the trees. Her heavily-lashed eyes, as clear as glass, assumed the hue of anything within a close proximity—the glistening green of emeralds, the deep blue of a bottomless lake or the rich brown of turned soil.

Even to this day, he could never quite figure out why she selected a painfully shy, country-to-the-core boy like himself to marry. And him poor at that. But she no doubt loved him, and took to country life like seed to sod.

There had been one sad spot, a void that darkened the young couple's happiness. Their marriage produced no children, and there had been no money for specialists to determine why. At times Myrtie would shed a tear or two at a glimpse of cavorting youngsters or mothers doting on their young. Unlike him, John recognized that she accepted the hands dealt her by life. She was not one to waste precious time and energy fretting over a situation that could not be altered. Accepting a childless fate, she threw her energies into nurturing unwanted animals—the sick, the injured, the orphaned.

As a child, John's man-sized workload on the isolated farm left little time for socializing and provided few opportunities to develop friendships. He had hungered for companionship and yearned for siblings. Those needs were never fulfilled. He vowed that someday the large farmhouse would ring with the clamor and laughter of his many offspring.

Unlike Myrtie, he was never able to swallow the disappointment of a childless life. Not that he would have traded Myrtie for a whole trainload of kids. But still, resentment against an unfair God had set in too many years ago to count and continued to roil his gut like a festering boil that refused to heal. In their old age, the joys of sons and daughters and grandchildren should have been theirs, but instead, he and Myrtie were quite alone in an overpopulated world with only each other for company.

The slow-moving tractor crept to a stop. John shifted it into neutral, climbed down and lowered the plowshare. He returned to the seat and sat for several minutes musing over his strange attraction to this small tract. Myrtie's words rang through his head: *Something ain't right about that land, John Wilkerson.* Only when dead serious did she address him as John Wilkerson. *Best you leave it be.*

Not that he wasn't tempted to heed her advice; nothing would have pleased him more than returning to the barn to tackle other pressing chores. But his course of activities had been dictated by the land itself, and in his mind, no other options existed.

The parcel was a rock-laden wasteland. Sparse clumps of Johnson grass and a few spiny cacti were the only plant life that managed to gain a foothold in the rocky soil. More than eighty years before, his father designated the area as a dump; the barren piece of land proved ideal for refuse burning and disposal of animal carcasses.

Last winter the land began an unrelenting pull on John. During a death-dealing ice storm he awoke in the dead of night to find himself perched on top of a large boulder centered in the field. His thin nightshirt afforded little protection. Gale-driven sleet battered him, bitter cold invaded his body like a ravenous heat-eating organism. He had never realized how painful the cold could be. Blinded by the blustery assault, he relied on sheer instinct to guide him back to the house.

Dr. Stein made it to the farm in thirty minute's time. Hypothermia put up a vigorous battle for John's life, but proved no match against the old doctor's skills.

Myrtie reacted to the situation like an overprotective mother hen, and instituted a routine that squelched future impromptu wanderings. John could not pee without her there to flush the toilet when he finished. Following six weeks of convalescence, he emerged with only a few scars on the soles of his feet to show for the ordeal.

They breathed sighs of relief as winter released its icy hold. Spring brought sunshine and temperatures in the seventies. Dormant plants and trees awakened from hibernation to welcome the warmth of the sun with bright green shoots. Throughout the countryside, newborn calves, fawns and colts performed spindly-legged celebration-of-life dances. Migratory birds blackened the sky.

The neglected piece of property seemed to gather strength from the new season and began a relentless tug at John. He often found himself wandering about the field or settled on the boulder, still in possession of the tool or item he had been using at the moment he was pulled away.

The words *Alzheimer's* and *tests* crept into Myrtie's vocabulary. He dismissed her worry. Being a simple man, he accepted that something in the land had an ability to touch his mind.

The purpose of land?

Cultivation, of course.

His farmer philosophy drew him to the conclusion that the land desired to be cultivated. Tiring of the periodic interruptions in his spring workload, he decided to test his theory. Brushing aside Myrtie's objections, he cleared brush and rocks from the parcel. Each day he managed to dedicate a small portion of time to this task. As suspected, the land seemed satisfied with the modest amount of attention, and the unpredictable wanderings came to a halt.

He guided the tractor forward and began furrowing the land for seed. Swirling clouds of dust marked his progress.

He watched Ditcher bound from bush to crevice. He shook his head when the dog began a furious dig at the base of the boulder. "Dang it, probably found a rabbit burrow. Be hauling a whole litter of babies home to Myrtie."

"Ditch, get away from there," he hollered.

Ditcher pulled something free from the substantial hole he had made, and then turned and ran.

"Dang dog."

Unable to ignore his complaining bladder, he stopped the tractor and cut the motor. The morning had grown hot and humid. Sweat-soaked clothes clung to his body. He flicked a large red handkerchief from his pocket and wiped stinging sweat from his eyes and forehead. After urinating from the side of the tractor, he reached down and loosened a plastic water bottle strapped under the seat and screwed off the cap.

"Damn it. Empty."

He put it back in place.

His mouth felt drier than Sahara sand. He had never been so thirsty. An image of his dehydrated corpse perched on the seat and clinging to the steering wheel popped into his head. It startled him—bad.

Where the hell did that come from?

Myrtie accused him of being over dramatic, but this was a bit much even for him. Attempting to dispel a woozy sensation, he closed his eyes and rolled his head about. The simple exercise helped. Shading his eyes with his hands, he scanned the area for Ditcher.

"Ditch," he shouted. "Time to go."

He spotted the dog lazing in the shadowy latticework of a large oak tree. He stood and cupped his hands.

"Come on, boy."

The dog did not move.

"What's wrong—" He attempted to shout, but dizziness drove him back to the seat.

The tree's dark shade beckoned.

"That's what I need, out of the sun."

With a tight grip on the steering wheel, he eased to the ground.

Wait a minute, old man. What the dickens do you think you're doing? House ain't no more than ten minutes . . . and all the water you want to drink.

The shade beckoned. He pushed the thought aside and started forward. With each step, the air thickened. On he struggled, one foot and then another. A sharp pain tore at this chest.

Can't breathe.

He sank to his knees.

The world revolved faster and faster. Swirling blackness engulfed him. Images danced through his head.

Apelike people draped in fragments of soiled fur shuffled through his mind. Fleas and other strange insects crawled over the hairy bodies and through matted hair. Inflamed bites covered their filthy skin. The creatures communicated with grunts and hand signals. The marauding beasts slaughtered others of their own kind. Hands dug into chests and tore out hearts. Drooling mouths filled with sharp teeth ripped bloody chunks from the still pulsing organs. Women shrieked as sharp stones sliced their bellies and fetuses were torn from gaping wombs.

Blood. The land ran crimson. Bright red flowers were everywhere.

He found himself in a wasteland. A person draped in heavy fur and clutching a bundle wandered into his vision. The figure turned and a young pretty face came into view. Wind danced wisps of shiny black hair about the captivating face. The woman's fingers worked at the bundle, unfolding layers of fur. An infant boy, the withered umbilical cord still attached, lay in the nest of warm fur. The woman grasped the tiny ankles and suspended the baby over her head. A lusty wail spilled from the child's mouth. A knife fashioned from stone appeared in the woman's other hand. With a callous smile, she stared into John's eyes. The sharp blade sliced delicate flesh. Flowers appeared—everywhere, red flowers.

He was then gazing at a brick wall of an old building. Unkempt men, women and children, trembling in fear, huddled against the brick. Large pleading eyes stared from sunken hollows in ashen faces. Skeletal rib cages extruded above concave stomachs. Bony knots protruded from joints. A yellow star was visible on each tattered garment.

Rat-a-tat-tat sounded, and grotesque wounds ruptured the emaciated bodies. People dropped to the ground like nimble rag dolls. The machine gun clatter stopped, and screams replaced the din of exploding bullets. Unmindful of growing pools of blood, men wearing black arm bands decorated with swastikas walked among the dead and wounded. They aimed pistols at heads, and one after another the screams stopped.

A small girl racked by sobs clung to the legs of a dead woman.

One of the arm-banded men picked up the child and hugged her close.

"It's okay," he soothed. His face was contorted with loathing, eyes narrowed with hate. Sadistic laughter spilled from his companions.

The child's cries waned. Then she was flying. Her head connected with the brick wall. The tiny body dropped to the ground. The misshapen skull trickled blood onto the pavement.

John understood he was looking upon actual atrocities, and was sickened to his very soul. For some unknown reason, the portals of hell had been thrown open for his private viewing.

"I HAVE ALWAYS BEEN! I WILL ALWAYS BE! I AM NOW!" thundered through his head.

The images disappeared. Memories of the experience slipped deep into his subconscious. He was standing under the oak tree with Ditcher at his feet pounding out a welcome with his tail. Dismayed, he glanced about. His last memory was climbing from the tractor. How did he get here? Of course, another episode— not free from his compulsive wanderings after all. Discouraged, he collapsed beside the dog. The stench of decayed flesh and excrement wafted over him. The stink seemed to emanate from an object clutched in Ditcher's jaws.

"Lordy, what you got? Stinks to high heaven. Drop it."

Ditcher's teeth bared and a warning growl rumbled in his throat. On his haunches, he backed away from John's outstretched hand.

"Ditcher."

The dog sprinted away.

"Well, that's another one for the books. Dog ain't never growled at me before. Maybe would have bit me." Shaking his head in disbelief, he followed the animal's retreat with his eyes.

Ditcher stopped and cocked his head as if listening to some distant sound. For a full minute he stood frozen, as if on point. He then turned and headed back toward John. With his tail wagging in high gear, he padded up to him and dropped the object in his lap.

His hand, halfway through the motion of brushing the repugnant thing away, stopped its descent and remained suspended in midair. He leaned close and stared hard at a leather pouch. With the tips of his thumb and forefinger, he picked it up and brought it to his nose. It smelled of turned earth and musty old leather.

"Nope, ain't this that stinks." The repugnant odor had faded. Confused, he leaned over and sniffed Ditcher. The dog snatched a sloppy kiss.

He dodged the wet tongue. "Smell just like dog. Course nothing says a bath ain't overdue."

Peeling layers curled on the leather pouch. "Old." He loosened the strap and turned it up. Dark red orbs spilled into his hand.

"I'll be damned. Never seen nothing like these before. Seeds, maybe? What you think, Ditcher?"

Before the words were out of his mouth, a sharp pain doubled him over. It felt as if his intestines were constricting into a tight ball.

"Lord," he moaned.

The cramp subsided enough for him to sit up. With tremulous hands he worked the seeds back into the pouch, strapped the opening and stuffed it deep in a pocket. On rubbery legs he worked his way back to the tractor. Then home to Myrtie.

Ditcher turned and trotted toward the woods.

CHAPTER 3

Parked on a high bluff east of Caddo, Jeffrey Chambers had a bird's-eye view of the entire community. The shade of an ancient oak did little to dispel the heat accumulating in the dust-covered patrol car. He started the motor and flipped the air conditioner to maximum. Tuning out the irritating static from the police radio, he leaned back and enjoyed the feel of cool air on his clammy skin.

The town, bathed in the hot white light of summer looked like a storybook village come to life. Sunlight danced from one shiny surface to the next, glinting like diamonds on the polished bumpers and windshields of the few cars braving the midday heat.

Jeff loved Caddo, its people and the status afforded by the position of Chief of Police. Through the years, he handpicked the twelve-man, two-woman police force. None of those wet-behind-the-ears-fat-diplomas-tucked-under-their-arms-and-I'm-here-to-save-the-bad-guys-from-themselves types on his police force.

He provided what the people wanted. Almost to a man, the citizenry fostered unshakeable beliefs in victims' rights. Criminals' rights? Well, criminals' rights were all but nonexistent in Caddo country.

He was a born politician with a genuine like for people and felt empathy for even their most negligible problems. Under his watchful eye and guidance, Caddo officers tread lightly with minor infractions of the law; heads were turned to petty traffic violations and slack was cut whenever possible. Jeff's underlings did a pretty fair job of serving as referees in disputes, whether between family members, neighbors or co-workers.

Major offenders of the law found the Caddo police to be brutal in their methods. Through the years, a few drug dealers and junkies attempted to infiltrate the local youth. Strong urgings from officers had these low-lives headed for more favorable settings, comforted that most of their teeth were still intact and four limbs still attached to their bodies. Not that all four limbs had always been in working condition, of course. Trips in backs of squad cars to secluded areas where irrevocable understandings could be reached had proven to be a very successful tactic in the war on drugs.

No fucking argument from me, man. I'm out of here.

Not that the tactic always worked, not in the late Daniel Harrison's case.

At the thought of Harrison, a black cloud of guilt rose in his conscience. "Stupid little bastard, gave me no choice." Something had to be done, and be damned if it plagued him the rest of his life.

On a sunny spring morning a year or so back Daniel Harrison rolled into Caddo in a silver Mercedes convertible, the top down and his dark hair fluttering in the wind. Heads turned and tongues wagged. He zipped into the parking lot of the Smithlake Hotel, and strutted into the lobby like a fantail peacock. Leaving an open departure date on the register, he offhandedly peeled cash from a roll of bills that could have choked a Clydesdale. "Don't believe in credit cards," he alleged to Terrance Clary, owner/operator of the historical establishment.

Daniel Harrison, *Mr. Cool* himself, attired in designer clothes and expensive sunglasses became a familiar sight about Caddo. Evenings he could be spotted at the Little Dipper lounge laughing and talking with a growing number of newfound friends. The heavy drinkers seemed to sense when the young man with bottomless pockets would appear at their favorite watering hole, and flocked in like flies to partake of his generosity. Daniel Harrison was quite a windfall for the alkies.

He was equally generous with the youth of Caddo. Fifteen minutes after school let out, he would show up at Pop's Burger House to mingle with the kids crammed in the place thicker than fleas on a mongrel.

"Hey, fellas, Dan-the-man is here again today."

"I'll have a double banana split and fries. That okay?"

"Me too, Dan?"

"Double cheeseburger and a chocolate malt."

The young man's extravagance with the young people did not impress Pop, not for a minute. Daniel Harrison may have fooled the kids and maybe some of the sots, but not the skeptical old man who had catered to more than four generations of Caddo youth. He damn well recognized a fox in the henhouse when he saw one. Pop needn't have worried. Jeff Chambers was not a man to let someone mess with *his* town or *his* people.

Harrison's rap sheet proved enlightening for Jeff. During his teens, he spent more time in correctional institutions than out. Offenses included auto thefts, possession of illegal drugs and burglary. The real biggie had been an indictment on kidnapping and aggravated sexual assault charges. Days before the trial, the sixteen-year-old victim developed a mysterious case of amnesia. The charges were dropped.

Late one evening Jeff slipped into the back entrance of the Smithlake hotel and up to the third floor. He picked the lock of Harrison's room. He discovered an interesting menagerie of drugs and associated paraphernalia. The supply was too large for personal use. The generous Mr. Harrison had come to Caddo on a recruiting mission. Boozers and kids his targets.

He filled a syringe with clear liquid from a vial, and then settled back and waited.

Harrison came humming his way down the hallway. The song: "When The Saints Come Marching In." Quite appropriate, one could say, for someone about to meet his Maker.

He did not appear surprised when Jeff flashed his badge and identified himself as Chief of Police. His expression read—*been through this before, different town, different police force, but the same old tiresome scenario.* His street savvy failed to alert him to his precarious footing in this particular situation. The fact that he had been drawn into a new and dangerous game sailed right over his head.

His eyes came to rest on the array of drugs laid out on the bed. He assumed a hangdog expression much like a puppy caught piddling on new carpet. "Well, what can I say? Got me dead to rights. If I can have a peek at your search warrant, I'll go ahead and give my attorney a quick call."

"No warrant. Being my town, didn't see a need for one."

Harrison exhaled a sigh. He glowed with exhilaration.

Jeff could read him like a billboard with fluorescent print and pictures to match: Hayseed. No fucking search warrant. Got him by the balls. Yep, that's where you got him, Danny-boy, by the balls. Damn well lucked out on this one.

Harrison grinned. "May as well go ahead and dump this shit down the toilet. Ain't no court in the great state of Texas will accept it as evidence." His head shook in mock disappointment. "Nope, most judges take a pretty dim view of illegal searches. And the Miranda statement? Nary a word has passed your lips about my right to remain silent and all that crap."

Jeff pinned him with a blank stare.

Harrison dropped into a chair, flipped open a gold case, removed a Marlboro and lit it. He sucked deep on the cigarette and then exhaled a slow stream of smoke.

Not a care in the whole stinking world, his relaxed air conveyed.

He nodded at his shoes. "See these babies? Cost more than you make in a week. I like nice things, and goodness knows there are a lot of *nice* things in your little town. Such *pretty* girls. Sure grow 'em good here. Juicy as Georgia peaches. Now, let's see if I'm figuring this right. You're entertaining the idea of me leaving your little burg, ain't you? Before sunup, like in the old westerns? I'm right, ain't I?"

Jeff nodded.

"You can put that thought away. It ain't gonna happen, not anytime soon. Ain't through having my fun yet."

Jeff smirked. "Oh yes, my friend, you *will* leave our little town. That's a given."

Harrison's features twisted into a mask of outrage. "Don't threaten me. I've heard about the methods you hayseeds use, even seen a few of the results. Think you're a real badass, don't you? Well, your beat-'em-up scare tactics ain't gonna work on me. I've got friends. Influential friends. Friends who would cut off your balls and fry them up for breakfast. And they're watching. One scratch, one fucking scratch, and this whole town is in a deep pile of stinking shit."

Jeff chuckled. "Can't count the times I've been up to my neck in shit. Always been able to work my way out of it." His voice hardened. "It'd be better for all concerned if you'd pack up and get on out of here. Don't look back, don't come back. Walk away a free man."

"Without a search warrant you ain't got nothing to hold me on. And like I said, ain't through having my fun yet."

Jeff unsnapped handcuffs from his belt. "Your choice. Can't say I didn't give you a chance. Stand up and turn around."

"Bullshit! Ain't takin' me to no boonies." His hand slid beneath the mattress and came out with a hunting knife, the blade thick and razor sharp.

Jeff rested his hand on the butt of his pistol. "Boy, didn't your mama ever tell you not to bring a knife to a gunfight."

The knife dropped to the bed among the drugs.

Harrison stood and Jeff snapped on the cuffs. In a fluid movement he darted the hypo needle into his prisoner's arm and pressed the plunger.

"You bastard. What the fuck you do to me?"

"Just a dose of your own elixir. Won't hurt you, will it?"

Harrison's knees appeared to give away, and he dropped into a chair.

"Shit, man."

After the young man lost consciousness, Jeff removed the cuffs and laid him on the bed. He maintained a thirty-minute death vigil. The youthful body took on the look of an alabaster statue forever frozen in time.

He slipped down the back stairs and into a cloak of darkness.

The following afternoon a maid on her cleaning rounds discovered the ripening body.

A quote from an article in the Caddo Weekly News:

"Based on the massive amount of drugs found in the dead man's system, accidental overdose was ruled out. The death was ruled suicide by the medical examiner."

Forcing aside the morbid memory, he watched a metallic-green Lincoln Town Car inch its way through the cemetery. It rolled to a stop in the shadow of a massive archangel statue. The imposing angel marked Homer Crowley's final resting place. The squat woman emerging from the car was the wife Homer had left behind at the time of his death some ten years ago.

He chuckled.

Some years back, the Ferrell brothers and some teenage buddies decided time was ripe for a Halloween invasion of the cemetery. The boneyard had not been targeted for more than twenty years. Imbued with courage, tenacity and a profusion of shovels, ropes and tools, the group of six arrived at midnight in a Dodge pickup.

Within two hours, eight headstones teetered in high branches of an ancient oak. Switched headstones assigned different partners to several of the dear departed. Florescent paint depicted new and improved epitaphs on a number of stones, some a little risqué for many people's taste.

How they had managed to transport old man Crowley's archangel statue from the cemetery to the front lawn of the courthouse in downtown Caddo was still a mystery. Even six strapping young men such as themselves should have found it impossible to heft a stone statue weighing better than a thousand pounds into and out of the pickup bed without damaging either.

Mrs. Crowley didn't find any humor in the prank. For several long seconds all she could do was point and sputter. Poor old thing grabbed her chest and turned the shade of an eggplant. Looked to be having one humdinger of a stroke right there on the spot. It didn't take long to uncover the culprits. One boy spilled his guts, and like a row of collapsing dominos, the others fell into place. In addition to divvying up six hundred and fifty dollars remuneration, the teens spent three months of weekends mowing the cemetery grounds and manicuring the graves. A couple of good citizens had the misfortune of dying during that time, and the boys were made to hand-dig the graves. Not one of them demonstrated any further desire for vandalism. They became living legends, though. Every Halloween their story sprang to life, and every year the tale was embellished with bigger and better feats.

Dean Calder's voice blared from the police radio. "Chief, you ready for lunch?"

Jeff picked up the microphone. "Affirmative. Starving to death. Meet you at Pearl's in ten minutes. Out."

Dean had appropriated a booth in front of a large picture window and had iced tea waiting when Jeff arrived. His face crinkled into a welcoming smile.

Jeff slid into the booth and gulped down half the tea. Pearl Turner headed their direction with an icy pitcher of tea to replenish his glass, her order pad tucked under her arm.

Pearl's two hundred and fifty pounds attested to her appreciation of her own cooking. Huge breasts rested on her massive stomach, and her chin was indistinguishable from the rolls on her neck. Despite her excessive weight, she displayed a remarkable ability to move fast and keep food and drink in front of her customers. Her smile was as quick as her witty remarks. Slinging hash or slopping hogs were her standing jokes with regulars. The café's authentic home cooking was legendary within a fifty-mile radius of Caddo. Nothing pleased the woman more than customers who consumed huge quantities of her food.

As Jeff placed a large bite of apple pie into his mouth, Dean leaned forward and whispered in a conspiratorial tone, "Don't look up, it's that Duncan woman. Appears to be headed our way."

Jeff scrunched down in an attempt to make himself less visible.

Naomi Duncan was the self-appointed caretaker of Caddo's moral fiber, and he skirted her complaints whenever possible.

His pie took on a bitter taste at the sound of her high-pitched voice. "Chief, Chief, you've got to do something about the filth that's showing at the Town Theater. Movie's full of naked people and vile language. Why, they're having sex right there on the screen. It's pornography. That Scott Williams is showing pornography, and I demand you arrest him."

Jeff worked to control a grin that tugged at the corners of his mouth. Snickers throughout the café were more than he could handle. He pressed his napkin to his mouth and coughed to cover a chuckle. He looked up with as serious an expression as he could muster. "Now, Naomi, calm down. We've been through this a hundred times before, and you know darn well Scott Williams has every right to show any movie that's not X-rated."

"I don't care how that movie is rated, I know pornography when I see it. Your daddy would turn over in his grave if he knew you were allowing this kind of filth to go on. And your dear mother would be appalled."

"Naomi, regardless of how you think my parents would feel, I can't do anything about Scott Williams and the movies he chooses to show. Now, if you want to take it over my head, the mayor's office is right up the street. Won't cause nary a hard feeling on my part."

"Jeffrey Chambers, I expected you to have high morals like your father, God rest his soul, but you're just like the rest. Turn your back on sin. God will punish. Mark my words, God will punish." Her face dark with anger, she turned and stormed through the crowded tables and out the door.

"Man, I don't envy you when the mayor finds out you sicced that demented woman on him. You'll be punished," Dean snickered. "Mark my words, you'll be punished."

Pearl approached the table and began clearing away dishes. "Crazy woman, only one oar in the water. Sorry I couldn't head her off before she got to you. Can you explain to me why she sits through all those movies if she's so all-fired offended? Talk has it she never misses one."

"I don't understand that either. But you know, sometimes people get so hooked on religion they're blind to everything else. Naomi is a sad case. She's to be pitied. Poor girl, raised on that isolated farm by a fanatical father. It's a wonder she's not worse than she is."

CHAPTER 4

Joyful yelps and animated leaps greeted Naomi Duncan at the front door. The hearty welcome lightened her mood. She reached down and swooped up the ball of black fur. "How's my Angel-wangel? Kissy-kissy for mommy-wommy? I wuvs my girl." Smooching with the dog, she strode across the living room and into the large kitchen. After one last affectionate smack on the nose, she deposited Angel on the floor. "Precious want din-din?"

The poodle wiggled and yapped.

"Sinners," Naomi complained while spooning Mighty Dog into a bowl. "The town is full of sinners and not one soul seems to care."

She placed the bowl on the floor and sank into a chair at the time-scarred oak table. Angel moved about the bowl sniffing at the contents. She began to take delicate bites of the food.

Despite the replay in her head of the humiliating scene at Pearl's Diner, she could not help but smile at her pet's familiar mealtime routine. "We know how to deal with sinners, don't we, sweetie? Those nasty old males came sniffing around my baby. We showed them, didn't we?"

Angel glanced up, writhing with delight.

"When that nasty old thing raped my Angel-wangel, we took care of him, didn't we, sugar? Won't go sniffing around anywhere else."

Naomi's mind drifted to faint memories of the mother who abandoned her when she was four years old. She could remember warm smiles, nursery rhymes and arms that hugged a lot. She pictured a white sun dress with large yellow and orange daisies. Mention of her mother always threw her father into a rage, and the fantasy that someday a pretty lady who smelled good would come to take her away died when she was still very young.

Every night, from her earliest memories, her father read the Bible aloud. Prayer was a never-ending routine. She could remember fighting to stay awake as her father lectured her into the wee hours of the morning. He ranted about classmates who would lead her down Satan's path to the gates of hell. At times he ripped pages from her school books, enraged at the blasphemous teachings he found.

She was never allowed to catch the school bus. Her father delivered her to school, and was always there in his old truck when classes let out. Extracurricular activities were denounced. Birthday parties, dances, football games, slumber parties—were forbidden fruit.

On her twelfth birthday, Sarah Nicholson, a devoted member of Crusaders Evangel Church, showed up at the Duncan home and told Naomi she was there to explain the curse put on women by Eve. Following Mrs. Nicholson's discussion, her father began including lust and sins of the body in his lectures.

At the age of nineteen, she was hired into a clerical position at Schilling Glass Company. As with school, her father deposited her at the front doors at eight o'clock sharp, and at five o'clock he was waiting for her to emerge from the building.

She found herself in a new world. A few men asked her out, attractive men at that, and female co-workers seemed eager to develop friendships. Even though the male attention made her feel awkward and left her with nagging feelings of guilt, she yearned to experience a date—something as simple as a movie or a hamburger at the local malt shop. At the same time, female camaraderie was an unexplored realm for her, and this, too, she found appealing. But she did not have the courage to face down her father, and so all social offers were rejected. Her reputation as a cold fish put an end to social gestures. Her co-workers gave themselves a pat on the back for trying, and then went about their lives without giving uppity Naomi Duncan a second thought. After a year, she quit the job that had been so promising in the beginning.

Then Don Miller entered her life.

On a crisp spring morning when she was twenty years old he showed up at their front door seeking work. The farm was in critical need of another strong back; barn and fence repairs had been neglected for years. The wood supply had dwindled during the harsh winter and acres of fields waited to be plowed and sowed. Tom Duncan was overwhelmed by the workload and hired the young man who agreed to backbreaking labor for room and board and a pittance of wages. Don proved to be in his element with farm work. He tackled any task, regardless of how menial, with enthusiasm. His new employer was impressed.

While under Tom Duncan's watchful eyes, Don showed no more than a passing interest in Naomi. When away from the older man's suspicious scrutiny, he glowed with admiration.

Naomi burned with embarrassment when caught in one of his visual inspections. When he grinned, revealing those perfect white teeth, his eyes sparkling with warmth and merriment, she melted. Often she would bow her head and mumble some excuse to go elsewhere.

"Smile for me, Naomi," he sometimes teased. "You're so pretty when you smile."

By early summer she stopped the excuses, and put herself in his company at any opportunity. She relished the stolen moments, and took pleasure in the fact she had managed to pull the wool over her father's eyes. For once, all-seeing, all-knowing Tom Duncan had been outsmarted. Unfortunately, she had no inkling of the price she would pay for these small victories.

In bed at night, Don's tanned face would flash through her mind. She imagined running her hands through his thick blond hair. She flushed with pleasure at the thought of his sensual lips against hers and her tongue probing, exploring his mouth, maneuvering across his beautiful teeth. Lying there in her little fantasy world, she could taste him. But the thoughts were bad. The warm stirring awakened in her groin by her sexual reveries was lust. Her father had warned her often about this atrocity against God. Lust was the devil's path to the soul. She prayed for the Almighty to remove these sinful thoughts. She prayed long and she prayed hard, but prayer didn't help; the thoughts refused to leave.

Early on a Saturday morning she stood watch until her father's pickup was a small black dot on the horizon. He was to pick up Brother Morgan at the parsonage, and then the two of them were off to Dallas on some kind of church business. The extended trip would keep him away from home until late afternoon.

She turned and walked to the barn. She stepped into the dim interior and searched out the man who was in her every waking thought. Her eyes devoured him. He flashed a knowing smile. Without a word, he took her in his arms and his mouth closed over hers. His probing tongue awakened sensations she never dreamed existed. He picked her up and carried her to the haystack where he laid her in a nest of soft straw. He removed her clothing, one piece at a time. A hot throb built in her groin. Her body tingled with anticipation.

"So beautiful," he moaned, his hands lingering on her bare flesh.

He suckled each breast. As his tongue circled a nipple, fiery sensations rippled through her like static electricity. His tongue continued its exploration, moving between her breasts and making its way to her navel. The instrument of pleasure worked its way to the fire between her legs. Her hips arched and an indescribable pleasure imploded inside her. She emitted a long, loud moan.

She lay there trembling while Don removed his shoes, socks and shirt. In one quick swoop he was free of his jeans and underwear. Work-hardened muscles rippled on his arms. Silky fluffs of golden hair covered his chest. His skin glistened a sun-worshiper's bronze. Her breath quickened.

He lowered himself on top of her, and guided his pulsing manhood between her legs. He applied pressure. A little more. Still more.

It hurt, but she found the pain exquisite. "No, no, it's okay," she told him each time he hesitated. She thrust her hips upward, forcing his manhood deep inside in one quick jab. Tears sprang to her eyes, and she managed to hold back a cry. And then the pain was gone.

Drenched in sweat, they cuddled in the hay. Don pulled her

against his chest and rocked her like a cherished child. "My sweet, sweet baby. My precious Naomi."

Tears of happiness flowed, someone at last loved her.

From that day forward, she would lie in bed at night, her ears tuned for the grating sounds of snores. Her father slept deeply, and even a full bladder rarely pulled him from bed during the night. His snores were her signal to slip down the hallway and into Don's bedroom. The blanched light of predawn sent her scurrying back to her own bed.

They would lie in each other's arms and talk for hours. He told her of exciting places he would show her. He described New Orleans with its beautiful old mansions and luxury hotels and historical cemeteries filled with ornate mausoleums. He strolled her down Bourbon Street and tree-lined avenues with wide sidewalks alive with fortune-tellers, entertainers and artists creating exquisite works right before your eyes. She pictured painted mimes frozen into living-statues or performing silly skits for crowds of tourists.

And the food.

Her mouth watered at his vivid narrations of strange sounding dishes. When she balked at a fare such as escargot or squid, he would tickle her until she promised to taste each and every morsel he would order for her.

He took her on mental trips to high mountains with crisp, flawless air. Towering pines stretched high enough to fondle feathery clouds. Don's laughter rang in her ears as he pelted her with imaginary snowballs. She shivered at the feel of frigid water in crystal lakes and spied fish swimming below the mirrored surfaces.

Her mind's eyes squinted against the blinding glare of sugary sand as she and Don walked hand-in-hand on Florida beaches. He took her on an exhilarating journey through Disney World. They cuddled close, feinting fear, as a tram carried them through the Haunted Mansion. She laughed at Goofy and shook hands with Mickey Mouse and saw lifelike pirates.

Her mind spun with the amazing sights Don brought to that

little bedroom in her mundane world. She loved him with her heart and soul.

One night as they lay in his bed with their bodies entwined, the door burst open. Her father, his face a mask of rage, stood in the doorway. His eyes bulged and gurgling sounds emitted from his throat. He backed away from the door. She scrambled out of bed and slipped her gown over her head. Don wrestled a pair of jeans up his legs. "Oh no. Oh Jesus." he mumbled under his breath.

Her father returned with a shotgun. Don backed out the door with his hands raised and the double barrels pressed against his stomach. "I love her and she loves me," she heard him explain as they moved down the hallway. "We're going to be married."

After an eternity, two shotgun blasts sounded, about ten seconds apart.

Don never returned. Her father burned his belongings. Clothes, photographs, a bedroll, leather work boots and a pair of athletic shoes dissolved to ashes in a smoldering fire.

Then came her first purging of sin. On her knees before her father, she cowered and covered her nakedness as best she could with her arms. He stood over her, a glowing soldering iron in a tight fist.

As ordered, she held her hands out, palms up.

"The sins of the mother are visited upon the daughter," he said. "You're like your mother, Naomi. You look like her. Her whoring blood flows in your veins. It's got to be purged or you'll be in hell's torment for eternity. This is nothing compared to burning forever in hell." He ran the hot iron across her right palm.

She fell backwards and attempted to crawl away, but he was on her, pinning her to the floor.

"FORNICATOR! WHORE OF BABYLON!" The iron bit into her other palm.

She shrieked.

"THIS IS BUT A TOUCH OF THE PAINS OF HELL!"

"No, Daddy. Please—please, no more." The pungent odor of seared flesh forced bile to her throat, choking back her piteous murmurings. Struggles were futile against the giant of a madman intent on causing her such agony.

"YOU UNHOLY DAUGHTER OF A WHORE!"

The searing rod ate its way into her breasts. When the iron cut a fiery swath across her pelvis, everything went black.

That night, as she lay in a semiconscious state, her wounds eating at her like millions of stinging fire ants, the fetus that would have been a little boy with twinkling blue eyes flowed from her body.

CHAPTER 5

For two days and two nights Myrtie Wilkerson maintained a vigil at her husband's bedside. Vomiting, diarrhea, high fever and chills had proven immune to home remedies and over-the-counter medications. Last night convinced her to call Dr. Stein. John suffered severe night-sweats into the wee hours; he tossed, turned and ranted about dead friends and relatives who waited for an opportunity to get at him.

The doctor came, toting his black bag.

With her husband no longer in discomfort and sound asleep, she sat across from Dr. Stein at the kitchen table, her eyelids heavy and shoulders slumped by fatigue. She appeared to give her undivided attention to the doctor's deep voice, but he may as well have been addressing the cow creamer that rested in the center of the heavy oak table. At the moment, she was elsewhere. She had retreated to a dark corner in her mind to mull over insurmountable problems. She was frightened. John's current illness was her major concern, but not the cause of her deep-lying fears.

More than fifty years of marriage had taught her every aspect of her husband—his likes, dislikes, wants, moods—the total man. And during his latest episode, or fugue as termed by Dr. Stein, he changed. Although the change was subtle, she detected a difference in him. It was as if something unclean had touched him, invaded his mind and soiled him. He was like a man possessed. His mind reached for something unremembered, something floating just beyond its grasp. No amount of humoring or cajoling could soothe away the demons that had taken hold in his imagination.

On more than one occasion she had expressed concern over John's fugues to Dr. Stein. The man was a healer who tended to treat the body rather than the mind. Sure of his diagnostic abilities, he had sloughed off her worries as nothing more than female foolishness. The mention of Alzheimer disease had drawn a stern lecture from him.

"Myrtie, get serious. There's a lot more to that disease than losing a few minutes of time. Hell, an older person gets a little forgetful, and they're tagged as an Alzheimer victim. It's natural to forget things as we age. So quit playing doctor, okay? That happens to be my job."

Despite Dr. Stein's skepticism, she knew that failure to treat John's mental state was a serious mistake.

She felt like a passenger on a runaway Amtrak; the years flashed by in a blur. To her dismay, John's golden years were advancing at a far swifter rate than her own.

Golden years.

The ignorance of youth had to have coined that phrase. Golden years. She could find nothing golden about old age.

Time had become her enemy. Powerless against its onslaught, she could only watch as bits and pieces of her husband's memory were snatched away. It wasn't enough that time was drawing the vitality from his bones and leaving behind a stooped, arthritic body. Or that day by day his skin withered and eyesight waned. No, the physical ravages were not enough. She knew the day was approaching when John's mind would retreat to some dark place within himself, and then he would be lost to her forever.

When that happens, Myrtie, what's left for you? Reckon what your fate will be? You know, don't you? Sure as the seasons change four times a year, you know. Your life will be spent ministering to a childlike man. Whole lot different from tending the babies you always wanted. Think how difficult the past two days have been. That will become your entire existence. All your time, all your strength and every ounce of energy will be spent caring for someone who probably won't remember who you are.

I can accept that. It's better than death. At least I won't be alone. He will still be of some solace, some comfort.

She realized death, too, was inevitable. Someday. She had read the statistics. By all odds, she would outlive John by ten years. Maybe longer.

She shuddered, frightened by the thought of spending her last years alone. There had been no siblings, and to her knowledge, there was not a person alive in the whole teeming world of six billion people who shared a drop of kindred blood with her. She would be alone in a world devoid of companionship and comfort. John was all she had. How would she ever survive without him? Without his love? His gentleness? His sense of humor? His crooked smile?

Worse things could happen, Myrtie, an inner voice warned. *Believe me, much worse.*

The thought unnerved her. Shivering from an internal chill, she shook her head to force away her morbid reverie. She found herself back in the sun-brightened kitchen.

"He picked up one hell of a virus from somewhere," Dr. Stein was saying. He snapped an oversized white handkerchief from a pocket, covered his mouth and coughed, a hacking, deep in the lungs smoker's cough. His face colored an unhealthy maroon.

"Damned things will kill you."

A Pall Mall balanced between two nicotine-stained fingers ascended to his mouth. He pursed his lips like a drawn purse string and sucked the slow working poison deep into his lungs. A look of immeasurable satisfaction crossed his features for a brief minute before the smoke once again awakened the painful sounding cough. In disgust, he stubbed out the cigarette.

Yeah, Doc, it's a shame something you love so much will kill you, popped into Myrtie's head.

Lord, where did that come from?

In one gulp Dr. Stein downed the remainder of his coffee, set the empty mug aside and stood up. "Well, gal, got to head back to the office. Full load waiting for me."

"Harry, are you sure he's going to be okay? Been retching something awful. Can't keep anything down. Lord, he's so pale, and weak as a kitten."

"Now, stop your worrying. Don't need you sick on me, too. Gave him a shot that'll take care of the vomiting. Vital signs are good and strong. I wouldn't leave if I thought there would be problems. John's a tough old bird. My bet is by tomorrow he'll be hollering for steak and potatoes. Probably have to hogtie him to keep him in bed."

"I hope so."

"Just keep poking Tylenol and liquids down him like I told you. And remember, I'm close as the telephone."

"I'll remember, believe me."

Myrtie stood on the porch and watched Dr. Stein fold his lanky frame into a small sports car. The engine roared to life, and the fun-loving teenager who still dwelled in the aged doctor's body manifested himself and skidded full circle. A choking cloud of dust and dry leaves cascaded behind the rear tires.

Men and their toys.

Dust devils marked the car's progress as it disappeared down the graveled road.

A loud yowl drew her attention to the barn.

"Just what I need, a cat fight. Too tired to deal with it—have to fight it out this time." Exhaling a sigh of resignation, she turned and walked back into the house.

She entered the kitchen and glanced out the window over the sink. The barn loomed. Pictures of wounded and bleeding cats formed in her mind.

"Dang. Okay, okay, I'm coming." She set a large enamel dishpan in the sink and flipped the water to cold. A good dousing never failed to discourage even the most aggressive of felines.

She headed out the back door, her arms straining to balance the cumbersome dishpan. Savage snarling and the high-pitched scream of a cat brought her to an abrupt halt. She looked up at the heavy barn door looming above her. On impulse, she turned and made several steps back toward the house with the intention of summoning John, then stopped. John was sick.

"Shoot."

Her arms trembled from the strain of the heavy pan. Water splashed the front of her dress and splattered her shoes. Disgusted, she set the pan down and headed toward the barn.

With a sharp tug, the door yielded about two feet. She stared into the shadowy interior, and as her vision adjusted to the dimness, a scene unfolded that she found difficult to accept.

A kitten dangled like a lifeless rag doll from Ditcher's bared teeth. A large black cat with her back bowed and claws protracted into talons, challenged the dog. Pitiful mews emanated from the kitten.

"Ditcher, no!" Myrtie screamed.

The startled dog dropped the tiny animal.

"You're a bad dog." She made her way to where he stood with his tail tucked and head lowered, and picked up the traumatized kitten.

"Poor little thing."

The mother cat took flight up a wooden post and into the safety of the hayloft.

With the downy ball of fur cuddled to her breasts, she scanned the cavernous room. Her eyes widened in astonishment at the scene of carnage materializing before her. Dozens of animal carcasses littered the floor. Her mouth agape, she stared down in disbelief at Ditcher cowering at her feet. Bloody saliva seeped from his mouth creating crimson streams down his jaws. Glossy red spheres formed on his chin and dripped to the ground.

He altered his supine position. His massive head rose and he pinned her with an astute gaze. Meekness faded from his unblinking eyes. An alien intelligence scrutinized her through the brown orbs. A rumble began deep in his throat and the lips pulled back exposing bloody teeth. The menacing growl heightened.

Hairs on her neck prickled. Her heartbeat quickened. The creature before her no longer resembled the gentle animal she had nurtured from a six-week-old puppy.

Get out. An inner voice commanded. *Now. Before it's too late.*

"Good Ditcher, good dog," she murmured, hoping against hope she could still reach the docile animal she knew still dwelled somewhere in the dog's body. Maintaining staunch eye contact, she took one tentative backward step. Then another.

The growl intensified.

Another step. Her shoe sank into something soft and squishy. Gas hissed from the bloated remains. She stood paralyzed, afraid to break eye contact with the demon dog. An army of flies assailed her legs.

She fought an urge to stomp her feet. Foul air filled her lungs. Saliva creamed in her mouth and her stomach flip-flopped. She belched sour bile.

Oh God, don't vomit.

Her throat muscles worked against her rebelling stomach. If she vomited, she would die. Not the close your eyes and ease into peaceful sleep kind of death. No, she would experience a terror-filled and excruciating pain kind of death; sharp canines sinking into living tissue and tearing away hunks of bloody flesh kind of death; a closed coffin kind of death; generations of children sitting in the dark and scaring each other with the gruesome tale kind of death.

Ditcher crouched, readying to push off with his muscular hind legs. Hate emanated from the animal's cold eyes.

"No, Ditcher," she pleaded, struggling to contain her hysteria. Her vocal cords seemed to be under the control of a complete stranger. The pitch of her voice rose shrilly and then fell to an almost inaudible whisper.

Ignoring the flies, the stench, the carcasses, everything except the spellbinding eye contact, she forced herself to continue her painstaking withdrawal. "One-two-three-four-five". She counted off each grueling step.

The kitten began a weak struggle for freedom, and its claws sank deep into her breast. Tears welled as she choked back a whimper.

She gave up the comforting count of steps for a different chant, one that bolstered her courage, kept her moving:

"I'm not going to die—I'm not going to die—I'm not going to die."

With each step, Ditcher paced her, as if he had fallen into some kind of sadistic game. The sun warmed her back.

The doorway.

She turned and darted through the opening. She expected to be forced to the ground by the weight of the huge dog—and then would come the brutal attack that would end her life. The death attack. But that didn't happen. She whirled with the agility of a prima ballerina and lunged at the massive door. It slammed shut with a loud bang.

The dog threw his weight into the weathered door, creating a narrow gap. His snout shot through the shallow opening. Slobbering and snarling, his lethal jaws chewed on empty air.

With the kitten's claws working her flesh and Ditcher's din bombarding her senses, the fear drained away. She had simply had enough. Outrage welled, and she did something very rare for her. She cursed. Loud and clear, she cursed.

"You son of a bitch! Not this time, you ain't." *Fuck you.* flittered through her mind, but even in her current state of furor, she could not make herself voice the F-word.

Her feet dug in as she strained against the heavy door. Inch by inch it moved, forcing the frenzied dog from the opening. The kitten clung to her, its claws buried in flesh. The door snapped into place. She slipped the bar into the brackets.

Ditcher fell silent.

The unexpected hush proved disconcerting. Gritting her teeth, she extracted the kitten's nails from her skin. Blood blossomed on the front of her dress. As fast as her rubbery legs could carry her, she made her way back to the house where she nestled the tiny feline in a dish towel and placed it in the deep porcelain sink. She needn't have bothered. One weak meow, and the kitten ceased movement. Tears sprang to her eyes as she smoothed the ruffled fur. "Poor thing. I'm so sorry. I just didn't make it in time, did I?" Refusing to cry, she sucked in deep, and then dialed the Caddo Police Department.

After placing the tiny corpse in a shoe box for later burial, she looked in on John. He was asleep. Offering a quick, silent prayer of thanks to Dr. Stein, she took up vigil on the front porch to await the arrival of a Caddo officer.

CHAPTER 6

Jeff Chambers emerged from the squad car to be barraged with a chilling tale about dead animals and Ditcher turning into a killer. He listened while Myrtie relived aloud her ordeal in the barn.

Ditcher a killer? Attacked Myrtie? Despite finding the bizarre story difficult to believe, he accepted every word related by the distraught woman as unexaggerated truth. He had known John and Myrtie Wilkerson most of his life. As a teen he had even worked summers harvesting cotton and other crops on their large farm. Myrtie was as down-to-earth and reputable as they come. If she told him the sky was falling, he would run for cover.

"Must be rabies," Myrtie insisted. "Like the dog in that story, Cujo. Ditcher never killed anything in his entire life. Was always bringing baby animals home, sometimes whole litters at a time. John accused him of turning the place into a gall-durn zoo, and was always fussing about all the wild critters underfoot. He never meant it though. Treated the little things like his own babies. Would mope around for days when one of his favorites was turned loose."

"Yeah, Myrtie, I know about John and his animals. Ditcher, too, for that matter. Can't imagine him turning bad. Why, he'd knock you off your feet to get a good slurp at your face."

"He ain't like that now. Caught rabies somewhere. Can't be nothing else."

Jeff shook his head in puzzlement. "Maybe so, but never heard of hydrophobic dogs bringing kills home. Strange behavior. Said yourself he had his vaccination. Always thought rabies serum was one hundred percent effective."

"In my seventy years, ain't never seen anything like this. I know I'm not crazy, but—" Myrtie hesitated.

"But what?"

"That's not Ditcher in there. Looks like Ditcher, but that creature in there ain't my Ditcher."

"A look-alike?"

"No. It's his body all right, but something else is inside it."

"Come on, Myrtie. We both know that's impossible." For the first time since his arrival, Jeff was beginning to question the old woman's mental soundness. "Maybe he turned bad. You know, like some pit bulls or rottweilers. Hear about them turning on their masters all the time."

Her eyes flooded with tears. "A gentle animal like Ditcher turning mean? Don't make sense."

Feeling awkward at the old woman's tears, Jeff looked down and studied a small mound of dirt he was forming with the toe of his shoe. He groped for something—*anything*—he could say that might comfort his disheartened friend. "Myrtie, I know how you and John love that dog, and with John sick and all, maybe we ought to call Doc Roland and—"

She blotted her eyes with a sleeve. "I'm sorry, Jeff. Being a sentimental fool about this whole thing. Don't matter what's wrong with him, rabies or turned bad, he's gotta be put down. Hate it falls on you. John would've handled it with no fuss at all. Since he can't, let's get it done, okay?"

Jeff nodded.

Country-graveyard silence emanated from the imposing barn. Sun hot enough to shrivel a rock beat down. Jeff's sweat-damp uniform adhered to his back like a thirsty leech. Dark circles marred the underarms of his shirt. He rubbed his sweaty palms down his pants legs, and then unholstered his nickel-plated .357 revolver. With a metallic click, the chamber popped open. Satisfied with the full load of ammunition, he snapped it shut.

With the bar lifted from the brackets, the door creaked open an inch or two. He widened the gap and stepped through into a steam bath of murky silence. "Shut the door, Myrtie, I'll let you know when I'm ready to come out."

Out-out-out echoed through the cavernous interior.

The door snapped shut shrouding the interior in darkness.

It's broad daylight, no way it should be so dark in here.

He turned on the flashlight he had brought from the cruiser.

Tools, discarded gunny sacks, cobwebs and assorted farm implements materialized and then dissolved into shadows as the beam swept the room. The light settled on the remains of an adult opossum; a short distance away the lifeless bodies of its half-grown offspring came into view. The traveling beam revealed more carcasses. Many more.

"Jesus H. Christ."

Ears tuned for a breath of sound, he moved deeper into the interior. A sigh of relief escaped his mouth when a light switch stabbed into view. He flipped it, and for a second light flooded the room, then with a sizzling pop, it went out.

"Dammit."

He continued to play the flashlight. Velvety shadows slithered from the bright beam with the fluidity of phantoms.

A voice, soft and sweet, sounded from a dark recess in a far corner.

"It's safe over here, Jeff. In the shadows. Safe, and I'm lonely."

"What the—?"

"Turn off the light, sweetheart. It bothers me, hurts my eyes."

"Molly?" Jeff wanted to believe his precious Molly was there, with his heart and soul he wanted to believe. But Molly had been dead over five years, and despite an inner voice insisting it could not be her, his arms dropped to his sides. The pistol hung in his right hand, the flashlight illuminated his feet. He took one tentative step toward the voice.

"That's right, my love. Now turn it off, the light."

No! his inner voice screamed.

He disregarded the command, and took another step. The flashlight dropped to the floor. A bright path arced before him. In that path lay dead animals: a small dog, no more than a puppy, its throat ripped open. A rabbit, two kittens, a raccoon. Slaughtered innocents. Icy fingers did a jig up his back.

This time he heeded the inner voice shrieking *Danger! Danger! Danger!* like a wailing siren in his head. Up came the pistol. He reeled backwards into a wall, flattening against the rough wood. With the .357 grasped by both hands, the nozzle jerked from one rolling shadow to the next. A vivid image slammed to mind. Massive jaws with long, sharp teeth closed on his throat. Blood arced from his severed jugular vein. A crimson fall colored his entire world bright red. His legs gave way and he slid down the wall. Splinters as thick as knitting needles tore into his flesh. He felt no pain.

The pistol wavered. He was unsure if he could find the strength to pull the trigger. An anguished cry broke the heavy silence.

"Dear Jesus, help me!"

He recognized the voice as his own.

Hearing Jeff call, Myrtie wrenched the door open. A figure leaped from the opening, taking her to the ground. This time, Ditcher did not threaten her. He bounded through the yard, across the road and into the freedom of the fields.

Jeff blinked against harsh sunlight. Disoriented, as if having been jerked from deep sleep, he glanced about in confusion.

He was sitting on the floor. "What the hell?"

He leaned forward with the intention of rising to his feet, and stiffened. His back felt as if it had been used for dart practice. Then he remembered the entire episode, the uncontrollable fear. *Molly? Did I really imagine her voice?*

A shadow lengthened at the doorway. Silhouetted by brilliant sunlight, Myrtie stood brushing herself off. "I'm so sorry, Jeff, I let Ditcher get away."

Jeff leaned back and laughed. Overflowing with relief and the pure pleasure of being alive, he laughed.

Myrtie stared at him in puzzlement.

CHAPTER 7

Once again January Rainwater found himself in the barren wasteland. A large boulder did little to protect him against the onslaught of brutal wind. His clothes were not suited for the frigid climate into which he had been thrust. The chill went so deep that he was certain he would never be warm again. He looked up to see the young woman, raven hair whipping at her face, appear on the horizon as she had so many times before. Nothing about the scene had changed.

Draped in heavy fur and clutching a bundle to her breasts, she labored to maintain her balance against the bitter wind. He watched her stumble and fall, then struggle to her feet. Exhaustion and pain were etched on her features.

She stopped within a few feet of where January huddled, her treacherous journey at an end. Bloodred seeds scattered about her feet kindled to life, glinting like priceless rubies in the gray environment.

January's stomach churned. He attempted to avert his gaze, but could not take his eyes from the drama playing out before him.

The woman knelt and placed the bundle on the ground. She unfolded layers of fur. A newborn infant, a boy, lay naked in the nest of warm fur. The baby began to wail, his chubby arms and legs churning. The young mother removed a stone knife from among the layers, and lifted the infant high by his ankles. She stood and turned to January, her face a mask of sorrow. Her tear-brimmed eyes pleaded for him to stop the madness, to save her child.

January could do nothing to thwart the atrocity that was about to take place; the scene had already been played out hundreds of years before. He was there in spirit only and was powerless to stay its reenactment. He watched with a mixture of anguish and outrage as the child was slaughtered. As blood trickled to the ground, the red seeds took root and sent forth bright green shoots.

January awoke. He remained in that frozen wasteland for a few seconds before the familiar chirp of crickets penetrated his brain and brought him home to his own bed. Contrary to the deep body chill he had imagined, the room was hot and sticky. Blotting sweat from his face and neck with the sheet, he sat up and flicked on the bedside lamp. A soft yellow glow chased away the darkness. 4:08 glowed bright green on the digital clock.

"Damn."

Realizing further sleep would prove impossible, he stood up and stretched, flinching as his sixty-seven-year-old joints popped and complained with sharp jabs of pain. He tied back his shoulder length gray hair with a beaded length of denim cloth, and then slipped into jeans and a T-shirt he had worn for the past two days. He padded barefoot down the hall and into the kitchen.

Sprawled in a straight-back wooden chair, he stared at flames licking the blackened bottom of the coffee pot, his mind searching out the message in his recurring dream. The young Indian mother shared the same blood; he recognized her as an ancestor. What could be so important, so dire, to have drawn her spirit from the grave to visit him in vision-like dreams?

Red seeds? Slaughter of an infant? What, what, what?

The savory aroma of the coffee roused him from his reverie. He turned off the burner, poured a mug of the steaming liquid and carried it outside to the front porch where he settled into a wooden, time-scarred rocking chair. Sipping the strong brew, he once again opened his mind to thoughts that fluttered at the edge of consciousness. He reached back into his memory for stories told him by his grandfather, stories that had been passed from generation to generation by his people. Despite the strong dose of caffeine, he was soon lulled to sleep by the hypnotic creak creak creak of the rocking chair and the mesmerizing chirp of crickets. He dreamed.

He walked in a primitive Indian village among his ancestors. Laughter and conversations filled the air. He understood every word of their strange tongue. In crude huts women nursed their young or squatted before fires where simmering food in stone bowls sent forth mouthwatering aromas. A number of young hunters, rugged and formidable looking, sat in a group forging arrowheads from stone and carving shafts for spears. They bantered as they worked.

He then found himself in a field of lush bushes adorned with breathtaking blooms. The flowers were bright crimson, the color of blood, and despite their beauty, emitted a nauseating odor that forced him to pinch his nostrils. His stomach gurgled and rolled. A belch filled his mouth with the bitter taste of bile. Icy fingers did a duck-walk up his spine, the hair on his neck prickled and gooseflesh rose on his arms. He was not alone. Hatred emanated from a hostile presence, an alien thing that was smelling him out. It was powerful, and he knew if he didn't move, and move fast, he would be obliterated like an insect under the heel of a work boot. He harbored no doubts that he could be killed.

He ran. The verdant shrubbery sprang to life and lashed at him with willowy limbs, leaving behind stinging, angry welts on his face and arms. Oblivious to the pain, he charged on, wheezing and panting. He felt the thing at his heels. His mind's eye could see massive arms reaching and enormous taloned hands flexing within inches of his back, ready to enclose him in a bone-crushing embrace of death.

He snapped awake, his heart hammering. His hands raised in tight fists, ready to do battle. Bright sunlight and the gentle sway of the rocking chair brought him back to the present. He felt foolish. His face reddened with embarrassment.

Did it again, didn't you, old man? Spent half the night on the porch. Old timers' disease has taken hold for sure.

Nothing to do with old timers' disease, he argued with that critical voice. *Had some thinking to do, that's all.*

From the look of the sun, he guessed it to be about seven-thirty. His cronies would already be gathering at Pearl's for a bit of bent-ear and breakfast. If he hurried, he could still join them, and maybe he'd be able to draw a fable or two from them about red flowers. The workings of several minds were better than one.

His fingernails worked at fresh mosquito bites dotting his arms as he carried the coffee mug to the kitchen where he deposited it in the sink. After taking a few minutes to relieve his bladder, give his teeth a couple of good swipes with a toothbrush, slip into a pair of scuffed black boots and lift a set of keys from a nail inside the back door, he emerged once again through the front door and onto the porch. Down the steps, and several long, deliberate strides carried him to his battered Dodge pickup.

The truck creaked and groaned as he settled his one hundred and ninety pounds into the seat. A grimy threadbare blanket did little to camouflage rusty springs that had worked their way through cracked vinyl seat covers. Rust-eaten cavities speckled dented fenders. Original blue paint had faded to a drab gray.

He slipped the key into the ignition, and contrary to the truck's outward appearance, the engine surged to life and purred like a contented old cat. He maneuvered through deep ruts and chuckholes cratering the two-mile stretch of gravel road leading to the highway.

CHAPTER 8

A doe fleeing from a large predator at her heels darted onto the roadway. An agonizing screech sliced the country-quiet and the stench of burned rubber filled the air. A massive object hurled past her. She bounded the yawning culvert paralleling the highway and disappeared into the safety of the forest.

"Son of a bitch!" January bellowed, fighting to maintain control against a 360-degree skid. A deep trench loomed before him. His body heaved into the air and his head exploded with pain. Under its own sway, the truck lurched to a stop with the back wheels buried in soft dirt, the windshield facing skyward and the front wheels spinning in the air.

Maintaining a death grip on the steering wheel, he stared hard at his white knuckles for a full ten seconds before his gaze traveled upward to peruse feathery clouds playing a slow game of tag against an azure backdrop. He let go of the steering wheel and slumped back in the seat. A cloud of dust settled about the accident site, wafting into the cab like a solid brown fog. A jagged cough exploded from his lungs. His eyes watered, and he swallowed with a throat as scratchy as sandpaper.

"What the hell?"

Then he remembered.

"Damn that deer."

Not the deer's fault. Should have been paying attention to business instead of letting your mind wander off somewhere in wa-wa land.

"Yeah, yeah. Damn well can't blame this on some dumb animal, can I? This fancy bit of driving ain't going to earn any points with State Farm." He patted his pocket for his cell phone, and then pictured it plugged in and charging on the kitchen counter.

His head felt as if an iron mallet was pounding a railroad spike into his skull. His fingers traced a deep gash he estimated four inches long. The wound ran like an open faucet. Blood poured down his neck and forehead. He wiped it from his eyes with the back of his hand.

"Damn thing's going to need stitches."

He popped open the glove compartment, removed a thirty-eight caliber pistol wedged in clutter and placed it on the seat beside him. "With my luck, the damn thing will go off and finish what the accident started." A large blue neckerchief peeked through the rubbish filling the tight space. "Aha, knew you were in there somewhere, you rascal." After folding the cloth into several thicknesses, he screwed up his features and sucked air through his teeth. He pressed the make-do compress hard against the laceration.

"Holy shit." It hurt.

After five minutes or so, he eased away the cloth. A little blood continued to ooze, but not much.

The door complained with a loud creak, but opened.

"Well, praise the saints and bless the Pope for this bit of luck."

He slid out the cab, supported by firm grips on the steering wheel and door frame. He eased his full weight to his left leg. It held without too much pain. A jagged tear in his jeans revealed a yellow-purple bruise already making an appearance and a battered knee cap that would no doubt swell to double.

"At least it ain't broken."

Laboring against grainy soil sucking at his boots, he made his way around the pickup. The rear end of the truck was wedged against the wall of the culvert, the tailgate entombed in a make-believe grave and the rear tires buried to the axle. He shook his head in disgust.

"Monkeyshit. Take a damn crane to get this son of a bitch out of here. If you ain't some kind of stupid Injun, January Rainwater."

His left knee paining enough to bring tears to his eyes, he began to climb the steep embankment. Tiny rocks and grit filtered into the tops of his boots. Nearing 100 degrees, the heat was dense enough to cut with a knife. To make matters worse, the head wound had reopened; equal amounts of sweat and blood streamed down his face and neck.

Nearing the top and gasping for breath, he stopped to rest. He attempted to flex his left leg. A sharp stab of pain killed the motion.

An elongated shadow fell across his line of vision. He looked up in expectation at his would-be rescuer. The biggest fucking dog he had ever seen loomed above him. Its teeth were bared and a rumble like a Mack truck gearing up to second built in its throat.

His heart hammering like a snare drum, January began a frantic crab-crawl down the incline.

The dog leaped, landing atop him and sending them downward in a tangle. Canines tore into January's left shoulder. He drove a hard fist in into the dog's head, sending it tumbling with shreds of bloody cloth clutched in its jaws. The dog stood, and almost humanlike, shook its head. Its eyes once again settled on January.

January dug his heels into the gritty soil and pushing hard, propelled himself backwards, never for a second taking his eyes from the dog. His buttocks slid over the loose soil. The effort moved him close to the pickup, but not close enough.

From a crouched position, the dog pushed off with muscular hind legs, descending like a hurling ball of death.

January coiled into a tight ball and kicked upward. His heavy work boots slammed into the massive chest and sent the dog catapulting. The somersaulting ball of fur landed with a loud thud several feet away. It rose to shaky legs, and then collapsed. This time it lay where it had fallen, its tongue hanging from its slack mouth and its eyes rolled back exposing the whites. Bloody saliva bubbled from its mouth as it struggled to breathe. The heavy boots had done a number on its rib cage.

January struggled to his feet, and stood for several seconds to allow a wave of dizziness to pass. It took four or five slow steps for his legs to find their balance. He made his way to the truck.

The face staring at him from the side view mirror could have played a starring role in The Walking Dead. Stringy hair, a mishmash of grey and crimson, hung about a blood-streaked, dirt-mired face. The top of the head appeared to have been the target of a mad hatchet man. The eyes were sunken black hollows and the mouth was drawn into a tight ring of pain. For a moment he stared in fascination. A slow smile cut through the taut features.

"Hell, old man, you got all dressed up like this and it ain't even Halloween. Yep, still got a lot of tough in you, don't you? Nary a dog alive who can best you."

Go ahead, January, act the fool. The way I see it, there ain't much to smile about.

I'm standing on my own two feet, ain't I? I'm alive.

Alive? Standing? For how long? That ain't buttermilk flowing out of your wounds. For your information, that's pure, high octane, unleaded, oxygenated blood. You lose much more of it and you ain't never going to jump-start again. And the dog? Reckon why it attacked you? The way I see it, there are only three reasons a dog would tackle a human being. Maybe if it's starved, it might. But that big fella doesn't look like he's missed a meal in a long time. And a dog will sure enough attack to defend its territory. Look around. Ain't much here worth protecting, is there? And of course there is always rabies. Makes no never mind whether it's a dog or a raccoon or a fox. A rabid animal will attack anything. Rabies, most likely. The way I heard it, the shots are painful and go on for—

A head shake forced away the unpleasant thoughts. He opened the pickup door and removed the blood-damp neckerchief from the seat. After folding it into a long, narrow strip, he pulled it taut over his head and knotted the ends under his chin. The blood slowed to a dribble.

"Now the shoulder."

The jagged tear in his shoulder made the cut on his head look like child's play. Testing for nerve damage, he flexed his hand. Fiery pain almost took him to his knees. Once awakened, the pain continued in scathing waves. He stood gritting his teeth and deliberating options for first aid.

His eyes scanned the interior of the cab and settled on the threadbare blanket.

Cut into strips? Pocketknife? Not too sanitary, but just might work. Hell, it'll have to work.

He stiffened at a slight sound of shifting soil. Before he could turn, the dog's teeth sank into his left calf. A quick grab of the steering wheel kept him from being dragged to the ground. His free hand groped about the seat and closed on the wooden handle of the pistol.

Time slowed to a crawl.

His arm came around, the pistol pointed downward. His finger tightened on the trigger. Fire shot from the barrel. An earsplitting explosion seemed to go on forever. The dog lifted and lingered in the air for what seemed an unending time. With the leisure of a leaf caught in a gentle breeze, the massive body floated to earth.

He stood frozen for a full minute, unable to take his eyes from the thing made of blood and fur. Realization cut like a razor through the heavy fog clouding his mind.

The dog. You shot the son of a bitch. You shot the dog.

With the pistol grasped before him, he limped to where the animal lay motionless. A jagged opening the size of a grapefruit in its side exposed a crimson mass of muscle and bone. Its heart pumped rivulets of blood from the wound. The eyes fluttered open and underwent a metamorphosis. Like a dying flame, hostility faded. The gentle eyes conveyed to January, *I really didn't want to hurt you. Something inside me did it. I would lick your wounds and make them better if I could.*

January's sad smile sent a message of forgiveness to the dying animal. In a gesture of acknowledgment, the dog's tail pounded the ground. A whimper escaped his slack mouth as he exhaled his last breath.

He dropped the pistol and turned toward the steep embankment. An unscalable wall loomed above him.

Got to do it. Have to climb that incline before you get any weaker. No time left to cut up blankets and tie off wounds.

Lots of cars use this old highway. Someone will hear me hollering.

Don't think so. It's too hot. In this kind of heat, people run with windows up and air conditioners at full blast. It's not like the old days. Nope, the only way you'll get help is to make it to the top of this ditch. Now, get your rickety old ass in gear and go for it.

Bowing to logic, he began the struggle upward. He seemed to slide back three feet for every hard-earned foot of progress. With pain and exhaustion eating at every nerve, every muscle and every inch of skin, he stopped for a breather. His hands, arms, clothes, even his boots were slick with blood—more blood than he knew his body contained. Life sometimes kicks a man in the gut, taking him to his knees and opening his eyes to his own mortality. Today, life had given him one hell of a boot, right in the balls, not only bringing him to his knees, but laying him out flat on his belly. For the first time since his truck had careened off the roadway, he realized he might die. Today. Right here, too weak to scale an incline that any determined three-year-old could master in forty-five seconds or less.

As an omen to his morbid insight, a death shadow swooped across the dry soil. He looked up. Two vultures circled above him, riding the air currents like ebony kites. He knew their numbers would increase.

Voracious feeders, January. When you stop moving, they'll come for you. The eyes. The eyes are what they go for first. Maybe not in your case, though. You have open wounds. Those sharp beaks will have something to tear into. Couldn't be much more painful than what you've already been through. Wouldn't think so, anyway. Know what else? After dark the coyotes will move in. Probably a few other carnivores, too. Raccoons, foxes. But you'll be dead by then. Vultures will see to that. Yep, the critters are out there waiting for nightfall. They'll clean up what the vultures leave behind.

Fury bubbled up like an erupting volcano. He shook his fist in the air. "You sons of bitches ain't going to get me!" he screamed. "Not today! Not ever! You hear me? Do you hear me, you godless flesh-eating devils?"

Rage fueled his determination. He forced his tortured body to continue its upward struggle. His head and shoulders cleared the top of the culvert, but his trembling arms were too weak to support his weight. He collapsed. For a time he lay gasping and thinking that each breath might be his last.

A vulture lit on the far side of the road. With its head cocked, its beady eyes studied January as if contemplating whether it was safe to move in for a meal.

A screamed obscenity and a tossed rock sent the bird into panicked flight.

By sheer resolve he pulled himself inch by grueling inch over the top of the embankment and onto the scorching macadam. The world evolved into a whirling carousel of greens, grays and bright white light. Indistinguishable images danced through his head.

Have to rest. One minute. Then I'll get up.

His head dropped to the scalding surface. Following a flinch, he stopped moving. Oily pools of blood formed around his prone form. His mind drifted to a soothing sea of blackness.

CHAPTER 9

"As I told Doc Stein, when I seen him sprawled out in the middle of the road in that pool of blood, sure 'nough took 'im for dead. Told myself a car run smack over 'im and just kept right on going. Then seen them strips of rubber leading into the ditch. Lordy, and that dead dog with a hole in his chest the size of my fist. Figured out real quick what happened. January wrecked his truck then got himself chewed up by that monster dog."

A stab of guilt speared Jeff Chambers in the solar plexus. The dog had to be Ditcher, and if he had killed him in the barn instead of zoning out like a snot-nosed rookie, January wouldn't be half dead now.

Atrell Jones, every rib on his bony chest well-defined, and zeroing in on the big seventy, couldn't have weighed more than a hundred and thirty pounds soaking wet. He looked as if he had just stepped out of a bloodbath. Red streaks of blood had found their way into his thinning grey balls of hair on his head.

"Atrell, January outweighs you by fifty or sixty pounds. How'd you ever get him into your truck?"

"He come around for a bit and I walked-carried him like this." His shoulders dropped and he shuffled forward a couple of strenuous steps, his arm around the imaginary January. "Wanted to call an ambulance, but he insisted I drive him here."

"Excuse me." They looked around into Dr. Stein's harried-looking face.

"January's going to pull through. And you, Atrell, are the one to thank for that. Did some pretty quick thinking. He was closer to meeting Jesus than I like to think about."

"Well, you know, Doc, raised a bunch of young'uns, and there wasn't no money for doctors when they got hurt. Me and the Missus patched them up the best we could. Did the same for January. Tore up my shirt and tied off where he was bleeding the worst. Pressed cloth against his shoulder and told him to hold it down tight while I drove. Course, never had a young'un chewed up like that old man was."

"You saved his life. Damn good job. Deserve a hero medal."

The doctor nodded at Jeff. "January keeps slipping in and out of consciousness, asking for his grandson. Reckon you could head out to his place and find a telephone number for the boy? Give him a call?"

"Yeah, be glad to. I'll phone Berkeley if necessary, understand he's been teaching there a couple of years now."

"Tell him his grandfather is out of immediate danger, but could use his moral support. The sight of that young man will do more for him than all the medicine we can poke down him."

"Don't worry, Doc, I'll get him here."

Dr. Stein gave Atrell a pat on the back. "Again, one hell of a job you did. I suspect January will want to extend his personal thanks as soon as he's able."

Atrell cleared his throat and looked down at the floor. "Wasn't no more than he'd have done for me. Tell him I'll be around in a day or two."

"I'll tell him." The doctor turned and headed down the hallway.

"Chief?" Deep worry lines etched Atrell's face.

"What is it? There a problem?"

"Kind of. You know I work for Larkin Ballard-and-and . . . well, you know how he is. Ain't going to take too kindly to my tore up uniform shirt. And lordy, when he gets a gander at that bloody van, he'll be on me like a duck on a june bug. Won't be no time for explainin'. Nosiree, he'll be just like a duck on a june bug."

In Jeff's eyes, Larkin Ballard was a prime example of a man's man, five-and-a-half feet of compact steel. Canon ball biceps and the thick neck of a three-hundred-pound lineman. When angered, he could prove more belligerent than a constipated bull with hemorrhoids. Not that his fiery Irish temper reared its ugly head too often, but when it did—Katy bar the door.

Despite occasionally short-circuiting, he was well liked. His imposing demeanor coupled with his colorful reputation as a brawler made him the ideal man to control the tough lot of truck drivers who manned the fleet of eighteen-wheelers coming and going on a daily basis from Schilling Glass Company. The majority of these drivers were independent, hard-as-nails types.

He agreed with Atrell's assessment of the situation. The bloody van would be like waving a red flag in front of a bull. Larkin would freak out.

"I see your problem. Tell you what, Jim McAllister and I are pretty good buddies—"

"McAllister?"

"Yeah, you know, head of security at Schilling."

"McAllister. Sure, we call 'im Mack.

"I'll give him a call, smooth things over before you get there."

"I thank you, Chief."

"Best you run home and shower off the blood. Put on clean clothes. And trash those pants, won't ever come clean. I'll see that Schilling springs for a new uniform."

After the call to Jim McAllister insuring that Atrell would receive a hero's welcome, Jeff headed for January's place. He discovered an address book in the drawer of a night stand, and called Michael's home number. Bingo, an answer on the second ring. Michael agreed to catch the first available flight.

CHAPTER 10

"George, you're going to love this house," Penney Sneider assured her husband for the umpteenth time as she maneuvered the minivan through the tree-lined streets of the aged neighborhood. "You can't believe how discouraged I got by all the dinky cracker-box doll houses Sharon Saunders kept dragging me to. Then this place. What a find."

Seven months ago George's five-month-pregnant sister had stopped at a convenience store in Houston to buy a Snickers candy bar, a craving she developed early in her pregnancy. That craving ended her life. An addict high on God knows what walked into the store with a pistol clutched in his fist. As he fired a shot into the ceiling, the clerk dove for the floor behind the counter. The shooter studied the stunned pregnant woman for a long moment, and then started babbling, "You're evil. Evil, evil, evil. Have to be destroyed." A highpowered bullet in her chest drove her backwards toppling a display of Lay's chips. The perpetrator turned and fled through the door as if Satan himself was hot on his tail. The clerk gave a full account to the police.

As a prosecutor with the Houston DA's office, George had seen too many senseless killings, and the death of his sister had been more than he could handle. With fear of the same thing happening to Penney or his children cemented in his mind, he insisted they move to a small safe town. After a few months of job searching he landed the position of Caddo City Manager. Although it meant a substantial cut in pay and Penney leaving behind family and friends—her support system—she reluctantly agreed to the move. She had lived in Houston her entire life and had not once felt threatened or been accosted. To relieve George's stress she was willing to make the sacrifice.

Three days ago she had driven to Caddo and spent the day with a realtor to look at homes. Only one house piqued her interest. At first glance she had been almost convinced it would be a waste of time to go inside. One step through the front door and she was hooked. Images of the shabby exterior diminished, and a love affair between her and the rambling old house was set into motion.

George tended to judge a book by its cover. Regardless of who or what the object might be—*even a house*—once influenced by that first impression, he rarely bothered to look below the surface. He may have been born with his instant judgment characteristic or perhaps too many years as a prosecuting attorney had cemented the trait. Maybe he had rubbed shoulders with too many dregs of society, listened to too many half-truths, saw too many devastating crime scenes—too much blood, too much brutality.

Penney never wasted much energy worrying about that aspect of his personality, she learned to work around it. During seven years of marriage she had become proficient in getting what she wanted, and she wanted the house. After all, being uprooted and moved over two hundred miles from friends and family deserved some compensation. She knew the shabby exterior would shade George's opinion and he would fail to see the dwelling's true potential. After a couple of days of chewing on the problem, she arrived at a solution. Present the interior first. Problem solved.

After slowing to read a street sign, she made a sharp right. "Okay, George, we're almost there. Shut those peepers, and no fair peeking."

"Mommy, do we have to close our eyes, too?" six-year-old Lauri whined from the backseat.

"No, only Daddy."

Penney slowed and maneuvered the minivan to the curb. Tires scrapped against concrete. "Damn. Don't dare look," she cautioned her husband.

"This is a plot. You're going to do me in for my insurance money so you can run away with the iceman."

Lauri unsnapped her seatbelt and climbed halfway over the front seat. "Mommy, who's the iceman? Are we running away with him?"

George and Penney crumpled over in laughter.

Three-year-old Jenni's eyes widened to blue saucers at the thought of her mother running away. Her tiny fingers went to work on the release button of her car seat. "Iceman? Why do you want an iceman, Mommy?" Despite a lack of attention to her words, she continued to jabber. "Saw lots of scuppers at the zoo. Remember? There was a tiger that looked just like Chocho, 'cept bigger. And-and a scary angel with a long sword. No iceman though." With a metallic click she was free. She climbed from the seat and tapped her father on the back of the head. "Daddy."

"What is it, pumpkin?"

"Wouldn't we have to keep the iceman in the frigerader? Else he would melt. You know, like the scuppers at the zoo?"

Scuppers? Zoo? Confused, George mulled over the words, and then recalled the ice sculpture exhibit at the Houston Zoo. Both girls had been quite taken with the display. "No, honey, an iceman isn't made out of ice. Years ago they used to deliver ice to homes. The man who delivered the ice was called the iceman. I was only teasing Mommy about running away."

Penney stepped out her door, hurried around the car and opened the passenger side. She took George's hand.

"All right, my frog, follow me and you will turn into a prince."

He croaked, "Ri-bit. Ri-bit."

The girls collapsed into giggles.

Opening the back door Lauri pleaded, "Wait. I want to help."

"Me, too." Jenni Parroted

"Please?" they implored.

"Sounds like an excellent idea to me. He's all yours." With a shrug, she turned and headed up the sidewalk. From the porch, she watched the girls struggle at extracting him from the front seat. She laughed. George was playing the disability of closed eyes to the fullest.

"No, Daddy. Lower your head. Bring your feet straight down. No, no, not like that."

Jenni turned to her sister. "Pull his other foot down."

His head lowered as ordered and both feet planted firmly on the ground, he was guided out of the van. The girls trekked up the sidewalk with their father in tow.

Peripheral movement drew Penney's attention to the house on the left. Curtains separated and a face surrounded by curly gray hair appeared at the window. Penney waved. The curtains dropped back into place.

A middle-aged ruddy-faced man stepped onto the porch of the house to the right. He was soon joined by a timid-looking woman with mousy brown hair. Penney could feel the man's eyes scan her body, undressing her as they traveled.

The creep.

At last reaching the porch, George complained, "Jeez, it's tough being blind."

"Oh, Daddy, you're not really blind."

He threw back his head and rolled out a loud guffaw.

"George," Penney hissed, "the neighbors are watching."

His eyes opened and his mouth dropped. He backed down the sidewalk.

Can't be. I'm in Caddo. I'm all grown up now.

Silvery streams of drool seeped from the corners of his mouth. He stopped his retreat, frozen in place, afraid to take his eyes from the house. The forbidding windows glowered like the segmented eyes of a spider. A loathsome greeting throbbed through his head.

Hi, George. I'm glad you finally came. I see you brought your little family. I've been waiting, and I'm so glad to see you.

Images of Jacky Jensen flooded his mind. The angry boy, always dressed in the same soiled T-shirt and tattered jeans, had been the scourge of George's neighborhood. Jerky the Jerk—his behind-the-back moniker—was into anything that would put a dollar or two into his pocket. Shoplifting. Petty thefts. Burglary. He was a bully and loved torturing weaker kids. His infamous reputation for retaliation against snitchers kept his cruel exploits free from the ears of adults.

Lost in a memory, George ambled toward his boyhood home. Street lamps blinked to life as dusk faded to night.

"Hey, assbrain, where you think you're going?"

Hoping the words were not directed at him, he quickened his pace. *Please, God,* he prayed. The slap slap slap of footfalls on the pavement behind him sent him scurrying, but too late. Jerky grabbed his collar and jerked him to a stop.

"I asked you a question, assbrain." His breath reeked of decayed teeth and nicotine.

"I'm going home. Don't want any trouble."

Jerky slammed their foreheads together. A lightning bolt of pain shot through George's head. He blinked against a kaleidoscope of bright specks performing loop-de-loops through his vision.

He wanted to believe that this whole thing was a case of mistaken identity. But deep down where the soul dwells, where bad experiences have a way of gaining a foothold, he knew he had been cast into the roll of Jerky's newest victim.

He attempted to wrench free, but Jerky held tight.

His eyes darted about in search of a rescuer. "Help me. Somebody, please help."

No windows brightened. No doors opened. No cars rolled down the deserted street. Cicadas and frogs ceased their calls. Homes sheathed in blankets of darkness had an abandoned look. Silence gripped the night.

Tears welled, and he began to cry.

"Itsy-bitsy crybaby don't want no trouble. Don't mess with me, you blubbering piece of shit. I need money and you better have it."

"I don't have any money."

"Too bad for you. Now you pay the consequences," Jerky's tone was a warning of things to come.

The grip tightened on George's collar, and he was propelled forward like a child in the hands of an angry adult. His legs pumped in an attempt to keep up the rapid pace.

Can't breathe.

Suddenly he was flying. His face slammed into a hard surface and the darkness exploded with pain. He lay where he had fallen, sucking air down his raw throat. His tongue explored a slice on the inside of his upper lip. His front teeth ached, but were intact. The coppery taste of blood turned his stomach. He coughed, gagged and spit out strings of bloody phlegm. He raised his head. Weathered wooden steps swam into view. He sucked in hard as his eyes continued upward.

The Brandon House.

Warmth ballooned in his groin and flowed down his legs. Urine saturated his jeans.

The front door creaked open. He strained to see through the thick blackness of the interior. Dense gray mist seeped from the opening, rolled across the porch and down the steps. It enfolded him. It touched him in private places, explored him, tasted him and prickled his skin. He crab-crawled backwards, his unblinking eyes fixed on the open door.

A sadistic smile worked Jerky's mouth as he watched the younger boy's retreat.

"Fucking coward, ain't you, assbrain? We're fixing that. You're going to walk right up on that porch and go inside. And you know what else, you're staying in there until I decide to leave. Yep, coward-boy, I'll be standing right out here watching."

"I ain't going in."

"Oh yes you are." An object appeared in Jerky's right hand. A click echoed through the stillness as a blade was released from its confines. The long steel blade glinted in the dim glow of the street lamp.

"As I said, little man, you are going in there, 'cause if you don't, I'll cut off your balls and stuff them down your throat."

A tinge of anger flickered to life in George—and grew. Fury ballooned until it filled every hollow. He brought his head up hard into Jerky's groin. The boy collapsed, curling into a ball and bellowing.

George scrambled to his feet and sprinted away like a gazelle under the claws of a lion.

"George, George." The sound of Penney's voice broke through his spell. Her hands gripped his shoulders. "What's wrong?"

He looked at her for a moment before turning his head to take in their surroundings. His eyes came to rest on a beefy man standing on the porch of a house next door. A rounded gut and bulbous red nose told him here is a guy who likes his beer. His grin was too wide.

A wisp of a woman stood beside beer-belly, frowning. She obviously did not find the Sneider family humorous at all.

He looked back at the place they had come to see. There stood a benign dwelling in need of repairs. All resemblance to the dilapidated Brandon house had vanished.

"You're shaking and white as a sheet," Penney fretted. She pressed her wrist against his forehead as if checking for fever.

Lauri stood several feet away, astonishment written across her features. His youngest daughter clung to his leg. He patted her on the head. "I'm okay, pumpkin, it's just the heat." To Penney, he said, "I don't really feel like looking at houses, let's go back to the motel, okay?"

Settled in the van and the air conditioner struggling against the ninety-eight-degree temperature, George laid his head back and closed his eyes.

"God, what was that about back there? You looked terrified."

"I guess I was." He raised up and glanced at the girls in the backseat. Both were engrossed in coloring books and crayons.

He lowered his voice to keep from drawing their attention. "At first glance, that place looked like the Brandon House."

"Brandon House?"

"Yeah, an old boarded up house in my neighborhood. Spooky place. All the kids were sure it was haunted."

Penney laughed. "You know, I guess most neighborhoods and small towns have at least one creepy old house that is dubbed as haunted."

"This was no ordinary haunted house. Its morbid history was enough to make anyone a believer. Hell, even some adults wouldn't go near it. Last guy that lived there slaughtered his family."

"Slaughtered them?"

"Wife and three kids. Then committed suicide."

"How awful."

"I went to school with the kids, two brothers and a sister. The oldest boy was in my class. Their father seemed to be a pretty nice guy. Coached little league sports and was PTA president for a couple of years. I guess one night he snapped."

Penney frowned. "How did he do it?"

"Cut their throats with a butcher knife, and as if that wasn't enough, opened the living room drapes and lined them up at the window. Hanged himself from a light fixture and—"

"Enough. Sorry I asked. I don't understand why at least one of them didn't get away. After all, four against one."

"Think about it. He was a devoted husband and father. Imagine your dad standing over you with a butcher knife, and for the sake of argument, let's make it a bloody one. What would you do? Run? Laugh? What?"

"Dad? A butcher knife?" She giggled at the picture. "In his wildest dreams, he could never do anything like that."

"I'm sure they thought the same thing, maybe took it as a joke. An old lady walking her dog spotted the bodies. She told the police that she thought it was some kind of prank, those bloody faces and all. Expected the whole group to burst out laughing until she got close enough to see the slit throats. And there was Mr. Brandon, suspended by the neck and glaring out at her. Claimed his bulging eyes were somehow alive, never moved from her face. Said he spoke to her. Insisted she could hear him plain as day."

"Come on in. Join the party. You'll love our little games."

"That's when the old gal started screaming. She ran one direction and the dog another."

"You made that up. Funny, ha-ha."

"Swear to God, that was printed in the newspaper."

"A talking corpse? She had to be touched in the head."

"Touched or not, us kids believed every word of it, especially when they started publishing accounts of other deaths."

"Other deaths?"

"I told you, this was no ordinary haunted house, lots of people died there. After the Brandon slaughter, public interest was piqued. Couple of reporters did extensive research. Probed old police reports, newspaper archives and even tracked down a few former residents. Everyday, for a week or so, some kind of hair-raising story was profiled in the paper. Better reading than a horror novel. Let's see if I can remember any of the details." His brow creased in concentration. "Oh yeah. In the early twenties a lady named Zar . . . no, Zorskey. Unusual name, it stuck with me for some reason. She drowned her two toddlers in a claw-footed bathtub, and then climbed in and slit her wrists. In the thirties, a woman baked arsenic-laced rolls and fed them to her husband. They found her kneeling by his convulsing body and singing "Bringing in the Sheaves" at the top of her lungs. Now in—"

"Stop. You've convinced me. That place would have unnerved me, too."

"Unnerved is an understatement of the effect it had on us kids. Even in broad daylight, we wouldn't go near that place. People claimed to see movements and flickering lights in there at night. I can still see Chase Little making a cross on his chest and vowing, Cross my heart and hope to die, hope my whole family dies, too, if I'm lying. I saw Mr. Brandon standing at a window and grinning, holding up that bloody knife."

"Did you believe him?"

"Oh yes, I believed him. Everyone did. To this day, I believe he saw something. Not Mr. Brandon, of course. Probably some old bum who had taken up residence in the place. Or maybe just shadows, who knows?"

CHAPTER 11

As days passed, a heavy pall settled over Caddo. Even-tempered people found themselves easily irritated; arguments over petty issues often led to blows. The sight of wives and girlfriends wearing large concealing sunglasses to camouflage swollen and bruised eyes became commonplace. Accidents involving children increased tenfold. Tumbles down stairs, bike wrecks, trips and falls were the excuses to explain away injuries. Nightmares plagued the community. People found themselves held prisoners in catatonic sleep, playing the lead roles in terrifying dramas.

Naomi Duncan trod through a realm of illusion without an inkling that none of it was real. She sat in bed with the sheet clasped against her breasts. Pallid moonlight illuminated the small bedroom. Furniture shrouded in shadows loomed as eerie phantoms. Her eyes darted about the room in search of movement. Instinct told her she was alone. She could feel in her bones that something monstrous walked the night sniffing her out. She deserted the bed and slipped into yesterday's jeans and blouse. Her impulse was to flee the house and seek safety somewhere outdoors, but the prospect of stepping into the impenetrable blackness of the hallway killed the thought. She attempted to raise a window, then another, but both refused to budge. She sought refuge in the clothes closet. Cloaked in darkness, she curled into a fetal-like ball amid shoe boxes, blankets and an olio of junk that had accumulated through the years.

She waited and she listened.

Lub-dub-lub-dub-lub-dub.

Minutes passed with her accelerated heartbeat as the only sound. Pain triggered by the viselike clamp of her jaws inched down tense neck muscles. A dull ache throbbed at her temples. She found the heavy, sultry air difficult to breathe. Musty odors of mildew, mothballs, wool and the leathery smell of old shoes mingled with the acrid stench of her own stale sweat.

Something crawled across her foot. She stiffened and attempted to brush it away. With a click, it dropped to the floor.

Don't move. Not a sound. The other thing will hear you. A cockroach. A nasty but harmless roach.

For several seconds no sounds emitted from her unwelcome companion, and then she felt something skitter up the bare skin of her back. Her hair stood on end as it scuttled up her spine, across a shoulder and then down again.

A spider?

She pictured a Black Widow scurrying unchecked about her body. She envisioned the bright red hourglass etched like blood on the plump, glossy abdomen. She sucked in hard at the thought of fangs poised to sink into her flesh. Then her imagination tugged another direction. Now a half-dollar-sized scorpion explored her bare skin. Brown markings stood out on the thick circular body. A stinger protruded from its segmented tail. In her mind, she watched the stinger draw closer and closer to her skin. She choked back a scream.

A fiery prickle brought her upright. Leaking tears, she pressed her back against the wall. The insect burst with a repulsive pop. Warm liquid oozed down her back.

She wanted to desert the claustrophobic closet and to crawl into a hot bath. She longed to scrub away the sweat and goo and soak away the tension. Fear of what might be exploring the house, lurking in wait for her, killed the urge. She leaned back, and within minutes drifted into exhausted sleep.

Clomp. Clomp. Clomp.

Heavy footfalls on the hardwood floor jerked her awake.

It's here. Her instincts recognized that something evil and deadly, something with no compassion and no mercy had arrived.

Clomp. Clomp. Clomp.

Thumpathumpathumpa. Her heart attempted to beat its way out of her chest. Woozy from fear, she squeezed her eyes shut.

"I know you're here, pretty girl."

Don? No, it can't be.

She scooted close to the door and pressed her ear against the wood.

"Naomi, you're so pretty when you smile," Don's familiar voice enticed.

Don came back?

She reached up and grasped the doorknob, and then jerked it away as if the metal was fiery to the touch.

It's a trick.

"New Orleans, Naomi. Remember? Painters on sidewalks. Mimes. Wonderful food."

New Orleans? No one but Don could know about New Orleans.

Her hand once again ascended to the doorknob, but fear refused to let her turn it.

"Mountains, Naomi. Remember how we planned to visit the mountains? And go to Disney World and see funny loveable Goofy?"

She turned the knob, flinching at the loud click. She pushed the door ajar. Afraid of what might be waiting to gobble her up, she placed an eye to the narrow opening. There Don stood, exactly as she remembered him, the same warm smile, startling blue eyes and curly blond hair. She rose to her feet, pushed the door wide and stepped from the closet. For a moment she stood on unsteady legs, her eyes devouring her long-lost love, then collapsed into his outstretched arms. She buried her head in his chest and inhaled his masculine scent. The tension drained away. She raised her head and his lips closed over her mouth. His probing tongue awakened forgotten passions.

Safe. At last I'm safe. Nothing can hurt me now.

No, you are not safe, an inner voice insisted. *Get out of here, get out now.*

She pulled away from Don's rousing kiss, the security of his arms. "We have to leave. Something is out there, and it's coming for us. I can feel it." She grabbed his hand and tugged toward the door, but he stood firm.

"Naomi, nothing is out there."

She increased the pressure. "Please, please. Don't you

understand, there is something out there, and it means to hurt us? I can't lose you again. I'd rather die."

"I'm glad to hear you say that." His voice came out in a monotone and icy enough to send a chill through her.

Confused by his coldness, she dropped his hand and stepped back. The man before her looked like Don, still possessed the same rugged handsomeness, but had been robbed of every trace of humanity. It was like looking at the shell of the person he had once been. His mouth twisted into a sinister sneer. Not a hint of warmth lingered in that malevolent smile. He studied her with the detachment of a scientist viewing a lab specimen.

"I have something for you. Something very special." He brought his arm from behind his back. "We will never be separated again."

Her heart leapt into her throat at the sight of a double-edged ax grasped in his fist. The blades were honed to razor sharpness.

She backed away. "Why would you hurt me? You loved me. I know you loved me."

"I still love you. I love you so much I couldn't stay away. You see, the only way we can be together is in death. You have to die. It's that simple. After all, you did say you'd rather die than lose me again."

His coldness, the detachment in his voice, grated her nerves. As he talked, she continued to inch toward the door, each timid step increasing her hope for escape.

"I'm only granting your—" In mid-sentence, he hesitated, his face contorting into a mask of agony. The side of his head imploded and his right eye disappeared into a bloody crevice.

Paralyzed to the spot, she could not tear her eyes from the Don-thing metamorphosing before her.

The hair and scalp disintegrated, the skull split exposing a pulpy mass of brain matter. His chest caved inward and stomach burst splattering strings of intestines and chunks of gore to the floor with sickening plops.

Those disgusting plops released her from paralysis. She turned and sprinted toward the door.

Whomp.

The door slammed shut. She worked at the knob. Her hands slid as if the metal had been coated with a layer of petroleum jelly.

Laughter filled the room. "Come now. You'd rather die than lose me again. That's what you said."

She wiped her palms down the legs of her jeans, and then tried the door again. Still, she could find no purchase on the stubborn knob.

Clomp clomp clomp.

She glanced over her shoulder. The Don-thing was no more than four feet away, the ax suspended over his ruined head.

She grasped the knob with the tail of her blouse, and this time managed a firm grip.

Thank God.

She twisted hard. The knob refused to turn. She willed it to give.

Turn. In the name of God, turn.

Despite the pressure, the knob would not move. Her arms dropped to her sides and head lowered in resignation.

"Your father did this to me. When I vowed I'd come back for you, he blasted me face-on with that double-barreled shotgun. Kind of messy, wouldn't you say? Guess he wanted to make double sure I couldn't come back. Double sure." He chuckled at the unintended pun. "A vow is a vow, my love. Don't you agree?"

Whoosh.

The ax descended.

Naomi awoke with a headache the size of Texas, a stark image of Don Miller etched in her brain. Tears leaked down her cheeks.

Jeff Chambers tossed and turned in an effort to rouse himself from deep sleep that held him captive in his own version of hell. He stood in a darkened hallway in the basement of Caddo Hospital. The double doors leading into the morgue loomed before him. The smell of disinfectant hung as heavy as rain in the musty air. His nose wrinkled at the underlying odor of stale blood.

The doors to the morgue swung inward. He stepped through the entry like a marionette controlled by the invisible strings of a sadistic puppeteer. A gurney shrouded with a white sheet stood in the center of the large room. The outline of a cadaver stood out in the cold illumination of overhead fluorescent lights.

He shuffled deeper into the room, each uncontrolled step drawing him nearer to the shrouded figure.

You really don't want to see what lies beneath that sheet, Jeff.

As if reading his thoughts, the sheet slid from the table and fluttered across the room where it hovered for a brief moment like a ghost butterfly before dropping to the floor.

The nude, marble-white corpse of Daniel Harrison rested on the stainless steel surface. The cadaver still wore the expensive black shoes worn on the day of his death, the day Jeff injected him with a lethal drug dose. Sutured autopsy incisions ran like railroad tracks from the chest to the abdomen. A jagged line encircled the corpse's head as if a blunt knife rather than a keen scalpel had made the cut.

Keep your cool. You've seen dead bodies before, bodies blown into pieces so small that a shoe box would have sufficed for a coffin. Bodies burned so badly that nothing remained but chunks of charred meat. You've seen eyeballs dangling from sockets and blood seeping from every opening. This is nothing more than a neat little cadaver, autopsied and ready for burial. Nothing to be afraid of.

The corpse's eyelids popped open. The cold dead eyes stared at him. The Harrison-thing chuckled. "Can't say I didn't warn you, Chief. One little scratch, remember?"

He struggled to back away, but his muscles refused to respond.

The cadaver sat up, dangling its legs over the side of the gurney. A white finger shot out and pointed at the expensive shoes. "I like nice things, remember? All those pretty girls in your nice little town. Don't you think they'll love the new me? I warned you, Chief. One little scratch."

The corpse slid from the gurney to its feet. It stood for a moment with its head lolling from side to side, too heavy a burden for the feeble neck. The eyes rolled back exposing the whites. The sinewy arms flailed and then stiffened. The fingers curled into tight fists. The knees buckled and the corpse dropped to the floor.

Weak with relief at the turn of events, Jeff reached out and supported himself on the side of the steel gurney. The Harrison-thing thrashed about on the floor, convulsed, twisted and jerked, its features contorted in pain.

No worries here. All feathers, no meat in this son of a bitch. Big talk. Couldn't harm a housefly with swatters in both hands.

Sprawled on its back, the corpse kicked one last time, then ceased to move.

Jeff nudged an arm with his foot. Gaining a bit of courage, he nudged harder. The arm flopped. The Harrison-thing was now as harmless as a dead rattlesnake. He exhaled a sigh of relief.

The corpse opened its eyes and chuckled. "Surprise, surprise, surprise." It arched its back and flipped to its feet with the agility of an acrobat. "How do you like our little game so far, Chief? Huh? Personally, I'm enjoying it immensely." The words carried the stench of putrefaction.

Jeff attempted to bolt for the door, but once again found himself under control of the sadistic puppeteer. Tears of frustration burned his eyes.

"Ahhh, you're not having fun, are you? Well, I say we make it a little more interesting."

The corpse moved away, its footfalls echoing in the cavernous room. It stopped at a steel top counter and stared down at a multitude of syringes and vials. It selected a large syringe, and with the expertise of a practiced drug addict, extracted serum from a vial. A bloodless thumb pressed the plunger. A glistening stream of clear liquid shot from the tip of the needle.

Jeff was reminded of a doctor preparing to administer an injection. But the Harrison-thing was no doctor, and he knew there was no benevolence intended here. The serum was deadly and had been concocted for him.

The corpse made its way back to the gurney, and with a quick jab, plunged the long needle into Jeff's chest. Jeff watched the serum disappear into his body. He found himself swept into a state of euphoria. He floated to the floor. Contented to the depths of his soul, he smiled up at the giver of such bliss.

The corpse smiled back, an expression of satisfaction on its bloodless face.

"Complete satisfaction," Jeff giggled. "Must have had a Dr. Pepper." He roared with laughter at his clever quip.

The room began to spin around and around and around. A brilliant propeller of multicolored lights flashed through his vision. A golden doorway formed in the center of the spectacular kaleidoscope. His father stepped through.

"Dr. Pepper is the friendly pepper-upper. Really, Jeff, I'm disappointed in you."

"Gol-dang, Dad, it sure is good to hear your voice. How—"

"I'm here to try to get you out of this tight spot, not for a social visit. So, man-up, huh? What's the right answer? Complete satisfaction?"

"Wrigley's spearmint gum, of course. Right?"

His father's head dropped to his chest. "All that money on an education, and you can't even correctly answer a simple question. Where did I go wrong?"

"You know I wasn't some nerd who never watched TV. I saw all the commercials."

"Maybe so, but one more strike and you're out. Strike-o. Bunk-o. Out-o. You ready to put your brain into first gear, to try again?"

"Hell yes, I want to try again."

"You don't have to get testy. I'm only here to help you. Answer the question?"

"I know the answer," a woman's voice proclaimed.

"Molly?" Jeff stared in disbelief at his dead wife posed in the golden doorway.

She graced him with a pretty smile. "Want me to tell you."

Jeff's father shook his head. "Molly, you can't tell him, it would be cheating."

Jeff nodded. "Dad's right. I can't let you tell me the answer.

You know I never cheat."

"If that's the way you want it," Molly said. "Always too smart for your own britches. *Always* a little smarter than anybody else. I certainly know when I'm not wanted." With a flourish, she turned and stepped back into golden light.

Jeff's heart broke at the sight of her disappearing in the golden hue. "Wait, please wait."

"She's gone. Now let's get this over with."

"Okay. Let's see. Coke or Pepsi? Pepsi, I think. Pepsi is the one that satisfies. I'm almost positive."

His father grinned. "That your final answer? Five seconds to change your mind. One-Mississippi, two-Mississippi, three-Mississippi, four-Mississippi, five-Miss—"

"Wait, wait. I've changed my mind. Coke is my answer. Coca-Cola completely satisfies."

His Dad's grin faded. "That's not right. You lose." His head bowed in defeat, he turned and stepped through the golden doorway. The magical door dissolved.

Jeff looked up at the Harrison-thing silhouetted above him in the harsh fluorescent glow. His sense of euphoria dissipated.

"No consolation prizes for losers."

A tingling sensation awoke in his toes, traveled up his legs, flowed into his torso and shoulders and shot down both arms and into his hands. Liquid fire replaced the tingling. He stiffened and his eyes bulged. His mouth stretched wide into a silent scream. Muscle and bone disintegrated under the fiery onslaught. His skin sizzled and popped like bacon thrown into a hot skillet. His eyes were consumed by the internal fire. He plunged ever downward into a bottomless black sea before jerking upright in his sweat-soaked bed.

Unlike other Caddo citizens trapped in terrifying nightmares, Mark Ferrell was once again a carefree teenager in a fun-filled dream cavorting with his brother Jeremy in a cemetery.

"Ruth Burton," Mark read in the bright glow of a Coleman lantern. "I found it. Come on, help me move it over by Wynn

Dobbs. Old lady Dobbs will shit when she sees this, everybody knows they were fucking."

They wrestled the cumbersome headstone twenty or so yards to the other grave site and set it in place. They stepped back to admire their handiwork.

"All right," they chimed, giving each other the high-five.

Mark picked up a shovel. "Let's get started on Adam Baxter. Shouldn't be too hard, just buried him last week. Dirt ain't had time to settle good."

Jeremy grabbed a shovel and followed his brother to the grave site.

At the clink of metal on the coffin lid, Jeremy stopped digging, leaned on his shovel and rested his back against the earth wall. "Whew, that's damn hard work." He sleeved sweat from his forehead, leaving behind a muddy streak. "I vote we forget this, ain't no way we'll get this big motherfucker out of this hole."

"Yeah, you're right," Mark said. "Didn't realize a coffin was so big." His brow wrinkled in thought, and then a wide grin brightened his face. "So we don't prop open the coffin against the gate. So what? We go to plan B. Right, little brother?"

"What the hell you talking about? There ain't no plan B."

"Sure 'nough is. Just figured it out. All we have to do is open the coffin and take the body out. Oh, the awesome possibilities. Maybe hang old Adam by the neck from that big oak at the entrance. Or tie him spread eagle to the gate, you know—like crucified. Hell, we could lay him in the middle of the road like a hit and run victim, then sit back and wait for a car to come along. Talk about blowing someone's mind."

"Bullshit, Mark. I ain't touching no dead body. Up yours. End of discussion."

"You're a pussy. The dead can't hurt you. The creep was a shithead, liked to feel up little kids. Nobody will care what we do to the bastard."

"I still ain't touching him."

"Big pussy. Didn't realize I had a titty-baby for a brother."

"Okay, smart-ass, if you're so brave, open the coffin. Once you see the corpse, if you still have the balls to tie a rope around him, I'll help heft him out. But you damn well better understand, I ain't touching no dead body."

"Your best offer, huh? Guess I don't have a choice, do I? If I'd known you were such a pantywaist, I'd brought Karl along. He'd eat this son of a bitch for lunch."

"Well, Karl ain't here, so shut up. I'll climb out and throw you the rope."

"Not so fast. Still more dirt to get out of here, and you can at least help me with the lid. Won't have to put your lily-white hands on the body, I'll take care of that part."

"Okay, let's get it done."

"Damn it all, next time I'm bringing Karl," Mark grumbled, attacking the loose soil with a vengeance.

With a loud crack, the lid sprang free. Putrid gas filled the grave. Hacking and gagging, their noses pinched, the boys blinked away stinging tears.

"Jesus."

Bitter gorge erupted into their mouths, and their dinners splattered the coffin.

They scaled the dirt wall. Mark's foot connected with the Coleman lantern balanced on a makeshift perch in a corner of their work space. The glass globe shattered against the metal coffin, plunging the grave into blackness.

His head clear of the opening, Jeremy sucked fresh air. His feet continued to plow earth as he groped about for a solid hold. Handfuls of brown, frostbitten grass pulled away, and he began to slide back into the grave. Icy hands closed around his ankles. His bladder evacuated. "Mark," he mouthed, before being wrenched backwards into the inky void. A bloodcurdling scream erupted from the grave.

Mark stiffened, almost losing his balance. He made a wild grab for the headstone. Maintaining a death grip on the heavy stone, he pulled himself free. He lay on the grass gasping for air. He found the strength to rise to his knees and lean over the grave.

"Jeremy?"

Silence.

"Can you hear me, Jeremy?"

Silence.

"JEEER-AH-MEE!"

He sat up and looked around. Shadowy contours of headstones and mausoleums speckled the moonlit grounds. Trees stood like specters against the sky.

There was a feel of abandonment about the place. Something was missing, something vital. The answer dawned on him; there were no chirps from crickets or croaks from frogs and toads. Only silence. He tried to recall if he had heard the familiar night sounds earlier, but could not remember. The depressing silence was almost heavy enough to bow his back. He shivered more from fear than from the coldness than had settled on the cemetery.

He rose to his feet and made his way back to the tree where they had dumped their equipment. He knelt and groped about in search of a flashlight. "Damn it to hell, stupid Jeremy probably broke his fucking leg or something. The old man ain't going to be happy about this. Gonna be hell to pay. Kick our asses all the way into the next fucking county."

He identified the water jug, their jackets, a pick and a rope.

"No fucking flashlight."

Then he remembered Jeremy's words. *Forget the flashlights. Lantern's full of fuel and will be plenty enough light.*

"The son of a bitch." His anger blunted his fear. "What am I suppose to do now?"

His eyes strained in search of the pickup. It may as well have been parked on Mars for all he could see.

Something flickered by the Johnson mausoleum. "Oh Jesus."

Nah, couldn't be anything.

Something is there, moving through the trees.

He conjured up the image of a vampire with glowing red eyes. A wide, cruel grin stood out on its alabaster face. Vicious fangs dripped the blood of an earlier victim, and now the monster was coming for him.

His heart palpitated. Limp from fear and near to fainting, he lowered his head between his knees and sucked hard on crisp air.

"Dammit, stop imagining things." The air had turned a bit nippy. He slipped on his jacket and patted about the pockets. He felt the box of wooden matches used to light the Coleman lantern.

"Yes, yes. Your mama didn't raise no dummy. Well, maybe one. Jeremy has Malt-O-Meal for brains."

The meager illumination of a single match bolstered his courage, but not enough to walk by the Johnson mausoleum to reach the pickup. Not with a vampire roaming around.

He draped the coil of rope over his shoulder, and guided by the flickering light cupped in his hands, made his way back to the grave site.

He knelt by the open grave.

"Jeremy, I've got matches and the rope. I can get you out."

Silence.

"Answer me."

Silence

"Dammit, groan or do something. Anything."

Silence.

He flattened to his stomach, suspending his head and shoulders over the hole. The stench of decay took his breath. He pinched his nostrils and breathed through his mouth. A vivid picture formed in his mind: Jeremy in the coffin entwined in the arms of the corpse, his mouth slack and head angled.

His blood turned to ice water and his heartbeat tripled. Sweat popped out on his forehead. A warning growl emitted from his churning bowels. The nausea returned full force.

"Oh God, not now. Not again."

He squeezed his eyes tight and swallowed hard. The nausea abated. He forced away the morbid picture, but another scene slipped into its place: Jeremy's lank form plummeted from the second story roof. With a thud and loud grunt, he landed on his back. Appearing stunned, he rose to his elbows and looked up. "Watch that step. It's a big one."

Fifteen feet, Mark calculated. Fell fifteen feet and not so much as a scratch.

The grave? Six feet?

Wait a minute. Halfway out when he slid back in. Two, maybe three foot drop. Couldn't be hurt.

Then why isn't he answering?

Of course, another of his practical jokes.

Sure he had hit on the answer, he removed a match from the box. It slipped from his trembling fingers and dropped into the blackness.

He removed several matches and scraped the heads against the side of the box. Blessed bright light flared in his face.

"Now, let's see what the hell is going on."

He lowered the miniature torch. Flickering shadows darted from the dirt walls. A chilling wind gusted upward extinguishing the flame. An icy hand closed around his wrist.

"Damn you, Jeremy. You and your childish jokes. Real funny. I'm kicking your ass."

The grip tightened and dragged him headfirst into the darkness.

Mark snapped awake with the image of earth spilling like a miniature landslide into an open grave. He shuddered and wiped away gooseflesh from his arms.

The children of Caddo dreamed of scary places alive with monsters and spiders and snakes. No matter how loud they cried or how hard they wished, their mommies and daddies would not come to rescue them.

Three-year-old Jenni Sneider dreamed of a mean-looking angel carved from glistening blue ice. The stern-faced creature hunted children and froze them solid with a touch of its long sword.

Lauri Sneider dreamed of first grade with ghouls for teachers. The punishment for any infraction of the rules was death.

Pearl Turner dreamed of poison food and angry customers and of a visitation by the rotted corpse of her dead husband.

Sharon Saunders dreamed of haunted houses and haunted cars where she was forced to take refuge against her dead mother who pursued her with the purpose of murder in mind.

People dreamed of cheating spouses and vengeful relatives and of dead things that go bump in the night.

Most awoke feeling less rested than when they had gone to bed. Many of these weary souls sought companionship. Any companionship would do, human or animal. Few people could face the prospect of being alone, even in broad daylight.

CHAPTER 12

Sharon Saunders scanned sheets of paper, and then dropped each reject back into the overflowing tray balanced on her lap. She reminded George Sneider of a raccoon rummaging through a garbage can; one cursory glance, and back into the clutter the unacceptable tidbit goes.

Twenty-five pounds of excess weight detracted from the middle-aged woman's attractiveness. Chestnut-tinted hair swept back from the face culminated in a French twist. A teal silk suit, not designer quality but from a finer department store complemented her flawless complexion. The expensive clothing and meticulous grooming gave her the look of success. She looked out of place amid the disarray of the cramped office. Stacks of paper and a staggering number of books ranging from novels to outdated real estate manuals claimed every available surface in the compact room.

George shifted in search of a comfortable position in the straight-back wooden chair. The dark mood that materialized on entering the stuffy real estate office deepened with each passing minute. An expanding knot of anxiety had settled in the pit of his stomach.

He did not want to be here. He did not want to talk about the house, to see the house and he damn well did not want to buy the house. Penney's cajoling and his need to please her had coaxed him here today. Yesterday afternoon they made the three-hour drive to Caddo and checked into a small motel that had seen better days. A noisy window unit air conditioner performed with the efficiency of a commercial freezer. To their surprise, the king-sized bed proved firm and comfortable. Still, he had slept fitfully. Plagued by nightmares and a nagging sense of wrongness about the town, he made several middle-of-the-night treks to the door and windows to assure all locks were secured. Drained of energy and in a cynical state of mind, he accompanied Penney to the midmorning appointment.

Penney had requested no more from him than a quick walk-through. If he then rejected the house, there would be no hard feelings. They would forget that place and resume their search for something acceptable to them both.

So, what's your problem, George? Appears to me you're holding all the cards. A quick look-see, and you're off the hook. Penney is a woman of her word. Lighten up, huh?

In an effort to dispel his grim mood, he leaned over and whispered, "If we stole her tray, betcha she'd go out of business."

"Hush. She'll hear you."

"Ah now, pilgrim," he drawled in a credible John Wayne imitation, "she cain't hear a thing over that fan blowin' right thar in her ears. Tell you what, pretend like you gotta use the toilet, and make it good. Lean over and groan, maybe turn a little green while y'ur at it. When she gits up to show you the john, I'll snatch the tray and bolt out the door. Five hundred dollars ransom is what we'll demand."

Helpless to contain a giggle, Penney rolled her eyes and gave him a *please behave* look.

"I found it," Sharon sang out in triumph. "Rosenberg, Robert, a hundred and twenty-five thousand. As I told you, best buy in Caddo."

"When was the house built?" George asked, gloom once again enfolding him.

"Well, let's see," she said, tilting her head to bring the lines into focus through her bifocals. "1988. Built when there was still genuine craftsmanship. Lots of real wood, not that pressed together stuff used today. Both the air conditioner and roof were replaced a little over three years ago. The deal of a lifetime."

"Let's get serious. Real wood or not, that house is falling apart. A pocketful of money will have to be laid out for repairs before it can be sold."

"Now, Honey," Penney chimed in, "from the outside it looks worse than it really is. I've seen the inside and it's in pretty fair condition. Nothing wrong that paint and elbow grease can't fix. The girls can have their own rooms. There's even a spare room for the office you've always wanted."

"I suppose it doesn't need new carpet and updated tile and new drapes and new—"

"Yes, it does, but for that price we can afford all those things. It's twice the house of any new ones I looked at. And those beautiful oaks and—"

"Hold it." Sharon interrupted. "I know something I think will make you both happy." She glanced about as if to assure they were alone. Her voice lowered to a degree that they had to lean forward to hear over the whir of the fan. "I trust you not to tell anyone I told you this, ethics and all. The owner lives in California and wants to sell the house as is. Doesn't want the hassle of fixing it up, him so far away and all. If you offered a hundred thousand, he'd grab it."

Penney's mouth broadened into a grin that gave her the appearance of a child who had won an all-expenses-paid family vacation to Disneyland.

A con, flashed through George's head like a bright neon sign in bold blinking letters. *A con. A con. A con.*

"New air conditioner, new roof and a little paint and elbow grease will fix this place up fine and dandy. This guy, out of the kindness of his heart is ready to give it away. A hundred thousand is ridiculous. There's something rotten out West."

Penney cleared her throat, her eyes wide in a plea of understanding. "It's no big deal. Something unpleasant happened in the house. People won't even look at it." She glanced at Sharon for confirmation. "We're the only ones who have shown any interest. Should've told you up front, but I wanted you to see the inside first. I didn't want some silly story to taint your perception."

Her explanation did little to assuage the irritation now bordering on anger or his feeling of being the butt end of a joke.

She didn't trust me to be adult about something unpleasant.

Clanka-clanka-clanka. The rhythm of an off-center blade in the fan grated like a bow string stretched between his temples. A dull headache was threatening to evolve into a migraine. The air felt depleted of oxygen. He needed out of here. "Sharon, we've taken enough of your valuable time. Give us the key, we'll drive over and have a quick look."

"Oh, no need. I'll be glad to drive you."

Penney came to the rescue. "No, that's not necessary. We need to make a stop by the motel."

"Well, if you're sure." She removed the key from a desk drawer and handed it to Penney. "I'll be glad to pick you up at the motel? Save you a trip back here."

George stood, grasped her right hand and pumped her arm. "You've done enough. Don't mind dropping the key by."

Once outside, he exhaled a deep breath. "That's the most persistent female I've ever met. Let's get the hell out of here before she decides to follow us."

Maneuvering the minivan into the street, he said, "What say we get something cold to drink and a hamburger? Take it back to the room?"

"Sounds good to me."

CHAPTER 13

Mouthwatering aromas issued from the paper sack decorated with a grinning Ronald McDonald. George unlocked the door and followed Penney into the motel room. They ate their high cholesterol meal in silence.

An overhand pitch sent the crumpled McDonald's bag sailing across the room where it dropped into the metal waste can with a dull thud.

Penney grinned. "Didn't know I married a Michael Jordan."

"I'm the man." His expression turned thoughtful. "Something is bothering me about this move and I can't put my finger on it."

She opened her mouth to speak, but was cut off by a hand gesture.

"This is probably the dumbest thing you've ever heard and I feel stupid telling it." He hesitated to consider his words. "No, stupid is the wrong word. Backward is the word I'm looking for. Backward like mountain people who believe in ghosts and witches and hexes. This town doesn't feel right. It's like my guts are telling me to beware. At first I related it to moving jitters, new job, new people. Now I'm not so sure. The Brandon house was my childhood fantasy of everything I thought was evil. Most kids picked Dracula or zombies or some sort of ghoul. Not me. I picked an old house. I let that place scare me so bad one time that I peed my pants. Haven't thought of it in years. It's perplexing why all of a sudden I'm flooded with all those old memories." Laughing nervously, he said, "The town just doesn't feel right."

He perceived no understanding in Penney's expression. Warmth from embarrassment invaded his face. Attempting to make light of the situation, he fell into a Boris Karloff imitation. "There's evil seeping into these here streets of Caddo."

With a grin she said, "That Karloff imitation needs work. As to this feeling you have, I haven't felt anything but warmth and friendliness. But that shouldn't account for much. I believe humans are endowed with intuition—a sixth sense, gut-feelings, whatever you want to call it," she said, gesturing with her hands for the right term. "Smart people should pay attention to these warnings. I believe these perceptions are normally on target and can save a lot of grief if heeded. It doesn't matter which of us picks up negative vibes, we should both be concerned."

Feeling relieved, he squared his shoulders.

"Well, my love, what now?" she asked.

"What I would most like is to hear the big secret about that house. My curiosity is killing me." He fell backwards on the bed, tore at his collar and emitted choking sounds. Feigning his last death throes, he tossed about with his legs churning the air.

She laughed. "Okay, clown, if you'll stop dying, I'll tell you the big mystery."

George sat up. "Okay, shoot."

"According to Sharon Saunders, back in the mid-eighties there was another house on the lot. It caught on fire in the middle of the night. A mother and two children were asleep inside. A little boy was trapped in a bedroom, and by the time the fire department got there, it was too late. The mother got out unharmed, but went back in after her kids. She managed to get the daughter out, but both of them were burned so badly they only survived a couple of weeks. Sharon said there were three funerals in a matter of weeks, saddest thing the town had ever been through. Not a dry eye to be found anywhere."

"What about the father?"

"I don't know, but for some reason he wasn't there. Sharon may have told me why, I don't remember. The poor man lost his entire family. Never got over it. Turned into the town drunk."

"Can you imagine what he must have gone through? I'd have ended up in the loony bin weaving baskets."

"Understand why I didn't tell you sooner? You know how you are, tend to take on everybody else's pain. I was afraid you wouldn't be able to get those poor children out of your mind and wouldn't really *see* the house."

"Know me pretty well, don't you?"

"There's still more. Sad, but not as tragic."

"Let's hear it."

"Another house was built there. For the last ten years or so an older couple lived in it. It's their son who's trying to sell the place. Probably doesn't want any part of it after what—"

"Okay, move on."

She threw him a smirk. "Sharon told me that last September the woman was preparing dinner, and keeled over dead. Heart attack, according to the coroner. Not according to her husband, though. The old man wandered the town babbling that the house was haunted, and *they* killed his wife. Whoever *they* are. He claimed her face was frozen in an expression of pure terror. Said she was so frightened, her heart quit beating. She was literally scared to death. Of course, nobody believed him. They were married forty-eight years, and the old man couldn't handle the loss. Went off his rocker. Quit shaving or bathing and wore the same dirty clothes for weeks at a time. Committed suicide. Shot himself in the head."

"Why didn't someone notify his son before it got so bad?"

"I asked Sharon the same question. She said the police did call him, maybe a month before the old man killed himself. His fair-haired child wasn't too concerned."

"You know, according to Sharon, nobody believed the old man's stories. Isn't it interesting that she can't get anyone to look at the house?"

The hint of an idea nudged its way into George's brain, and then germinated into full understanding. Love, hate, pain, fear—strong emotions, linger long after a person dies. The soul enters a new universe, but like the physical body, unharnessed energy remains behind. So much pain. So much suffering. The energies left behind in the house manifested his worst childhood fears. Caddo was no different from any other small town with its past tragedies. Nothing here to be afraid of. No bogeyman in Caddo.

Wait a minute. For days you've been worried, half scared out of your mind. And now you're ready to accept the first half-baked theory that pops into your head.

Half-baked, hell. Sound reasoning is what we're talking here.

Despite a lingering wariness, he was sure he had figured out the source of his fears, and was flooded with a sense of relief.

"You ain't going to believe this, but I think I may have figured out my problem. I'd try to explain, but it's a little complicated, and I could be wrong. Since we're here and have the key, what say we go have a look-see at that house?"

Penney shrugged in submission. Making a quick circuit of the room in search of her purse, she glanced into the bathroom and behind the bed before spotting it in a chair by the door. She opened the clasp and checked the zippered pocket for the house key. She slipped the purse strap over her shoulder. "Let's go."

George eased the van to the curb, and sat for a moment with the motor running to study two immense oaks that ate up the front yard of the large brick home.

"Damn, can't believe I missed them last time."

While Penney headed for the front door, he wandered the exterior. Curls of peeling brown paint looked like colonies of roaches on the sagging eaves and warped shutters. Knobby, overgrown shrubs crowded weed-infested flowerbeds. A few anemic begonias struggled for life among the weeds. He squatted to examine the yellowed lawn. Handfuls of dried grass pulled away.

Penney hollered, "I'm going in. See you in a minute."

He waved, and then trotted toward the front porch. He stopped for a moment to visualize the house painted a cream color, the useless shutters discarded and the windows polished. His mind's eye could see the huge oaks reflected like surreal paintings in the gleaming glass. The lawn was transformed into a thick emerald carpet. An assortment of ornate shrubbery and a mélange of bright flowers flourished in flowerbeds. The picture in his head was so real he swore he could hear honey bees and wasps buzzing about the imaginary flowers.

Stepping into the entry was like being welcomed by an old friend. He knelt and ran his hands over the cool smooth surface of the neglected floor. He envisioned the marble restored to its original elegance. His reflection stared back at him from the gleaming stone.

He wandered into a large den where a massive fireplace claimed more than half of a wall. A brick hearth large enough to support fireplace implements as well as the bulkiest of Penney's potted plants extended into the room.

"Could park the minivan on that sucker."

He reached up and brushed away cobwebs from the mantle. An appreciative whistle escaped his lips at skillful carvings embodied with delicate blooms and entwined with intricate vines. The miniature flowers appeared to have been picked and transformed to wood. Chubby cherubs with plump arms and legs and rounded bellies decorated the corners of the heavy mantle. Graceful wings flowed from the figures, and angelic eyes stared into the heavens. Euphoric expressions had been captured on the childlike faces.

In a flash, the innocent faces distorted, grew ugly and menacing. Alien eyes radiating hate mocked him. Fear surged through him, leaving his knees almost too weak to support his body. Fueled by an urge to find Penney and flee the house, he struggled against a force that had him cemented in place. He attempted to scream, but could muster no more than an inaudible squeak. The paralyzing pressure relented, and he collapsed on the large hearth. Too terrified to move, he waited for the *they* the old man had babbled about.

As if a stopper had been pulled, the fear flowed away. A sense of euphoria settled on him. His senses sparkled with life. Basking in heightened awareness, he relaxed and let his body go limp.

The tranquil crackle of burning logs emitted from the empty firebox and the pleasant fragrance of wood smoke permeated the room. Despite the ninety-degree temperature, he hugged himself for warmth against frigid wind assaulting the doors and windows. He visualized Penney posed on a blanket, coaxing him to join her. The soft glow of firelight accentuated the sensuous curves of her body.

Laughter and the clinks of dinnerware dissolved the erotic vision and brought him to his feet. The savory aroma of roast beef drew him toward the dining room. His stomach gurgled. The taste of Penney's rich burgundy sauce bloomed in his mouth.

He stepped into the spacious room where an array of expensively attired people was seated at a large dinner table. The bejeweled, coiffured women had the look of fashion models. The fragrances of high-dollar perfumes and colognes tinged the air.

Fred Zimmermann, Caddo Mayor, whose stern demeanor bespoke money and power, appeared to be the center of attention. Beside him sat Jeff Chambers, his boyish grin fixed. The entire city council along with their spouses had seen fit to attend this social gathering.

Penney, her face aglow with a perfect hostess smile, was by far the most beautiful woman in the room. Coppery hair, afire with shimmering highlights, rested in intricate curls atop her head. Her hazel eyes, transformed to emeralds by her velvety green gown, moved about the table as she responded to bits and pieces of conversation.

Flickering candlelight played an array of iridescent hues through crystal carafes of Cabernet Sauvignon placed at each end of the table.

Antiquated drapes, threadbare and containing enough dust to throw an asthmatic into respiratory failure, had been replaced with fashionable shades. The mute peach and seafoam green tints of the window treatments accented a large area rug on which the dining table had been centered. Outdated wallpaper had been stripped and the room painted. The creamy, peach-colored walls gave the room an air of warmth and spaciousness.

Lauri and Jenni, scrubbed and smelling of perfumed soap and looking like pixies in identical granny gowns, entered the room. He watched as they hugged and kissed their mother, then turned and curtsied with shy goodnights to the guests.

"Aren't they darling?"

"How well mannered."

"Such beautiful girls."

Lauri glanced back as she followed her sister out of the room. Her aquamarine eyes twinkled with mischief. George recognized the look, and knew his oldest daughter longed for a last minute invitation to join the festivities. Jenni, his shy one, flushed with embarrassment at the free flowing praise, kept her eyes glued to the floor.

His deepest instincts told him he belonged here. He had come home.

"Hey, George, where are you?" returned him to the shabby dining room.

"I'm here," he shouted, heading toward the sound of her voice. He located her in the kitchen, on hand and knees, exploring the inside of a cabinet. Backing out, first her shoulders came into view and then her head. Cobwebs and fluffy dust balls clung to her hair looking like a crown of snowflakes. She shook her head and ran her fingers through her hair. "These cabinets are wonderful, solid wood and sturdy as the day they were built. I guess this is what Sharon meant by lots of real wood."

"I've done some pretty close checking, too, and you know, at a hundred thousand we'll be screwing this guy without even kissing him."

She grinned. "You certainly have a way with words, Mr. Counselor. Have you seen the bedrooms yet? The master is huge. The master bath you won't believe. Glass shower large enough to hold a family meeting with room left over for refreshments. And a gorgeous marble tub."

"Well, dummy, are you going sit on the floor babbling or show me?"

She raised a hand. "Here, help me up."

Groaning like a body builder straining at an overloaded barbell, he pulled her to her feet. "Gained a pound or two have we?"

"No, I haven't, so I guess you must be getting a little too old for the likes of me." Wrinkling her nose and sticking out her tongue, she skirted away, but not quick enough to avoid a pop on the butt.

Following her through the den toward a darkened hallway, he

detected the lingering aroma of wood smoke.

In the master bedroom, harsh white sunlight streamed through wide French doors, creating an elongated checkerboard pattern on the carpet.

The small patio proved as hot as a preheated oven. Waves of stifling heat snaked upward from the baked concrete. Blue and orange hues issued from blistering glass panes like open flames. The brutal Texas sun had sucked every drop of moisture from the soil and left behind a barren yard dissected into a network of deep cracks and dotted with sparse clumps of dead grass.

After a compulsory tour of the master bath—bathrooms not his forte—he settled on the ledge of a six-foot bay window to pursue his favorite pastime: watching Penney.

He recognized her look. In her mind, she was already decorating the room. She walked about, marking off areas for furniture, envisioning paint and window treatments. She prattled aloud, seeking his opinions, but not waiting for replies before her mind darted in another direction.

Leaning back and throwing an occasional "Uh huh" "Yeah" or "I think so," he became aroused. He grew hard. Delicious heat coursed through his veins with the force of an electrical current. Enticing waves of female scent washed across the room; the erotic fragrance invaded his lungs and left him gasping for air. A lifetime of desire unfurled in his groin. He was consumed by sheer animal lust, a sexual drive that demanded gratification.

As if guided by unseen hands, he stood and made his way toward Penney. He seemed to glide in slow motion as if suspended inches from the floor, his feet making no contact with the solid surface. He reached her, and forced her tight against him, his fingers burying in the flesh of her thighs. His need elevated to an unbearable level, and a bestial groan swelled in his throat.

Startled by her husband's unexpected roughness, Penney attempted to pull away, but was held prisoner in his rigid arms. The face staring down at her no longer resembled the man she had shared her life with for seven years. Only a touch of blue was visible around his dilated pupils. The sinister black orbs studied her. Purple-blue veins bulged on his neck and throbbed with each heartbeat. His temples expanded and then contracted with each pulse.

Thump-thump-thump. She was unsure whether the heartbeat pounding through her head belonged to her or to her husband.

His face began a slow metamorphosis. The right side of his mouth drew upward into a grin that traveled to his eye. The left side twisted into a deep frown. The bizarre features revealed two distinct personalities, total opposites, and neither belonged to her husband.

It dawned on her that the old man's stories had been true, and the negative feelings George had described such a short time ago had been on target.

There is evil seeping into the streets of Caddo.

She attempted to push him away, but his hold tightened, bone-crushing hard.

Can't breathe.

He forced her to the floor, and began tearing at her clothes. All six buttons on her blouse went flying as he jerked it open. One hard tug and her lacy bra ripped in two. Then off came her panties and jeans in one fell swoop.

"George, stop it. The front door is unlocked."

"George, stop it," he mimicked in a voice sounding remarkably like her own.

Rape. This is rape.

Not if it's your husband.

Yes it is.

Thoughts of how to repel an attacker ran through her mind: A knee to the groin. The heel of her hand sharply up into the nostrils. Fingers in the eyes. And scream, scream, scream.

She brought her knee up with the intention of disabling him, but could not bring herself to do it. This is her soul mate, the father of her children, not some sicko who would ravage and torture her then toss her broken body aside like so much garbage.

Succumbing to the inevitable, she relaxed.

His mouth was on hers, pressing harder and harder, his hands exploring her body. The taste of copper filled her mouth as her teeth cut into her lip. His tongue stabbed down her throat. As if the probing organ was a catalyst for primeval lust, the same undeniable hunger claiming ownership of George flowed into her. Her body exploded with sexual hunger. What could have been a brutal rape evolved into a mutual act of carnal mating.

George and Penney Sneider now belonged to Caddo.

CHAPTER 14

Wailing babies, brilliant red blooms and sad starved faces reeled through a nightmare landscape slick with blood. The images faded and John Wilkerson found himself standing on a deserted roadway. Billows of heat coiled from the blistering blacktop like transparent vipers. An aged pickup truck zigzagged into the picture and bore down on him, the souped-up motor howling like a banshee. Ditcher sprinted into the scene. The dog yelped in anguish as he skirted killer tires. The bumper connected, tossing him high in the air. He struck the hood with a metallic thump and rolled to the macadam. He bounced several times on the hard surface before landing in a rumpled heap at the side of the roadway. The high-pitched shriek of tires biting into pavement and the stink of burned rubber filled the air. The truck skidded full circle before screeching to a stop amid a cloud of acrid smoke.

The driver's door opened, and January Rainwater slithered from the cab. A steel blue pistol glinted in his right hand. The man's depraved eyes searched out the limp form of Ditcher. He strolled to where the dog lay. A whimper escaped Ditcher's throat as the dark man pointed the pistol downward.

"No! No! No!" John screamed as exploding bullets ripped the life from his beloved pet.

"Wake up, John. Wake up. You're having another nightmare."

His eyes opened, and there stood Myrtie silhouetted in golden lamplight like a benevolent angel. Still in the grip of the nightmare, he glanced about the room in search of phantoms he was sure had followed him out of the dream. Everything was in place; nothing menacing caught his eye. The antique bureau displaying Myrtie's array of precious knickknacks stood in the corner. The dresser with the blotched mirror passed down from his grandparents rested against the far wall. Familiar curtains danced in a mild breeze. The serenade of crickets and frogs told him everything out-of-doors was in sync. The night was in harmony.

Rising to an elbow, he grasped Myrtie's arm. "I'm telling you,

January Rainwater shot Ditcher. I saw him as clear as I can see you. That no-good Injun shot my dog. You've got to believe me."

She didn't believe him. He could see it in her face. He so wanted to reach her, make her understand. Attempting to sound rational, he began to repeat the same story he had told her so many times before.

With a gentle nudge, she coaxed him back to the pillow. "I know, sweetheart, I know," she crooned, tuning out the incoherent garble spilling from his mouth. She freed the twisted sheet from his legs and straightened it over his chest. She collapsed into a bedside chair. "Yes, yes, I understand. A dream, John. A bad dream."

Sleep reclaimed him, and after a few minutes she turned off the lamp and crept back to her own bed in the adjoining bedroom. Separate beds was the only way she could get any rest.

At the sound of a throat clearing, John opened his eyes and smiled a welcome at the man sprawled in the bedside chair. Tossing aside the covers, he sat up and flicked on the bedside lamp. "Hi, Pa."

This was the third visit by his father, and he did not puzzle over the fact that the man had been interred in the family burial plot for more than twenty years. He did not question where his mother might be or wonder why Myrtie was excluded from these late-night reunions.

In the next room she slept the sleep of the innocent, ignorant of the corruption weaving its way into the fiber of John's soul.

"Well, son, I see she still don't believe you. Too bad. But I seen it. I seen that dirty redskin murder your dog. And you know, I think—" Zachary's voice trailed off as if his better judgment had taken control of his tongue.

"You think what, Pa?"

"Don't matter. Ain't my business."

"Come on, Pa. What's on your mind?"

"Now you gotta remember, this is only my thinking and ain't worth so much as a dead flea. I know a little more than I'd like to about your wife. And—well—ah. Do you suppose maybe she—?"

"She what?"

"Well, have you considered that she might know a little more about Ditcher's killing than she's putting on?"

The absurd statement struck John as funny. Rib-tickling funny. Try as he may, he could not hold back a hearty chuckle.

Zachary cleared his throat and shifted. "Like I said, wasn't worth a dead—"

"Pa, Myrtie loved Ditcher much as me. He ran away, and there ain't no possible way she could know what happened to him. Take my word for it, if I could somehow make her understand, she'd be every bit as upset as I am."

"You don't know?"

His father's tone plunked a chord of concern in his gut. "What? What don't I know?"

"She called the law on Ditcher. Locked him in the barn and then sent Jeff Chambers in to shoot him. Dog was too smart for them, though. That's the reason he ran away. I thought you knew."

"Myrtie? My Myrtie who cares for every orphaned critter within a hundred-mile radius, and crawls out of bed every two hours to bottle-feed? My Myrtie shoot Ditcher? Never."

A cloud of suspicion descended on him. His brow drawn in concentration, he studied the lined face of his visitor. Straight white teeth glistened in the man's generous mouth. He pictured his father's ill-fitting, yellowed dentures. And that mat of thick gray hair? Pa's all right—at the age of forty.

Pa, take my hat. Ma warned you about burning your bald dome. Show up looking like a lobster head, and she'll be some kind of mad.

The room had turned bone-chilling cold.

That's not your Pa, an inner voice insisted. *It's not even human. Send it away. Make it leave. Tell it to get out.*

Shivering as much from fear as the icy atmosphere, he opened his mouth to speak. *Get out* lay on the tip of his tongue, but the thought slipped away as if claimed by a silent wind. With the same frustration as walking into a room to get something, then forgetting what you had gone there for, he strained to remember what had been on his mind. The thought hovered at the edge of his memory, darting at his mind with the persistence of a moth struggling to penetrate glass to get at a flame. Deciding it couldn't have been important, he shrugged in resignation.

"You hear what I said, son? Myrtie ordered that policeman to sho—"

"I heard. You're talking crazy, Pa. She loved Ditcher. What on God's green earth could make you think she'd do something like that?"

"Watched it happen. That's how I know. Can't rightly say why she did it, but she did. As I told you before, I know a few things about Myrtie that ain't too kind."

"Ain't kind? Can't imagine what you'd be talking about. Why there ain't a sweeter, gentler person alive. Look how she's taking care of me. Fusses day and night. Can't get any rest with a thermometer always jammed in my mouth, or a pill stuck down my throat, or being force-fed some kind of hot soup."

Zachary frowned, and looked down at his hands. He seemed intent on lacing and unlacing his calloused fingers.

Here's the church, here's the steeple reached out for a second or two from John's childhood memories. Uncomfortable with the heavy silence, he said, "Look at me, Pa. You've been talking real strange. Now tell me what you're holding back."

His father raised haunted eyes.

This was not going to be a friendly father-son talk. There would be no bragging about the biggest fish caught, or reliving the taste of Ma's apple pie, or groaning over falling cotton prices.

You don't want to hear this, John.

"You been sick a powerful while now. Reckon why you ain't got much better? Kind of makes me wonder what's in all those pills. By my way of thinking, you should have gotten a little of your strength back by now."

"My God, Pa. You're talking about Myrtie. And-and Dr. Stein gave her the pills. You-you-you—" John sputtered, unable to find further words.

"Dr. Stein," Zachary snorted. "Yes, I'm fully aware we're talking about Myrtie. I have my reasons for what I'm saying. There's something I swore I'd never tell you. Swore to God and swore to myself. Vowed I'd never cause you pain. Lived with this thing gnawing at my guts year after cursed year. Intended for you to go to your grave never hearing it, but now I'm afraid for you. Don't feel right about what's happening around here. Ditcher shot, you sick and all. You have no idea what you're living with." His voice broke and tears leaked down his cheeks. "Couldn't stand it if something happened to you."

John's throat muscles constricted into a tight ball. He understood that a bomb was about to detonate and blow his life into a million tiny fragments. He could do no more than stare at the crying man.

Zachary removed a large handkerchief from his pocket and mopped perspiration from his brow. After snorting into the cloth, he turned watery eyes to John. "Son, there ain't no painless way to say this. Me and Myrtie . . . well, ah, she . . . we. Hell, ain't no other way to say it, I had her. I had your wife in the biblical sense. God forgive me, I had her lots of times."

Despite the words rolling around in his head, John's mind refused to accept their meaning. He tossed aside the thought like a pair of dirty socks.

Pa and Myrtie?

He shook his head in denial. His mind rejected the vague image of his wife and father in an impassioned embrace. Then the hazy picture began to materialize, the blurry edges became distinct outlines and focused into full clarity.

Pa? Myrtie?

The lewd picture of Myrtie and Pa pounded at his brain. Bitterness, like the foul contents of a witch's caldron, boiled inside him.

"What the hell do you mean, you had her?" He rose to his feet, his large hands clinched in fists.

Zachary recoiled. Cringing, his arms up to protect his head. "Please don't hit me. Wasn't my fault. She's the one that done it.

Myrtie's the one that come after me. And others, too. She had lots of others."

With his arm drawn back for a blow, John realized his father had no reason to lie. How could he have been so naïve for all those years? His anger slipped away, and his arms dropped to his sides. He collapsed to the bed. His keen filled the room.

Zachary stood and enfolded him in his arms. With a large calloused hand, he pressed his head against his chest. "I'm so sorry. I know how it hurts. But can't you see, I was afraid for you. Had no choice but to tell you the truth. Forgive me. Please, please, forgive me."

His father's touch was cold, contaminating. He pulled away from the embrace. As if the old man's touch had been a catalyst for self-righteous anger, he was once again flooded with rage. Immersed in a sea of indignation, every fragment of self-pity vanished. "You had her?" he asked in a tone icy enough to freeze blood in the veins. "What's the matter, Pa? Can't you come out and say it like it was? You fucked her. Isn't that what you meant? And just who else fucked her?"

"Son, please. It ain't important."

"You bastard. Don't you call me *SON!* You tell me. Tell me everything. NOW! Or I'll rip your ugly face off."

"Okay, you have a right to know."

The man's sympathetic tone made John want to spit in that disgusting face.

"I'm surprised you ain't already heard it. Everybody knew about her. And everyone of them laughed behind your back. God strike them dead, they laughed behind your back."

"Tell me."

With a sigh of resignation Zachary launched into his fabricated account. "With me, it happened shortly after you was married. While you worked in the fields and Ma was busy cooking or washing, Myrtie would come to the barn where I was. You've got to believe me, I resisted her. For a powerful long time I resisted her. She worked on me, worked on me hard. She'd pull her blouse open and massage her breasts, pinch her nipples right there in front of my eyes. Lift her dress high with no panties on. Everything showed. She'd press her naked self hard against me, panting how bad she wanted me. Pleaded time and time again for me to take her. She was so young and pretty, I couldn't stand it no more. I was like a starving man being offered a whole table of food. Couldn't help myself. And once I took her, I couldn't get enough. I hated myself and I hated her, but I couldn't get enough."

"Who else?"

"I'll tell you, but first you've got to know how the guilt ate at me. Like maggots, it ate at my guts. I told her, 'No more.' I told her, but she kept right on tempting me. Told her I'd tell you. And Ma, too. That scared her off of me. After that, she'd glare at me with those angry eyes, but she quit bothering me. Then I seen her leading pickers into the barn, and I knew it had started again."

"Pickers?"

"Yeah, every summer she would have her fun with the pickers––or anyone else for that matter who she could lure into her clutches. She slowed down when Doc Stein started hanging around. He was like a dog in heat, and Myrtie went for that. Yep, Doc cut quite a figure in his young days. I'd watch her flit around you, blink those big blue eyes and act so sweet and innocent. Played you like a fiddle. Still makes me sick to think about it."

"Dr. Stein? Impossible."

"It's true all right, and still going on. Why do you think he comes running every time she picks up the telephone? Shoot, busy practice and more than he can say grace over, but one word from Myrtie and he drops it all. Open your eyes, son. Dammit, you ain't blind, are you?"

He ran through the times he could remember Dr. Stein in their home through the years.

Hundreds of times.

"She used him, too. Yep, she used Doc Stein good." He leaned forward until their faces were inches apart. "Didn't you ever wonder why there was no babies?"

John shook his head.

"Well, there was babies all right. Three of them. Three

different times Myrtie carried life in her belly. She didn't want them. Nope, wasn't about to mess up her life with shitty diapers and a bunch of screaming kids. She had Doc Stein in her spell, and he ripped them out of her. All three of them. Your children. My grandchildren."

John's Adam's apple bobbed at his effort to swallow the lump in his throat. "Why didn't you tell me?"

"I threatened to tell you, but couldn't. I was scared of her. Myrtie would have destroyed anybody or anything to protect herself. She told me that she'd claim I raped her. Doc Stein would have backed her up. She'd have done it. It would have put your Ma in her grave. Think back, son. Way back then, who do you think you'd believed? Me or Myrtie?"

"Myrtie."

"I've been carrying this burden nigh on fifty years, and I'm tired, bone-weary tired. These awful secrets have kept me from my final rest far too long. I hate to leave you with this heavy cross to bear, but considering everything that's happened, you had to be told. Seeing as how I've finally shed this burden, ain't coming back no more after tonight. Going to be with your Ma. You'll have to deal with this knowledge the best you can. You're my son and I love you."

John did not hear the touching farewell. His mind had retreated to a world within himself where a panoramic vision played out before his eyes. A young and vital Myrtie with golden tresses surrounding her beautiful face lay unclothed on a soft mattress of hay. Entwined in her arms was a sweat-shiny young man whose muscular body pumped as he thrust his erect manhood deep inside her. Moans of pleasure filled the heavy air. And then her lover began a rapid metamorphosis. His features evolved from one masculine face to another. He stared in disbelief at the ever changing faces of men he had known for years.

The scene moved on. Myrtie lay on an examination table, her legs elevated and feet in stirrups. Dr. Stein, seated on a low stool at the foot of the table, brandished a bloody scalpel. "Here it comes." A baby, a ruined infant, popped from her. The baby boy landed with a sickening plop on the metal surface. And then the tiny body of an infant girl landed with the same repulsive sound. Another boy. The baby girl's eyelids blinked open and her dead eyes focused on John. Her rosebud lips parted. "Daddy."

The show continued. A crowd of men—neighbors and longtime friends—milled about his large front porch. A number of women in the front yard huddled together in a tight group.

Billy Gladstone, the hellfire and brimstone preacher from the Pentecostal church, stepped forward, a worn Bible tucked under his arm. His eyes narrowed to thin angry slits. He raised a sinewy arm and pointed at John. "You brought a temptress amongst us." His finger sliced through air toward the men. "She tempted them. Led them down Satan's path. Look at the women, John Wilkerson. LOOK! Myrtie committed adultery with their husbands. Fornicated. SINNED!"

"I had her," one of the men shouted.

"Me too," another admitted.

"And me," a third confessed.

"And him."

"Both of us."

"ALL OF THEM!" the preacher lamented, his face a mask of outrage. "The whore had them all. The poor wives. All of them fine Christian women. Do you see them, Brother Wilkerson? Do you see the WIVES? Your whore took from them what was rightfully theirs. What do you say to that?"

Mortified beyond words, he hung his head and shrugged. Tears of humiliation stung his eyes.

"Jezebel! Whore! Slut!" sounded from the cluster of women. Condemnation hung in the air like dense black smoke.

"Bring her out," Billy Gladstone ordered. "Bring the adulteress out. You see, Brother Wilkerson, all of them had her, and I didn't. Bring her out. I want my just due."

"Yeah, John," one of the men shouted, "the preacher needs some pussy."

Laughter swelled from the men, sidesplitting, knee-slapping

laughter. The men hooted and catcalled; some added vigor to the drollery with suggestive hip movements.

The women giggled and pointed and dabbed their eyes with little lace handkerchiefs.

John's rage was absolute. He sat on the bed, his eyes cold blue orbs of seething anger. He could not see his visitor's self-satisfied grin nor hear the gleeful chuckle spilling from his mouth.

The figure of Zachary Wilkerson disappeared through the doorway and dissolved into darkness.

CHAPTER 15

At the sound of an approaching car, Millicent Forbes tossed her sister a disdainful smirk and hurried to the large picture window that claimed eight feet of the front living room wall. She pulled aside the velvet drape and leaned over the window seat for a clear view of the street. A red Mustang with a heavy-footed teenage boy at the wheel zipped by and disappeared down the block. Her shoulders slumped.

"Dang."

Six, maybe seven, trips to the window this morning had resulted in the same letdown. She leaned further, her neck craned to scan from one end of the street to the other. As if on cue, a white minivan made a sharp right onto the block. In seconds it reached the neighboring house and wheeled into the driveway. A yellow and green Mayflower moving truck crept into view. Its huge tires thumped over the high curb as the driver maneuvered the tight right turn.

"Ouch."

The truck lumbered up the narrow street and eased to a stop at the curb next door. George Sneider emerged from the driver's door of the white minivan, and despite his stiff movements— fatigue from long hours behind the wheel Millicent assumed—his face was animated by a bright smile. Being a dedicated student of people-watching, she detected a smidgen of adventure in the buoyant grin. The man was happy to be in Caddo.

Penney was next out of the van. Her shoulder-length hair glinted like spun copper in the brilliant sunlight.

Twenty to one, ain't a drop of coloring ever touched that beautiful head of hers.

Two young girls piled out of the back seat. With the energy reserved for the young, they launched into a game of Ha-ha, you can't catch me. Their gleeful shouts and laughter brought a grin to Millicent's face.

"They're here," she shouted over her shoulder.

"For heaven's sake, lower your voice," her sister scolded. "I'm not deaf, you know. And come away from that window. I'll swear, I don't know how you got to be so nosy."

"I ain't nosy," Millicent retorted, maintaining her position. "Just curious, as you should be. It ain't everyday we get new neighbors."

"Ain't. Your grammar is atrocious."

"Priscilla, sometimes you make me crazy. I ain't one of your students, and I would appreciate it if you would quit treating me like one. For your information, I will say *ain't* any damn time I please."

"Okay, okay, a truce. Now please come away from the window."

Irritated with herself for lacking the grit to refuse her sister's directive, she took one last look at the activity next door. Feeling disheartened, she walked across the room and plopped into a blue wing chair facing Priscilla.

Not bothering to look up, Priscilla continued knitting; the needles clicked with the steady rhythm of a miniature typewriter. Her features were drawn into a tight scowl of concentration. Frown lines furrowed to her chin. Her thin lips disappeared in the whitened draw of her mouth. Crows-feet cut the corners of her short-lashed, too small, eyes. A pasty complexion etched with a spider web of fine blue veins attested to her aversion of the sun. Patches of scalp could be seen through thin lifeless hair.

That hairdo. Millicent groaned, reaching up and patting her own thick curls. *A tight bun, just right for the old maid school teacher she is.*

Despite the onset of years, she refused to let her appearance slip. After all—unlike her sister—she still had her pride. Every Friday, like clockwork, she appeared at Shear Talent House of Beauty to be fussed over by none other than Mr. Anthony himself.

Tired of being ignored, she asked, "Aren't you the least bit excited about the new City Manager moving in next door?"

Priscilla raised her eyes and fixed her with a frosty glare over the top of her magnified half-glasses. "No, it doesn't matter to me who moves in as long as they clean up that trashy place. It's an eyesore, and I can't imagine why a young couple would want it. Mark my words, it'll look just as shabby a year from now."

"I happen to know better. If you'd bother to take a look, you'd see they're a clean-cut couple. Sharon Saunders has told some of their plans for remodeling. Old Max Klein and his boys will start painting next week, soon as they close on the house."

"Close next week? Strange they'd be moving in now."

"Worked out some kind of lease agreement, I understand. Guess they wanted a little time to settle in before he starts his new job."

She needn't have bothered to explain, her sister's attention had returned to her knitting. Her words drew nothing more than a disinterested "Hum."

She stood up and headed toward the kitchen.

"Where are you going now? More snooping, I suppose?"

"Look, whether you agree or not, I think it would be neighborly to welcome them with something cool to drink. It's hot, and I'm sure they're exhausted."

"You are just being nosy. Please leave those people alone. They're too busy to be bothered by the likes of you."

"It's not *those* people. They have names. George and Penney Sneider. Their daughters are Jenni and Lauri, and cute as buttons on a Sunday-go-to-church silk blouse."

"I see you've done your homework. You aren't fooling me for a minute. I know what's on your mind, and don't you dare do it. I taught school for thirty-eight years and I won't be hassled by kids hanging around here. I'm telling you, don't get it in your head to start inviting those little girls over here."

Millicent pivoted and stormed into the kitchen. "Crazy. You make me crazy!"

"That old dried up prune thinks she can tell me who I can or cannot invite into my home. I'll invite Fidel Castro if I take a notion. Yeah, or the Kennedys and all their kids. Whole damn clan, for that matter. Let's see how she'd like that."

She opened a cabinet and removed a large silver tray and a serving platter embossed with tiny pink and red roses. A variety of homemade cookies was soon arranged on the platter. Earlier she had made iced tea and lemonade in anticipation of the Sneider's arrival. She stared into the refrigerator. *Tea or lemonade?* Little girls would prefer lemonade, she decided, and removed the frosty pitcher.

She picked up the tray laden with goodies, paper napkins and plastic glasses and headed out the back door.

Rounding the corner of the house, she came face-to-face with Red Meyers. She fumbled the tray, but managed to balance it with only two of the cookies dropping to the ground.

Red stood motionless, mesmerized by the activity at the house next door. He reeked of soured sweat, cheap whiskey, unwashed hair and stale urine, all rolled into one unsavory package.

Breathing through her mouth, she backed off several paces. The man's zombie-like demeanor proved more disconcerting than his foul body odor. "Red Meyers, what in the world are you doing here?"

Unable or unwilling to hear her, he continued his glassy-eyed vigil.

Her arms were beginning to tremble from the weight of the tray. With a mixture of frustration and uneasiness, she stated forcefully, "Red, I asked what you're doing here? You know you don't belong here."

He turned unblinking eyes to her. "Tell them they can't stay. I had a dream, they have to leave."

"I know about your dreams. Drunken stupors are more like it. Don't need to be around here frightening those nice people. Now go on, get out of here."

His eyes blinked several times as if waking from deep sleep. He stared at her in confusion. "Millicent Forbes? Tell them, Millicent, tell the pretty lady to take her babies and go. Please. They don't belong in that house."

"I'm calling the police if you don't leave."

"The police? No, not the police. Call the fire department. The house is burning!" he cried, dancing from foot to foot. "Good Lord, can't you see the smoke? The flames?"

Wringing his hands, he pleaded, "Call the fire department."

Light years from reality. She then pictured the fire that had consumed Red Meyers' home so many years before: rolls of thick smoke billowed from the blackened structure and enfolded the neighborhood in an eye-stinging, suffocating fog. Windows shattered like detonating hand grenades. The crowd, thrill seekers and neighbors clothed in anything that had been close at hand—bathrobes, rumpled housedresses, shorts, jeans—breathed in collectively before scattering to avoid glass and wood splinters transformed into missiles. Internal explosions thrust debris hundreds of feet in the air. Fiery blasts of heat scorched upturned faces. Tentacles of hungry flame snaked from the structure, demanding to be fed. And the screams.

No more. Can't stand it. She shook her head to force away the images. She turned teary eyes to Red, and her heart melted.

How could I have forgotten? Poor man, lost his entire family.

Only his stink stayed an overwhelming urge to set the tray down and enfold him in a comforting embrace. "I see it, Red. I see the smoke. You wait here while I call the fire department, okay?"

"Please, please hurry."

"I'll hurry." She turned and headed for the kitchen.

"Yeah, Dottie," Millicent said into the receiver, "Red's over here and having one of his episodes. Sure, sure, I'll wait with him until someone gets here. Uh-huh, my thinking, too, can't have him scaring the bejiggles out of the Sneiders. Some welcome, huh? I agree, nobody should have to go through what he's been through. Bye."

She hurried out the back door to find the driveway deserted. She walked to the front of the house and scanned the street in both directions. Gone.

"Well, I tried."

A patrol car wheeled into the driveway and braked within a foot of where she waited.

"Howdy, Miss Forbes," Dean Calder said, emerging from the car. He glanced about in confusion. "Red Meyers, I thought—"

"He was here. Wandered off when I went in to call you."

Dean jotted an occasional note on a clipboard as she recounted her strange encounter.

"Don't look like he's bothered the Sneiders. Busy as bees over there. I'll drive around the neighborhood, see if I can spot him. Not that he's a danger, but can't have him wandering around here in his present state."

As she hurried back to the kitchen, Dean backed the squad car into the street.

"What's going on out there?" Priscilla hollered from the living room. "What in God's name are the police doing here?"

Not bothering to answer, Millicent picked up the tray and headed out the back door.

"Millicent."

She giggled. "Let that old biddy stew in her own curiosity for awhile, see how it feels."

Dean circled the block, and then cruised through several alleys. He pulled up to a driveway where a rowdy group of ten- to twelve-year-old boys were entrenched in a game of basketball. The boys tossed aside the ball and crowded about the squad car.

"What you doing, Dean?"

"Can I sound the siren?"

"We do something wrong?"

The excited boys were intent on out shouting each other.

Dean raised his hands. "Whoa. Hold it a minute."

The boys stopped their banter.

"That's better. Any of you seen Red Meyers wandering around here?"

"Nope."

"What'd he do?"

"Gonna arrest him?"

He raised his hands again to quiet the barrage of questions. "No problem. He's not in any trouble. Looking for him is all."

"Take us for a ride," several voices beseeched in unison.

"Sorry, guys, can't do it right now. Tell you what, get permission from your folks and I'll be back in an hour or so. We'll go for a spin in the country, sirens, lights, the whole bit."

"Yes. All right. Wow. Cool," echoed from the youngsters as they scattered toward respective homes.

Somewhat puzzled by Red's elusiveness, Dean eased away from the curb. *How far to Red's shack from here? Five miles?*

He guided the car out of the middle class neighborhood and followed the route he suspected Red would walk home. Within ten minutes he eased the vehicle into Red's junk-strewn yard.

He sat there a moment thinking he had wasted his time in coming here. No possible way Red could have made it home by now. "What the hell, may as well check it out since I'm here."

As he stepped from the car, an unkempt, underfed dog with its tail wagging appeared from under the porch. Dean mounted the rickety stairs, the mongrel at his heels. He stood at a weather-beaten door hanging by one hinge. He could have leaned forward and peered inside through an ample space between the door and frame. But even someone like Red Meyers deserved his privacy. He knocked.

"Red, it's Dean Calder. You there?"

"Yeah, yeah, hold on," a drowsy voice responded from the interior. Following a moment or two of muffled sounds, the door creaked open. Clad in a yellowed undershirt and dingy, threadbare briefs, Red stood in the doorway rubbing sleep from his eyes.

"What you want, Dean?"

"I wake you?"

"Yeah, from the strangest dream. I was wandering around my old neighborhood."

"Doing what?"

Red shook his head. "Don't know. I can't remember."

CHAPTER 16

Michael Rainwater held his grandfather's arm until he was settled in the front seat of the car. "Talked to my boss today. I'm officially on leave."

"I'm glad you're staying a while. Don't think I could face this thing alone."

"Please, let's just forget about this evil stuff and concentrate on getting you well."

"Evil stuff? It's real, Michael. You'll come to realize it soon enough."

"Whatever you say, Gran, but right now my first worry is you."

He eased the car out of the parking lot and into the street. Picking up speed, he glanced at January. The man appeared to have aged ten years. His unkempt hair, thinner than he recalled, had faded from silver to a colorless white. Lines cut deeper into the leathery face. His shoulders slumped in a posture of defeat. Skeletal cheek bones stabbed from the hollowed face. Dull eyes, marked by dark circles, had been robbed of the vitality he remembered so well. Swallowing hard, he returned his attention to the road.

Within twenty minutes he made the right turn onto the gravel road leading to his grandfather's house. He maneuvered the rental car around potholes that looked substantial enough to swallow a cow. He coasted into the shade of a huge oak and cut the motor. "Wait there, Gran, I'll come around to help you out."

"I ain't no invalid. I can get out on my own, thank you very much."

Grinning to himself, he waited for his cantankerous grandfather to maneuver from the front seat. He matched him pace for pace to the porch and up the steps without offering an assisting hand.

January opened the front door.

Michael stiffened. A sensation of danger slammed into his gut with the potency of a fury-charged fist. He jerked the older man away from the door.

"What the hell?"

"Something's wrong,"

Then January appeared to feel it too. Color drained from his face and he shivered as if icy fingers were performing a dance up his spine.

"Jeff Chambers gave me your pistol," Michael said. "I put it in the trunk. Wait here, I'll get it."

He sprinted up the stairs with his eyes locked on the open cylinder of the revolver. "Five bullets." He snapped it shut.

"Hollow points," January told him. "Can do a lot of damage."

The pistol in a two-handed grip, he kicked the door open. A metallic bang echoed through the dank interior as the door knob struck the inside wall.

Drawn shades impeded the bright sunlight, leaving corners and recesses cloaked in tenebrous shadows. He reached inside the doorway and groped about until locating the light switch, and flipped it. An overhead fixture blinked to life, washing away the gloom. He scanned the living room. Every nook or cranny that could conceal an intruder stood empty. Everything appeared to be as he had left it earlier that morning. A pair of shoes, one upright and the other on its side, lay in front of the leather recliner where he had kicked them off the night before. Yesterday's shirt was still draped across the back of the couch and a folded newspaper rested on the heavy wooden coffee table where he had left it.

No bogeyman.

Despite the normality, the feel of danger continued to radiate with the force of a high frequency wave. Silence hung in the air like a bloated storm cloud holding its lightning in temporary abeyance, waiting for the right moment to release its fury.

With his forefinger planted on the trigger, he made his way to the kitchen. Anemic sunlight outlined dirty dishes cluttering the sink. A jar of mustard with a spoon protruding from the crusted opening rested on the counter top. Nothing had been disturbed. He backed out of the kitchen, vigilant for the slightest noise or movement. He reached the hallway leading to the bedrooms and flipped the light switch.

The narrow passageway remained shrouded in darkness.

"Damn."

The eerie blackness seemed to repel light, as if a thick velvety drape had been drawn across the entrance.

Not afraid of the dark, are you, Michael?

Damn right. At this moment I am. Shouldn't be that dark in the middle of the day.

Shouldn't have closed the bedroom doors, would have been plenty of light.

I don't remember closing them.

Sure, sure. Shut by themselves. No other way to the bedrooms. What you gonna do, leave poor injured January on the porch all day?

"May as well get it over with." His guts wound as tight as springs, he stepped into the darkness. It was like descending into a black hole. With his back pressed against the wall, he moved blindly, one slow step after another.

Shsssssssssssssssss.

He froze. His stomach constricted into an icy ball and his mouth dried. Beads of sweat popped out on his forehead. He tightened his abdomen muscles to block urine escaping his bladder.

Rattlesnake.

A shadow separated from the floor. Black on black, swaying and weaving. Then another joined the first. Another. And another.

"Oh God." He fired down, again and again and again, until the explosions were replaced with the clicks of the hammer snapping on empty chambers.

Shsssssssssssssssss.

Rattles sounded from every direction. He plunged toward where he hoped to find a bedroom door. Wood splintered under his impact and the door burst inward. Sunlight—blessed ever-loving sunlight—stung his eyes. Then his eyes widened to saucers. His heart stopped in mid-beat as if frozen solid.

A dense carpet of rattlesnakes churned the bedroom floor.

He mouthed the only prayer he could call to mind. "Now I lay me down to sleep, I pray—"

A sting to his left calf jerked him from his paralysis. He looked down, and with a "Holy Jesus" his bladder lost control. A large snake hung from his leg like an appendage; the creature coiled, uncoiled, and writhed in its struggles to free its fangs from the denim of Michael's jeans. He forced his hand downward, grasped it behind the head and jerked it free. The scaly body coiled around his arm. He slammed the snake into the slithering mass on the floor, and took flight. Two quick leaps and he was on the bed, balanced atop the firm mattress.

A large rattler coiled around a footboard leg. Death ascended. The forked tongue flickered in mesmerizing rhythm, tasting air, seeking the body heat of its victim. Cold hooded eyes seemed to glow with triumph as it slithered onto the mattress. It coiled in readiness to strike.

Michael flexed his body, and with the determination of an Olympic hopeful, dove for the window. Glass shattered, and his right shoulder slammed on hard ground. He rolled, and was on his feet and sprinting around the house.

The front porch was alive with reptiles. They dropped two and three at a time to the ground and glided toward January.

January backed toward the car.

Michael increased his speed, his legs pumping like a fine-tuned machine. Within seconds he closed the distance to his grandfather. Without a decline in speed, he snatched his wrist and continued the mad dash. He reached the car and yanked open the driver's door. After cramming in January headfirst, he twisted in behind and slammed the door. January's butt held the position in the seat reserved for his head; his head and shoulders rested at a crooked angle on the floorboard.

The snakes dropped in hordes from the porch. Like one living organism they came, a flowing river of death.

"The keys, the goddamn keys." Michael patted his pockets.

"Fucking buffalo balls." January cursed, as he struggled to an upright position.

THE IGNITION! Michael's mind screamed. With trembling hands, he turned the key. The motor whined. He worked the accelerator.

"Oh God, please."

Snakes disappeared under the car. Others glided around the sides.

Ping. Ping. Ping. Ping.

It sounded like sleet pelting metal, but Michael knew it was fangs attempting to penetrate steel. He jerked back as a large rattler slammed into the side window. Streams of clear venom cut trails down the dusty glass.

He continued to work the key. The whine of the motor escalated to a rumble. He jerked into gear and slammed the accelerator to the floor. The back wheels spun in place, creating plumes of dust and dry leaves. The tires found purchase, and the car shot forward.

This time he did not maneuver around potholes. The tires slammed into deep depressions, drawing protesting groans from the shocks and jostling the two occupants like a daredevil carnival ride. On reaching the highway, he eased the car to the shoulder and stopped. His stomach churned and a dull ache pounded at his temples. The backs of his eyes hurt. He expelled a sandpapery cough. Numbness crept up his throbbing leg.

"You all right, Gran?"

"A little rumpled, but no worse for wear, I guess."

"One of the damn things got me on the leg. Need something for a tourniquet."

January pulled the denim strip from his hair. "Use this. And get your ass over here, I'll drive."

"No, look at your shoulder. I'm in better shape than you are."

January looked at blood saturating his shirt. Pain awakened that felt like a red-hot branding iron burning its way into his flesh. "Must have tore out some stitches. If this ain't the shits. Should never have let you come here. Got us both in a mess now."

"Dammit, if I hadn't been here, you'd probably be stone-cold dead by now. How do you think I'd have felt? So knock off your guilt trip. You hear." Sheepish-looking, January leaned back with his throbbing arm cradled against his chest.

After knotting the cloth above his left knee, Michael slipped the gear to Drive and pressed the accelerator to the floor, fishtailing onto the roadway.

"Michael?"

"Yeah, Gran?"

"It tried to get us both today. This thing means business and our lives aren't worth a plug nickel if we don't do something soon."

He gave his grandfather a sideway glance, but did not respond.

"You know I'm right, don't you?"

"What happened today was strange, but I can't believe some unknown entity sent a horde of snakes to ambush us."

"That's exactly what happened, believe me. The rattlers were sent to kill us."

"Get serious."

"I'm more serious than I've ever been in my life. From the beginning of time serpents have served as man's epitome of evil. Cold-blooded creatures, shunned and feared, deserted at birth and forever committed to crawl the earth on their bellies. No emotions, no reasoning. What easier recruits? And what deadly weapons. Veritable killing machines. What more effective assassins than venomous snakes could the evil send against its enemies?"

"The dog? How do you explain that?"

"That one's a little tougher. I suspect it came into direct contact with the evil and all the being had to do was play into its natural instincts."

"Okay, for the sake of argument, let's say your theory is right. Why didn't this thing come after us itself and squash us under its thumbs like bugs? Or better yet, why didn't it send a man? A sharpshooter? We wouldn't have stood a chance against a high-powered rifle."

"I don't think it's strong enough yet to possess a human being. But it's gaining strength, I can feel it in my bones. You can be sure it will be sending someone for us. Probably several someones. Not only for us, but other unsuspecting people as well."

"How can you know that?"

"Legends. The legends passed down through hundreds of generations of our people. Until now, I never believed the old Indian superstitions. But you've got to admit, they made for entertaining stories. Remember how we used to sit around a campfire or build a roaring blaze in the fireplace? Those tales would have you jumping out of your skin."

"Yeah, I remember," Michael said, with a nostalgic smile.

"Those legends warn of an evil entity, an enemy of mankind. Our people coined this being the Evil One. Christianity made the entity a *he,* and coined him Satan or the devil . . . the Anti-Christ. Every religion has its own term or name for the Evil One. Indian legend has it that the Evil One gains power through a certain flower-bearing plant. Plants and flowers the spawn of the devil? Ridiculous, huh?"

"Yes. I do find that hard to swallow."

"Think about our Christian beliefs. Satan took the form of a snake and enticed Eve into eating an apple. With that single act, using one insignificant piece of fruit, he managed to destroy man's paradise on earth. Doomed us forever to pain, suffering and death. Why would flowers be less likely than an apple? What could be less suspect or more enticing than beautiful flowers?"

"Regardless of how sensible you make it sound, it's still Indian legend. Pure superstition."

"You're wrong, Michael. I've had dreams. No, more like visions or-or—" he hesitated, searching for an appropriate term. "Dream-visions is about as good a terminology as I can think of. In these dream-visions I'm there among our ancestors. Their primitive lodges reek of body odor, charred meat, animal grease. Fires are contained in pits in the centers of the dwellings. I breathe the smoke, it stings my eyes." His features crumpled in a look of anguish. Tears welled in his eyes. "I watched a young mother slaughter her newborn. I could hear his wails, see the wound, smell the blood. I stood in a frigid wasteland and watched the child bleed to death. When blood splashed the ground, tiny green shoots shot from rock-hard soil." He pulled a handkerchief from his pocket, wiped sweat from his forehead, blotted his eyes, then snorted into it. "I'm scared. Scared out of my wits. You have to believe me, these revelations are not figments of my imagination. They're too real not to be true. The snakes, the dog, only bear it out."

Michael looked into a face that had the look of a child who knows that a monster resides in his closet, and no one will believe him. A door creaked opened in his mind. A door of truth. Revelations unfolded in his head and pushed away his skepticism. He accepted that his grandfather's statements were not the ravings of a mind that had been touched by the finger of senility. His complexion faded several shades.

"You've convinced me. I believe you. What do we do now?"

"I honest to God don't know. For the time being, stay alert and prepared for anything."

He brought the car to a stop at the hospital emergency entrance. The two of them, arms around each other, limped through the automated double doors. The receptionist looked up in surprise at the two men. She flinched at the sight of January's bloodstained shirt. "Mr. Rainwater, we just released you."

"You ain't going to believe this."

CHAPTER 17

Dean Calder leaned back, tilted the wooden chair against the wall and propped his feet on Jeff's cluttered desk. "Could have dropped my teeth when Red came to the door. Not twenty minutes before, old lady Forbes claimed the man was in her driveway ranting about a fire. Ain't no way he could have been there. He'd been asleep for a couple of hours."

"You know Millicent, warden of the block. Saw someone who looked like Red and took it on herself to get him out of the neighborhood."

"Could be. But claimed she stood next to him, at least until his smell drove her back a-ways. You know as well as I do, ain't nobody stinks like Red Meyers. She said they carried on a conversation."

"Flowered it up for your benefit. That's the only logical explanation."

Dottie Hodges' pixie head popped into the doorway. "Jeff, it's Doc Stein on line one, sounds upset."

"Thanks, I'll get it."

Jeff picked up the receiver and pressed the blinking button. "Yeah, what's up, Doc?" He could not help but grin at the unintentional cartoon line. His grin faded. "Hold it. Let me make sure I understand. Hundreds of snakes?"

Dean's chair plopped upright.

"That's what they told me," the doctor said. "Gave Michael an antivenin injection, but he's going to be a sick puppy for a day or two. He got pretty excited and did some running. Spread the poison like crazy. January managed to tear out a bunch of stitches. Admitted them both, need to keep a close eye on them for a day or two."

"What in hell do you think is going on?"

"You tell me. I'm busier than a one legged man in an ass-kicking contest. Can't get off the phone for people calling and demanding something for nightmares. Half the kids in Caddo are afraid to sleep alone. Driving their parents crazy and the parents are driving me crazy. On Tuesday I stopped by to check on John Wilkerson. He caught some kind of nasty virus that kept him down for a while. He was up and around, but acting strange. Distant and icy. Myrtie looked like hell. Had one humdinger of a shiner and was covered head to toe with bruises. Claimed she slipped and fell off the front porch. Bullshit. The finger-bruises on her arms were plain as day. Somebody's been beating on her, and it's John. Nobody out there but those two. The son of a bitch is beating the shit out her and I don't know what to do about it. Now we have rattlesnakes traveling in packs. You tell me what the fuck is going on, Chief."

"Look, I'll be right over, see if we can figure out something to do for Myrtie. If it's okay, I'd like to get the story straight from the Rainwaters."

"Sure, sure, they aren't going anywhere. Reckon they'd be glad to see you. Talk to you in a bit." Dr. Stein hung up.

"What's going on?" Dean asked.

"It seems a pack of snakes attacked the Rainwaters. Friendly dogs going crazy, little old ladies carrying on conversations with people who aren't there and the whole town is having goddamn nightmares. Hell, I'm having them too."

"*Snakes?*"

"Rattlesnakes. And to top that off, it appears John Wilkerson is using his wife for a punching bag."

"I don't believe it. Not a mean bone in that man's body."

"Well, you better believe it. Doc Stein saw finger-bruises. The hell of it is, we can't do a damn thing about it. Told Doc she fell off the porch. Wait a minute, have an idea." He flipped open a dog-eared Rolodex, picked up the telephone receiver and keyed in a number.

"Mary, hi. Doc Roland in? Sure, sure, I'll hold." Jeff listened to Elvis belting out "Don't Be Cruel" for several seconds before the doctor's voice came on the line.

"Yeah, Chief?"

"Howard, you got anything back on Ditcher yet?"

"Yep, and like you suspected, no sign of rabies. Called Dr. Stein first thing this morning to tell him January won't need the shots."

"Find anything else wrong with him?"

"Nope. Even checked for a brain tumor. Physically, there was nothing wrong with that dog."

"Called the Wilkersons yet?"

"Tried, didn't get an answer."

"Hold off on that. What'cha you know about snakes?"

"Can't say as I've treated any, but did some study on them in college. In fact, I still have an old reptile textbook around here somewhere. Why?"

Following the conversation with the veterinarian, Jeff hurried to the squad room and removed three shotguns from a tall oak gun cabinet. He rummaged four boxes of shells from the deep bottom drawer. After placing the weapons in the trunk of his squad car, he and Dean drove to the hospital.

He did a quick fill-in to Dr. Stein on a planned visit to the Wilkerson farm, and then headed for January's room. Michael was as sick as the doctor had predicted, and incapable of anything beyond a weak wave of his hand. January was as hyper as three-year-old on a sugar-high. His tale of the snake attack had their hair standing on end.

After leaving the hospital, they made the five minute drive to the animal clinic. Dr. Howard Roland emerged with a red leather book tucked under his arm. He climbed into the backseat, his face animated by an excited grin. "Ready to do a little rattlesnake hunting?"

"Yep," Jeff said, "after a quick visit with Myrtie Wilkerson."

CHAPTER 18

Myrtie's body clock pulled her from sleep at five o'clock in the morning as it had for some fifty-plus years. She discarded her nightgown, slipped into a faded housedress and worked her feet into a pair of terrycloth slippers. Through gray daylight, she made her way down the hallway. She stopped dead at the sight of her husband hunkered at the kitchen table. She sucked in deep and forced herself to step into the room and then made her way around the perimeter, maintaining maximum distance from him. She could feel his icy stare follow her, but was too frightened to look up and meet his eyes.

Overnight, John had become an angry, unpredictable stranger. In a few short days her life had evolved into a living hell. At first it had been icy stares and indifference. Then degrading names— whore, slut, cunt, bitch, murderess. Shortly into the name-calling, came the physical abuse. The assaults intensified day by day. Stinging words, hard fists and other painful abuses were now a part of her daily routine. Pleas or attempts to appease him only fueled his rage. Her nights were filled with frightening nightmares, but the days were worse. Much worse.

She had vowed for better or worse before friends, family, minister and God. For the most part, her marriage had proven for the better. The worse? Her life was now beyond any worse she could have imagined. Shame prevented her from discussing her dilemma with another soul.

Accept and endure. Her bruised mind gave her no other alternatives.

Attempting to make coffee with tremulous hands, dark grounds spilled from the unsteady spoon. She tensed, holding her breath.

Stupid. Stupid and clumsy.

Frozen in place and afraid to exhale, she waited. Her stomach churned and her heart performed wild palpitations. She blinked back tears.

No sounds from the table.

No scraping chair.

No angry accusations.

No painful blows.

She exhaled and let her body relax. Using a damp cloth, she erased all evidence of the spill.

The coffeepot ready with no further mishaps, she set it on a burner to perk, and dared a furtive glance at her husband.

He appeared mesmerized by the strange red seeds scattered on the table. She knew that look. Had seen it countless times through the years when she had caught him unawares staring at her. Adoration. What she wouldn't give to again see that gleam in his eyes for her.

She poured a mug of steaming coffee and carried it to the table. He watched her approach with chilling indifference. Like a ceremonial peace offering, she set the mug before him. He first looked down at it, then up at her. His lips curled into a disgusted smirk.

Realizing his intent, she threw her hands over her face and lunged away. The coffee scalded its way down her back. Mewing against agonizing pain, she jerked her dress over her head and let it fall in a rumpled heap to the floor.

His lips were spread in a sadistic smile and his eyes gleamed with wanton pleasure. "Stupid bitch."

She cowered against a wall, swallowing her cries, afraid the slightest whimper would draw his attention.

This time she was lucky.

His attention once again fixed on the seeds, he seemed to have forgotten her presence. He scooped the seeds back into the worn leather pouch, secured the opening and stood up. Without so much as a word or backward glance, he stalked out the back door.

She staggered to the table and dropped into a chair. The burn proved more painful than the worst of slaps or hard punches.

"Why, why?" She rocked in misery.

The old Ford tractor roared to life, rattling the windows. The din decreased and faded to a barely discernable rumble.

Clutching an improvised cold pack put together with ice cubes and a dishtowel, she made her way to the bathroom. Unmindful of the clutter spilling about her feet, she fumbled through the medicine cabinet until she found a large brown prescription bottle.

PERCODAN, the label read. ONE TABLET EVERY SIX HOURS AS NEEDED FOR PAIN.

"Thank goodness." The narcotic had been prescribed for John last winter to relieve the pain of swollen and sutured feet. He had required only one or two of the strong painkillers, and she had been almost sure the unused portion had been tossed in the trash.

She twisted off the cap and worked three of the yellow tablets into her palm. One by one, she washed them down, grimacing at the bitter aftertaste.

Lying in bed with the cold pack pressed against her throbbing burn, she forced her mind to happier times. Within moments, soothing darkness enfolded her.

She found herself in the sunlit kitchen humming her way through lunchtime preparations. A symphony of bird songs, joined periodically by the tat-tat-tat-tat of a woodpecker, floated on a gentle breeze. The mingled scents of mown grass, peach blossoms, jasmine and roses perfumed the air. Ditcher dozed at her feet, his legs working as if giving chase to a dream rabbit. She stepped over him, careful not to disturb his slumber, and began setting the table.

Each day by dawn, John's demanding workload pulled him from the house. By eleven o'clock he reappeared, tired and famished, ready for lunch and a two-hour respite.

She stepped away from the table, and then hesitated to listen to a low distant rumble. The noise was strange, maybe like the reverberations of an earthquake or the repercussions of a faraway bomb. The birds fell silent.

Ditcher rose to his feet and stood dead still, his ears perked. He whimpered and looked up anxiously. The hair on his back bristled and a low warning growl built in his throat.

The room darkened as if the sun had crept behind a thick cloud layer. Covered with gooseflesh, she hugged herself against a chill that had taken possession of the room. The rumble escalated to a roar, pounding at her skull with the force of a ball-peen hammer.

Ditcher tugged at the hem of her dress, urging her away from the windows. She followed the dog's lead into the living room. The room was alive with warm sunshine. He continued to pull her toward the front door. Unable to contain her curiosity, she turned to look behind her. Her mouth dropped.

A black fog churned from the kitchen. Like a dark avenging angel, it advanced into the living room, swallowing the back wall and console television. The couch dissolved in the swirling mass. John's threadbare recliner was next to be devoured, then the cluttered coffee table.

Ditcher dropped her hem and lunged forward. He darted about, barking and snarling. A smoky tentacle materialized from the churning mass and descended on him like a shadowy serpent.

She attempted to shout a warning, but managed no more than a silent scream.

The tentacle coiled around Ditcher like a mammoth python. Fur and flesh dissolved. The animal's high-pitched howl of pain was cut short. The blackness was infused with bits of flesh, fur and bloody bone.

She jerked the door open, fled down the steps, across the yard and onto the gravel road. Aged, brittle joints screamed at the pressure. Biting pain coursed through her knees and calves. A sharp tic worked its way into her side. Her lungs threatened to explode. Gasping for breath, she staggered to a stop. Leaning forward with her hands braced on her knees, she sucked hard on air. Her temples throbbed and her heartbeat raced double time.

Black death swirled from the windows and doors of the house. Her home imploded. Tentacles snaked upward and snatched birds from the sky. Trees, plants and bushes disintegrated in the onslaught. The huge barn was devoured. Rays of sunlight, drawn like metal to a magnet, disappeared in the inky maelstrom. Daylight dissipated into a moonless winter night. The tenebrous mass, its crescendo mounting to an earsplitting level, closed on her.

Her feet lifted from the ground and she floated upward, as if cradled in loving hands. With the buoyancy of a helium balloon, she rose higher and higher, distancing the monstrosity gobbling the earth below. A warm breeze washed away the chill that had worked its way into her bones. Downy white clouds floated past her. A sapphire sky spanned the horizon.

Wham. Wham. Wham.

"Myrtie!"

Her ascent slowed.

"Myrtie!"

Head over heels she tumbled, plunging downward, faster and faster.

Wham. Wham. Wham.

She plunged ever downward. The unearthly blackness rose to meet her.

She screamed.

Her eyes popped open, then blinked shut against blinding sunlight.

Wham. Wham. Wham.

"Myrtie!"

The pounding, the shouts, that awful roar, had followed her from the nightmare. She clamped her hands to her ears. Then, like a precision-sharpened scalpel slicing through diseased flesh, realization cut through her confusion.

Someone's at the door. And John's tractor.

"Myrtie, it's Jeff Chambers. You there?"

"Jeff," came out as no more than a weak whisper. Then the nightmare filled her head in full clarity. Like the pages of a book turning in her mind, the dream's meaning unfolded.

Ditcher didn't catch rabies. Something was in him, just like she told Jeff.

And whatever got Ditcher, now had John. How many more would this evil thing, whatever it was, take possession of? She was certain the nightmare was a premonition. She was next. Jeff Chambers might be her last hope.

She struggled to sit up. "I'm here." Her head dropped back to the pillow like a solid lead ball.

Get up. You only have to make it to the front door, a trip you've made a million times before. Now, get up.

She managed to half-rise.

That's it. Come on.

The room swam out of focus, and a wave of nausea washed over her. She swallowed hard, determined not to throw up. A sour belch gave the nausea a firm foothold, and vomit gushed from her mouth. It saturated her gown and formed into greenish-yellow pools around her on the white sheet. She collapsed into a semiconscious state, too weak, too sick and too drugged to continue her struggles. The Percodan had done its job.

CHAPTER 19

From his high perch on the tractor, John spotted a dust cloud created by the progress of a vehicle on the gravel road. He eased to a stop, and with growing irritation studied the car's headway. At the sight of the unwanted visitor turning into the driveway, he bellowed, "Fucking son of a bitch!" His complexion darkened to a deep, stroke-threatening red.

He slammed the accelerator, and the tractor reacted with a teeth-shattering jerk. He wheeled in the direction of the house. The aged motor wailed. The rusted tailpipe rattled and erupted soot and black smoke. The agitated machine bounced and jostled him, but anger refused to let him ease pressure on the accelerator.

Amid a choking cloud of dust, the screaming tractor rounded the house and screeched to a halt within inches of Jeff Chambers' squad car. John killed the motor.

Stupid bitch. Called the goddamn law.

He crossed his arms and waited for the three men to descend the front porch steps.

"What you want?" he demanded, pinning the men with an icy stare.

"In the area," Jeff answered, "thought we'd stop by and give you the report on Ditcher. Doc got the results back this morning."

"Yep," Howard Roland said. "Nary a sign of rabies or anything else for that matter. Mighty strange what could—"

"Figured as much. Now if you'll be on your way, I got work to do."

The three men stood slack-jawed and stared at a man who appeared to have been stripped of every trace of innate warmth. His cold eyes glinted with hate.

Jeff cleared his throat and shifted uncomfortably. "Look, John, sorry we showed up unannounced. This time of year, should've known you'd be up to your ass in alligators. We'll let you get back to your rat-killing while we visit a spell with Myrtie. Promised I'd talk to her when Ditcher's results came back."

"She ain't here."

"Ain't here?"

"No, she ain't, visiting a sick cousin in Dallas. I'll tell her what you said. Like I told you, got work to do. You can just be on your way."

"Dallas?" Jeff questioned. "When did she go to Dallas? Didn't even know she had a cousin."

"Damn right she does. Been up there two days now. Apparently a lot you don't know about us." With an irritated toss of his head, he reached down and pressed the starter. The engine roared to life, drowning any possibility for further conversation.

The three men retreated to the squad car.

CHAPTER 20

Backing onto the gravel road, Jeff said, "Jesus, if looks could kill, we'd be getting dressed up for our own funerals."

"Strange behavior," Dean agreed. "That old man usually talks your ears off. Hundred times he's said to me, 'Won't you sit just a spell longer?' And you know what else? Can't remember ever leaving that house without a bag of Myrtie's homemade goodies. Don't understand it. Never seen John Wilkerson too busy for a friend. Hell, for that matter, even for a stranger."

"Never seen any kinder people than those two," Howard said. "Can't count the times one or the other called me concerning some injured animal. The way he treated us today, can't imagine him giving a rat's ass about any kind of animal. Sounded hard as nails. Something put a burr under his saddle."

Dean said to Jeff, "You look worried."

"I'm positive there's no cousin in Dallas. Known those people most of my life, and never heard either of them speak of an aunt or uncle. Without aunts and uncles, there sure as hell aren't cousins."

"I hear what you're saying, but if Myrtie was there, why didn't she come to the door?"

"Damned if I know. Could be she didn't want company. Yeah, especially if she's bruised up and doesn't want anyone to see her." Jeff eased the car to a stop on the shoulder and sat with his brow creased. "If something is wrong, we can't drive off and leave her. What if she's injured and couldn't come to the door?" He hesitated. "And maybe I'm letting my imagination run a little wild. Who knows, if John's been knocking her around like Doc Stein said, maybe she left his ass. That would explain why he's so pissed. Can't see Myrtie doing that after all their years together, but you never know about people. What say we go on to January's place and try calling from there. If she's home, surely she'll answer the phone."

"And if she doesn't?" Dean asked.

"Then we'll stop on our way back and not turn loose of that old man 'til we talk to her."

"Sounds good to me, but don't think he'll be happy to see our smiling faces again."

"Tough titty."

"Hey, fellows, ready to hear about rattlesnakes?" Howard asked. "Found some pretty interesting stuff here."

"Shoot," Jeff said, guiding the car back onto the roadway.

"In this part of the country, chances are good we're dealing with diamondbacks. Can grow up to eight feet long. Highly venomous. Live births. Broods of up to a dozen." He snickered. "Maybe one of those big mamas is in the throes of hard labor and all twelve of the little buggers are coming out breach. You'll get to witness a snacearean section."

All three men howled with laughter.

Laughing so hard he could hardly talk, Howard pointed at Jeff. "I forgot the frigging ether. You'll have to hold the big mother down while I cut."

"Not me. You're on your own," Jeff said, sleeving away tears.

"Nope, you're the one who hauled me out here, so it's your responsibility. I suggest you be careful what part of your body you get close to her." He nodded at Dean. "He's going to suck out the poison if you are bitten."

"You is gonna die," Dean cackled, his eyes wide in mock distaste. Through sinus clearing snickers, he added, "I'll pull the babies out, Doc, but it's your job to check their little bottoms to see what sex they are."

"Hell, yeah. Wouldn't want a George named Sally and have him grow up with a complex."

"Enough, enough," Jeff pleaded. "My sides are splitting."

"All right, serious time," Howard said, unable to wipe away a grin. "Let's see if there's anything else of interest in this big red book." Following a several minute pause, he began to read. "Rattlesnakes cannot tolerate extreme heat or cold. In hot areas they become nocturnal, avoiding the heat of day in protected shelters such as burrows. In winter they congregate in slides or crevices to hibernate."

Jeff scratched his head."Doesn't make sense. With this heat, ain't no way hundreds of them should be congregating in a house. I don't perceive rattlesnakes as social creatures."

"You're right; they're loners. Don't see a thing in here that gives a clue to their unusual behavior."

Jeff made a right turn onto the gravel road leading to January's house.

Howard snapped the book shut. "Looks like we may be able to figure it out soon enough."

CHAPTER 21

John Wilkerson remained perched on the tractor until the patrol car disappeared amid a cloud of swirling dust. He killed the motor, and climbed down. Puzzled why Myrtie had not opened the door to the three men, he stood for a moment with his brow wrinkled in thought.

Afraid? Yeah, that was it. Stupid cow heard the tractor and was too scared to come to the door.

The thought gave him a deep sense of satisfaction. The long morning atop the tractor and the jostling ride had taken their toll. Before ascending the porch, he took a moment to flex stiffness from his arms and legs. He scaled the steps and opened the front door. From lifelong habit he began to wipe his feet on the grass-simulated welcome mat, and then realized what he was doing. With a burst of irritation, he kicked the mat aside.

"Piss on it."

He stepped through the doorway and made his way across the living room and into the kitchen, unconcerned by a trail of dirt and dusty footprints left behind on the polished floors. Taken aback by a lack of cooking aromas that always permeated the house by midday, he jolted to a stop. His eyes traveled to the vacant stove, scanned the bare counter tops and came to rest on the oak table where spilled coffee had dried to brown splotches. He scanned his memory for the last time Myrtie had failed to prepare a hot lunch and came up blank. His stomach gurgled.

"Stupid lazy whore." He slammed a fist into the nearest wall. It tore through Sheetrock and crammed into a wooden beam. He howled and danced about, sucking bloodied knuckles.

Her fault.

He whirled and stormed into the living room.

"Teach that lazy whore a lesson she'll never forget."

Later, John, an inner voice insisted. *You can deal with her later. Now you need to eat.*

Several long strides carried him back to the kitchen and across the large room to the aged Frigidaire. He jerked open the door and fumbled out yesterday's partially eaten roast. The antique bevel-edged platter, a cherished heirloom passed from Myrtie's maternal grandmother, slipped from his grasp and shattered to the floor. He managed to catch the meat in midair. He tore into it with the gusto of a starved lion ripping into the flesh of an overdue kill.

When the meat had been devoured, he returned to the refrigerator, snatched a quart carton of milk and ripped open the top. He turned it up. Milk cascaded from the sides of his mouth, saturating his clothes and puddling in sticky pools at his feet. The empty carton landed with a hollow thud amid the remains of the platter. Next, he seized a raw egg, held it over his widened mouth and squeezed until the brittle shell collapsed. Velvety liquid slid down his throat. More and more egg shells joined the clutter on the floor.

Sated, he sank into a chair and stared down at the normally fastidious floor as if attempting to figure out how such a nasty mess had gotten there. A loud belch broke his spell. His eyelids drooped, and he eased his head to the table.

"Take myself a little nap."

NO! a booming voice demanded. *YOU CANNOT SLEEP NOW! THERE ARE THINGS TO DO!*

He jerked upright and scooted the chair back. "Myrtie, I'm home. Where are you, sweetheart?"

CHAPTER 22

Jeff brought the car to a stop in January's yard.

Other than the front door standing ajar, nothing seemed amiss.

At a sudden movement in front of the car, all three men jerked and gasped. A squirrel skittered passed the passenger door. It stiffened. Ears perked and tail fanned, it gave out a chattering distress call before darting to the safety of a tree.

"What scared him?" Dean asked. "Don't see a thing."

"Only one way to find out," Jeff said, and opened the driver's door. Out of the car, Jeff took the lead, and stopped after walking several yards. "Here's what spooked him." He poked at a dead rattlesnake with the toe of his boot. "See the tread marks. Got run over."

"Jesus, the size of that sucker," Howard said. "Five feet if it's an inch." He glanced about nervously. "January said there were hundreds of them."

"Sure as hell aren't going to find them standing here." Jeff popped open the trunk and started handing out weapons.

Shotguns in hand, they made their way up the front steps. Jeff nudged the door open with the barrel of the gun. The interior was as silent as a tomb on a frigid winter night.

"So far, so good." He stepped through the doorway and stood dead still absorbing the atmosphere, his ears tuned for a breath of sound. Instinct told him the house was empty. He relaxed, and throwing caution aside, strolled to the kitchen.

Dean and Howard, jittery as preteens at their first boy-girl dance, tread behind.

They opened drawers, cabinets, rooted through a small pantry, even pulled the refrigerator away from the wall, but found nothing more dangerous than dust balls and a few dead bugs. Single file, Jeff maintaining the lead, they headed for the bedrooms. In the hallway they stopped to poke and prod at corpses of three more snakes.

"Holy shit, look at this one, would you?" Dean said. "Hollow points were what Michael used. Sure did the job. This sucker is cut in half."

In all three bedrooms they overturned mattresses, rooted through closets, and explored bureau drawers. No reptiles. The two bathrooms were vacant.

Jeff shook his head in puzzlement. "Considering the dead snakes, January's story checks out. If there'd been so much as a roach in this place, we'd have found it. Where could hundreds of snakes have disappeared to?"

"Must have disbanded," Howard said. "Strange things happen in nature. We'll probably never figure out why they choose to congregate here, one of those unexplainable quirks. Have to admit, it's the weirdest thing I've ever heard. Maybe someone at A&M could shed some light on the subject. I'll give them a call this afternoon."

"Sounds good," Jeff said. "You two can have a look around outside while I gather a few things for Michael and January."

"I'll get their stuff," Dean offered.

The tilt of Dean's head and his fidgety hand movements around the stock of the shotgun told Jeff that he did not want to be left alone in the house. The offer had been no more than a subordinate-boss show of respect.

"Will the both of you get out of here and let me get to work. You ain't needed here." He grinned as they turned and disappeared through the door.

Dean tromped around the right side of the house while Howard proceeded a bit more cautiously to the left. Howard's belly churned with frustration from a case of mixed emotions. He was relieved that they had not been accosted by a horde of deadly snakes, but at the same time he was disappointed. A busy work schedule had been laid aside for the opportunity to see the mass of rattlers. He had looked forward to the adventure as much as any boy anticipated that first overnight camping trip. Exploring the house had been a little scary—downright nerve-racking if the truth were told. Dang it, he had every right to be exasperated. Not so much as one live specimen had been spotted.

Howard, no different than most people, was fascinated with snakes. Three years ago while on vacation he and Marilyn had driven long desolate miles through West Texas. For a span of two hours, signs popped up against backdrops of sand-washed landscape:

VISIT THE HOME OF THE RATTLESNAKE ROUNDUP
SEE VENOM MILKED.
FRIED RATTLESNAKE & RATTLESNAKE BURGERS
RATTLESNAKE SOUVENIRS

Titillated by the signs' exotic promises, they had stopped in the town and checked into a motel for the night. The following day, every thrill promised had been fulfilled. They had stood in a crowd of spectators as a burly, ruddy-faced, Levi-clad, western-booted snakebite victim was rushed away in an ambulance. In addition to horror on lookers' faces, he detected a touch of elation.

The overconfident cowboy had gambled and lost.

Some people had come with the hope to see the worst happen, and their appetites had been fed.

Neither he nor Marilyn could stomach the thought of yummy-promised reptile meat, and had survived the day on French fries, beef burgers and five-alarm chili. The spicy concoction liberally called chili had hung in his gut for days. In the heat of the moment, he had purchased a snakeskin belt on which the serpent's head served as the buckle. On their return home he had tossed it into a bottom drawer to be forgotten. The exorbitant price paid for the barbaric souvenir had refused to let him trash it.

Howard kicked in frustration at a small mound of dirt. Tiny pebbles pinged against the base of the house. He spotted an ajar panel and knelt down. Laying the shotgun aside, he peered into the narrow opening. Blackness.

"Darn, should have brought a flashlight." He grasped the thin wooden edge with his fingertips and gave a sharp tug. His fingers slipped off. "What the heck. Nothing there anyway."

Howard Roland. What happened to that desire for adventure?

Got nothing better to do, anyway. May as well go ahead and check it out while you're here.

He fished a bone-handled pocketknife from his pocket, snapped open the heavy blade and inserted it into the narrow opening.

Better call Dean. Never know what could be behind there.

He withdrew the blade.

Get real. Since when are you such a pantywaist? Even if there happened to be a snake or two behind there, what could go wrong? Shotgun in easy reach. Remember, that handler said snakes are more afraid of you than you are of them. They'll slither away every time if given the chance. Never bite before sounding a warning rattle. Unless threatened or trapped, won't strike. He pushed a whole pack of them around with his boot. And you know how Dean is. Hell of a nice guy, but sometimes a little pushy. Sure as shootin', he'll shove you aside and take over. He is the authority here. You're nothing more than an invited guest. Yep, it'll be all over town how he solved the big mystery, that's to say if there is a mystery worth solving behind that little panel.

Convinced he would find nothing more than cobwebs and a few spiders, he went to work with the pocketknife. With a sharp creak, the panel loosened enough for a sturdy handhold.

Jeff stood in the kitchen tapping a finger on the counter top and listened to the Wilkerson's telephone ring for the tenth time. He hung up. "Damn, got to stop again." He tucked the shotgun under his arm and picked up a large black suitcase packed with shaving items, toiletries, underwear, socks, shirts and jeans. He emerged from the front door, sprinted down the porch steps and to the car where he deposited the suitcase in the trunk. He headed around the house and spotted Howard kneeling on the ground tugging on a wooden panel.

A bolt of knee-weakening panic knocked every ounce of air from his lungs. He opened his mouth to shout a warning, but managed only a weak squeak. He sucked in deep, and as the panel gave way, screamed, "Nooooo!"

A dark shape shot through the opening, and fangs sank into Howard's neck. He threw up his arms. More shapes darted from the opening, like a multiheaded monster. Fangs found homes in Howard's arms, legs, hands and face. Again and again the snakes struck.

Dean sprinted around a corner of the house in response to Jeff's scream. The sight of the rattlesnake attack stunned him into paralysis. With his mouth slack, he could do no more than stare in morbid fascination.

Jeff rushed forward, clutched Howard's collar and jerked him away from the deathtrap. Dean sprang into action. He raised his shotgun and fired into the opening.

Jeff tossed Howard over his shoulder and bolted for the car. Behind him, Dean continued to fire one shot after another; earsplitting explosions reverberated through the woods and sent wildlife scurrying for cover. He pushed Howard into the backseat, and within a breath's time, Dean slid in beside him.

He hurled his large frame into the driver's seat.

The yard now churned with snakes, and like a single living organism, they glided as one toward the car.

"God in heaven," Jeff breathed.

The souped engine purred to life with a single twist of the ignition key. He fishtailed out of the yard, and like January and Michael, they experienced a daredevil ride over deep ruts and jarring potholes. He flipped on the revolving emergency lights and siren as the car skidded onto the highway with a rubber-burning shriek. He pressed the accelerator to the floor. At speeds of more than one-hundred and ten miles per hour, the police car wailed into Caddo.

CHAPTER 23

The burrr, burrr, burrr of a telephone goaded Myrtie from sleep. With determined effort, she managed to sit up. Woozy and disoriented, she waited for the room to swim into focus. Her mouth was coated with vile-tasting film and her throat tender. She ran her parched tongue around dry, cracked lips. Heavy footfalls in the hallway drew her attention to the doorway.

John stepped into the opening. His angry look drew into a grimace.

Myrtie looked down at the vomit streaking her gown and pooled on the bed. "I-I-I—" she stammered. "I was sleeping . . . must have got sick."

"I can see you did. Stinks worse than a shit house in here. Hawking phlegm, he fixed her with a steely gaze. "Filthy slut. Gonna wallow all day in your filth like some sow?"

Her eyes swam and she swallowed a lump in her throat. "I'll clean it up . . . right away."

She relaxed and allowed the hot tears to spill as he stomped away. Segments of a nightmare tumbled about in her head. An image of Ditcher flicked to mind.

Ditcher. . . and, and—?

Someone at the door.

Who?

She felt it was crucial to remember who, but a name or face refused to surface. The harder she strained, the further the impression drifted from her. As dreams often do after waking, the fleeting images slipped away. "Don't matter, only another nightmare."

Holding the headboard, she stood up. Her knees threatened to buckle. "Easy does it." She took one slow step. Then another, and another. At last in the bathroom, she stripped off the reeking nightgown. After brushing her teeth, she rinsed and gargled again and again, then downed two glasses of water. She could not remember anything tasting so good.

Her image in the mirror brought a wince. A tangled mass of oily lifeless hair framed her pallid face. Dark circles accentuated her puffy eyes. Deep worry lines added ten years to her age. She was reminded of desolate bag ladies who wandered the streets of large cities. "Dear Jesus."

You get a good look at yourself, Myrtie? What's happened to your pride? No wonder John's been such a bear. You taken a good whiff of yourself lately? No, not just the vomit. How long since you bathed? For smell, you could match the rankest of bag ladies. At least they have an excuse. Know what else? You've become a mealymouthed whiner. Who could blame John for his behavior? Reacting no different from any other man under the same circumstances. He's a good man. Got to clean up your act. Maybe develop a backbone. Ain't a man alive who likes a sniveler, especially one who stinks.

She swooped up the reeking nightgown and flung it into the bedroom. After turning both shower handles full force, she stepped into the inviting spray. The steaming water bit like live embers into her scalded back. With a twist of the hot water handle to off, an icy flow deadened the throbbing burn. Covered with gooseflesh and her teeth chattering, she adjusted the temperature to a comfortable level. The soothing water washed away most of her fatigue and cleansed her mind of the fogginess that had followed her from sleep.

Invigorated by the long shower, she towel-dried her hair, then brushed it until it gleamed. She applied light makeup and dabbed Passion cologne behind both ears. Rummaging through the closet looking for something attractive and loose-fitting to accommodate the burn, she found herself humming.

Clad in a figure-enhancing powder blue dress with intricate lace encircling the neckline, she stepped in front of the mirror. The earlier image of a fatigued crone had faded to oblivion. She turned and twisted about like a teenager admiring the look of her new prom dress.

Primp and preen all you want. Getting all prettied up won't work. John has changed. He won't even notice.

I've changed too. Marriage problems aren't one-sided, you know. I'm equally to blame. Why, if only I had—.

Get serious. You may have overdone it with all that kowtowing and playing the martyr. Pissed him off more. You did nothing to make him turn on you. You've known for a long time that his mind was slipping. Admit it, his brain finally popped out of its socket. Sure as God exists and the Pope is Catholic, he's toppled over the edge. And he's not childlike and docile like you expected. Some articles you read painted a pretty bleak picture, remember? A few Alzheimer victims go beyond forgetful and disoriented. Some drift into a world of paranoia and anger. Looks like John had the bad luck to draw that card. You need to be honest with yourself and do what has to be done. Leave, get away from him.

And go where? To a rented room in town? And live on what? Welfare? And how do I manage to face our friends? Why, tongues would wag so hard and fast there wouldn't be an idle telephone in the entire county.

Stop being dramatic. You gotta do what needs doing. It's really very simple. Call Dr. Stein, he'll handle everything. You saw the look on his face, didn't believe for a minute you fell off the porch.

John would be committed. I couldn't allow that. I'd be alone.

There you go, overdramatizing. So what if he's committed for a while? In this day and time there are miracle medicines that would likely take care of his problem. And being alone is not the worst of fates. You keep screwing around and he will hurt you bad. Your old body can't take much more abuse. Doesn't heal like it used to. Pick up your purse, march down the hallway, trot out the front door and climb into that old truck and get the hell out of here.

You may be right. But what about the backbone theory? He might relent if I showed a little grit. It could work. And I do owe him that much.

If it doesn't work? How long do you intend to play this deadly game?

Tomorrow. If things aren't better by tomorrow, I'll go see Dr. Stein.

Her mind made up, she refused to entertain any further daunting thoughts. She glanced in the mirror for a last appraisal, and liked what she saw. Her silver hair glistened like a new dime. Makeup had performed a minor miracle on the dark circles under her eyes. Powder and a hint of blush had given her complexion a healthy glow. The worry lines had all but faded.

"Not bad for an old gal."

For the first time since the onset of John's illness and his black moods, she felt pretty, alive and hopeful.

She stripped the sheets, shaking her head in disgust.

"Three Percodan. What could I have been thinking?"

The mattress would have to be disinfected with Lysol, and then carried outside to air. She tossed the soiled sheets in the corner atop the discarded nightgown.

Her shoulders back, and a newfound purpose to her step, she made a spunky entrance into the kitchen where John sat at the table. A bit of resolve slipped away at his steely glare. Her step faltered, and she looked away. Her eyes fell on the filth-strewn floor. She recognized glistening fragments of her grandmother's antique platter. For the first time in weeks, genuine anger popped to the surface.

Whoa. You're blaming John unfairly. You know how he is in the kitchen. Mr. Butterfingers. Who in their right mind would put a hundred-year-old antique into a refrigerator. If you hadn't swallowed that fare-thee-well dose of Percodan, you'd have been up to make lunch and the platter wouldn't have gotten broken. Best you chalk this one up to experience. Clean it up and forget it.

She turned with the intention of fetching a broom, but the sight of the leather pouch stopped her dead in her tracts.

Empty.

The limp pouch appeared more loathsome than when bulging with the peculiar red seeds.

Empty.

A bone-chilling tale of suffering and death emanated from the crumpled piece of leather, and she knew that by some bizarre quirk of fate she had been cast as the story's leading character.

Pick up your purse, march down the hallway, trot out the front door, climb into that old truck and get the hell out of here.

The soundness of her own advice came too late to help. With astounding clarity she understood her last chance for survival had been tossed to the wind like so many ashes.

"I-I forgot to—" she stammered, backing toward the door.

John was on his feet and across the kitchen in a shot. He lifted her off her feet, and with a cruel-sounding laugh, thrust her backwards.

A sharp crack like the snap of a dry branch sounded as she landed on the floor amid the shards of her cherished platter. Crimson egg shells floated about in a swelling pool of blood.

He stared down at the woman writhing about in blood and garbage. Jagged bone from a broken hip tented the material of her dress.

Memories of a young beautiful Myrtie with corn silk hair and sparkling blue eyes forced their way through the dense fog that had clouded his mind for days. He envisioned nights of gentle lovemaking and whispered promises of undying love. He glimpsed sunny day picnics, teary funerals, quiet dinners, peaceful wintry evenings by a glowing fire. Lazy afternoons in the porch swing. Countless moments and events that made up the very essence of his adult life played through his head. It dawned on him that the injured woman sprawled on the floor was his Myrtie, the giver of untold years of happiness. The color drained from his face.

"My God in heaven, what have I done?"

He dropped to his knees and cradled her head in his lap. "Baby, please forgive me." He brushed hair from her eyes, and then eased her head to the floor. With the agility of a man thirty years his junior, he sprang to his feet. "Please hold on. I'm calling an ambulance." He ran to the telephone and snatched the receiver. With trembling hands, he depressed nine-one, and then hesitated. A picture of a pale infant who had been denied the right to draw life's breath formed in his mind. One heartrending word reverberated through his head.

Daddy. Daddy. Daddy. Daddy.

His features hardened, and he replaced the receiver in its cradle. His rage returned twofold. The old John Wilkerson was gone forever. He ambled to where Myrtie lay on the floor panting like a woman in the throes of hard labor, her features contorted in agony

"You're a real tart. Had me fooled for a minute or two there. Yep, almost pulled it off. Well, this old man is on to you. Your fooling days are over. Ain't never going to fool a man again." He leaned over and grasped the front of her dress. A hard jerk and she was upright.

A shrill scream died on her lips as she collapsed into unconsciousness.

CHAPTER 24

Myrtie found herself on a raft floating on gentle waters. A distant rumble worked its way into her tranquil world. The modest waves picked up intensity. The raft rocked and tipped, threatened to cast her into the tumultuous sea.

Her eyes opened, and blinked hard against blinding sunlight. Her head lolled to the right. Fascinated, she studied an arm tethered to—*to what? A tractor seat? John's tractor?*

She cut her eyes to the left. Another tethered arm.

My arms? Yes, of course, my arms. I'll be darned. Imagine that.

She slipped in and out of consciousness. Her broken body should have been racked with unbearable pain. Perhaps a deep state of shock blocked the pain or maybe her mind had advanced beyond physical sensation. Regardless of the reason, she was detached from the suffering and fear associated with dying; her last few minutes on earth proved to be a pleasant experience.

"Up and down, up and down," she giggled. "Bouncy, bouncy." She and John were having quite the time riding the swells on his old tractor. Her head lolled forward. She was surprised to discover clods of dirt beneath her feet instead of water. She stared hard at wide bloody swaths across both her ankles.

John, she called in her mind. *You've got to stop the tractor and look at this. How do you reckon this happened?*

As darkness closed on her vision, she saw tiny green shoots peek from the furrowed soil as her blood flowed to the ground.

CHAPTER 25

January Rainwater fought against velvety blackness pulling him into its embrace. The sound of retching pulled him back from the void. For a confused moment, his glassy eyes moved about the sterile hospital room, then settled on his grandson who was in the adjacent bed. Michael was vomiting into a stainless steel pan, his knuckles white from pressure on the side bar. An ebony angel, clad in a crisp white uniform, held the container for him. With each new spasm, his bloodless face drew into a grimace. The nurse brushed hair from his eyes and bathed his forehead with a cool cloth.

"That's good, sweetie. Get that nasty stuff out. You'll feel much better."

The dark angel in white had been scurrying all afternoon with a bedpan, vomit pan or a fresh ice pack. Michael's system had decided to expel anything from his body that was not attached. When not on the bedpan or throwing up, he lay lifeless with a damp cloth draped across his forehead and an ice pack resting against his swollen calf.

Look at him. Why did you allow him to go into the house alone?

Wasn't thinking. He's an excellent shot, and had five bullets and—

And what? Worried about your own worthless hide, weren't you? You sensed the danger. Didn't even try to stop him. Nearly sent him to his death. About time you got off your lazy old ass and arrange to get him out of here.

Damn right. Not a soul alive worth Michael's little finger. The hell with them all. I'll send him back to California where he belongs.

Now you're talking.

Critical scenarios had played through January's head untold times since admission to the hospital. Guilt ate at him like piranhas feeding on an animal unfortunate enough to enter infested waters. A shot Dr. Stein had administered was plying its magic, tugging him toward healing sleep. Despite his valiant efforts, the remote darkness proved to be overpowering. Further and further he descended into the comforting embrace of sleep.

Send Michael to—

Peaceful. Dark. He ceased fighting and drifted away from his thoughts, away from the guilt, away from Michael. He floated on a cloud of well-being. Down and down he drifted, as if in the arms of a gentle breeze. He came to rest in the center of a sun-brightened clearing. Lofty trees adorned with emerald foliage ringed the plush sanctuary. Lush shrubbery, elaborate ferns and plants bursting with spectacular blooms flourished all about him. A latticework of dazzling sunshine rippled through the dense canopy; the forest twinkled, as if illuminated by thousands of flickering candles. The clearing was alive with butterflies that appeared to have been brushed with iridescent paint. Some sported wingspreads equal to the length of his forearm. The graceful insects danced and darted and lit on exotic blooms.

He offered an arm, and a number of the elegant insects converged, their touches as light as snowflakes.

As if on command, the butterflies merged into a swirling orb of extraordinary colors before him. The orb exploded in flame. He attempted to back away, but his feet appeared to be rooted to the ground.

Flaming tentacles danced hundreds of feet in the air. The ghostly flames licked at him. The unearthly fire was like the embrace of benevolent arms.

"Fear not, January Rainwater," emanated from the firestorm. The voice, as soothing as cool rain on a sweltering summer day, dissipated his fear. He understood he was no longer a prisoner in this strange drama. If he chose, he could turn away and return to the security of the hospital room. He did not want to leave.

As if sensing his decision, a figure materialized in the conflagration. A man as naked and pure as a newborn stepped out.

An overwhelming desire to be linked forever to the purity and love of this being washed over him.

"No, January, you cannot stay here. This is but a temporary summons. Ultimate evil has entered the world, and mankind is in mortal danger. This evil is hungry for souls and innocents. It is a voracious feeder. From the moment of man's creation, this malevolent being has plagued the world. Untold times it has invaded earth to corrupt humanity and inflict suffering and death on millions of innocents. This ancient enemy is strong, and conquers through illusions and deceit. It seeks to destroy all that is good. It would rule the world. But understand, this evil is not omnipotent. It is limited to drawing on the corruption in man to achieve its aims as my Master must draw on the goodness in man to protect creation. You, January, among all men have been chosen to face this evil being."

"Me? Why me? Look at me, I'm an old man. Weak. I don't have the strength to fight this thing. This evil."

"Do not deceive yourself! You have the strength and the wisdom to do battle with this enemy of man."

"I can't. Twice I've faced his emissaries. Don't you understand? It's too much to ask of me."

"You still walk the earth, do you not? As expected by my Master, you faced this being's corrupted agents with courage. It was no accident you were found on the roadway or that your grandson was there to pull you from the fangs of death. The Master sees all, and sends forth protectors. From the day of your birth you were destined to face this enemy. You must accept your destiny, all that you love is in the balance. And understand, January, the Evil One fears you and will not rest until you are destroyed."

"I don't know how to do this thing you ask. How can I confront a nameless, faceless thing?"

"You will know the enemy. Search out the plants brought forth by human blood, as seen in your dreams. You will find the red flowers spawned by the evil pleasing to the eye. The weak in spirit and the corrupt will find the scent of the blooms beguiling. Impure souls will embrace the evil with relish and thrive on their newfound freedoms. Unspeakable acts against nature and humanity will befall earth. Find and destroy the plants, January."

"Alone. How can I?"

"You are not alone. There are others. Like you, they are plagued by fear and confusion. Time is short. Your adversary will attempt to enter your minds. The evil will venture to recruit each of you. Above all, it must be resisted. Now look upon the just and pure of heart. Gather them to you, for they are in danger."

With this final declaration, the man turned and stepped back into the inferno. A feeling of loss settled on January as the figure dissolved. The flaming tower dwindled to the size of a small campfire, and darkness descended on the forest. The modest flames struggled against the pressing blackness.

A number of people took form about the fire, their features eerie in the illumination. Michael was among them. Next to him sat a sad-faced teenage girl. The bulk of Pearl Turner occupied the space next to her. Myrtie Wilkerson and Howard Roland were next. A small girl, no more than three or four years old, huddled in the lap of a stunning woman with flaming red hair. Red Meyers hunched beside the mother and child, his rheumy eyes and ruddy complexion communicating decades of alcohol addiction. Others he knew, but a few faces he had never seen before.

"Women and children?" he exclaimed "A drunkard? Only a few strong men? No. This can't be right."

The figures of Myrtie Wilkerson and Howard Roland began to waver as if being viewed through rain-shrouded glass. Their flesh began to degenerate. Veins and blood vessels came into view, muscles and tendons bare. He watched their exposed lungs expand and deflate. Their eyes pleaded to him from naked sockets. The maddening thumpthumpthump of their runaway heartbeats vibrated in his skull. He clamped his hands over his ears, but could not block the sound. With each beat, the reverberation grew louder. Unable to turn his eyes away, he stared in horror as decaying flesh melted and formed into slimy pools. Their skeletal mouths stood open in silent screams. For several seconds the skeletons sat upright before the small fire as if seeking refuge from the darkness, and then collapsed. The bones disintegrated, leaving behind two small mounds of dust.

A chilling wind blustered into the clearing and descended on January. Phantom fingers, as frigid as ice floes, explored him, sending ripples up his spine and covering him with gooseflesh.

The wind then swept down and swooped up the remains of Myrtie Wilkerson and Howard Roland. Forming into a dust devil, it danced off into the night.

He stared in disbelief at the barren positions in front of the fire.

Death, January. You saw it. Felt it. The raw face of death. Myrtie and Howard are both dead.

"No," he groaned.

CHAPTER 26

January awoke to the sight of Michael sprawled in a chair by his bed.

"What the hell are you doing up?" he barked.

"Well, well, look whose back among the living."

"Damn it, boy, get your ass back into bed."

"Lower your voice, Gran. Going to wake the whole floor. Everyone but the nurses, anyway."

January thrust a finger at him. "To bed."

"You can caterwaul all you want, I am not getting back into that bed. Fifteen hours flat on my back was quite long enough, thank you. And believe me, there is nothing more the old diarrhea and vomit monsters can do to me."

"Fifteen hours?" January glanced at the dark windows.

"Yep, going on four o'clock. Now, for a little good news." He extended his left leg. The swelling had almost receded. He flexed his knee. "All better, see?"

"I'll be damned, looks brand-new. How you feel?"

"Hungry. In fact, so hungry I could gnaw the balls off a brass billy goat. We're paying steak and lobster prices for crap they serve disguised as food. You know what I get? Crackers and gelatin. Green gelatin, at that. Yuk."

The light banter meant Michael was well on the road to recovery. January grinned with relief, and then sucked in deep to stifle a yawn. Eyes at half mast, his mind wandered back in time.

After graduating high school he headed for North Texas State University to pursue a degree in journalism. But Caddo refused to release her native son. Four years later, a degree under his belt, he was drawn back to his roots like a salmon compelled to return to its spawning grounds. Harboring no regrets about the lucrative journalism career that might have been, he happily went about earning a rewarding and profitable living pursuing interests closest to his heart. At a young age he developed an insatiable thirst for knowledge in Indian folklore and nature. He published several books depicting American Indian history and never lacked for city-bred greenhorns with fat wallets seeking his skills as a hunting or fishing guide. He was indeed a colorful character who walked the walk and talked the talk of a rustic outdoorsman possessing a unique insight to the ways of nature. His love for nature often rubbed off on hardened hunters, and from time to time, these men could be seen trudging from the woods struggling under the weight of an orphaned fawn or with a litter of wild animals—raccoon, fox, squirrel, rabbit—snuggled in their jackets. Occasionally, January faced the frustrating task of convincing a hell-bent-on-adoption individual that a garage or backyard, regardless of how large, was no place to raise wild animals. Myrtie Wilkerson, without exception, welcomed these displaced critters with open arms to be nurtured to adulthood and released back into the wild.

He married Catherine, his high school sweetheart, and within two years, Angelina Rainwater made her debut. At first glimpse of the porcelain-skinned infant with Catherine's rosebud lips and large dark eyes, he lost his heart. He now had two beautiful women to cherish.

He found the next fifteen years to be as full and perfect as a human being could ever hope. His home rang with laughter and overflowed with affection. In his eyes, Angelina fulfilled the role of a perfect child. She maintained decent grades in school, and did not experience preteen awkwardness or a complexion ravaged by the pubescent acne that plagued many of her friends. She was endowed with her mother's beauty and her father's zest for life. However, under the overindulgent tutelage of doting parents who refused to see her slightest flaw, she became both manipulative and self-centered. She adopted the attitude that the world was there to serve her. Shortly following her fifteenth birthday, she was arrested for shoplifting. It was the first of many arrests for petty crimes. Possession of an illegal substance, driving without a license, drunk in public—the list went on and on.

She said a hundred times if she said it once, "I'm not going to rot in this hick town with its hick people and hick cops. I'm beautiful, and someday I'm going where I'll be appreciated. I could be a famous movie star."

True to her word, two years after her first arrest, she took off for Los Angeles. No amount of argument could stay her course. Although she never returned home, she would occasionally call pleading some kind of emergency and needing money. January knew his daughter had descended into the drug world, and was now beyond their reach. They allowed her to use them as only a drug addict can. Never giving up hope that someday she would turn her life around, he always wired whatever cash she requested.

Catherine was inconsolable. Powerless against her torment, he watched helplessly as her mind and body dwindled away. In sleep, death claimed her. A stroke is what the death certificate read, but he knew better. Catherine had grieved herself to death.

Life turned as sorrowful as it had once been happy. He existed in a dismal routine of long sleepless nights and endless days. He was never hungry. When an inherent voice insisted he nourish his body, he downed whatever was at hand—a can of corn, a raw potato, dry cereal washed down with tap water, stale crackers, a shriveled apple. It didn't matter what he ate, food was food.

He received a telephone call from Captain Sammons of the Los Angeles Police Department, and for the second time he lost Angelina.

His beautiful daughter had died of a drug overdose, and to January's dismay, he discovered her one last deception: she had left behind an eight-year-old son. There was no husband in the picture, and the father's identity was impossible to trace.

A wondrous gift of a grandson dropped in his lap and gave him a new lease on life. With his two beautiful women laid to rest, he turned his emotions and energies to rearing Michael.

Under his guidance and unconditional love, Michael flourished. Winter evenings were filled with crackling fires and storytelling, summers with hunting, camping and fishing. Michael wore skinned knees, bruises, scratches and insect bites like badges of honor. He excelled academically and outclassed his peers in sports. His life abounded with friends. He headed off to college with academic and football scholarships to his credit. January gave up the vivacious young man to the world and a career far from Caddo.

His complaining bladder pulled him from his reverie and back into the sterile hospital room.

"Decided to join me again, huh?" Michael said, glancing up from a dog-eared magazine.

"Sorry, guess I must have drifted off."

"You need the rest. Go back to sleep."

"Couldn't go back to sleep if I wanted to." He threw back the covers. "Need to pee so bad my teeth are floating."

"Hum," Michael grunted in the absurd Indian dialect depicted in so many old western movies. "You like English Indian. Drank forty cups of tea a day and drown in own teepee."

January could not contain a guffaw. "Dammit, Michael, shut up or I'll never make it to the pot without wetting myself." He stood up on legs as stiff as tree limbs, and made his way to the bathroom. By the time he had emptied his bladder, washed his hands and brushed his teeth, his joints had limbered to some degree. With a lighter step, he returned to his bed to find a cup of steaming coffee on the nightstand.

"Thought you could use that," Michael said.

January glanced about quizzically. "You not having any?"

"Can't, not on my diet yet."

"Hell, it won't hurt you. Here, take this." He extended the cup and reached for the call button.

"Wait. Something happened you need to know about." Michael's somber tone plucked a chord of concern in his gut.

"Howard Roland . . . he's dead. Went out to the house with Jeff and Dean yesterday afternoon, and got more than twenty-five rattlesnakes bites. Nobody could have survived that."

The dream slammed into January's head; he stared at a picture of Howard Roland and Myrtie Wilkerson with their skeletal mouths open in silent screams.

"Myrtie Wilkerson," he croaked.

"Gran, what's wrong? What about Myrtie?"

"Just a minute," he said, snatching up the telephone receiver. "I have to call Jeff Chambers."

CHAPTER 27

WHAM-WHAM-WHAM!

The sound of pounding on the front door snatched John Wilkerson from deep sleep. He jerked upright, and for a moment his eyes darted about in confusion.

WHAM-WHAM-WHAM!

"Goddam it," he muttered. "Go the hell away." Exhaustion tugged him back to a prone position. He burrowed his head under a pillow like an armadillo tunneling into a decaying drift of leaves. He dropped back to sleep.

Yesterday evening after bleeding out Myrtie, he struggled the deadweight of her body into a wooded area where he spent backbreaking hours digging a grave. He dumped her corpse into the gaping hole and refilled it. Another hour was spent to haul large stones and dead branches to conceal the mound. He pushed his exhausted body to clean the kitchen floor and scrub away evidence of spilled blood. In the wee hours of morning he shed his clothes and dropped into bed. Despite fatigue, restful sleep was denied him. Even in that twilight world, the unrelenting master demanded his attention. There was still much to do.

WHAM-WHAM-WHAM!

"Damn." He tossed the pillow aside and sat up. Yawning, he snatched up yesterday's crumpled overalls and began working them up his legs.

"Holy shit," he blurted at the sight of dark brown stains marking the denim. He kicked free of the pants. His undershorts and work shirt were also matted with dried blood.

WHAM-WHAM-WHAM!

"YOU SON OF A BITCH!" he screamed. "GET THE HELL AWAY FROM MY DOOR!"

"Jeff Chambers here," sounded from the front porch. "Come on, John, open up."

He stripped off his bloodied undershorts, and then stood for a moment, unsure of what to do with them. In desperation, he stuffed the entire bundle of telltale clothes under the mattress.

WHAM-WHAM-WHAM!

He snatched a pair of undershorts from a dresser drawer and drew them on. From a nail inside the closet door he retrieved a pair of twice-worn but blood-free khakis. Barefoot, shirtless and zipping his pants, he headed for the front door.

Someone discovered the body.

Impossible. Grave was too well concealed.

Animals could have dug her up. Fox, coyote, raccoon. After all, she wasn't embalmed. Someone could have stumbled across her remains.

Ain't no way animals could move those rocks, unless a goddamn grizzly wandered by. Not a grizzly within two thousand miles of here. Nope, that bastard cop is just sticking his nose where it don't belong. That big nose is going to get him in more trouble than he bargained for. A few days and ain't nobody going to be too concerned about one dead old woman, anyway. Don't reckon a dead cop would draw too much attention either.

Careful. Wouldn't do to have people out here looking for him.

Stifling a yawn, he opened the front door. "What the hell is so all-fired important that you'd drag a man out of bed at five in the morning?"

"Sorry, John, figured you'd be up by now. I need to talk to Myrtie."

"Myrtie. Goddamn, told you yesterday, she ain't here."

"I understand. If you'll give me the telephone number to reach her, I'll be out of here. Call her from the office."

"And just what is it you need to talk to her about?"

"Now, John, if I discuss this with you, I wouldn't need to talk to Myrtie, would I?"

"Anything you have to talk to her about is my business too. Been married a mighty long time and ain't got no secrets."

"To be honest, I'm concerned about her. Got a call from January Rainwater this morning. He's concerned, too. Had a dream she might be in some kind of danger."

"January Rainwater? You takin' him serious? You're stupider than you look. Can't believe you'd wake a man because of some foolish dream. Let me set your mind at ease. Myrtie called last night and sounded as spry as a spring chicken." He shook his head in exasperation. "Can't believe you drug me out of bed 'cause some dumb Injun had a scary dream. Tell you what, you go back and tell that superstitious ass that Myrtie's fine. And tell him, by God, I'd appreciate it if he'd keep his nose out of my business. You too, for that matter." He slammed the door.

"John, open this door. One way or another I'm coming in for a look around. You hear?"

"You're full of shit, too."

"We can do it the easy way or the hard way. Suit yourself. Not aiming to be difficult . . . a little look around, that's all. Judge Cole will issue a search warrant for the asking. And I'm warning you, if I go to that trouble, I'll do more than just have a quick look-see."

John opened the door. "All right, you win. Keep in mind I've been bachen' for a few days, house is a mess." With the slightest hint of humor in his voice, he added, "Fraid Myrtie ain't going to be too pleased when she gets back. It'll take her a month of Sundays to clean this place up. And you better know, she's gonna be damn well pissed when she finds out I let you see the house in this shape. She'll skin me alive."

"That why you didn't want me to come in?"

"Damn right. That old gal can be as feisty as a bantam rooster when she gets her dander up."

"I won't tell her if you won't." Jeff was pleased to hear a touch of the old John Wilkerson in the man's tone.

He walked from room to room with the old farmer on his heels. He stepped into a bedroom, and gagged. "Shoo, what happened in here?" He backed out of the room fanning the air with his hands.

"Had a touch of that dang virus again and threw up. Stripped the sheets, but ain't sure how that dadburn washing machine works. Figured to keep the door shut and let Myrtie handle it when she gets home."

In a bathroom, Jeff found an array of medicine cabinet items cluttering the floor, and looked at John questioningly.

"Did that looking for something to settle my stomach. Wasn't feeling too spunky at the time, and a little bit of a mess was the last thing on my mind. Think I'll be able to handle this cleanup without Myrtie's help."

He hesitated at the kitchen entrance. A couple of coffee mugs and several pieces of silverware rested in the sink; the counter tops, table and floor were spotless. "Appears you've done a pretty fair job in here."

"Ain't really my doing, pretty much as Myrtie left it. Been living on TV dinners and sandwiches. No way I'd try my hand at cooking, probably burn the place down." He glanced down to discover dark brown stains in the linoleum creases. In bright sunlight they stood out like a flashing neon sign. His shoulders sagged and beads of sweat popped out on his forehead.

Stupid fool. How in the fuck could you have been so damn careless? No choice. Have to kill the son of a bitch if he spots it.

January Rainwater sent the man out here. That thickheaded Injun would have the whole goddamn town out here looking for him. You did it up good this time.

Jeff strolled into the room. Halfway across the room he stopped to examine the sole of his shoe. "Sticky, and feels like I may have stepped on a piece of glass."

"To-tomato juice," John stammered, his heart slamming at his chest with the force of sledgehammer blows. "Dropped a whole pitcher, glass and juice went everywhere. Damndest mess I ever did see. Thought I got it all up. Goes to prove I'm pretty much thumbs when it comes to woman's work."

Jeff turned, and then hesitated to stare at something out the window. "What's that?" he asked, pointing into the distance.

John crossed to the window, and scanned left then right. "Where? What you talking about?"

"That red . . . out in that field."

His eyes locked on the field afire with bright red blooms; he sucked in deep. The sight wiped all concerns from his mind. The Master's real work could now begin.

"What's growing out there?"

John felt he could stand there for hours, but at present he had no choice but to deal with his uninvited guest. "It—it's flowers," he stammered. A thought hit him. "That, my boy, is our latest crop. Flowers. Hybrids, a newly-developed strain. Our secret's out."

"Flowers?"

"Yep. Real beauties. I'll tell you about them, but first I gotta get some caffeine down me or drop here on the spot. Suppose you have a seat on the front porch while I put together a pot."

"Sounds good to me, never turned down a fresh cup of coffee."

At the sound of the front door snapping shut, John dared to breathe. He fumbled the coffee pot from the cabinet, filled it with water and dumped a generous helping of Maxwell House into the basket. He left the pot with flames licking the blackened bottom and hurried to the bedroom.

You were lucky this time, old man. Play it cool, and in two or three days it won't matter what he sees. Then let the cocksucker march his smart ass out here. He'll get one hell of a welcome.

John pictured the naked corpse of Jeff Chambers suspended high by its ankles from a sturdy oak limb. Empty sockets—robbed of the eyes by crows—stared out from a bloated face.

Jeff settled into a time-scarred rocking chair on the front porch, but was soon looking about for the source of an awful stench carried by a mild breeze."

"Lord, have mercy, what's going on here?"

Animal carcasses in the barn? Heat doing a number on them? Not like Myrtie, her first priority had been to burn them in the event of rabies. Septic overflowing?

The breeze abated, and the reek diminished to a tolerable level.

As he rocked, uneasiness settled on him. He had the feeling of being watched—no, more like being studied. The tiniest trickle of fear skittered up his spine. He rose and paced the full length of the porch, scanning the area. Then the silence hit him.

"What the hell?"

The place should have been teeming with birds. Even ever-present sparrows had deserted the area.

The watched-feeling intensified. His uneasiness escalated to fear. It was all he could do not to sprint for the safety of his car. At a sound behind him, he jerked about, his fists raised.

"Hey, careful there, don't hit me." John stood in the doorway holding two mugs of steaming coffee. "Didn't intend to startle you."

"Caught me a million miles away," Jeff said with an embarrassed grin.

John extended one of the mugs and nodded toward a chair. "Now sit, dying to tell someone about them flowers."

John settled into a chair, and inhaling deeply, an aroma surged through his blood, tingling his nerve endings and leaving him breathless. Steeling his mind to deal with his unwanted visitor, he began to spin a tale. "A young fella, salesman by the way he was spiffed up, come knocking at our door some months back. You know Myrtie, couldn't turn him away without a cool drink and listening to his spiel. That man went into the damnedest pitch we ever heard. Started spreading out books on the kitchen table and pushing colorful brochures in our hands. Talked so hard and fast, I venture to say he didn't take a good breath for better than five minutes. Insisted we'd make a fortune growing this new strain of flowering plants his company developed."

"I've seen the type. Insurance pushers usually . . . but flowers?"

John pictured the decomposing corpse of the man perched beside him. The rope creaked as the body swayed in a strong gust of wind.

Lovely.

"Yep, that fella was as proud of those plants as a brand-new daddy." John was amazed at how easily the lies rolled off his tongue.

Ignorant hayseed is swallowing the whole pile of shit—hook, line and sinker.

"Got that young man to hush long enough to find out where

he got our name. Seems Myrtie thought she was ordering a packet of seeds that caught her eye in some magazine. As it turned out, she'd requested a company rep."

Jeff threw his head back and laughed. "Didn't buy that heap of horseshit, did you?"

"Had to. It was checked right there on the order form he showed us. Myrtie sure enough requested a personal visit. We felt right bad about it, him making the trip and all. Shoot, they were asking an arm and a leg for those seeds, and we weren't about to throw away a chunk of our hard-earned money on some hair-brained scheme. Not us."

"But what about—?"

"Don't get ahead of me. Ain't finished with the story yet."

"Sorry." He raised his hands in supplication.

"As I said, the guy was pushing those flowers for all he was worth. The more he talked, the more sense he made. Me and Myrtie began to catch a little of his fever. If the stated facts were true, there was a pile of money to be made. Fella said we didn't have to take his word for it. Gave us a list of his customers from all over the country. Greenhouses, farmers and such. Suggested we contact them. Soon as we pushed him out the door, we picked up the phone and started dialing. Got the same story from everybody we talked to, making money hand over fist. We figured old age would be a whole lot easier with a pocketful of money. Decided to draw out a wad of savings and give this venture a shot. Bought us a supply of them seeds. Not near what that young fella wanted us to buy, but reckon he made himself a good enough commission."

"You sure kept this to yourselves. First I've heard of it."

"Damn right we kept it to ourselves. Didn't want to be the laughingstock of the whole damn county if we fell flat on our faces. And you know how folks are around here. At the smell of a profit, they'd been ordering those seeds like crazy. Couldn't afford for that to happen. Made that salesman fella promise he'd stay out of the area until we got this thing rolling. Reckon by next spring his face will be a common sight around town. You seen that crop of beauties out there. Fact is, you're the only one who has seen it. Appears we pulled it off, don't it?"

"You old rascal, appears you did at that."

"Prettier than long-stemmed roses and twice as hearty. If this thing goes right, them flowers will be our only crop. Be shipping them all over the country. Can you imagine an old dirt farmer like me growing something as sissy as flowers?"

"Of course I can. Nothing wrong with growing whatever makes the most money. Proud of your spunk. Don't know anybody who deserves a megadose of good fortune more than you and Myrtie."

"Haven't made people too welcome around here for a spell now, trying to keep this a secret and all. Been downright rude to folks who come by for no more than a neighborly visit. Reckon our friends think we've turned plumb unsociable. Ain't a fitting excuse, I guess, but we sank a lot of money into this project, and it's been powerful heavy on our minds. Even Billy Gladstone got a taste of my tongue."

"Billy Gladstone?"

"Yeah, especially ashamed about that one. Fine, well-meaning man. But that old preacher's more gossipy than any four of the cluckingest hens in the county. Never no mind what we'd say, he'd have most likely spread our glad tidings from the pulpit. Reeee-joice for the Wilkersons, brothers and sisters!" he mimicked in a sterling imitation of the preacher's commanding voice.

Jeff laughed.

Making a donkey out of the dumb-ass cop.

"Soon as Myrtie's back, we'll be having the preacher over for one of her special Sunday dinners. Kind of smooth things over."

"John, never heard either of you speak of a cousin in Dallas."

Pictures of an old woman with her mouth drawn on the left side, a distraught young man, a Christmas card and a sign reading New Haven Retirement Home flickered through John's mind. He understood the meaning. The Master was guiding him. "Nope, guess we ain't talked much about Sadie. Fact is, there's some doubt in our minds that we're even related. Five years or so back, we got a letter from her saying she'd traced her family tree. Claimed Myrtie was a cousin of hers, four or five times removed. We never pursued any kind of relationship, her living in Dallas. Christmas cards and such was about the extent of it. Couple a days ago her son called and said his mother had a mild stroke. Old lady wasn't ailing bad enough for a hospital, but a mite too feeble to stay by herself. No money for a full-time nurse, and he'd get fired if he took off work. Said he'd found a rest home that Medicaid would cover, but they couldn't admit her for another two or three days."

Yuk, yuk, yuk.

"You know Myrtie. Nothing to do but go up there and take charge. Damn flowers coming to bloom and more than we can say grace over, but there was no talking her out of it. Threw a few clothes in a suitcase, and Sadie's son drove down and picked her up."

"That's our Myrtie all right. When you expect her home?"

"Today, thank God. Supposed to check the old woman in the nursing home this morning, but won't be no getting her out of that place until she's satisfied with everything about it. Me, I'd drop the old gal in the lobby and be gone. Not Myrtie. She'll snoop through the kitchen and interview half the staff before she turns loose. Probably come traipsing in here about midnight."

"You're probably right."

For a long moment, the two men sat rocking and sipping coffee. "Something else on my mind," Jeff said. "Dr. Stein told me he—"

"Dammit, I knew I was right. Told Myrtie as much, and she pshawed me. Doc thinks I beat her up, don't he?"

"Yes, he does."

"In my wildest dreams, I wouldn't lay a hand on that woman. Why, that feisty old gal would sew me in a sheet and beat the living tar out of me."

Jeff chuckled at the thought.

"No, sir, wouldn't touch that woman. I knew what Doc was thinking, could see it plain as day on his face. He kept squinting his eyes, you know how he does, and studying Myrtie. He was for sure in some kind of a twitter, and I can't blame him. I'd have thought the same thing. Myrtie looked pretty bad. Can't wait to tell her about this, it'll make her day."

"John, what did happen to her?"

"She took a bad spill off the porch. All my fault, too. I came in bone-tired one evening and kicked off my work shoes right there on that mat. Next morning, barely turning light, came out with my coffee and took a rocking chair. Stepped over the shoes, but know now I should have pushed them to the side. A few minutes later Myrtie comes charging through that door like a locomotive. Needless to say, she didn't see the shoes, and tripped. Before I could take a breath, she took a swan dive right off the porch. Scared me half to death. Thought for sure I was having the big one right then and there." He clutched his chest for emphasis. "The next day I had to look hard to find a spot on that old gal that wasn't black, blue or purple."

"Doc said something about finger-bruises on her arms."

"I didn't notice any, but wouldn't be surprised. I was so shook, I rushed down the steps, and without thinking, yanked her to her feet. The way I grabbed hold of her, I could sure enough have added a bruise or two."

John read belief in the policeman's face, and smiled inwardly. *No problem here, old man.*

Jeff glanced at his watch, and stood up. "Sorry for barging out here like a damn fool, but after what happened yesterday, I overreacted to January's call."

"What happened yesterday?"

"Howard Roland was killed by rattlesnakes."

John's mouth dropped, his face a mask of shock. "But he was here yesterday. How? Where?"

"At January's place. Michael and January are both in the hospital, barely escaped the house with their lives. The place was teeming with rattlesnakes. Michael was bitten and January managed to tear out some stitches. When we went to check it out, Howard discovered their nest, and was bitten more than twenty-five times. Didn't have a prayer of surviving."

Yes, Master. Culling the enemy.

"The poor man. Hard to understand something like that happening to such a nice person."

"Yeah, it's tough all right. Appears we got a rattler epidemic on our hands. Be extra careful in the fields, and keep a shotgun handy."

"I'll watch my step, and you can take that to the bank."

"A whole battery of volunteers are burning up the phone lines passing the word around. Hate the scare we're laying on people, but can't chance anyone else getting bitten, or God forbid, killed."

The breeze picked up reawakening the foul odors. Jeff swallowed against a wave of nausea. "Think maybe you may have a septic problem. Want me to help you check?"

"No, that old rascal can be contrary sometimes. I'll take care of it."

"Okay if you're sure. Give Myrtie my love, huh?"

"I'll do it."

He failed to turn and see the satanic grin on John Wilkerson's face as he descended the porch steps.

CHAPTER 28

Naomi Duncan put aside her bread making and hurried to answer the door. Angel raced ahead of her, dancing about and yapping.

Who in the world?

After a quick wipe of floury hands on her apron and a couple of pats to her hair, she opened the door. She could not help an amused smile at the comical sight of John Wilkerson cradling an enormous bouquet of flowers in his arms and shifting from foot to foot. He looked like an aged suitor come to woo her.

Angel saw something different. Contrary to the dog's normally exuberant tail-wagging greeting to friend or stranger, she cowered and backed away. With a warning growl, she turned and sprinted down a hallway.

Naomi shook her head. "My goodness, never seen her act like that before. Sorry." She opened the screen. "Come in, come in."

"No, thank you. Just dropped by to give you these flowers." He extended the bouquet. "Grew them myself."

"Oh, Mr. Wilkerson, thank you." She swept the flowers into her arms.

Without another word, he turned, walked down the steps and climbed into his pickup. Fourteen minutes later the pickup careened to a stop in front of Ferrell's Supermarket. John emerged from the passenger door and strode inside. He reappeared within minutes, Tuck Ferrell at his side. A quick flip of a threadbare canvas covering the truck bed revealed an array of brilliant red flowers. Tuck's hands disappeared into the crimson mass.

From a block away Red Meyers recognized George Sneider, the new City Manager. The man stepped into the street without looking either direction and hurried toward a group crowded around a battered pickup parked in front of Ferrell's. Red flinched as an old model Buick skidded to a stop within inches of the careless pedestrian. The man appeared to be oblivious of almost being plowed down and turned into blood soup. The driver's door opened and Millicent Forbes stepped out. Without a glance at the man she had almost hit, she bee-lined into the crowd. The car remained in the middle of the street with the door standing wide.

"What the hell?"

He was looking at more people than he had seen in one place since—*since when?* He stood groping through the fog in his mind.

"Fourth of July picnic."

He glanced down at the near-empty pint bottle clutched in his hands, then back at the crowd. He grinned.

"Your lucky day, Red old boy."

A crowd that size would be good for enough handouts to replenish his liquor cache for four or five days. Maybe a week. He was already looking forward to the days ahead when he could languish in his shack without a care in the world. Yes siree, he and Old Mr. Crow were about to have themselves a high old time. He stuffed the bottle in his pocket and headed toward his unexpected windfall. His unsteady gait carried him to the perimeter of the milling group. He spied his first easy touch. With his perfected poor-me face donned, he sidled up to Millicent Forbes.

People normally backed away from him, more often than not pressing a dollar or two into his hands. Millicent stood her ground. No one was evading him. Not one single person. Some even pressed against him, elbowing and jockeying for a position nearer the truck. It appeared he had become an inconsequential presence in a group whose minds had fused into a single entity. The giant mind had only one thought, and that thought had nothing to do with him. This was a new experience—not being noticed.

He craned his neck to see what had everyone so excited.

"Flowers?"

Then a stench hit him—festering sewage, excrement, putrid

meat, charred flesh. He backed away.

"Sweet Jesus."

Sure his knees would buckle, he staggered into a nearby alley and reeled against a wall. He vomited. Each time he attempted to straighten, the nausea hit again. He rubbed his nose against the awful stench that had settled in his nostrils. He fumbled the whiskey bottle from his pocket and unscrewed the lid. He put the bottle to his lips, but did not turn it up.

He stood staring at the amber liquid that had been his lifeline for so many years. He shook his head as if waking from a trance. He didn't want it. Overcome by a sense of righteous anger, he hurled the bottle at a brick wall. The sound of shattering glass and the cascade of whisky on the brick felt good, really good. He looked down at the filth caked beneath his fingernails. He stared hard at his soiled shirt and grimy pants. He took particular notice of the side-worn, broken-down shoes and lack of socks. His hands explored his unshaven face and thin oily hair.

"Oh God. What have I done to myself?"

The stern face of January Rainwater popped into his head. Instinct told him the old Indian had answers. Life and death answers. He knew where to find him. Contrary to popular belief, booze had not deafened his ears to what had been on everyone's tongues for the past several days. Nope, the drunken stupors had not affected his hearing in the least. Old January got himself chewed up by a monster dog. That demon dog turned him into one big hunk of hamburger meat is what the stories told. A dollar to a dime, he was still in the hospital whiling away the hours propped up in a fancy bed and being waited on hand and foot by pretty nurses in starchy white uniforms. Yep, those ladies were no doubt scurrying hither and yon seeing to his every need. But he did not envy January his bit of imagined luxury. He hated hospitals. For more than twenty-five years, he had made wide berths around any buildings that housed medical facilities. All those many years ago he had been forced to sit by while lethal burns sucked the life from both his wife and daughter. He had lived their pain—every excruciating second of it. That bitter dose of hospitals had been enough to last a lifetime.

He pictured himself stepping through the large double doors of Caddo General. He could hear the squeak of rubber soles on polished floors and the clatter of food trays. Medicinal odors hung heavy in the air. He began to tremble.

"I can't. Can't go in that place." More than anything, he wished to crawl back into his old skin and curl up with a bottle in some dark corner.

Can't-go-in-that-place, an angry voice from deep inside mocked. *Going to wallow in self-pity the rest of your life? Take another good hard look at yourself. A drunken spineless worm is all you are. You're disgusting.*

He hung his head.

Been running away for better than twenty-five years now, his pride-voice taunted. *About long enough, wouldn't you say? If you can't walk into a building that's nothing more than a pile of brick and mortar where people seek medical treatment, then I suggest you step back into that crowd. Shouldn't take long to beg enough change for another pint. Who knows, maybe your old liver still has a few good years left in it.*

"Don't fret, darling. You don't have to go into that old hospital."

His head jerked up. He stood with his mouth agape, staring into the beautiful face of his wife. Her teeth glistened like iridescent pearls. Eyes as green as emeralds glinted with mirth. Her thick auburn hair was tied back casually in the ponytail that had never failed to peel away years and give her the look of a teenybopper. She was wearing his favorite dress, a white sun dress with royal blue piping ornamenting the shoulder straps, pockets and hem.

"Linda." Tears sprang to his eyes. He reached out for her.

She backed away. "No, no, you can't touch me yet. I've come to take you to a place where there is no sadness. No pain. The kids are waiting for us. They ask for their daddy every day."

He dropped his arms.

"The bottle, sweetheart. The one you smashed on the wall."

His eyes moved to the shards on the ground. He understood her meaning.

"It won't hurt much. A slight sting is all. Then we can be together, a family again."

He walked to the wall, dropped to his knees and picked up the broken bottle neck. The sharp edge glistened in the bright sunlight.

"That's right, darling," Linda's soft voice encouraged.

He had contemplated suicide untold times. On a number of occasions he had stood on the very abyss, but always, the words of the nuns from childhood catechism classes jerked him back from the edge. He could still picture the stern faces of the no-nonsense women clad in their stark black habits.

People who commit suicide burn in Hell for eternity. Only God has the right to take a life.

The threat of Hell never instilled fear in him. Despite his staunch Catholic upbringing, he harbored serious doubts that either Heaven or Hell existed. But uncertainty always remained with him. Maybe the nuns had been right. After all, billions of people, many much more intelligent than he, believed in an afterlife. This uncertainty coupled with his firsthand knowledge of loneliness had made him unwilling to risk an eternity devoid of his wife and children. Now Linda was here and eternity with his family was at his fingertips.

"Do it, Red. For me and the children."

He drew the sharp edge across his left wrist. A crimson thread appeared.

"Deep. You have to cut deep."

He pressed the hungry edge to his skin. But still he hesitated.

"Now! Do it now!"

He glanced up into a destroyed face. Thin wisps of hair clung to a charred scalp. Flesh hung in layers from raw open wounds. Fingers ended in blackened stumps, and the warm smile had changed to an ugly leer with lips burned away and the teeth rotted stubs.

He squeezed his eyes shut. The bottle neck dropped from his

hand. When he dared to look again, he was alone. He struggled to his feet, and with determination and purpose to his step for the first time in years, he deserted the alley. Like a frightened child pursued by demons, he moved past the mob competing for the reeking flowers being distributed by John Wilkerson.

Forty minutes later he rummaged through the maze of junk in his yard. It never bothered him that the citizens of Caddo had selected this particular area to dispose of worn-out appliances and other items that garbage men balked at carting away.

He hefted a heavy oblong metal tub on its side.

For watering cattle?

He brushed a city of cobwebs from the interior, paying little mind to startled spiders skittering for cover. Although dented, it appeared serviceable. He dragged it to the porch, stopping twice to catch his breath. For too long he had lifted nothing heavier than a liquor bottle. After mopping sweat from his face, he hauled it up the steps and through the doorway of the shack that had served as his rent-free home for more years than he could remember. The shack had once sheltered a variety of animals— raccoons, rats, mice, opossums, armadillos. Bird nest remnants still claimed space in the sagging rafters. The patched roof did little to block the sun at the peak of summer or the bone-chilling wind and rain of winter. Spring and fall were usually comfortable, except for the hordes of houseflies and biting-stinging insects that found the roof a welcome mat into the dank interior. On occasion, during his more lucid periods, he found it within himself to crawl on top of the shaky structure and cover the larger holes with odds and ends of sturdy cardboard or any other scavenged material that would hold a nail.

His water source was an old stone well built in the twenties by an immigrant German mason who had intended the structure to stand for centuries as a monument to his skills. The well tapped an underground spring with a perpetual supply of the purest, sweetest and damn-coldest water imaginable.

At the thought of the icy well water, he glanced wistfully at the wood-burning stove. He considered firing it to heat the water, but rejected the idea. The room already had the feel of a preheated oven, and would take on the fiery temperatures of Hades itself. With a shrug, he accepted the inevitability of a cold bath.

After several exhausting trips lugging a leaky metal bucket to and from the well, the tub was half-full. He stripped, and then tossed the bundle of filthy garments out the front door. "Burn them later, by God."

A bar of Lava soap was located among an array of outdated but clean clothes in a large plastic garbage bag that had been left on his porch by one of Caddo's do-gooders. He eased a foot into the icy water.

"Yikes!"

Gooseflesh streaked from his toes to the top of his head. He placed his other foot into the numbing bath. Then sucking in deep, plopped down hard. His testicles shriveled to the size of prunes. He began to scrub.

CHAPTER 29

Naomi closed the door after John Wilkerson's hurried descent of the porch steps. She turned and made her way back to the kitchen, cradling the bouquet like a cherished infant. The indescribable scent wafting from the blooms seeped through her pores and surged into every cell of her body. She sank into a chair and placed the flowers on the table. The bouquet splayed like an ornate fan bejeweled with priceless rubies. The brilliant blooms added a flair of color to the austere room.

She stiffened, as if forced upright by an electric charge. Her hands dropped to her sides. For more than twenty minutes she remained as motionless as a stone statue, her gaze fixed on something light years away from the dreary kitchen.

Plunk. Plunk. Plunk. Every five seconds, a drip of water struck an upside down aluminum pot that lay in the sink amid a clutter of breakfast dishes. A housefly worried about her nose and slack mouth before buzzing away to explore a mound of bread dough that had expanded over the edge of the counter top and was creeping down the face of a drawer. Angel padded into the room and curled into a ball at her feet. A dog barked in the distance. Angel let out a sharp rejoining yap.

None of this penetrated the world into which Naomi had retreated. In her mind, she was four years old and perched on her mother's lap. She wiggled about excitedly as page after page unfolded the fairy tale of Cinderella. She experienced righteous anger at the wicked stepmother and her two selfish daughters. She fell in love with the fairy godmother who, with a simple wave of a wand, transformed mice into elegant white horses and a pumpkin into a beautiful golden coach. Her eyes widened in disbelief at the handsome face of the prince. Familiar blue eyes stared up at her from the storybook.

Who?

And then, as if the fairy godmother had swished her magic wand, she was transformed into a grown woman and found herself in the prince's enchanting embrace.

Me—and the prince.

No, not the prince. She stared raptly into the handsome face. This enchanting man with adulation in his eyes was Don Miller. He kissed her ever so sweetly.

How could she have ever forgotten the exquisite feel of his kisses, his touch. She basked in contentment, like the feel of snuggling down into the warmth of a down comforter on a frigid winter night. She had been granted very few pleasures during her life, and until now, had forgotten that wonderful feeling of good.

Her father's stern face replaced Don Miller's. That wonderful feeling of good was replaced by fear.

She was on her knees and naked, cowering under his wrathful gaze. She flinched at the heat of a glowing soldering iron he waved before her face. "This is but a touch of the fires of hell!" he yelled. The fiery rod cut a path across her right palm.

She screamed, and her eyes blinked open. The stink of seared flesh followed her from the trance and into the kitchen. Her hand continued to throb. Blinking back tears, she looked at her palm, but found only the scar from that first purging so many years before. The pain clicked off.

The faintest rustle jerked her attention toward the door. Her mother stood there smiling warmly.

Naomi squeezed her eyes shut, and after a long minute, opened them. Ellen Duncan was now sitting across the table from her.

"Don't be afraid, little cricket."

Naomi stared dumbly at the mother she had not seen in more than twenty years. She was identical to the picture etched in her memory. Everything was there, the carrot-colored hair swept back from a pretty face dotted with a hint of freckles, large hazel eyes heavy with dark lashes, and the white sun dress with a splatter of yellow and orange daisies.

She deserted you. Cared more for some fast-talking salesman than she did you.

"You can go back where you came from. You're not welcome here."

"Please, baby."

"Please, baby," Naomi mocked. "I don't know what you expected to find here. Over twenty years and not so much as a phone call, not even a postcard. Go on back to your lover."

"Is that what your father told you? I left him for another man? Deserted you? And you believed him?"

"It's true. He would have no reason to lie to me."

Her mother smirked. "Lie? No reason? Your father's life is made-up of nothing but lies. I. Did. Not. Abandon. You."

"Yes you did."

"No. I love you, and I've been right here your entire life."

"You think I'm stupid? Nobody's lived here but me and Daddy."

"Oh yes, I've been here. I saw everything that cruel son of a bitch did to you. The burns. The beatings. You can't imagine my elation when you found Don Miller. But your father took care of that little situation, too, didn't he?"

"Don? What do you know about Don?"

"I know he loved you. I know the two of you would have been married, had children. And I know your father made damn sure that didn't happen."

"I don't understand."

"I think you do. Go to the barn. The answers are there."

The figure of Ellen Duncan began to waver like a wisp of smoke in a mild breeze. "Have to leave now, little cricket."

"No. Please don't go. I didn't mean it."

The chair back and counter top oozing dough bled into view through the translucent figure.

One final whisper, "The barn," and she vanished.

Naomi sat for a moment fighting an ache that pounded at the back of her skull. Unable to push aside her mother's directive she hurried out the back door and headed for the weathered barn.

She forced the heavy door wide, and stepped into the musty interior. A shaft of sunlight bleeding through a narrow gap in the wall pinpointed a slight mound in the northwest corner of the cavernous building. To the unpracticed eye it would have looked like a natural rise of the dirt floor. To her, the slight elevation conveyed a story—a story she wasn't sure she wanted revealed.

She removed a shovel from the storage bin, and began to dig. A hole grew. Three feet. Four feet. Her only hesitations in the backbreaking labor were to sleeve stinging sweat from her eyes. Blisters formed and burst on her palms. She was oblivious to the pain.

The blade clinked against something hard. She tossed the shovel aside and began to scoop away soil with her bare hands. A human skull appeared. Wisps of curly blond hair clung to the moldered scalp, and the once beautiful white teeth had taken on the brown of the grave.

She could not cry. A river of lost-love tears had already been shed for Don Miller; none remained. Only emptiness existed in the part of her where he had once resided. She took comfort in knowing that since their time, no other woman had enjoyed the warmth of his arms or borne his children. He would remain solely hers forever.

She continued to work the soil, and another skull webbed with carrot-colored hair came into view. Yellow and orange daisies were still recognizable on the tattered remains of a sundress.

Her hands began to throb. She climbed from the makeshift grave and stood with her shoulders slumped as if carrying the weight of the world.

"He didn't even have the decency to provide separate graves. The secret's out, at least you can now rest in peace." The cavernous room swallowed her whispered words.

She was unsure of what to do about the morbid discovery.

Call the police?

Come on, Naomi, an inner voice chided. *Just what do you think would happen to that wonderful loving father of yours? Prison, perhaps?*

Yes, the rest of his life in prison—or maybe the death penalty.

Not so fast. I think it's about time you use a little of the common sense God gave you. People kill people all the time. Every minute that passes, a life is stolen. You read the papers, some murderers don't do so much as one day of jail time. Sad, isn't it?

Who's to say he wouldn't implicate you?

No one would believe him. For God's sake, I was four years old when Mama was—

She could not bring herself to say the word murdered.

A sharp butcher knife in the hands of a four-year-old could prove lethal to a sleeping woman. A mother, let's say. Don't make the mistake of underestimating your father. You know he's a convincing liar.

Her father's voice played in her head.

Yes, officer, she was always a strange child. Forever drifting into . . . moods, I guess you could say. Blackouts, wide-awake blackouts is probably a better way to put it.

Fugues? No, can't say as I ever heard the term.

Committed? Oh yes, thought about it many times. Prayed hard over it, too. Couldn't do it, though, not to my only child. Could you?

You bet I did, slept with one eye open. Laid down hard rules, too. No friends.

Cruel? Yeah, guess you're right. Made for a pretty lonely childhood. But to my way of thinking, not near as lonely, or for that matter, as cruel as wasting away in some institution. Don't you see, I had no choice. Couldn't let what happened to her mother happen to an innocent playmate.

I know, I know. Don Miller. Slipped by my vigilance. Can't say I feel much remorse for that one, though. Nothing more than a penniless drifter. Never dreamed of an involvement there, at least until it was too late. In my daughter's defense, that young man was a pure opportunist. Took advantage of her naiveté. Used her up, then tossed her aside like a five-dollar whore. Not that he deserved to die, of course. But you know what they say: Hell hath no fury like a woman scorned. My fault as much as hers. I should have seen it coming.

She shivered. "No. He could never pull it off."

His voice continued to drone through her head.

Mentally ill . . . born that way. Every last one of you have seen her craziness. At school board meetings. Council meetings. Satan, sin and punishment is all that spills from her mouth. Ain't nobody immune to the bitterness of her tongue.

You're right, she's gotten worse in the last year or two. For some time now, been locking my bedroom door at night and wedging a chair under the knob. Man shouldn't be afraid in his own home, should he?

He wouldn't do that to me.

Sure he would. To save his own hide he would. Face it, you're expendable, just like your mother was. Let's say for the sake of argument he leaves you out of it or by some stroke of luck, he's not believed. A good attorney would have no problem convincing a jury the murders were crimes of passion. No premeditation. Know what he would get? Two, maybe three years of soft prison time. Today's prisoners are coddled. Color TV's in cushy cells, three squares a day, recreation rooms, libraries—

"That's not fair. He should suffer."

The system won't mete out the slightest bit of suffering, especially where a contrite old man is concerned.

"No, they won't, will they? This is a family matter. Should be handled by family." She grinned. "Daddy dearest, ready for a little fun? Me and you are going to play a game. You'll rue the day I was born."

That feeling of good returned full force.

In the time it took to refill the grave, a plan was laid out in her mind. Simple. Simple but effective.

She removed the chainsaw from a high shelf in the storage shed, and topped the tank off with gas. She carried it back to the house and set it on the porch.

Twenty minutes later, after luxuriating in a hot shower, soaping again and again, the stink of death and grime had been washed away.

CHAPTER 30

Smelling of shampoo and Ivory soap, Naomi sat on the trunk of a fallen oak and waited for her father's return. With a lover's touch she explored the sharp teeth of the chainsaw positioned across her lap.

For months, Tom Duncan had moaned about the need to render the oak's massive trunk for firewood. He would be pleased to see she had taken on the task.

She recognized the chugging sound of his ancient pickup, and smiled. She stood, and yanked the starter cord of the chainsaw. The small motor roared to life. The vibrating blade cut shrilly into the massive log.

The pickup squealed to a stop. A door creaked open, and then slammed.

The shriek of the saw drowned the sounds of her father's approach, but she could feel him, every step he took. She knew when he slowed his pace to give his sweaty crotch a soothing scratch. And then he was behind her. She could feel him reach out to tap her shoulder. She sucked in deep and turned. The blade sliced as effortlessly through denim and flesh as a knife through warm butter. She killed the motor and dropped the chainsaw to the ground, her features distorted in horror.

"Oh my God, Daddy. I didn't know you were there."

Blood arced in a crimson fall from the wound that had laid his lower thigh open like a gutted fish. She slipped the neckerchief from around her neck and knotted it above the cut. In the short time it took to bind the leg, her hands and arms were slick with blood.

Too much blood. Way too much. You murdering bastard, don't you dare bleed to death. I won't let you die that easy.

"Sit, sit, take off the pressure." She coaxed him to the log and elevated the leg. The blood-flow ebbed. She turned and sprinted for the pickup.

The truck bounced over ruts and potholes to where her father sat rocking and grimacing. After half-carrying and half-dragging his two hundred pounds of near-deadweight, she managed to push him into the idling truck. At a high run, she leapt into the driver's seat and slammed the gear to Low.

Don't die. Don't die. Don't die, played through her head as the old vehicle was pushed almost beyond its endurance toward Caddo.

CHAPTER 31

At the sound of a throat clearing, the receptionist forced her eyes from the torrid novel that had held her prisoner for two days and the better part of two nights. She donned a tired smile. "May I help you?"

"I'm here to see Mr. Rainwater," Red Meyers said.

He expected the young woman's features to screw up in distaste and to hear the humiliating words, "I'm sorry, you can't come in here." He expected her hand to disappear below the desk drawer where a hidden button tapped into security. Within a matter of seconds a burly guard with an *I-don't-take-no-shit* smirk would swagger into the lobby. The rent-a-cop's beefy arms would cross over a prominent beer belly, and he would glare at Red with the superiority afforded by a cheap tin badge. With a quick jerk of his head, he would say, "This way, buddy." It would not be like in the movies where an iron-clutch to an elbow forces an unwelcome intruder to tiptoes while being paced to a door. No, the intimidating guard, who would reek from an over-application of aftershave, would avoid soiling his hands. Red would be escorted out, but fragrant old beer belly would maintain a minimal distance of two or three feet. The few other people milling about the lobby would fan out, creating a wide swath for his slump-shouldered exit.

None of that happened. The receptionist said, "Just a moment, sir," and keyed the name into her computer. She looked up. "Rainwater, January and Michael, both in room One-Forty-Eight. Hallway to the right, halfway down on the left."

She dismissed him by flipping open the thick paperback.

He headed toward the indicated hallway. The receptionist had been his first encounter since his unexplainable reformation. Direct eye contact had been made, but he knew she had not really seen him. Quite a different scenario would have unfolded if the old Red Meyers had been standing there. Oh yes, that pretty nose of hers would have wrinkled and the corners of her mouth dropped into a deep frown. And then that look—disgust, as if a rubber stamp had been used to ink the same debasing expression he had seen untold times on other faces.

At the sight of a nurse charging in his direction, he stopped dead in his tracks.

Here it comes. Entering the hospital unchallenged had been too good to be true.

He cringed as the woman neared. Peg Wilmeth, RN, stood out in bold black letters against the silver backdrop of a name tag displayed on her right breast pocket.

No problem here, Peg old gal. Right as rain, neither of us wants a scene.

He turned, readying to submit to the forthcoming demand to leave the hospital, but harried Nurse Wilmeth skirted around him, leaving behind a sharp glance of irritation.

Out of my way you doddering old fool.

Red felt as if he had stepped into another man's skin. It was like being welcomed back to the human race after long years of exile.

It felt strange being seen as someone no less or no more remarkable than any other person walking the streets of Caddo. He liked this new role, the role of ordinary. Twenty some odd years of individuality had been quite enough. The unpretentious John Doe look fit just as snug and comfortable as an expensive pair of kid gloves.

He strolled down the hallway reading room numbers and stopped in front of door 148.

The part of him that had been allowed a twenty-five-year grip on self-pity had maintained a low profile for the past several hours. Now that the time had arrived to slice the turkey and taste the meat, Old Self was stirring in agitation. He sensed that his long reign was nearing an end, and was not about to go down without a fight.

Not a good idea to go in there, Red. They'll think you tipped the bottle one too many times and laugh you out of the room. We've done all right, haven't we? Never gone hungry. No need to spoil it now. Let's turn around and find us a Good Samaritan who will part with enough change for a bottle. You only think you don't want a drink. I know better. Remember the taste, the tingle, the exhilarating burn to the throat. And lordy, that wonderful gray place where nothing can touch us.

No. You've sacrificed enough, his pride voice argued.

Old Self scoffed. *Sacrificed? Linda and the kids are the ones who sacrificed. Not you. They gave their lives because of your make-a-buck philosophy. A man is supposed to protect his family, make sure the home is safe, smoke detectors in working order. You didn't do that. Traipsed out of town and left Mama and the kiddies behind to burn to death.*

He moaned as guilt stuck sharp talons through his heart. He backed away from the door. Pride voice spoke up. *Your being there wouldn't have changed a thing, except you dying with them. Fire Chief and everybody told you the house exploded in a fireball. Gas leak. You didn't die, and that's just the way it is. Don't blow your last chance to get on with your life. Go in, see January Rainwater.*

Old Self worked to keep the guilt churning. *You'd likely be a grandpa by now if you hadn't let them die. Becky would have been how old now? Thirty-five. And Jon-bo—*

Red pushed the door open. An aura of goodness spilled from the room with the force of a six-foot wave. He staggered back a step. Old Self wound down like an old Victrola running out of juice.

CHAPTER 32

"Naomi, he's going to be just fine. Nobody blames you, accidents happen. For heaven's sake, please quit your crying."

"Oh, Dr. Stein, I saw him drive up. Never dreamed he'd walk up behind . . . with-with me using that chain saw."

"It's okay. Now hush and listen to me. Your father really needs to stay in the hospital for a day or two, but he's refusing. Hell, a blood transfusion wouldn't hurt. Maybe if you talked—"

"Me, talk to him?" she sniveled. "That stubborn old fool would come closer to listening to you than me."

"I guess we can't force him to stay, can we? Stitched him up best I could, and he shouldn't experience too much of a problem if you do exactly as I tell you." He plucked a gold Cross pen from a desk set and began to scribble on a prescription pad.

Handing her two forms, he instructed, "Don't need him sitting around while you get these filled. Take him home first, then go to the pharmacy. I gave him a potent pain shot and he should sleep like a dead man for the next two or three hours. One of the prescriptions is an antibiotic, two every four hours, day and night, understand?

Naomi nodded.

"Set an alarm. Don't want him missing so much as one dose. You hear?"

"Yes, sir."

"The other is for pain. Believe me, he'll be hollering loud and clear for relief. Regardless of how much he frets and fusses, no more than one tablet every three hours. Clear?"

"Clear."

"And keep a close watch on that wound. Some redness, swelling and a little drainage are normal. If the redness intensifies or spreads or the drainage develops pus, takes on a rancid odor, you call me immediately."

"I will," she tearfully agreed.

"Sending a wheelchair with you, a loaner. Don't want him standing on that leg until I see him again. When he's up to it, maybe wheel him outside for a little fresh air, but don't let him overdo it."

"I'll take real good care of him, I promise."

Glancing down, the doctor spotted her blistered hands. "Good Lord, child, what have you been doing?"

She drew her hands away from further scrutiny. "I guess I got a little carried away with cutting wood."

"I'll swear, that's what work gloves are for. Now let me have a look."

"They're fine."

"Open up, you hear? I don't have time for silly games."

Reluctantly, she moved her hands into the bright illumination provided by a desk lamp.

He lifted her right hand and studied it thoughtfully. "Hum." Then the left. "How did you get these scars? Burns?"

"They're nothing, really. A childhood accident."

"Looks like pretty deep lesions. What happened?"

"I fell. Caught myself on the stove and my hands came down on an electric burner."

"Kids. It's a wonder any of them survive." Once again he began to scribble on the prescription pad. "Antibiotic salve. Those hands look pretty nasty. Under the circumstances, wouldn't do for them to get infected."

Naomi stood dabbing her eyes, and watched the aged doctor hurry down a corridor. She smiled. *Oh yes, Dr. Stein, you can safely lay all concerns aside. I'm going to take real fine care of my Daddy.*

CHAPTER 33

January and Michael looked up at the man standing in the doorway. His scraggly home-cut hair was combed back in a style that had been left behind in the seventies. A green polyester shirt, as outdated as the hair, hung over the waist of baggy jeans. White socks peeked over the tops of black wingtip loafers; an obvious effort had been made to polish away years of use from the side-worn shoes. A hint of Old Spice hung in the air.

The man brought to mind a labor-intensive farmer who had slicked up for that infrequent visit to town. Despite his earthy appearance, January was sure this man had never in his life climbed on a tractor or spent so much as one day with a cotton sack strapped to his back; the deeply lined face spoke of hardships unrelated to the backbreaking labor of the fields. There existed a countenance of better days, of affluence that had been lost or left behind. Something about the man—the draw of the mouth, tilt of the head, the stance—struck a chord of familiarity.

Who? Where?

The questions bounced about in his head for a moment before seizing on a memory. He zipped back in time to last night's dream; a modest campfire illuminated the features of the group huddled against oppressive darkness. His eyes were drawn to the face of a rheumy-eyed drunk.

Can't be.

He blurted, "You are . . . hell, are you Red Meyers?"

"In the flesh."

January could tell Red was taken aback by both his and Michael's haggard and worn appearance. No doubt, they looked to be one step from death's door. He stiffened when the man backed away from the threshold.

"Look, I shouldn't have come here. A mistake—"

"No mistake," January said. "We've been expecting you."

"Expecting me?"

"Damn right. You and several others. Didn't necessarily expect you today, but knew you would eventually show. Get your ass in here. And shut the damn door."

Red stepped meekly into the room.

"That chair," January indicated with a sharp thrust of a finger. "Pull it over here."

Like an insecure student under the scrutiny of a ruler-wielding teacher, Red scurried across the room, picked up the straight-back wooden chair and plopped it between the two beds. He dropped into the hard seat.

January snorted. "That's better."

Michael chuckled. "Come on, Red. Don't let him intimidate you. Gran's a feisty old man, but that tiger temperament of his is all show."

January puffed up in mock exasperation. "Why would you go and say a thing like that?"

They all laughed.

"Michael's right," January said. "I may have been a little cantankerous, but thought for a minute there you were going to take off. Couldn't let that happen. We need you here."

"Don't ask me to explain, but something led me here. I somehow knew you could help me. Damn crazy things are happening."

"Appears to me you've been doing a pretty fair job of helping yourself," January said. "Just look at you. Hell, last time I saw—"

Red's face colored. "No need to say it, I know how I looked. And how I smelled. But something strange happened today that made me take a good look at myself. I know you won't believe it, but I lost all desire for alcohol. Been boozing it for better than twenty-five years, and now, for my part, they could dump every ounce of that shit down the sewers and melt down the stills. You know as well as I do, it's impossible to lose an alcohol craving at a snap of a finger. Once an alcoholic, always an alcoholic."

January nodded. "Last few days has convinced me anything's possible. Been having nightmares, haven't you?"

"Yes, the same one over and over, and each time it progresses to a higher degree of horror. The dreams are so vivid, I would swear I'm physically there and scared shitless. Almost afraid to close my eyes anymore."

"I understand. Almost like dream-visions. I suspect the whole damn town is experiencing them."

Michael asked, "Red, what happened to kill your alcohol craving?"

"It started with me puking in an alley. I was going to take a drink, you know, to wash away that terrible taste in my mouth. I couldn't. I was as repulsed as much by the whiskey as I would have been by a plateful of maggots. I threw the bottle against a wall." His features took on a look of deep, unrequited longing as he described his dead wife in a white sundress, her beautiful smile and thick auburn hair. He showed them the paper-thin cut on his wrist. "She wanted me to die so I could be with her and our children. And I wanted to. *Bad.* Had the broken bottle neck pressed hard to my wrist and ready to cut deep enough to sever a vein. If I hadn't looked up and saw what was standing there, I'd done it."

"What did you see?" January asked.

"A charred rotting corpse. I'm not crazy. It was there, and looked every bit as real as either of you."

"No, Red, you're not crazy. God help us, the evil is growing stronger by the minute if it's capable of doing that. I was warned The Chosen were in danger. This only proves it."

"The Chosen?"

"In a dream, I was visited by an angel, not my perception of an angel, of course. No halo, no wings, but he couldn't have been anything else. The purity and love emanating from him was unbelievable. He told me I had been chosen from birth to defeat an ancient enemy. He showed me the other chosen. You were among them, Red"

"This is getting weirder by the minute."

"It gets even weirder. As ridiculous as it sounds, we are to locate a field of beautiful red flowers and destroy them."

"Holy shit!"

"What?"

"The flowers, I saw some this morning, a whole pickup load."

"Holy contaminated rat shit," January cursed, the words pushed out by a spectrum of emotions ranging from excitement to dismay. "Good God, man, why didn't you tell us before now?"

"Flowers? How was I supposed to know flowers were important? Didn't see any reason to mention them. Their stink is what made me puke. Figured I was allergic, me being the only one sick and all. Must have been twenty people crowded around that truck, and the odor didn't bother anyone but me."

"Can't believe it. Stuck in this hellhole of a hospital and the devil himself marches into Caddo as pretty as you please. Right under our noses. Lord, help us. Lord, help the whole cursed world. Where the hell was the pickup?"

"In front of Ferrell's."

"The owner?"

"Seen that old truck rattling around Caddo for years. Belongs to John Wilkerson."

"John Wilkerson. That black-hearted bastard. Explains the out-of-town story he dumped on Jeff, doesn't it? The son of a bitch bled her dry before Jeff ever got there."

"Bled her dry?"

"Like a slaughtered hog. Human blood germinates the flower seeds, and John used Myrtie's blood. She's dead just like I dreamed."

"Gran, it's not your fault. Couldn't have been prevented."

"Like hell. I was warned she was going to die, and I let it happen."

"Not true. You dreamed that both she and Howard Roland were already dead. That's what you told me, remember?"

"You're right. I couldn't have saved her or Howard, could I?"

"Nope."

"At least there's one thing in our favor, we know where the cursed field is located. Red, you sure it was the flowers that made you sick?"

"Oh yes. That stink made me sicker than a dog with

distemper."

"Can you remember who was there?"

Red rubbed his chin, his brow wrinkled in thought. "Millicent Forbes for sure. Wasn't really paying much attention, but if I think hard about it, could probably come up with more names."

"Good," January said, tossing aside the sheet and slipping out of bed. "We need to get out of here, got things to do."

"Whoa, hold your horses, Gran. Just where do you have in mind we go? Can't go back to the house, it's a deathtrap."

"Well damn, a motel then."

"Too public. You heard what Red said, a good-sized crowd was attracted by the flowers, and most of them are probably under that thing's control now. Unlike animals and snakes, people have access to guns, knives and God knows what other kinds of weapons, and the smarts to ferret us out. We'd be sitting ducks in a motel."

January collapsed to the side of the bed. "Can't stay here, no safer than a motel." His eyes traveled nervously to the door. "Dallas? No, wouldn't work, have to stay close to those flowers."

"Don't nobody come to my house," Red said smugly. "Nice little shack. Most of the comforts of home and it doesn't attract many visitors."

January's face lit up. "Why, you old rascal, if you ain't the smart one. Did anybody see you come in here?"

"Why sure, lots of people."

"Then your place won't work."

"Sure it'll work. Nary a soul recognized me. A bath, shave and clean clothes was like stepping into a disguise for me. Didn't draw a second glance from one single person."

"Phew. That's settled then. Now listen, don't be getting too overconfident about that new look of yours. Took me a minute, but I figured out who you were. Someone else could too. You need to slip out of here and keep your head down. Michael, give him your car keys."

Michael fetched a pair of jeans from a closet, removed the keys from a pocket and tossed them to Red.

Red caught the keys and stared down at them as if he were holding a brown recluse spider in his bare hand. "I-I-I," he stuttered. "It's been years since I was behind a wheel."

"Hell, you ain't driving nowhere," January snickered. "Those are so you can get in the car and wait for us. The exit at the end of the hallway dumps into the parking lot. In the second row, look for a tan Ford Taurus, a rental car. And for Pete's sake, try not to be seen. Won't take us long to throw our crap together and get out there."

Red walked to the door.

"Stand straight. That pathetic slump is a dead giveaway."

CHAPTER 34

Naomi Duncan charged down an aisle of Elliot Pharmacy toward the prescription counter. Frank Elliot glanced up at the woman's approach. He stiffened, bracing for an upcoming tirade.

What would it be this time? Condoms?—a tool conceived by Satan to entice the weak into fornication and adultery. Magazines? Redbook? Readers Digest? Ladies Home Journal? None were immune to Naomi Duncan's hit list. He searched his mind for recent issues that might have mentioned sex and came up with two. And of course, there were always the paperbacks with brightly illustrated covers of scantily-clad women who promised readers erotic journeys into fantasy worlds. A new shipment of romance novels had been added to the rack that very morning.

Poor timing, Frank.

She could be on her high horse over tobacco products—snuff, cigars, cigarettes. In her twisted mind, tobacco—Satan's destroyer of the Lord's temples—ranked just below the debauchery of sex.

Naomi stepped up to the counter and with a mind-boggling smile extended three prescription forms. "How long will these take?"

"Five, ten minutes at the most."

She stood for a short moment with her features creased in thought.

Get ready. Here it comes.

Then that disarming smile again. "Take your time. Got a little shopping to do." She turned, and with an animated lilt to her step, strolled toward the cosmetic counter.

Shocked motionless, he could do no more than watch her retreat.

Beverly Elliot stepped from the front checkout counter and hurried to offer Naomi assistance. His wife's quick, jerky pace was a dead giveaway of her apprehension.

As Frank worked, he found it necessary to resist an urge to desert the tight-walled cubicle and go—*go where?*

To cosmetics. He could not control curious glances. Open smiles and friendly nods confirmed the women's amiable interaction. He ached to join the conversation—hear their words, their opinions, to offer his thoughts.

What's gotten into you? This is what you'd expect from that nosy Millicent Forbes. Those two gals are only having a friendly chitchat, and it's none of your concern. Besides, you don't even like Naomi Duncan. Never have. So keep your mind on your business, huh?

His wife caught his eye. You are not going to believe this, her expression read.

Thirty minutes later Naomi carried a loaded shopping basket to the prescription counter. She stood with a pen poised over an open checkbook as the purchases were totaled. In near-shock, Frank scanned an unbelievable array of beauty aides—lipsticks, blush, foundation, nail polish, colognes, mascara, eyeliner, eyebrow pencil, talcum, perfumed soap. Each time he looked up, she offered him an easy smile.

CHAPTER 35

Naomi entered the kitchen through the back door. Gravelly snores and occasional snorts emanated from her father's room.

Good. Still asleep.

Angel charged into the room, whimpering and jumping up Naomi's legs.

"Get down. That hurts."

She dropped the smaller of two plastic bags on the table and carried the larger one to her bedroom. As if fearing another scolding, the dog padded behind, tail tucked and ears down.

As she dumped her purchases on the bed, a tremor of excitement fluttered her belly at the sight of the brightly colored packages. She had never been allowed to experiment with so much as a tube of lipstick; makeup had never touched her skin.

Face Paint. For Satan's whores.

Beverly Elliot had been kind and generous with advice. She had explained the use of creams, cleansers, powder base—the entire spectrum of complexion care. Naomi yearned to sit down before a mirror and practice the makeup ritual that was commonplace to millions of women throughout the world. She picked up a gilded jar of bath salts, unscrewed the lid and breathed the wonderful fragrance. She glanced at Angel. "Bath tonight, sweetie. Not a shower, a long hot perfumed bath. Then we'll play with the rest of this stuff. What you think?"

Angel wiggled in reply.

"More important things for now." She swooped up her pet. "Want to help mama," she crooned, hurrying back to the kitchen. "Huh, do you, sweetie?"

Angel was in pure heaven until Naomi sat down at the table and put her on the floor. She attempted to reclaim a position on Naomi's lap.

"Go away. Don't have time for you."

Her tail tucked, Angel skulked out of the room and took refuge under Naomi's bed.

Naomi upended the plastic bag. She set aside a can of Drano, an economy-sized jar of petroleum jelly and a tube of antibiotic cream. The two large prescription bottles contained capsules rather than tablets. "Oh yes, these will do."

So far, luck had been with her. Everything, to the tiniest detail, had gone as planned. Well, almost everything—her father's heavy blood loss hadn't been counted on. But even that had worked to her advantage. It had weakened him, and that's how she wanted him, weak.

Working slowly, savoring her labors, she replaced the powder contained in each of the capsules with tiny Drano crystals. She spooned the entire measure of petroleum jelly into a bowl and added a steady stream of salt.

"Little Drano, you think?"

"Sure, why not?"

In went a sprinkle of crystals. Bowl and spoon in hand, she headed out the back door, scanned the ground and squatted over her discovery.

"Angel-precious, just look what you did for mommy."

The dog's recent droppings were scooped into the bowl. Five or six stirs, and the fecal matter dissolved in the salve.

After returning to the house, she arranged a tray with two capsules, the salve concoction, a glass and a pitcher filled with water drawn from a toilet bowl, and then settled in a comfortable recliner and waited for her father to awaken.

CHAPTER 36

Peg Wilmeth tapped on the door, and then pushed it open with a hip. "Time for shots boys," she sang out. The sight of vacant beds brought her to an abrupt halt.

"January? Michael?"

Her smile drooped. After setting the tray containing two syringes and alcohol swabs on a nightstand, she checked the bathroom; damp towels, soggy washcloths and soiled hospital gowns littered the floor. The lavatory shelf had been cleared of razors, combs and other grooming aids. A plastic bottle of Prell shampoo lay on its side in the shower. The thick emerald liquid veined the door glass and tile walls. Mucky green footprints stood out on the white tile floor.

"Cleaning crew is going to be royally pissed when they see this mess."

The clothes closet was empty. In the top drawer of the nightstand were several packets of salt and two bananas—black and fragrant—and in the bottom drawer a pair of smelly white socks. The only other item left behind was a sick-looking ivy dehydrating on a window ledge.

"Damn, Damn, Damn."

She slipped the syringes in a pocket, and hurried to the reception desk.

"Shelley, room One-Forty-Eight is empty."

Shelley Carroll looked up.

Peg recognized her expression. The ditzy blonde called her Wicked Witch of the West Wing behind her back, and sought any opportunity to get under her skin. The gal's doddering old supervisor, J. J. Johnson, always turned a deaf ear to her complaints about the bimbo's insubordination. She steeled herself for a confrontation.

"Yeah, I know," Shelley said, offering an innocent smile.

"Well?"

"Well what?"

"You know damn well what." Her eyes glinted fire and her fingers flexed in agitation. For a long moment they appeared to be participants in a stare-off.

"The goddamn Rainwaters," Peg blurted, breaking eye contact. "Where the hell are they?" Her angry words drew curious stares from a number of people milling about the lobby.

"Oh, them. Checked out an hour or so ago. And you know, Peg, neither of them seemed the least inclined to update me on their future whereabouts. Why, what difference does it make?"

"No difference. Surprised they were gone, is all." She spun on her heels and stomped away. "Dammit, nobody around here ever bothers to tell me anything."

Shelley chuckled as a few onlookers threw her smiles of appreciation for the bit of entertainment.

Peg Wilmeth stuck her head into the nurses' lounge. She took in the large table with chairs askew and the muck-encrusted microwave oven that had evolved into a war of wills among the staff on who would finally break down and clean it. Her gaze moved to the cluttered counter top and stainless steel sink with its drippy faucet. The door to the restroom stood open. She scanned the hallway in both directions before stepping into the room. She crossed to the flip-top trash receptacle and plunged the syringes containing lethal doses of insulin deep into the day's accumulation of rubbish.

"One measly hour. A lousy hour sooner and we'd have been shed of those troublesome Rainwaters."

CHAPTER 37

At an unvarying speed of fifteen miles per hour the Ford Taurus consumed two miles of gravel road fronting the Wilkerson's farm. January, Michael and Red stared in astonishment at a veritable army of townspeople gathered there. The field with its lush red blooms was visible from the roadway.

"Damn," January said. "They're breathtaking."

"One good whiff would kill that thought real quick," Red said. He belched. "Hell, just looking at them is making me nauseous."

"Michael," January barked, "let's get the hell out before Red vomits or somebody takes serious notice of us."

The car shot forward, leaving behind swirls of dust and leaves.

"Hell, did you see all the guns. It's an arsenal."

Michael tossed January an exasperated glance. "Yeah, we can scratch the idea of slipping in unobserved. Couldn't get within a hundred feet of that field. No bonfire today."

"Should have known the bastard would have the place guarded better than Fort Knox. Take my word for it, we'll get to those profane plants, sooner or later. Just going to take a little more planning is all. We have to arm ourselves. There are handguns, two shotguns and four rifles at the house. Plenty of ammo. We've got to go there, no choice."

Icy fingers danced up Michael's spine. "No. It's a deathtrap. The snakes are still there. Can feel it in my bones. We'll have to buy what we need."

"Ain't right. A man barred from his own home. Pisses me off. I don't have my checkbook. Drive to First National and I'll draw out enough money to get what we need."

"Too dangerous. We can't go anywhere in Caddo. A bank teller could prove every bit as deadly as a rattlesnake. I have credit cards."

January frowned. "Credit cards it'll have to be. I'll pay you back every dime of it."

"I'm getting a job when this is over," Red said. "I'll put in my part too."

Michael stopped the car, and turned to face them. "Listen you two, let's get something straight. I don't need your money. My job pays well, and I can afford anything we need. No mouth. No arguments. Understand?"

January and Red both nodded, and then tossed each other conspiratorial glances that read: This is something that can be hashed out later.

Michael turned west on Interstate 20 toward Dallas. Two hours later, the horizon ablaze with a spectacular sunset, he whipped into the parking lot of a large shopping mall.

CHAPTER 38

Two salesmen, lounging behind a counter and chatting amiably, glanced up as three men entered the sporting goods store. The senior salesman eyed them with distaste. The eldest of the three, undoubtedly in his seventies, had an unhealthy cast to his skin. He walked with a pronounced limp and periodically flinched. His features, especially the high cheekbones, were dead giveaways to his Indian heritage. A beaded cloth, no less, had been used to tie back his thinning grey hair.

Straight off a reservation.

The middle-aged man in outdated, ill-fitting clothes looked as if he had wandered off of skid row.

Heavy boozer, that one.

The boozer stopped to stare at a rack of colorful golf shirts.

Please, don't touch.

The third and youngest man's dark complexion and longish black hair also hinted of Indian ancestry. He moved with confidence, and had obviously fared better in life than his much older companions. Although rumpled, his clothes were trendy and appeared to be expensive.

Probably a lucky find at some thrift shop. Dollar to a donut, the three together couldn't scrape up enough change for a Happy Meal at McDonalds.

He busied himself straightening the work area, and with a disdainful smirk and a flick of the head, directed his subordinate to handle the dubious-looking customers.

Glen Lowery approached the men and offered a bright smile. "May I help you find something?" The words carried a genuine like for people.

"Yep," January replied. "Got us a list here."

Glen accepted the crumpled sheet of paper. His mouth dropped as he scanned the penciled high-dollar items. "Right this way, gentlemen."

After checking January's drivers license for Texas residency, the salesman laid out three Defender 1100 shotguns and a case of twelve gauge double-aught shells on the glass counter top. Four AR15 rifles along with Bushnell scopes and twenty high capacity magazines joined the shotguns.

"Binoculars?"

"Absolutely."

Two sets of Bushnell Binoculars in leather carrying cases appeared on the strewn counter.

"Knives. What did you have in mind?"

"Hunting, the best on hand."

Red stood idly by with his hands in his pockets as January and Michael poured over an ample knife display. He was intimidated by the three large Spyderco hunting knives they selected, and refused when January encouraged him—just for the feel—to heft one of the lethal weapons.

Regardless of the circumstance, he was certain that he could never bring himself to plunge one of those sharp blades into another human being. He was content in this knowledge. During his early years—his affluent era before his family died and alcohol gained a stronghold—when rifles and shotguns were affordable, he was not in the least smitten with the sport of hunting as were many of his friends. In his mind, the wanton slaughter of wildlife was barbaric and cruel. Except for a pesky mouse or two, he had never killed a warm-blooded animal.

He glanced at the older sour-faced salesman who was staring at the expanding quantity of expensive items.

Commission sales, huh, Pop?

The man's distaste had been obvious when they had entered the store. Red hadn't missed the haughty wave to the junior salesman to serve them. The old boy now looked a bit green about the gills.

Never too old to learn a new lesson, huh, Pop?

Six high beam Maglite flashlights, an ample supply of batteries, two Coleman lanterns, three cans of fuel and spare mantles completed the list.

"Sure that's all?"

"What about sleeping arrangements," Michael asked Red.

"There's only one cot. Plenty of sheets, pillows and blankets though." Color crept up his face as he stared down at his shoes. "You know how it is, people tend to give me that sort of stuff."

Two queen-size air mattresses and a self-contained air pump were added to the supplies.

Weighed down by an array of boxes and sacks, and Michael's American Express bill bloated by several thousand dollars, the three men walked from the store.

Michael handed a shotgun and box of shells to January, then stowed the remaining acquisitions in the trunk. He slammed the lid, and as he turned to walk to the driver's door, an icy breeze swept down on him. The scene before him grayed out as if the entire world had been bleached of color. Sure he was about to drop into a dead faint, he reached out to brace himself against the car. In that twilight void a figure swam into focus, and then his mother was standing before him.

He melted under her stern expression.

"Son, what are you doing here?"

His shoulders slumped and head dropped. His chin almost rested on his chest.

"I asked you a question. What's going on here?"

"I-I—we're going to destroy John Wilkerson's flowers."

Her brow drew in confusion. "Why in the world would you do that? They're beautiful. How do you think that old farmer is going to feel when his livelihood goes up in smoke? Really, Michael, I don't understand you."

"Gran said the flowers are evil, and John Wilkerson killed his wife to grow them."

"I swear, your grandfather is still making trouble. Him and his ridiculous superstitions. I grew up listening to that Indian legend garbage. Got sick of hearing it, nearly drove me nuts. You're such a bright young man. Can't believe you fell for that crazy old man's fantasies. Look what he made you do, squander all that money. Thousands of dollars to feed his sick illusions."

"Mama, I—"

"Michael, snap out of it."

He blinked in bewilderment at the distant sound of January's voice.

"Don't listen to him. I'm here because I love you. I want to protect you. Please, son, give me some time. He'll make me go away."

An ache the size of Texas hung in his heart. "I love you too, Mom."

A hand appeared from nowhere and landed a stinging blow on his cheek.

"Damn it, wake up."

"Michael," she implored as she faded away. January's worried face loomed in her place. He drew away from the unpleasant odor of his grandfather's stale breath and scanned the parking lot, his eyes darting from one face to another.

"She's gone."

"Who?"

"My Mother."

"Angelina?"

Michael's hands balled into tight fists. "Where is she?"

"No one's been here but me and Red."

"Don't be an ass. You know damn well she was standing right here not more than a minute ago."

"No, she wasn't."

"You're lying. You drove her away. She said you would." Murder glinted in his eyes.

"Michael, please listen to me. Your mother is dead. Remember what Red said about meeting his dead wife in the alley? She wasn't there anymore than Angelina was here."

A discernible expression of doubt took form on Michael's features.

"The woman or whatever you saw could not have been your mother. She's dead, and as much as we might wish for it or want it to happen, people do not return from the dead."

An image of a flower-draped coffin filled his mind. Sad faces. Subdued whispers. He watched his boy-self scoop up a handful of loose earth. A mild breeze carried away puffs of dust as it filtered through his fingers to the silver coffin below.

"You're right. Mother's dead. What happened to me? I don't understand."

"That cursed thing entered your mind and used Angelina's image to get to you, just like Red. This far away, thought we'd be immune. Underestimated the son of a bitch. Let's get out of here, huh? Finish this conversation in the car."

Shrugging in submission, Michael turned and opened the driver's door.

"I'll drive," January said, nudging him aside. "You need time to pull yourself together."

Michael handed over the keys and heavy-footed it around to the passenger side. A nagging feeling of loss, of unspent grief, lay heavy on his heart.

CHAPTER 39

For several long minutes Michael sat watching traffic whiz around them and chewing on the episode with his mother. "Gran, I think I have a good feel for what happened to John Wilkerson. This demon is powerful and very persuasive. It picks out your weaknesses and plays on them."

"You're right about that," Red said. "That thing nearly made me commit suicide."

"Point taken. This is hard to say, but under the circumstances, I think I need to be honest. Gran, I thought you had driven mother away, and for a moment there I wanted to beat you to a bloody pulp. If you hadn't talked me down—"

"You didn't, and if it came right down to it, don't think you could have, no more than Red could have committed suicide."

"Answer me this," Red said. "Why are we hiding if this thing can touch minds from a hundred miles away?"

January scratched his head in thought. "According to the dream-angel this evil one is not omnipotent. It's attempted to wipe the human race from the face of the earth since its inception. To my way of thinking, it's done a piss-poor job of it so far."

"Wait a minute," Michael said. "Look at history, all the havoc."

"I'm not saying it hasn't done a pretty good number on us a time or two, but for heaven's sake, take a look around you. Mankind is thriving. There are more than six billion of us treading good old mother Earth."

"Dang, never looked at it that way."

"Kind of puts things in perspective, doesn't it? Now, let's try to figure out how it managed to touch you from such a distance. Couldn't know our physical location or we'd have already been overtaken by its converts. From the size of that unruly mob milling around the Wilkerson's farm, it had plenty of recruits to draw from. Nope, we'd been stone cold dead by now if it knew where to find us. Maybe it picks up thought waves, you know, like radio signals."

"If that's the case," Red said, "how did it know where to send the rattlesnakes? And what about the dog? Kind of blows a hole in your theory, don't you think?"

"Not really. The dog? I think that was simply a case of me being in the wrong place at the wrong time. Keep in mind, the accident happened fairly close to home. I suspect he was headed there when I conveniently presented myself. And the snakes? That's easy. The evil son of a bitch reached into John Wilkerson's head and plucked out the location of my house. Sent the rattlers to kill us."

"Makes, sense, I guess."

"It's still a mystery to me how that thing took over John Wilkerson," Michael said. "I'd have bet my legs, arms and tossed in both eyes to boot that he couldn't have been taken in by even the foremost legions of hell."

"You're right," Red said. "Take a good look at me, a weak slobber-faced drunk. Wasn't nobody more genuine or hardworking than John Wilkerson. Doesn't stand to reason how he could be influenced to slice up his wife, and me, one of the Chosen? Isn't that what you called us, January, the Chosen? There's something drastically wrong with this whole scenario."

"Never know what's in a man's heart. John apparently wasn't what he appeared to be on the surface. As for you, Red my friend, stop selling yourself short. The way I see it, you're about as strong as they come."

"Strong?"

"Yes, strong. Who did you blame for that awful fire?"

"Wasn't no one's fault but mine."

"Listen to yourself, would you? A weaker man would have conjured up an endless list of people to blame. The builder, the fire department, gas company— God. A man lacking in character would have laid the fault at any door but his own. Not you. Shouldered the entire unmanageable load by yourself. Unjustly, if I may say. Why do you think people have remained sympathetic to you all these years? Hell, we live in the heart of redneck country. Caddo people don't usually tolerate weakness, not blatant weakness, anyway. Live and let live is definitely not their philosophy. Under any other circumstances, they'd have dumped your ass in a freight car and shipped you off to parts unknown. Don't you see, subconsciously they recognized a strength in you most don't possess. Faced with your kind of tragedy, many people would have given up on life, put guns to their heads, hunted up a thirty story building to jump from or became antisocial husks. Granted, you had some tough coping to do. Maybe alcohol was your only means to work through it, but you survived, and pretty well in tact. You certainly don't hate the world or bear a grudge against the human race or God."

"Oh yeah, I'm really some kind of hero, aren't I? Well, I'm not the only person in the world who has lost loved ones. You lost a wife and daughter, didn't see you hitting the bottle."

"No, I didn't turn to the bottle. But, you know, if Michael had not been there I probably would have or something worse. I honestly don't know what would have become of me. Fortunately, I had a lifeline and—" A glance at Michael's expression stopped January in mid-sentence.

"You never told me any of this. You always took everything in stride, never missed a step. And you were always so up. So strong. Why didn't you—"

"You had your own pile of shit to contend with," January blustered. "You were just a kid, and more than anything, needed consistency and good old-fashioned adult guidance, not another taste of human frailty. So dammit, get off your high horse and be thankful we both got what we needed. You hear?"

"Okay, I'll leave it alone for now."

"Good. Now back to matters at hand. Considering how John Wilkerson was taken in, we're going to have to lay aside all of our friendships. Can't afford to second-guess who might or might not be immune to the Evil One's influence. Far as I'm concerned, the only safe people are the ones shown to me in the dream. Agreed?"

"Agreed," Red and Michael affirmed simultaneously.

"I can't overemphasize the danger of outsiders discovering our hidey-hole. It would probably come down to them or us."

"Something else," Red said. "People would get suspicious if I dropped out of sight or showed up in town all spiffy and sober. Need to crawl back into some filthy duds and do a little panhandling. No telling what I might learn. Drunks are perceived as stupid and deaf, you know."

January grinned. "Wouldn't have thought of that in a million years. Ain't you the smarty-pants."

"Shhhmart as they come."

January said to Michael, "Think about your episode. Try to remember everything about it, to the tiniest detail. Maybe we can figure a way to keep the devil out of our heads."

"Already given it some thought. First thing I remember is an icy breeze hitting me just before I went under. All color faded, and then Mom was standing there. She looked as solid as a piece of granite."

"Describe her, clothes, everything."

"Let's see," Michael hissed, staring at the picture in his head. "Young, early twenties I would guess. Her hair was long and black and shiny as coal. Her eyes were almost as dark as her hair. She was wearing a white blouse with a large lace collar and an ankle-length aqua skirt."

"You're describing the photograph hanging in the living room. I took it a month or so before she left home. You used to stand and stare at it for minutes at a time. She barely resembled the beautiful girl in that picture when she died. Her hair was chestnut, not black. Eyes light brown. Both appeared dark in the photo. You made the image in that picture the memory of your mother."

"You're right. That's exactly how I remember her." He turned to Red. "When you saw your wife, was there anything unusual about her?"

"Yes, now that you mention it. She'd turned twenty-nine one month before the fire, and looked her age. You know, two kids and all. In the alley she looked like a teenybopper, no more than eighteen."

"You two have hit the nail on the head. It uses its victims' own memories. Plucks images from heads, and bingo."

"That explains the hallway," Michael said.

"Hallway?"

"The hallway where the snakes were waiting. Remember how afraid of the dark I was as a kid, always had to have a nightlight. That thing picked up my childhood fear, and made the hallway dark."

"I bet you're right. Nobody ever said the devil plays fair, did they? Think about this. If you recognized an image as somehow wrong, could you push it out of your head?"

"Might be possible."

"I know it could be done," Red said. "When I hesitated, resisted plunging the glass into my wrist, I glimpsed up and saw the thing for what it was. Snapped right out of the trance."

Michael grinned. "Maybe we should start imaging our deceased relatives as buck-toothed with a big hairy wart on the end of their noses. That would sure enough strike a chord."

Laughter filled the car.

"I know you're joking," January said, "but it's not a bad idea. Anything to spark the conscious mind. Yes sir, the Evil One may be in for a big surprise next time it attempts to screw with one of our heads. Might find we're capable of a little ass-kicking of our own."

Michael's stomach gurgled. The early morning toast and oatmeal had overrun its course by a number of hours. "Anyone else hungry?"

"Me," January and Red chimed in unison.

CHAPTER 40

A large glowing Kroger sign appeared on the horizon like a lighthouse beacon. Bright blue letters heralding *Deli-Bakery* bled into view. Michael's stomach reacted with another audible rumble.

January snickered. "That belly of yours just doesn't take kindly to missing too many meals, does it?" He made a right turn into the large parking lot.

They emerged from the car and marched purposely toward the entry. A liquor store nestled next to the sprawling supermarket drew Red's attention. He slowed his pace.

BEER WINE LIQUOR glowed a pink neon invitation.

He changed direction toward the liquor store and picked up his pace.

Hold it, you fool. Just what in blue blazes do you think you're doing?

He stopped. Perplexed and scratching his head he stood in the large lot unmindful of anything but the pink neon invitation. His mind tumbled backwards to yesterdays, the days of cheap wine and rotgut whiskey, the era of numbed senses. He stared in fascination at an image of himself tremulously unscrewing the lid from a pint of Old Crow. The bottle rose to his lips. Pungent liquid filled his mouth and burned a fiery path down his throat. Warmth bloomed in his belly.

He grimaced, then sputtered and spit against the imaginary taste.

His fascination with the liquor store had nothing to do with the need for a drink—a quick fix, so to speak. Without a doubt, that addiction was every bit as dead as a country dog who dared to challenge the unforgiving tires of a speeding eighteen-wheeler.

What then?

The answer teased, tantalized, darted at his mind, but refused to germinate. Frustrated, he chalked up the uncanny pull of the liquor store to old habit. Discarding the unborn thought, he hurried to catch up with January and Michael.

Mouthwatering aromas welcomed the men as they stepped through the automated door. January commandeered a shopping cart, and let his nose lead him to the hot food deli.

"Everybody like fried chicken?"

Red and Michael both nodded.

Without further deliberation, January barked out an order for a twenty-one-piece box of fried chicken, eight rolls, a family-sized order of seasoned potato wedges and three large cokes.

Ellie Vaughan touched January's hand as she handed him change from a twenty-dollar bill. She jerked, surprised by a tingle that shot up her arm and charged through her body. "Static electricity," she chuckled in embarrassment.

Feeling nothing but a nondescript brush of skin, January offered her a confused smile, but did not bother to take a good look at her.

She watched the men settle at one of the wrought iron tables provided for diners. She smiled as the boxes were torn open and the scruffy trio dug into the food. Yes indeed, she appreciated huge appetites, and these fellows were a joy to behold. In her forty-eight years, cooking had evolved as her only perfected skill. Not that the high cholesterol fast food offerings of the deli provided a fair sample of her culinary abilities, but under her talented hands, even that fare took on a definite flair. By manipulating a few spices and tossing in a healthy dose of TLC, she managed to work a touch of magic on the simple array offered to a guileless public.

Stretching, working at the kinks in her body, she rose to full height. Her hands moved to the dull persistent ache torturing the small of her back. Although none of her days were pain-free, some proved worse than others; today had been one of the bad ones. Early this morning, following an anguished night of tossing and turning, she had literally rolled out of bed to hands and knees. She had managed to pull to her feet with a precarious grip on the headboard. The ability to bound out of bed, rested and eager to face the challenges of a new day, was a bygone luxury. Some years ago, like a boorish relative, Mr. Arthritis came to visit, and she found there was no getting rid of him.

But Ellie was a tough little lady. She resolved from the very beginning that the debilitating monster that had laid claim to her joints would never get the best of her. She had faced other tragedies. You bet she had. A blown tire on a rainy road-slick night had not only claimed her husband of twenty-two years, but also her eldest son. That had been the Cyclops of tragedies. But God did not take all; He left her one teenage son. For the most part, she had been able to lay her grief aside to lead the devastated boy through his misery. The loss of a father and an only sibling coupled with the mood-swinging onset of puberty proved a full load for him. Back then, teen suicides had been the rage, and too often her knees had gone weak at the late-night ring of the telephone.

For a long while following the deaths, an eternity it seemed, she struggled hard with the *Why?* When she came to grips with the answer, the bitterness and disillusionment dissolved and allowed her to get on with her life. Not that the enlightenment by any means eradicated the jagged emotional scars, but time proved to be a valuable helpmate in that area.

The *Why?*

Simple really. When the Almighty decides to call a soul to Himself, that soul has no choice but to go. God allows no opportunity for argument, and never mind the people left behind, that is just the way it is. Accept Him or reject Him. Although she suffered a bit of bewilderment and doubt during the very hardest of times, deep down she clung to religious beliefs developed in childhood: *To those who wait and keep the faith, God replaces what He has taken away.* Ellie Vaughan fit as snugly as a fine pair of shoes into the category of those who wait, and God did not disappoint her; He took two, He gave three. Healthy, cherub-faced triplet granddaughters were born one month ago to the day. And as for Mr. Arthritis? The heartless brute would have to take a backseat to the new additions to her family. Ellie refused to play the role of doting grandmother from the confines of a wheelchair.

Glancing at the clock, she was surprised to discover that twenty-five minutes had slipped by. A mere half hour remained until the deli closed. Thankfully, her day was fizzling to an end. She sighed at the thought of carting the heavy steel food containers into the walk-in refrigerator. That particular duty always proved to be a test of physical endurance, but had to be done. She turned with the intent of opening the cumbersome stainless steel door, and then hesitated. For a full minute she stood immobilized, reluctant to move. Her mind denied what she felt. More accurately, what she did not feel.

Only your imagination, Ellie. Take a step or two, and you'll see.

She was not experiencing the slightest discomfort—not in her back, wrists, knees, ankles. Nowhere. Ever so carefully she raised her right leg. Gritting her teeth at the expected shock of white-hot pain, she rotated her foot.

Nothing. Not a hint of pain.

She experimented with the left foot.

Still no discomfort.

She splayed her fingers. Her hands appeared alien. The joints were no longer twisted. The gnarled knuckles had somehow straightened. She flexed her fingers. The easy movement felt wonderful.

You're dreaming, my dear. Took one too many of those high-powered pain capsules at bedtime. You're a big girl now—wishes come true only in dreams. Face it, you're in bed in the midst of the finest and sweetest dream you've ever had.

I smell food. Can you smell in a dream?

She looked at the three men who were stuffing leftovers into a tall flip-top trash can. Their voices came through clear. The stainless steel counter top felt cool to the touch. *Pinch yourself to make sure you're not dreaming.* She gathered a hunk of arm flesh between thumb and forefinger, and twisted. Hard. She gasped.

"A miracle!" she screamed.

She would not remember the electrifying touch of the tall dark-complected man until several hours later. In the quietness of her home she would relive the moments leading up to her miraculous cure.

CHAPTER 41

A teenager struggled to take control of the overloaded grocery cart. "Sir, it's my job."

"Not tonight it ain't," January said, propelling the overloaded cart down a sidewalk ramp.

Michael tugged the frustrated boy aside. "My grandfather likes to do for himself, hates to admit he's getting old. What say we humor him, huh?"

The words drew a conspiratorial smile from the teen.

"Appreciate it," Michael said, pressing two dollars into the boy's hand.

With a quick grin, the kid turned and headed back into the store.

Chuckling at the exchange, Red double-timed it to catch up with a fast-paced January and the load of mostly nonperishable food items. Michael had taken it great, and January fairly well, when Red had informed them that a refrigerator could not run without electricity and electricity was not a luxury to be found at his place. Dairy items, frozen foods, fresh meats and such had to be excluded. It was beyond January to let something like that slip by without a bit of grumbling. While hurrying by the butcher counter, he had gouged Red with a murmur about powdered steaks.

Red had laughed. He found January's feigned hardness an endearing quality. There was nothing phony about that old man, one always knew where they stood. And Michael? Now there was a young man anyone would be proud to claim as a son. After Red disclosed the fact he had a dog, Michael had tossed a forty pound bag of Alpo into the cart. Despite Red's objections, the canine vittles stayed. Dog was no more than a flea-bitten mutt not worth a second look, but Michael would not hear of feeding him only scraps.

Dog was no ordinary dog. Some years back, the mongrel

wandered up to Red's shack, made himself a nest under the porch and there he stayed. He and Red became fast buddies. All meals, regardless of how meager, were equally shared. Fruit, bread, potatoes, it didn't matter to Dog, what his master ate, he ate. Until Michael and January entered the picture, Red had considered Dog his only real friend.

The sight of the pink neon sign—BEER WINE LIQUOR—pulled him from his reflections. He studied the glowing words for a moment, and then slapped his forehead in comprehension.

"Dang."

He latched onto Michael's arm. "Come on, we need to go in there, and I don't have any money."

"I don't think that's a good idea."

"Ain't going to drink the crap, going to wear it. Can't wander around Caddo without the smell of booze hanging on me."

"Damn right you can't," January said. "Come on, let's get these groceries loaded in the car, then we'll all go in. You two can shower in that stuff if you want. Me, I'm going to drink it."

At ten o'clock the rental car coasted to a stop within four feet of Red Meyers's sagging porch.

In the bright glow of a Coleman lantern, the men made short work of unloading the car. Aided by glasses of scotch whiskey, January and Michael settled into assembling the weapons. After popping open a can of Coke, Red got on with the task of putting away groceries. He was soon frustrated.

What the hell does a man do with a zillion pounds of groceries?

By midnight, the scotch bottle was down by half. Content with the world, Dog lay under the porch with his belly distended from a hog-sized portion of Alpo. Two loaded shotguns rested against opposite walls. The remainder of weapons had been stored in the only closet. A four-foot shelf above the rusted sink sagged from an overload of canned goods. Plastic grocery bags nestled in a corner served as overflow for food and ammunition. An inflated air mattress invited January and Michael to lay down their tired bodies. Lastly, and of high priority from January's standpoint, a twelve-pack of Miller Genuine Draft and a case of Coca-Cola had been lowered into the icy well water for next-day consumption.

Resisting the temptation to gather about the scarred wooden table to relive the day's events, they dowsed the lantern and collapsed into their respective beds. Despite fatigue, each lay staring into absolute blackness and munching on private thoughts. The steady drone of insects and a remote train whistle soothed and lulled. Bare minutes elapsed before snores filled the room.

CHAPTER 42

While the three men slumbered in Red Meyers's modest quarters, depressing darkness crept into Caddo. The dazzling array of stars that normally dressed the midsummer sky was obscured by a dense cloud cover. Street lamps and security lights did little to penetrate the shadowy gloom that blanketed the town.

An occasional car or pickup traveled the deserted streets, but for the most part, people took refuge behind locked doors. Many people downright denied or attempted to laugh away an inexplicable fear that had slithered like nesting vipers into the pits of their stomachs. After all, fear of the dark was a phobia left behind in childhood.

Despite the stifling heat and the suffocating humidity, the night carried an underlying chill. "A goose walked over my grave," was a colloquialism uttered by more than one to explain away a sudden shudder. Not that the innocent words were believed, of course. Caddo people were no different from the world's general populace when it came to the question of mortality; death was an eventuality meant only for others, not a personal reality. Deluded by this naive concept, most discounted an unshakable foreboding to recurring nightmares which the imaginative would describe as mental sojourns into the depths of hell.

The disquieting atmosphere made it impossible for many to take to their beds and once again face those terrifying dreamscapes conjured during sleep. People engaged in a multitude of activities to fill the endless hours. Those with an innate need for gab who found themselves alone or could not rouse a receptive ear in present company took to the telephone.

The couch potato types preferred the familiar solace of television. Curled in favorite recliners or with weary bodies extended on comfortable old couches, those lethargic individuals stared bleary-eyed at flickering screens. The unappealing fare of old movies, idiot-class talk shows and formatted sales spiels—

"Went from panhandler to millionaire in just six short months"— did little to dispel the somber thoughts, the gloom that had settled as thick and murky as river silt in minds and hearts.

There were the households that had been contaminated by the captivating scent of beautiful red flowers. From these abodes, almost without exception, spilled loud ugly arguments. Harsh cruel words, screams and the unmistakable cracks of stinging blows filled the air. Some disputes escalated to weapons. Hands groped for anything that could be used for protection or to maim, disable or possibly kill. Terrified children, forgotten by heretofore loving, easy-tempered parents, cowered in beds or huddled with siblings in dark obscure corners. The young, in their innocence, could feel the malignancy that had invaded their homes. Oh yes, in their minds, ogres lived in the dark recesses beneath beds, monsters resided in closets, ghouls, vampires and werewolves stalked the night. And now the innate security and protection afforded by solicitous parents had been snatched away from them.

As the night progressed, the police switchboard became clogged with calls from hysterical citizens, each call seeming more urgent than the one before. Emergency vehicles created bloodred backdrops as they raced from one crisis to the next. The anguished howls of dogs melded with the high-pitched wails of sirens.

Lackey's Garage and Body Shop burned to the ground. The best efforts of ten volunteer firefighters proved impotent against the raging inferno that had a mind of its own. Two barrels of spent oil and a foot-high pile of soiled rags had occupied a back storeroom. The rags went up first, and when a flaring tongue licked the oil, a flaming monster evolved that refused to die until the entire building had been devoured. A harried and brave battle ensued until the firefighters bowed to the inevitable and moved away from the blaze. While eight of the brave team elected to wrestle high-pressure hoses to saturate surrounding areas, two of the so-called courageous firemen maneuvered into the crowd of spectators who had been transformed to eerie phantoms by the inferno's ethereal glow. The two idlers, devouring the spectacle with their eyes, exhilarated by its sheer power, wished their peers would toss the hoses aside and allow the fire to have its way with the rest of the town.

Within two hours of the first alarm, the garage was no more than a smoldering pile of ashes. Three charred hulls of late model cars that had been locked in the building for early morning repairs stood as grim reminders of the fire's intensity.

Few people would dispute the fact that Frank Lackey's mechanical prowess outranked any competitor within a two hundred mile radius. With an ear tuned to an idling engine, the man could pinpoint even the most negligible malfunctions. No doubt about it, Frank was the Van Gogh of auto repair, but he had one major flaw; he cheated customers. Big time. Overstated costs for unnecessary work or nonexistent repairs proved the rule rather than the exception. Customers were no more than sheep for the shearing to Frank Lackey.

Fire Chief Cal Allen harbored no doubts that someone, possibly several someones, had taken it on themselves to even up the score. He understood their motivation, even appreciated it. The old crook had been long overdue for a taste of his own medicine, and a walloping bitter spoonful had been crammed down his throat.

As the night crept at a snail's pace toward dawn—the craziness—as some termed the chaos that gripped the town, heightened

A profusely bleeding Nelda Hammond was rushed by ambulance to Caddo Hospital where she received sixty-two stitches in her left buttock and thigh to close gashes inflicted by a butcher knife. Positioned on her stomach, she explained to Jeff Chambers, "The argument got a little out of hand is all. Silly, arguing like that over some trivial thing. But you know my husband. Always has to make his point." Nelda Hammond was known for her irrepressible sense of humor.

A blow from a twelve-inch iron skillet shattered Wanda Cole's lower jaw into about fifteen different pieces. "Self-defense," Nate

Cole insisted. "The bitch intended to bash in my head with the damn thing. Took it away from her and showed her how it's done, showed her good." Pumped full of morphine and powerless to work her jaw, Wanda was unable to comment.

Fifteen-year-old Blinky Pierce shot his father in the right shoulder with the family's High Standard .38 revolver. The pistol had been acquired some years back by Mr. Pierce for protection against the unsavory sorts that were so common in today's godless society. The teen's intent had been a bullet between the eyes, but the gun's recoil spoiled his aim. "The old man stays on my back all the time," Blinky complained when arrested. "Never lets up. Rags day and night. By god, just couldn't stand no more." As he climbed into the steel-screened backseat of a police car, he mumbled, "Too bad I didn't aim a little more to the left."

Four people ended up as paying guests in the hospital; twelve others were treated for sundry injuries—cuts, abrasions, sprains, a painful but not critical burn—and then released.

CHAPTER 43

Timely medical attention and a dose of pure good luck thwarted the hand of death during the craziness night, that's to say if one chose not to consider Bear, an affable Great Dane.

By any standards, Bear did not deserve the fate that befell him. Not a mean bone existed in his gangly body. He loved people. The sight of a human, young or old, would set his lanky tail to wagging. A friendly word or affectionate scratch would have him begging for more. At the merest hint of a belly rub, he would flop to his back, legs flailing and body wriggling in abandonment.

An old rogue raccoon brought about Bear's demise. Rascal, as the raccoon had been tagged by animal loving citizens, would emerge from his den at nightfall and make for Caddo. A blueprint etched in his brain led him to homes that commonly proved easy pickings. Natural inquisitiveness and a never-ending quest for new morsel yielding territories were what led him to the yard where Bear resided. The strong canine odor sent him scurrying for the very tree to which Bear was tethered by a twenty-five-foot length of rope.

Bear picked up the chase, baying like a hound on track.

Cut off from the tree, Rascal skirted toward a large farmhouse. He found himself cornered in a three-by-three nook against the house. Seeking a haven on the roof, he leapt and pawed at the wall, but his sharp claws could not find purchase on the slick vinyl siding. Accepting the futility of escape, he turned on his adversary. Back reared and teeth bared, he readied to do battle.

The huge dog did not attack. It dropped to its haunches, and with its head cocked, stared in rapt wonder. When the dog aimed a playful slap, he was rewarded with a deep-throated growl and a snap of sharp teeth. Rascal charged for safety.

Bear took to the chase, barking and howling. He suddenly jerked backwards and tumbled to the ground as if slamming headlong into an invisible barrier. It took a second or two for

Rascal to realize the dog was no longer in pursuit. He stopped and watched the large animal labor against a restraint about the neck.

The quest had proven quite exhilarating. Not being one to turn down any opportunity for fun, he added Bear to his nightly itinerary.

The Mason's master bedroom backed up to the yard where Bear resided. The frequent wee morning uproars proved disastrous to Lonnie Mason's fragile sleep habits. Once roused, he was up for the rest of the night. Solitaire, boring TV reruns or perusing books and magazines often filled the endless predawn hours.

At his wit's end, Lonnie decided a friendly discussion with Bear's owner was in order. Determined not to alienate his neighbor, he chose his words carefully, even tended to make light of the situation. Stan Hill took no offense whatsoever to the complaint. Lonnie felt an empathetic and aspiring to please Mr. Rogers had stepped out of a television set for the very purpose of the chat.

"That Bear's one feisty animal," the kindly old widower told him. "A bit overzealous at times, but no sweeter dog alive. Sweet or not, can't have him keeping you and the Mrs. up half the night, can we? I'll have me a little set-to with that scamp. He won't be a problem no more, I can promise you that."

That evening, feeling proud of his finesse in handling the uncomfortable situation, Lonnie slipped into deep restful sleep, and did not rouse until the alarm clock sounded at six o'clock. He blinked against the glare of sunlight spilling through the windows.

Thank God for small favors.

His thanks proved a bit premature. Not eighteen hours later, Bear's lusty yowls and barks cut short the night's tranquility. Repeat performances followed, night after night.

A second but not so beneficent discussion was held with Stan Hill. The old man laid on contriteness as thick as Blue Ribbon syrup. "Don't understand," he said in a confused voice. "Thought for sure I had that big galoot settled in. Tell you what, and you can bet your silver belt buckle on this, I'll shut that big trap of his one way or another. No sir, ain't no dog of mine going to disturb nice folks like you and that pretty wife of yours."

Not until the third discussion did it occur to Lonnie that maybe the old codger was missing a few critical brain cells. Not a man alive could have appeared as sincere as that old gent, and then turned his back on the problem, not unless he had a serious head problem.

CHAPTER 44

On the arrival of that ill-fated craziness evening, Lonnie forewent the ten o'clock news in favor of the needed comfort of bed. He lay dead still with a million thoughts pounding in his head. A dull throb worked unmercifully at both temples.

He glanced at the bedside clock.

Jesus, only ten-fifteen. He would have sworn an hour had crawled by since his retreat to the bedroom.

Each sweep of the second hand seemed to drive his headache up a notch. He considered going in search of a bottle of Tylenol, but the mere thought of lifting his head from the pillow heightened the agony.

Call Phyllis.

Sure, Lonnie. And what do you think your sweet little darlin' would do? March straight in here like a good little wife, maybe show a degree of sympathy, then rush right out to get her huggybear some pills and a glass of cool water to wash them down with. Get real. She'd tell you to fuck yourself.

How in the hell could his life have slid into the toilet in the matter of a few short hours. He was hung with a pissed-off wife and a goddamn headache with the penetrating power of a nuclear blast. He scanned through the day's events.

The morning started out well enough. His workday at Schilling Glass unfolded as smooth as silk, and he left the plant tired but content. While maneuvering through traffic, he caught a glint of red in Ferrell's large display window, and slammed the brakes. A half-ton purple and black pickup with imposing yellow and orange lightening bolts stabbing down the side panels squealed to a stop within a hairbreadth of his bumper. Horns blared. He did not hear them, nor did he glance in his rearview mirror and see the red-faced driver of the truck stabbing double-handed birds at him.

With the entrance into the supermarket's parking lot behind him, he glanced about for a vacant street space.

Nada.

Intent on snagging the first available opening, he eased forward, alert for backup lights. A slow block away he lucked into a parking space and pulled in. As he stepped from the car, a black and purple pickup jerked to a stop in the roadway. The passenger window hummed down. A hippie-looking guy, late thirties Lonnie approximated, stretched his lean frame across to the open window.

Figuring him for an out-of-towner needing directions, Lonnie donned an obliging smile.

"Hey, asshole, where in the fuck did you get your driver's license, at a nursery school?"

Lonnie's mouth dropped.

Horns blared.

"Shit," the man bellowed. "Do everybody a favor, cocksucker. Keep that sissy pile of tin off the fucking road!" He slammed to low gear and jammed the accelerator to the floor. The truck fishtailed and the shrieking rear tires left behind two feet of burned rubber.

Lonnie watched the truck make a sharp right at the next corner. He honestly could not figure a reason for the verbal attack. Shoulders slumped, he ambled toward the supermarket.

Twenty-five minutes later, he eased the back door open and stepped into the kitchen. Phyllis was leaning over the oven prodding a roast with a long-pronged fork. He cleared his throat as the oven door snapped shut.

She looked around and grinned. "Well, if you don't look like the cat that swallowed the canary." Assuming a stance of mock reproof, she said, "For your information, Mr. Bird Eater, that's roast beef in there. Blood rare. Don't you be giving me that wistful look. Won't work. Nary a bite for you until you fess up."

"No, no, not bread and water. Not again. A cruel woman is what you are. Cruel and heartless. Ah, but I have something that will force you to mend your wicked ways." Bowing eloquently, he swept a large red bouquet into the open.

"Oh my goodness," she breathed, taking a forward step, and

then stopped. Her smile faded. "That smell."

Fighting and an impulse to backhand the disdain from her face, he hurled the flowers to the kitchen table and stomped down the hallway to the bedroom.

Frothed with arguments, the evening deteriorated. Even Lon Jr. managed to wriggle into the act by playing a nonstop role of spoiled brat. A hell-tide temper tantrum at the dinner table drove Lonnie beyond reason. He stood, jerked off his belt, yanked his son up by an arm and proceeded to beat some manners into him.

Phyllis attacked with the fury of a wildcat protecting her young.

And now, an entire side of beef could be flash-frozen by her iciness.

A few lousy flowers and one measly spanking, well deserved at that, and Phyllis loses it. By God, kids need to learn boundaries. Ain't no better teacher than the biting end of a belt. No sir. Spare the rod, spoil the child. Who can argue with the Bible?

The Number One Bitch can, that's who can. One hell of a note to be taken to task for dishing out a healthy dose of good old-fashioned discipline. Sure as the sun shines in July, that boy will end up a pansy, a limp-wrist queer. May as well go ahead and buy him a pair of lacy pink panties with MAMA'S BOY embroidered on the butt.

His first impulse had been to make the aging hippie the fall guy for the miserable evening, but now he realized the loudmouth bastard had been no more than an irritant, a tiny fly in the ointment. Nope, none other than his lovely wife held the reins to his downward spiral. The insight washed away the headache, leaving behind an invigorating feeling of liberation. He was now ready to face the world on his terms, and no other terms than his own. At last tension free, he drifted into blessed oblivion.

At 3:10 a.m. Bear's sharp yelps and lively barks jerked Lonnie upright. Confused and blinking away sleep, he fumbled the lamp on. For a long minute he sat there squinting at the bright yellow glow, then snapped fully awake. The time was here to take control of his life. The old used and abused Lonnie Mason ceased to exist, and rue the man, woman, child—or dog—who dared to defy the new and improved version.

Mumbling obscenities, he tossed the sheet aside. "Enough is enough."

Phyllis rose to an elbow. She watched him slip into a blue cotton robe. "What are you doing?"

"Ain't no business of yours, so shut your goddamn trap."

He turned and stomped from the room.

After rummaging a flashlight from a kitchen drawer, he tromped out the backdoor.

CHAPTER 45

Hearing the door slam, Phyllis put on her robe and hurried outside to the stoop. Shafts of light streamed from the lean-to where yard equipment was stored.

Lonnie came home from work yesterday with an altered personality. It was almost as if an embittered stranger had stepped into his skin. Never had he raised a hand to her or their son, and for the hundredth time she argued the possibility of overreaction on her part. But even now, through an objective eye, she knew she was right, he was out of control and dangerous.

He stepped from the shed, and in his right hand was the machete used to hack away unwanted undergrowth and to lop off the heads of snakes that slithered too close to the house.

He leered at her. The machete came down in a savage arc, cutting air with an audible whoosh.

You want some of this? Huh?

She tried to back into the house, but her legs refused to move. She sagged against the doorframe.

He turned and stomped into the woods.

She watched the dancing flashlight beam ignite trees and bushes as he made his way toward Stan Hill's yard. The dog was barking. The machete's target dawned on her.

"My God."

She staggered on rubbery legs into the kitchen and collapsed in a chair. Her shoulders sagged and her head dropped into her hands.

He's out of control. Maybe he's still hung up on teaching Lon some manners? The whelps on his legs are child abuse, and there won't be no stopping him next time.

She sprang from the chair, vaulted down the hallway to the master bedroom and straight to the closet. Her hand groped about under sweaters on a high shelf until closing on the wooden handle of a pistol. She snapped the clip release button. It had a full load.

Sitting at the kitchen table, she concealed the pistol under a dish towel and awaited her husband's return. Her fear drained away. She was now in a mindset to kill if necessary.

At the scent of a human's approach, Rascal shimmied up a massive oak, not slowing until safely nestled in the uppermost branches. He gave a warning chatter.

Encouraged by intensified chatter from above, Bear energized his barks and leap walked a good six feet up the tree trunk before dropping back to earth. A bobbing light caught his attention. With his tail wagging in high gear, he loped off to meet his new visitor.

Lonnie heard Bear's approach, and tightened his grip on the machete. "That's right you son of a bitch, come to Lonnie, got something for you."

Bear bounded into view.

"Ready to meet your maker, are you, big boy?" Lonnie said in a friendly tone. "It's payback time."

Bear writhed in pure joy, peeing himself. Sure of a belly rub, he plopped to his back.

"Just like your master, short a brain cell or two." Lonnie swung the machete, targeting the massive skull.

A split second too late Bear attempted to dodge the descending blow. The blade sliced through his left shoulder and bit into bone.

Lonnie reached down and jerked the machete free. The second forceful blow split the substantial skull. Not yet satisfied, he continued to hack at the remains. Breathing hard and drenched in gore, he finally moved away from the carcass. With a sprightly step and whistling a favored ditty, he returned to the house.

CHAPTER 46

Phyllis's hand twitched toward the dishtowel when Lonnie stepped through the door. His bloody robe and the dripping machete were sufficient to make her crave the security of the gun, but his jubilant smile kept her hand at bay. He propped the machete in a corner as offhandedly as setting aside a broom.

"Took care of that little problem. Maybe a man can get some sleep around here now." Without a second glance her direction, he headed to the bedroom, shedding his robe as he went.

For more than five minutes she could not bring herself to desert the security zone established at the table. Her eyes kept traveling to the bleeding machete.

Took care of that little problem. Maybe a man can get some sleep around here now. Took care of —

Madness. The man is insane.

She crept down the hallway, the pistol held before her in both hands and stepped into the bedroom.

"Lonnie?"

The sounds of steady breathing and a nasal snort that would not qualify as a snore were her only replies.

Two thoughts hit her simultaneously: *He's mad as a hatter. Don't disturb him, he needs his rest.*

In her current state, the thoughts appeared logical. She backed from the room and pulled the door closed. After swooping up the bloody robe from the hallway floor, she hurried to the laundry room and dropped it in the washer along with a scoop of Cheer.

Cold water?

Yes, cold water removes blood.

She clicked the dial to Cold and pressed start. The metallic sound of water striking the tub snapped her from her pall. She remembered picking up the robe and her driving need to wash it before the blood set, but for the life of her, she couldn't understand why it had seemed so important.

The flowers were displayed in a crystal vase standing on the folding table. The vase had been Lonnie's doing, and despite a stern warning—*keep your goddamn hands off*—she had removed it from the den the minute he went to bed.

Why did their awful stink not bother him?

Swallowing against a sweat-popping wave of nausea, she fingered one of the colorful petals.

Flesh????

She twisted the entire bloom, hard. It clung to the stem without so much as sustaining a bruise.

"What in the world?"

The truth slapped her sharply in the face, and she jerked away from the flowers that weren't really flowers. She was certain she had stumbled on the source of Lonnie's bizarre behavior.

Why am I not affected?

Male hormones? Some chemical particular to men?

Regardless of the answer, they had to be destroyed. Holding the bouquet at arms length, she hurried outside and dropped it into the trash-burning barrel.

Hold it a minute, her cautious side spoke up. *Maybe you should think this thing through before doing something hasty— something you might later regret. How do you think Lonnie's going to react to you burning his flowers? Huh? Consider what happened to Bear. And for what? Barking?*

She returned to the kitchen and dropped back into her security zone at the table.

Put the flowers back in the vase, was her first thought. *He'll never know you touched them. He seemed happy enough a while ago. Who's to say he's not back to normal. After all, that dog has been driving him up a wall for weeks now. He simply snapped is all, and maybe it's out of his system.*

No, her skeptical side insisted. *Sane people don't hack up animals. A person could be driven to shoot a dog maybe, but not what he did.*

Okay, let's say he's still a little off kilter, he surely wouldn't hurt you. He loves you. A little temper shouldn't be too hard to live with.

Of course not, Miss Skeptical offered, *if you want to carry a pistol around all the blessed time, and make sure he's never alone with Lon for more than five seconds at a time.*

Miss Cautious wouldn't give up. *Burning the flowers may be the only practical solution. Take away the influence, and bingo, a good as new Lonnie. Worth a try.*

She glanced at the machete, and shuddered. The sight of the bloody knife cleared her thinking. Precious time had been wasted grappling for an easy fix to an unfixable problem. Something cold and cruel had latched onto Lonnie's emotions and was capable of influencing him to kill even her. Destroying the flowers would not change that fact. There had to be more where those came from. She loved Lonnie, and if not for her son and the fetus developing in her womb, she would stand against whatever had slithered from some dark hole to disease his mind. As it was, he would have to slay his own dragons or perish.

Forty minutes later she carried her sleeping son to the Dodge Neon and laid him in the backseat. The car's minuscule trunk had been stuffed to capacity with clothes and other items she snatched during hurried packing. She knew in the days ahead that an endless list of left-behind items would be sorely missed, but that couldn't be helped. She opened her billfold and made a quick inventory of its contents: Visa card, checkbook, Bank of America ATM card and a grand total of eighteen dollars and fifty-three cents. She could rummage more folding money from Lonnie's billfold, but was unwilling to go back into the house. The ATM and Visa card could be used to increase her cache of cash. She did not want to be caught high and dry in the middle of nowhere during the long drive to Florida. Her parents would be beside themselves at her arrival and their only grandchild would put them in a dither that would last for hours.

She sprinted to the trash barrel where the red flowers had already been soaked with an entire jug of Gulf Lite fluid. A tiny flare of a match, and lapping tongues of flame leapt high in the air. Then something scary happened, hair-raising scary. A howl erupted from the barrel, a shriek of rage.

She was sure her feet did not touch ground in her flight to the car. No longer concerned with noise, she lunged into the driver's seat and slammed the door. The small car tore down the driveway amidst a cloud of dust and gravel pings. She knew Lonnie could easily catch her in the fifteen-year-old gas-guzzling Buick parked in front of the house. It far outranked the Neon in horsepower. Her eyes continued to dart at the rearview mirror in search of advancing headlights. Amazingly, her son did not so much as whimper throughout the entire ordeal. One less crisis, thank God.

In the deep sleep of exhaustion, Lonnie incorporated the shrill wails issuing from the barrel into his vivid dream and dozed on peacefully.

Next door, Stan Hill snapped awake to escape a machete-wielding demon, a new twist to his recurring nightmare. He sat up, and in the muted glow of Phyllis's fire, fumbled about the nightstand for the hearing aids that would unlock the world of sound for him.

The compact car barreled along at seventy miles an hour through darkness so dense it seemed to reflect the glow projected by the high beam headlights. A flicker of intuition delivered Phyllis's foot to the brake pedal. The car slowed. Fifty. Forty. Twenty. A dirt road bled into view on the left. She coasted to a stop.

Without understanding why, she turned onto the road, easing around sizeable pot holes. After a hard mile or so, a shack loomed in her headlights.

What in God's name are you doing? You've gone as crazy as Lonnie.

Two men evolved from the darkness like eerie phantoms.

She slammed the brakes.

Braced against the men's shoulders were rifles aimed at her head. A blinding light flared in her face. She had always heard that at the split second of death you experienced a flashback of your entire life. Not so. "Oh shit," was her only reaction.

January nodded his approval, and Michael lowered his rifle. Red snapped off the high-beam flashlight. All three men stood smiling like fools at the latest of their elite force to arrive.

CHAPTER 47

Naomi Duncan lay back in a recliner, a leg dangling over the chair's velvety arm and a telephone receiver pressed to her ear. She admired the image staring back at her from a hand mirror. She pursed her lips and lowered her eyelids to half-mast in an attempt to capture the sultry look she had seen in so many movies. There it was—that tantalizing come-hither stare.

Come up and see me sometime, Big Boy.

For three nights her father's constant complaints had cut into her sleep. Not that she had minded, of course; his laments and struggles with pain were pure sweet music to her ears.

She was surprised at how fast his condition had deteriorated. In a few short days he had grown too weak to make the short steps to the bathroom without assistance. Twice she had changed soiled bedding in order to maintain her role as a concerned caregiver. Last night, while stuffing the second set of fouled sheets into the washer, she had decided enough was enough.

No more dirty work.

He had grown frail enough that she could proceed with the next phase of her plan. The time had arrived to add bit of mental anguish to his physical discomfort.

This morning, following a hurried breakfast of buttered toast and coffee, she had donned spike heels and a short red dress that conformed to her body like a second skin. The amount of money laid out in the past three days for new clothes and essentials every woman should own would have put her father into congestive heart failure. Considering that his last few days on earth were in their final countdown, her extravagance was a moot point.

After a couple of quick turns in front of the mirror, she had gone to work with makeup and a curling iron. She looked as if a young child had been turned loose in her mother's cosmetics cache. Emerald green eye shadow blanketed her upper lids. Heavy uneven eyeliner bordered her ample eyes. Double applications of mascara clumped her long lashes, giving them a false look. Dark brown extended her overplucked brows almost to the hairline. Slashes of bright red blush matched glossy lipstick layered on her full lips. Considering her novice status, she had faired well with the curling iron; soft waves and loose curls slashed away years and freed her natural beauty.

Following her elaborate makeup session, she had carried a hand mirror to the living room where she settled into the large recliner to call Dr. Stein. Wouldn't do to have him drop by unexpectedly.

She continued to admire her reflection as the doctor droned on. The image staring back at her possessed the allure and loveliness of Liz Taylor and the voluptuousness of Marilyn Monroe. Oh yes, heads would turn when she finally presented herself in public.

Take a gander at that beauty over there. Haven't seen her around before. Where do you suppose that honey has been hiding?

She is a looker okay. But you know, there's something familiar about her. Seen that face before. Where?

Never adjusting her gaze from the femme fatale reflection, Naomi said, "Nope, hardly any redness at all. Pink and healthy-looking."

She ran her tongue around her full lips.

"Yep, been resting like a newborn baby. Sleeps the night through. Uh huh, appetite as good as ever."

Damn it, lipstick on my teeth.

"Sure did, an hour ago. Ninety-eight-six on the nose. Monday, ten o'clock? I'll try, Dr. Stein, you know how stubborn he can be. Says the Lord is his healer and he doesn't need some fool doctor messing with him anymore. Like I said, I'll try for Monday, but can't promise anything. Thanks. Bye."

She hung up the receiver. Her lips spread into a smug smile.

Swinging her hips provocatively, she carried a tray down the hallway to her father's bedroom. The stink that met her at the doorway brought her to an abrupt stop.

Lord.

"My goodness, Daddy, you mess yourself again?"

The dazed figure in the bed stirred and murmured in the low whine of an ailing child, "Couldn't help it. Kept calling. You wouldn't come."

She walked to the bed and placed the tray on the nightstand. The stink was nearly unbearable. Breathing through her mouth helped a little, but not much.

"Sorry, Daddy. I was so tired when I fell in bed last night, must've been dead to the world."

He reached out, groping about like a blind man until he found her arm. "You call the doctor like I told you? It hurts. Hurts real bad. Something ain't right. The doctor needs to come."

Not for a second did she doubt his pain. His red veined eyes were worn raw from leaking tears and his mouth seemed permanently drawn into a marble white circle of agony. She was sure she could smell his pain, much as an animal can detect the scent of fear.

"Just hung up from talking to him."

Tom exhaled a heavy sigh and his features brightened.

"Told me some pain was to be expected. Gave me strict orders not to pay any mind to your constant complaining. He said, and I quote, 'Men are big babies when it comes to a little discomfort. Worst patients in the world.'"

"But, but—"

"Hush. I'm not listening to any more of your bellyaching. Here, take your medicine, It'll make you feel better."

You betcha, Daddy. These pills going to fix you right up.

He let go of her arm and accepted the extended capsules. After a low grumble about "quack doctor" and "ain't working" he washed the pills down with a glass of water.

"Now, let's have a look at that leg," she said, unscrewing the cap from the salve jar.

"No, No!" he bellowed, wriggling to the opposite side of the bed.

"Stop it." She leaned over and jerked back the gauze dressing.

Stitches were breaking under the pressure of swollen flesh. A few of the more tenacious threads cut deep into tissue. A veritable river of greenish-yellow pus oozed from the wound; angry red lines snaked in several directions. But the icing on the cake, so to speak, was the tiny white worms wiggling through his flesh. Oh yes, this was much more that she had hoped for.

She scooped a sizable dollop of salve from the jar.

"No. Please, please. It hurts too bad when you do that."

"You're making me mad, Daddy." She gave the leg a sharp slap.

For a second or two he sucked air like a surfacing swimmer, and then let out a wail. His back arced in spasm.

"That's better." She daubed the light brown ointment on the foul flesh.

Through watery eyes, Naomi's image swam into focus. For the first time since she had entered the room, he actually looked at her.

"Harlot!" he bellowed, rising on his elbows. "Painted whore!"

But even anger couldn't maintain his elevated position for long. He collapsed to the pillow.

Naomi was ready to reveal the gravity of his situation and knew her sexy appearance would drive it home as nothing else could. She struck a seductive pose. "What's the matter, Daddy, don't you like my new outfit?"

"Scrub your face and burn that sinful dress."

"Sinful? Why, I thought you'd enjoy it. After all, you've always wanted me. Isn't that right, Daddy?"

He shook his head.

"Come on, let's be honest with each other, huh?" She leaned close, cleavage spilling from the low cut bodice. "All my life you've lusted after me. Your sanctimonious teachings wouldn't let you take me, would they? Not in the biblical sense, anyway."

He clamped his hands over his ears and squeezed his eyes shut.

"You better look at me or you'll be in more pain than you ever imagined possible."

He dropped his hands to the bed.

"Don't give me that injured look, you hypocrite. Oh yes, Daddy, you fooled me. For a long time you fooled me. But I can see through you now. You couldn't stand it when you saw lust for me in another man's eyes, could you? When Don wanted me—" She paused, and then said, "Took is the word I'm looking for. When Don *took* me, you went crazy jealous. He took something that belonged to you. When you stuck that shotgun in his belly he was terrified, wasn't he, Daddy? If you had told him to go away, he'd have done it. But that wasn't good enough. He loved me, and you couldn't take the chance he'd come back for me. So you killed him."

"You're talking crazy. He didn't love you. Ran like a scared rabbit when I fired in the air. Trash. That piece of yellowbelly trash didn't have the guts to come back for you,"

"No, Daddy. I know what you did. Shot him down like a rabid dog. And me? I wasn't your sweet little virgin anymore, was I? In your sick mind, I was tainted, and you figured since I was soiled anyway, a few liberties would be okay. Lust was in your eyes when you forced me to strip. I saw it. Lust. You raped me. With your eyes, you raped me."

"No!"

"Had to make sure no other man would want me, didn't you? And I had to be punished. So you took the soldering iron and taught me a lesson I'd never forget. Those terrible scars eased your mind about other men wanting me. My screams were pure pleasure, weren't they? I bet you masturbated after I passed out."

"No. I was saving your soul. You sinned. Fornicated. Condemned yourself to the fires of Hell. God commanded I save your soul."

She chuckled sarcastically. "My soul? Remember the awful sores, the drainage? Remember what you told me? 'Pray. Thank almighty God that the sin and corruption are spilling from your body.' Well, it's your turn now. Look at your leg. There's a whole river of sin boiling from you."

"Stop this crazy talk." He stabbed an index finger at the floor. "On your knees, girl. PRAY for your salvation. PRAY for forgiveness."

"That doesn't work anymore. You're the sinner in this house, not me. We have more to talk about. I want to discuss my mother."

"NO. That whore will not be discussed under this roof."

"Did you torture her, too?" Her voice dripped with venom. "Tell me, before killing her, did you torture her?"

"I've told you time and time again, the whore ran away. Deserted us, went lusting after another man. Gave her soul to Satan."

"Liar. Liar. Liar." She slammed a fist again and again into his injured leg.

A tortured howl spilled from his throat. His right arm shot out like a striking serpent and he grabbed a handful of her hair. With surprising strength, he jerked her head backwards, forcing her to the mattress. His other hand closed on her throat, cutting off her shrieks.

She attempted to roll away, but was pinned in place. The grip on her throat tightened and darkness began to close on her vision. She thrashed about, groping for a handhold on anything. Her hand touched something soft and wet. She squeezed and dug, twisted and tore at her father's festering wound until her fingers were buried to the knuckles.

His grip loosened and she jerked away leaving behind thick strands of hair entangled in his fingers. Capturing her breath in short, quick gasps, she backed away from the bed, her dripping hand held before her like a hard-won trophy.

"Stop your lying. In the barn, Daddy. They're both there, right where you buried them."

She could see by the horrified expression on his face that he understood his position, the calculated accident, the festering wound. It had at last dawned on him that she was extracting her pound of flesh.

"You stole my life. I'm taking it back now, and there is nothing you can do about it. I'm going to do all the things you denied me. First, I'm going to find a man and bring him home to my bed.

While you lay there rotting, I'll be right in the next room with him."

Tears ran down his face as he swallowed back sobs. "Please, you don't understand. It was my only choice. Your mother was going to leave me and take you with her. You were my baby, I couldn't let you go."

"Just like Don Miller was going to take me away?"

"He wasn't right for you. He was a godless man and would have led you into a life of sin and unhappiness."

"I loved him, and that was my choice, not yours."

"Baby, we have money, lots of money. We'll do anything you want. Travel, buy a new car, one of those fancy sports models. A new house. Whatever—"

"Too late. After you're dead, the money will be mine anyway. Sorry, can't stand here listening to anymore of your blubbering. Gotta go find me a boyfriend." She turned and walked from the room, closing the door behind her.

He flinched as the lock clicked into place.

CHAPTER 48

Ed Barnes had not hit his wife in more than four years. Not that her big mouth had not pushed him to the very brink countless times, but his survival instinct had always managed to stay his hand. This morning, however, something black and formidable had risen in him and temporarily wiped away the threat that had haunted him for so many years.

Four years ago, in a drunken rage, he had sent eight months pregnant Sandra to the hospital with multiple contusions, a fractured right arm and in premature labor.

Ed quickly learned that in Jeff Chambers' town one does not beat his wife, especially his pregnant wife. A little set-to with the chief of police left him with a broken nose and a fractured jaw that resulted in a two day hospital stay one floor above where Sandra was recovering from her injuries and the birth of their son. Jeff had made him a promise, and Jeff Chambers was a man known to keep his word: *If you ever hit Sandra again, I will break your back. Snap you in two like a twig.*

That little confrontation proved a life altering experience for Ed. He harbored no doubts that a slip of temper where his wife was concerned would land him in a wheelchair sipping gruel through a straw for the rest of his life. Even on those occasions when he partook too heavily of the spirits and was falling down drunk, that promise—*If you ever hit Sandra again, I will break your back. Snap you in two like a twig*—killed his natural tendency to settle differences with his fists.

At the break of dawn Sandra crawled from bed with the intention of doing what she had done almost every morning for the past six years. Ed expected a steaming cup of coffee on the nightstand when soft music from the clock radio roused him from sleep.

Yawning, she opened the cabinet door and reached on the top

shelf for the can of Folgers.

Folgers, the only coffee for a real man.

She groped empty space.

"Oh no."

She ran back to the bedroom, shedding her robe. As quiet as a mouse in the company of a dozing cat, she slipped into a pair of denim shorts, a white sleeveless cotton blouse and worked her feet into a pair of navy slip-on sandals. Without so much as giving her disheveled hair a glance in the mirror, she rushed out the backdoor, billfold and car keys in hand.

In less than twenty minutes she returned with a can of Folgers crooked in her arm and an extravagant bouquet of red flowers cradled to her breasts. While preparing the coffee, she took momentary breaks to bury her face in the strikingly beautiful blooms. Their wonderful fragrance drew her again and again.

"Where the fuck is my coffee?"

She flinched. "It's almost ready, had to run to the store. We were out of coffee."

"Damn you, woman," Ed cursed, propelling the Folgers can from the counter with an sweep of his arm. The can clanged and bounced, spewing grounds in every direction. "Too damned lazy and stupid to do something as simple as keeping a little coffee on hand. He snatched up the bouquet and brandished it like a club. "What the fuck are these?"

"Flowers. I bought them this morning at Ferrell's. Now please, give them to me, they're mine." It was going to be one of the really bad mornings, she could already tell. Her mad dash to the store had been in vain.

"Had time to shop for flowers, huh? Well, I'll just get rid of them."

"No. They're mine. Now please, give them to me."

Glaring at her, he held the bouquet high out of reach.

In an attempt to salvage a bit of the morning, she turned, filled a cup with coffee and extended it as a peace offering. "Here. Now please give me my flowers and go get ready for work. Breakfast will be done in a jiff."

"Dammit, quit changing the subject. I'm getting rid of these."

Rage rose inside her, fury so thick and black it was almost tangible. She had to contain herself to keep from snatching a butcher knife and driving it into his belly. Nothing would have pleased her more at that moment than seeing his body writhing on the floor in a river of blood. For the first time in their marriage she was ready to do battle. "No. I told you they're mine. Now give them to me, and get the hell out of my sight."

She barely saw the blow coming. Ed's rock-hard fist slammed into her right cheek, sending her sprawling and the coffee cup flying. He hovered above her, his hands clinched into fists. She knew that look and stiffened for another punch or a hard kick to the kidneys.

Instead, he spun on his heels and stomped from the room. He reappeared shortly, clothed for work, her coveted bouquet held against his chest. Without so much as a glance in her direction, he stalked out the back door.

She sat on the floor and listened to his car back out of the driveway. She lowered her face to her hands and began to sob.

"Mommy. Why are you crying? You spill the coffee?" The sound of her son's stressed voice dried her tears.

"You hurt yourself?"

"No, of course not." She rose to her feet, brushing at clinging coffee grounds. "I slipped and fell down is all. Now, come here."

The child sprinted across the room and flew into her outstretched arms. She lifted the small body and sat down at the kitchen table.

"If you didn't hurt yourself, why were you crying?"

She wiped moisture from her face with a paper napkin. "Just a little sad. But you know what?"

"What?"

"I feel a bunch better since you're here." To her surprise, she really did feel better. Narrowing her eyes, she glanced furtively about the kitchen. "Reckon there are any hugs laying around here that don't belong to anybody?"

A giggling Jason squirmed from her lap and dashed about the

room in search of lost hugs. He glanced in cupboards, behind the refrigerator, under the table and in the dishwasher before coming to a stop. "I found one," he squealed, grasping the imaginary hug in his tight fist and stabbing the air triumphantly. "A big one. Do you want it?"

"Yes."

His small arms wrapped around her neck squeezing tight, tight, tight.

"Wow. I believe that's the biggest hug you ever found."

He settled back into her lap. "Pretty big, huh?"

His animated grin slackened as he stared at her face. "Your cheek is red . . . and there's blood on your mouth." He reached up and touched her puffy face.

"Daddy and I had a little argument is all. It doesn't hurt, I promise."

"Daddy's mean." His tone was much too venomous for a four-year-old. "I don't like him. I wish he would go away and never come back. Never, never, never."

"You really don't want your daddy to go away, do you, Jason?"

"Yes, I do. He hurt you. And he hollers all the time. Won't ever play with me. Just gets all mad and tells me to go away. I wish he would be the one to go away."

"Well, sweetheart, if that's the way you really feel, maybe I just might be able to make that happen."

She stationed Jason in the family room at the coffee table with a bowl of Frosted Flakes and a glass of orange juice. She clicked on the television. "Going to the garage for a few minutes, Jason. Stay right here, okay?"

"Uh huh."

She left him munching cereal and engrossed in a cartoon with robots blasting each other to smithereens and then miraculously piecing themselves back together.

She carried a three rung stepladder into the detached garage and scanned a high shelf. Her heartbeat quickened when she spotted a strip of bright yellow peeking from behind a large red gas can.

"Yes. I knew it was still there."

Stretched on tiptoes atop the stepladder, she was able to work the gas can aside, but only managed to push the yellow box further out of reach. For all practical purposes the box may as well have been located in another country.

"Damn. It's hell being short."

She stepped off the ladder and stared up in exasperation at the lofty shelf.

What'cha going to do now, Sandy-girl?

Her sense of humor kicked in as it often did during stressful times. She stood in the neglected garage eyeing the box and giggling like a schoolgirl. She hiccupped. That was even funnier. Doubled over, belly-rolling laugher spilled from her mouth.

Talk real sweet to tall Ed and have him reach it for you.

Hey, big boy, you wanna climb up and get that little ole yellow box for little ole me? Why, thank you, sweetheart. Now, you just go get all comfy and watch your game while I prepare a nice big surprise for you. A really big surprise. Ha, ha, ha.

Sandra. This is serious business. Stop your clowning.

The stern internal voice sobered her.

Think. Think hard.

The wooden ladder stored against the chain link fence came to mind, but she rejected that idea. The ladder served for outside work and was several feet too long to fit upright in the low-ceiling garage.

She stood for a long moment racking her brain and eyeing the gray canvas tarp protecting a restored 1957 Ford Fairlane. Her belly tightened in resentment of the money Ed had dumped into that old car—money that could have refurbished the house that was all but falling down around their shoulders. But nothing less would do than a hand-mix paint job to match the original color, rechromed bumpers, special order whitewall tires and custom made seat covers. Nope, nothing but first class all the way when it came to that useless pile of metal.

That's it! Zip up on the roof of the car, and presto, the box.

Don't know. I'd have to move it closer to the wall. Looks like a pretty tight squeeze. Ed would kick my ass all the way to Kentucky if I put so much as a teeny-weeny scratch on his precious toy. No, better pull in the Oldsmobile. Another ding or two on that old tank wouldn't make a bit of difference.

Come on, Sandra, where's your grit? About time you develop a little backbone, don't you think? It'd be a lot more fun to screw around with Ed's precious money-gobbling piece of green shit. And besides, why worry about what he thinks? Get to that little box, and he won't be thinking nothing about nothing anyway.

"No, he won't, will he?" She headed back to the house, and returned shortly with the car keys dangling from an index finger. After tugging off the tarp, she climbed into the driver's seat and slid it forward to where her feet could reach the pedals. It was a mystery how such an old car could smell brand new, almost as if it had rolled off the assembly line only yesterday. She wiggled her butt, enjoying the feel of the expensive fabric, the fabric that could have purchased a new washer, dryer and refrigerator in one fell swoop. It dawned on her that this was her first experience behind the wheel. Fact was, she could recall only three occasions when she had been extended passenger privilege. And Jason? The child had never—not once—been allowed inside the car.

Kids touch things, leave smudges and prints everywhere. Make messes and have accidents. Won't have my car smelling like piss.

She hawked and spit. The gob of phlegm landed on the dash and oozed down the metal leaving behind a slimy trail like a snail. It dripped on the custom floor covering.

That was funny. The giggles returned, but before they could get too far out of hand, she remembered Jason alone in the house.

"Time to get down to business."

She inserted the key in the ignition and twisted it. The fine-tuned motor purred to life. After all, a cool grand had been laid out to rebuild it. After backing out of the garage, she inched forward with no more than a hairbreadth between the front fender and doorway post.

Side mirror clear.

Her heart jumped into her throat at the sound of metal scraping wood.

"Shit."

You damn well better get to that box, 'cause when Ed gets a gander at this, he'll sure enough kill you deader than a twelve-point buck on opening day of hunting season.

Squinting and her jaws cinched, she continued forward, the screech biting into her nerves like the sound of fingernails scraping down a blackboard.

At last the car was in. With her heart beating double-time, she sat for a moment to give her trembling hands time to steady. She then scooted across the bench seat, exited through the passenger door and found it very simple to scramble up the hood and onto the roof of the car. She plucked the box from the shelf. Brushing away a thick layer of dust, RAT POISON and a skull and crossbones became clear on the cardboard jacket.

"I have a rat that needs killing. A big fat rat."

The ugly deep abrasions extending from the front fender to the rear taillight filled her with a profound sense of satisfaction. She ventured a guess that new door panels and probably a replacement fender would be required for repairs. Lord, would she love to see Ed's reaction to this. Oh yes, what a show that would be. A giggle could not be suppressed. But good sense reigned. She concluded it would be best—safer, at least—if Ed went to his death ignorant of the damage to his precious automobile. She replaced the tarp, satisfying herself that it was exactly as she had found it, and hurried back to the house.

Monster robots had been replaced by Tweety and Sylvester scurrying about the bright screen amid a chorus of zings, bongs and whams. Several minutes later Jason wandered into the kitchen where his mother was standing at a counter stirring the contents of a large bowl. Strewn bake goods—brown sugar, vanilla, flour, butter—meant that some kind of sweet treat was in the offing.

"What'cha making?"

She squatted down in front of him and placed her hands on his fragile shoulders. "Cookies. Big people cookies. These are special cookies for Daddy. You can't eat them. In fact, Jason, you mustn't take even a tiny taste of one. Understand?"

His eyes swam in tears. "Why only Daddy?"

"Sweetheart, these cookies have pecans in them. Lots and lots of pecans."

His face crinkled in distaste. "Pecans are yucky."

"Pretty awful. Tell you what, when I get through here we'll go to Ferrell's and you can pick out any kind of cookies you want. What'cha think about that, sport?" She gave his hair an affectionate ruffle.

"Any kind I want?"

"You bet'cha. Then we'll stop at McDonalds for lunch."

"Yea."

An hour later she wheeled into Ferrell's parking lot. Her heartbeat quickened at the sight of the crimson display in the large front window.

CHAPTER 49

George Sneider stopped his ascent of the courthouse steps to stare at a throng of motorcycles slicing a path up Main Street. People gathered at storefront windows and stepped from doorways to view the spectacle. A number of pedestrians appeared to be frozen in place by the deafening roar. Motorists made beelines for open slots or inched within a hairsbreadth of parked cars to make way for the monster bikes and their brawny drivers. It was indeed a remarkable sight, the traffic parting like the Red Sea to let God's children pass.

The riders drew a few smiles, a wave or two from teenagers and youngsters, but for the most part, people glared at them in disgust, as if Caddo had been invaded by a pack of diseased dogs.

George Sneider was among the smilers. Staring in open admiration, he savored the sight of the graceful high-dollar machines eating up the roadway.

"Sweet machines. Damn things cost more than my car."

A rush of envy cut through his pleasure. The earsplitting roar and the nonchalant ease with which the bikers propelled their colorful chariots awakened a long dormant yearning; a forgotten boyhood dream flickered to life. He imagined the vibration of a metallic red machine beneath him, experienced the sensation of wind on his face, bask in the curious and often envious stares of other motorists as he navigated through mile after mile of ever changing terrain.

Penney's fault, an inner voice chided. *She's the culprit. Sweet, darling Penney, the lady with the dollar sign eyes. She took that Harley dream and crushed it under her heels, then kicked it aside like so much garbage. Don't recall her being there during those long, hard years at law school. Nope, she didn't contribute one thin dime to your education. Pranced into your life when the money got good and took over. Been drawing those purse strings tighter than a virgin's pussy ever since. That's to say unless there happened to be some little expensive something she desired, like that diamond ring. And what about the minivan? Better yet, the house. Haven't put a pencil to paper yet, have you? Complete renovation—how much you think? Sixty thousand? Seventy? Considering her taste, probably more like eighty. Eighty big ones, George. May as well face it, won't ever be enough money for a Harley. Ever.*

As the lead cycle reached the courthouse, it skidded full circle and maneuvered to a stop at the curb. A black-clad figure dismounted and set the kick stand as the dozen or so other motorcycles thundered in around him.

"I'll be damned, it is you," sounded from the mirrored visor. Lifting off the smoke-colored helmet, the giant of a man made several quick strides up the steps.

"George Sneider," he exclaimed, grasping George's right hand and pumping his arm. "Recognized you the second I seen you." The man's idiot grin was filled with greenish-brown teeth and sprinkled with dark gaps. The reek of body odor and stale nicotine hung on him like a contaminated aura. A snake tattoo coiled down his right arm; ripples of sinew and muscle gave it life. Oversized fangs appeared to be buried in the large hand and pumping a perpetual flow of venom into its willing victim.

Dismissing the distaste on George's face, the guy said, "Oh, don't pay any attention to that. We all got 'em. Me and the boys," he clarified, nodding toward the other cyclists. "Vipers. Vipers is what we called our band. Never made a go of music, but still got our tattoos. Anyway, George-my-man, nearly shit my pants when I looked up and seen you. Yep, recognized you instantly. Seen your picture at least a dozen times in the Houston paper. Always showed my buddies. Told 'em how we grew up together."

George stared hard at the bearded face, racking his brain for a name. He could not come up with a clue.

"Well hell, don't recognize me, do you?"

"I'm afraid not."

"Jacky Jensen. Jerky to you."

George's eyes widened in disbelief. He moved back a step. "Jerky Jensen."

The giant guffawed. "Yeah, in the flesh. Always knew you fellows called me Jerky the Jerk. Kinda fits, don't you think?"

A pretty blonde, not more that five feet tall, sidled up to Jerky. She looked maybe seventeen years old. Her features were hard-set and permanent lines had already begun creep in around her eyes and mouth. George considered she might be as young as fourteen or fifteen, but running with a gang like the Vipers, abusing drugs and alcohol, exposure to sun and wind astride a motorcycle and existing on junk food had in all likelihood stolen three or four years of her youth. He had seen it before. At her current pace she would be lucky if she passed for forty by the time she reached the age of twenty-five.

Jerky swallowed the petite girl in a burly arm. "My squeeze. Ain't she a dandy?"

"Nice to meet you," the girl muttered.

"Come on, George old buddy, you ain't still sore at that little joke I pulled, are you? It was all in fun. Didn't mean no harm."

George opened his mouth with the intention of telling his boyhood tormentor, *Damn right I'm still pissed, and as far as I'm concerned, you can go straight to hell.* The words wouldn't come out.

George Sneider, an inner voice chided, *what's the big deal? It was a practical joke. Think about it. All he really did was try to make you enter an old rundown house. Remember, you butted him square in the balls, sent him to bed for two or three days. Don't see him carrying a grudge.*

He had a knife.

So? Always did carry a knife. Never heard of him using it. Come on, you were being such a blubbering crybaby, who could blame him for milking the situation for all it was worth? Circumstances turned, you would probably have done the same thing.

That house was haunted.

Get real. You're a big boy now. Don't tell me you still believe in ghosts? Admit it. The only problem with that house was your wild imagination. After all, Jerky did end up with the short end of stick. You busted his balls good and proper.

He pictured Jerky clutching his groin and writhing in pain on the ground. For the first time since the mind-scarring incident occurred, he saw the humor in it. A warm smile filled with nostalgic memories brightened his features. "Of course I'm not mad. Never was."

"Glad to hear it."

"What in the world are you doing in Caddo?" George asked. "Last place in the world I'd expect to run into you."

Jerky shrugged. "Hell if I know. We were sitting around jamming last night and somebody came up with the idea of a trip. Well, here we are." He hesitated to eye a police car pulling in at the curb. "Uh-oh, here comes the man."

Jeff Chambers emerged from the car and slammed the door.

"No problem," George said. "I know him."

"Don't kid yourself. Look at his face. He's not taking kindly to a bunch of bikers in his town. Probably thinks we're here to pillage and rape. Besides, the natives are getting restless."

Tossing nervous glances at the tall cop, the bikers had already begun to mount their machines.

Jerky gave George a friendly poke on the shoulder. "See you, buddy." He then scrambled down the stairs with his squeeze tucked in close.

Jeff strolled up to George, and the two of them watched the roaring horde of bikes disappear into a shimmering river of heat.

"What they up to?" Jeff asked.

"Just traveling, I guess. The big guy is a childhood chum, stopped to say hi."

"Where they headed?"

"How the hell would I know? No one appointed me their keeper." George turned and stalked away, leaving Jeff scratching his head in puzzlement.

Approximately five miles beyond the Caddo city limits sign a stooped old man in worn overalls stepped onto the roadway and waved his arms. Jerky coasted to a stop within a foot of the old gent. The other cycles roared in around them.

"A problem?" Jerky asked.

"Nope. Could hear you coming a mile away. Figured you might need a place to camp. Name's John Wilkerson. Got a farm with the perfect spot if you're interested."

For some inexplicable reason the offer appealed to Jerky. Without bothering to consult his companions, he said, "Sounds good to me."

"Follow me." The old man hurried to his battered pickup parked on the roadside.

CHAPTER 50

Ed Barnes pulled into the driveway and shut off the motor. He sat for a moment mulling over why Sandra had not notified Jeff Chambers of his little slip of the fist.

Maybe didn't hit her as hard as I thought.

He picked up the red flowers and inhaled their intoxicating scent. The aroma surged though his veins like a main line heroine shot. He then laid them aside and swooped up a bouquet of yellow roses. Yellow Roses had always been Sandra's favorite.

He stepped into the kitchen with the roses held out before him. His lower lip hung nearly to his chin.

Sandra looked around from the sink where she was rinsing a pan.

He cringed at her puffy, discolored cheek and swollen black eye. Oh yes, Jeff Chambers would have been on him like a rooster in a cock fight if he'd seen this.

Sandra grinned. "Flowers for me?" She walked over and put her arms around his neck and kissed him, a long tongue probing kiss that promised more exciting things to come.

Ought to give her the old wham-er-oo a little more often.

Ed couldn't remember a more delicious meal. Content their little disagreement had been settled so easily, he laid back in his recliner and stretched out long and lazy. Despite his full belly, he couldn't resist one of the homemade cookies Sandra placed on the side table. "Sweets for my number one man," she said, with an affectionate tweak of his nose.

"Damn, I do believe you make the best chocolate chip cookies this side of the Mississippi." He gobbled down the first one and reached for a second. Crunching and spewing crumbs, he said to Jason, "Boy, come here. You gotta try these."

Tossing his mother an uneasy glance, Jason stood up and wandered over to his father.

Ed slapped a cookie in his hand. "It's great. Give it a taste."

"These are big people cookies, has pecans. I don't like pecans. Mommy said I didn't have to eat one. Not even a bite."

Ed's face darkened. "Eat the goddamn cookie."

Jason put it to his mouth, his eyes swimming in tears.

"Ed, please," Sandra said, flying across the room and taking the cookie from her son. "He doesn't want it."

He stiffened, readying to get up and give her—give them both, in fact—a taste of the same medicine he had dished out that morning.

I'll break your back. Snap you in two like a twig.

The thought sobered him. Luck had been with him to get by with his earlier spurt of temper—wham, bam, thank you very much, bitch—and only a fool would tempt fate twice in one day. "All right, all right."

Sandra gave Jason a gentle shove toward the bathroom. "Come on, sweetie, time to take a bath."

"Making a damn pantywaist outta that boy," Ed grumbled, picking up another of the best cookies this side of the Mississippi.

CHAPTER 51

Penney Sneider scraped her untouched dinner into the sink and set the plate on the counter. The throb pounding at her skull with the impact of a ten-piece percussion band seemed to worsen by the minute. For two days now both girls had been absolute terrors.

"She pushed me."

"Did not."

"Did too."

"Mama, she—"

There seemed to be no end to their squabbling. And George? The man had turned into an unreasonable ogre. It was almost as if a stranger had stepped into her life.

Ogre? Stranger? Come on, Penney. A little strong, don't you think?

No, it's true, she told herself even while realizing her nasty headache might be clouding her judgment. *His precious flowers stink, make me sick. But does he care? Bother to show a little understanding? A bit of sympathy? No.*

Not being fair. He did shut them in his study.

Doesn't matter, they still stink.

Give the man a break. After all, his intentions were good. Bought them for you. Looked as proud as a peacock when he stepped through the door. And what did you do? Rejected them.

'George, they stink.'

Hurt his feelings. Him refusing to trash them is his way of saving face. Doesn't make him an ogre. He's simply a man, and like most men, has a mind of his own. Can't fault him for that. Admit it, the flowers are beautiful. You're allergic, is all. Or maybe you're pregnant.

"Lord, no," she groaned, groping for the date of her last period. The early months of her previous pregnancies had been pure torture; she had spent the first few weeks hanging over the commode, especially with Lauri.

Lauri.

Let your temper get the best of you, didn't you?
For Pete's sake, it was only a little slap.

Massaging her temples, she sank into a chair.

For three days now she and George had maintained an uneasy truce. Even though he had shut the flowers in his study, their reek seeped through the walls and followed her to every part of the house. The sickening odor even pursued her into the shower under running water. Not an inch of her home was immune to that awful smell.

Tonight at the dinner table, the stink hanging in the room like a sulfurous cloud and tension as thick as London fog, Lauri had acted the brat once too often. Despite having been exiled two different times to lengthy timeouts, her belligerent attitude lingered. "I hate chicken," spoken so rudely, so haughtily, had not elicited the little slap, the unthought shot of temper. Even her hurled plate and the sound of china shattering had not pulled that little slap from Penney. No, the sight of gravy oozing down the recently refinished cabinets—days of backbreaking labor on hands and knees—sapped the last iota of her control. She could no more have stayed the hand that shot out and laid a stinging slap on her daughter's cheek than she could have plugged a major leak in Hoover Dam with the tip of her finger. For a long moment absolute silence dominated the room, and then Lauri had let go with an overplayed heartrending wail.

Penney had felt disconnected, like a stranger viewing an unfolding drama. George shot to his feet. His chair fell to the floor, clattering like dry bones on the tile. Lauri flew into his arms and clung to his neck as if her very life depended on his protection. With her face buried in his shoulder, she piteously wept. The touching scene would have melted the coldest of hearts.

George's glare of pure hatred drove Penney back several steps. "Bitch," he spit out, then turned and stormed from the room. Lauri smirked over his shoulder. "Gotcha," that self-satisfied grin conveyed.

George had come within a hairsbreadth of striking her. Reliving the ugly episode upped her headache several agonizing degrees. She glanced about the cluttered kitchen, cringing at the dirty dishes piled in the double sink. The splattered gravy had begun to jell on the cabinet doors. No way could she face this mess now. Maybe later, but not now. What she needed more than anything was another hefty dose of Tylenol, a bed and a cold compress for her forehead.

As she walked through the den, neither her husband nor Lauri acknowledged her presence. Their eyes remained glued to the television screen where Kevin Costner was performing some kind of Indian dance around a blazing campfire.

The sound of Jenni's voice in deep conversation brought her to a stop.

Two voices?

She hesitated a moment, listening hard, then pushed the bedroom door open.

"Who you talking to, sweetie?"

Sitting cross-legged in the middle of the bed with a baby doll clutched to her chest, Jenni looked up. "Jonathan."

"Jonathan?"

"He's my friend."

"Your doll?"

"No, Mommy, my doll's a girl. Jonathan's a boy."

You've done it now. Got her so traumatized she's making up imaginary friends.

She sat down on the side of the bed and drew Jenni onto her lap. "Jonathan's nice, huh?"

"Uh-huh."

"Tell me about him."

"He used to live here. Says the house is different, though. His real house burned down a long time ago."

Penney sucked in hard at her daughter's words.

Burned. How could she possibly know?

Then Jenni hit her with another unsettling statement. "I don't feel good, Mommy. My stomach hurts and it stinks in here."

CHAPTER 52

"No, be there like I told you," Mark Ferrell bellowed into the telephone receiver.

"Look, the least you can do is tell me what's up."

"I told you. Just a little joke. Karl and Wayne didn't give me an ounce of flack, and just listen to you. This once, can't you simply do as I ask?"

"Really, Mark, we're a little old for practical jokes, don't you think? And what am I supposed to tell Liz when I go traipsing out of here in the middle of the night?"

"You're smart, little brother. I'm sure you can think of something."

"All right, against my better judgement, I'll be there. Cemetery at midnight."

"Don't let me down, Jeremy."

"I won't."

"Always so damn difficult," Mark grumbled, hanging up the receiver. He glanced down at the sheet of penciled names he had put together and smiled. The smile escalated to a chuckle, then a laugh. He leaned forward and drew in a long whiff of the red bouquet centered on the dining room table.

"Tonight is going to be a hoot. A real hoot."

CHAPTER 53

"Tuna fucking casserole," Homer Knoll bellowed. "I work my ass off all day, and what do I come home to? Tuna fucking casserole." He snatched the Pyrex baking dish from the table and marched to the backdoor. With an overhand toss, the bowl sailed through the air, performed a graceful loop-de-loop and landed upside down in the middle of the yard.

"Let the goddamn cats eat it. Going where I can get me a decent meal." He stomped down the stoop and to his car.

Thelma Knoll sat with her hands fisted in her lap and listened to her husband's car squeal out of the driveway. Homer took her for some kind of stupid. Well, Thelma Knoll's mother didn't raise no dummy. No, she did not. That act of his—ranting, raving and overplaying the role of a mistreated husband—didn't fool her for one second. That ploy had been used no less than a hundred times during their miserable marriage. It looked like he could come up with something a little more creative when he wanted out of the house for a tryst with Miss Hot Crotch. No need to toss perfectly good food into the yard like white trash.

"What the neighbors must think?"

He certainly didn't have to spoil her dinner. She had had a taste for tuna casserole.

"Well, let him have one last evening with Miss Hot Crotch. Hope the bitch is worth it." Exhaling a sigh of resignation, she got up and removed a ballpoint pen and notepad from a drawer. "Let's see," she mused, easing once again into her chair. With her brow creased in concentration, she began to write.

Johnnie Walker
Budweiser
Wine. Red? White?
Rib Roast
Super Glue
Nylon Twine

Beauty Parlor
Go to bank.

She laid the pen aside to review the list. "Oops, veggies and dessert."

CHAPTER 54

Fred Zimmermann eased his Lincoln Town Car to the curb and killed the headlights. Darkness enfolded him like a thick shroud. Half a block down, tenebrous shadows cloaked a one story medical complex. A right rear window radiated like a beacon for weary travelers. A cloud of insects mantled the lot's only working security lamp; three other darkened lampposts dotted the large parking area. Fred assumed the bulbs had burned out, but favored the idea that the globes had been the targets of rock-wielding pranksters. The thought that some type of mischief aided in tonight's venture added to his enjoyment.

A white Cadillac Seville, transformed to a sickly yellow by the overhead glow, was the only vehicle occupying the lot.

Fred grinned. Dr. Alan Payne's newest romantic liaison had drawn him back to the office for a late evening romp. The dentist's lone car told Fred that the blue-eyed and provocative Miss Kemp had already departed. He made a mental note to send the little lady, anonymously, of course, a couple of dozen roses. After all, her boyfriend would be spending few evenings at his office if not for her carnal appetite.

"Time to extract a little revenge. Extract!" He snickered at the unintended pun.

Like a phantom, he glided through the darkness to the back entrance of the building. The knob turned easily. Tightening his grip on a six-inch hunting knife, he eased the door open and stole down a darkened hallway.

Dr. Alan Payne, settled at a massive mahogany desk perusing a patient chart looked up as Fred Zimmermann stepped through the doorway. "What brings you here at this late—." He fell silent at the sight of the knife in Fred's hand.

Fred strolled across the room and dropped into a green leather armchair. He placed a large brown shopping bag on the corner of the impressive desk, and for a long moment looked about at the expensive trappings. Like the Cadillac, the office decor trumpeted success.

"What's this about?"

"Just a little settling up, Doc, that's all. Just a little settling up."

CHAPTER 55

Several men eyed an attractive woman sitting alone at the bar. Her short red dress exposed long shapely legs that seemed to go on forever. Despite too much makeup, she was exceptionally pretty. Ample cleavage spilling from her low cut dress brought a number of penises to full attention.

"Mind if I sit here?"

Naomi Duncan glanced up at a not really handsome but nonetheless attractive face. Curly blond hair and even white teeth brought Don Miller to mind. The light was too dim to make out his eye color.

"Why no, glad to have some company."

Too forward, she chided.

"Cliff Thorne," he said, offering his right hand.

She accepted a warm handshake. "Naomi Duncan."

"Tell me, Naomi, why haven't I noticed a pretty thing like you around here before."

Not sure how to handle the compliment, her words came out in a stammer. "Well, it's my first time here."

"Tell you what, pretty girl, lady luck is with me tonight. Spotted you before one of those gamey yahoos who make this place a second home managed to get his paws on you."

He's hitting on me, the new look works.

"What'cha drinking?"

"Pepsi."

"Don't drink?"

"No, not opposed to it, just never have. Don't know a thing about drinks and stuff. Had no idea what to order."

"I think I can take care of that." He set her glass aside, and with a quick wave caught the attention of the bartender.

"Pina colada for the lady. Chivas on the rocks for me."

In minutes a frothy white drink in a tall stemmed glass decorated with a bright pink paper umbrella appeared before her.

Two maraschino cherries and a chunk of fresh pineapple speared on a toothpick hung on the rim. She had never seen anything quite so pretty. Tentatively, she drew on the straw. Her taste buds exploded with pleasure.

"Like it?"

"Like it? I love it. It's Delicious."

Cliff grinned. "How about moving to a booth? Give us a little privacy."

Naomi nodded.

CHAPTER 56

Fred Zimmermann played his thumb along the sharp edge of the hunting knife. "Tell me, Alan, what'd you have for supper tonight?"

"Supper? What the hell kind of question is that?"

Fred shot across the desk, jerked Dr. Payne upright by the collar and pressed the knife against his bobbing Adam's apple. "Don't want to use this, but one more outburst like that and this blade will taste blood! Now, answer my question."

"I'll answer anything you want. Please sit down."

Fred eased back into the armchair.

"I had steak. A sirloin, grilled."

"And the wife and that sweet daughter of yours?"

"The same."

"What else you have?"

"Caesar salad and a baked potato."

"Dessert?"

"No dessert."

"Nothing?"

"I usually eat some kind of fruit before going to bed, an apple or something."

"This apple, peel it and cut it in slices?"

"No. Just wash it and eat it."

"Well, Alan my friend, any idea how long it's been since I took a big bite out of a crisp apple? Or the last time I chewed up, and I mean really chewed up, a man-sized hunk of beef?"

"Oh hell, so that's what this is about. Having a problem with those choppers again, aren't you?"

Fred chuckled and dropped the knife into the shopping bag. "Didn't take you long to catch on."

"Damn, you can put on one hell of a drama. Really had me going there."

"You know me, can't bypass an opportunity to jerk someone's

chain."

"Whew, nearly crapped my pants when you stuck that knife to my throat." He stood up. "Don't usually treat patients at this late hour, but in your case, always willing to accommodate. Come on, let's get you in a chair and have a look at that mouth. Don't forget this," he added, nudging the brown shopping bag with his hand.

"Thanks." Fred fell in step with the doctor as he headed down a hallway.

As Alan stepped through the treatment room doorway, he was hefted as easily as a child and slammed into the dental chair. His arms were wrenched behind his back and cold steel enclosed his wrists. He jerked upright at the sound of metallic clicks.

"What the hell?"

Fred moved around to the front of the chair. "Appreciate you making it so easy for me. Thought I'd have to drag you in here kicking and screaming. Comfy?"

"Take these things off. You hear? This has gone far enough."

"Soon enough, soon enough."

"Right now."

Fred frowned. "I suggest you settle down before you find yourself in a world of hurt. Believe me, you won't like my methods."

Alan shut his mouth.

"That's better. Now, how about we finish our little discussion. Apples? That's what we were talking about, wasn't it? Apples?"

Alan stared stonily ahead.

A wistful expression crossed Fred's features. "Nigh on twenty-five years since I clamped my teeth into a crisp apple. I know it doesn't seem like such a big deal to you. It is, though. A man misses something like that—misses it bad. Misses chomping away at a big wad of gum. Those things won't happen for me again. And why? Because you pulled every tooth in my head, Mr. Big Dentist."

"For God's sake, Fred, there was no choice."

"Seems you have a slip of memory there, Doc. Let me refresh it. Nineteen hundred dollars is what you had to have to fix my teeth up right. One Thousand, nine hundred greenbacks. Sound familiar? I was going to pay it, six hundred down, the balance on time. Remember what you told me?"

"How can you expect me to recall something from twenty-five years ago?"

"Come now, you gotta remember. 'Sorry, Fred, don't do business on credit. Full payment in advance.' That's what you told me, word for word."

"Please, that was a long time ago."

"Know what I found out later, after you'd done your deed and my gums were slick as a newborn's? Payment plans were set up for some patients. A lot of them, in fact. But you weren't willing to take a chance on a dirt-poor farmer like me, were you? Nope, much easier to yank out my teeth and be rid of me. Over, done, problem solved."

"Let me explain."

"Ain't no explaining. You know what you done. I know what you done. 'Pull 'em, Fred' is what you told me. 'Going to lose them someday anyway.' Hell, I was just a kid, twenty-two years old. Didn't know any better. But you knew better. Took my six hundred dollars, nearly every penny I had to my name, and yanked them right out. Added a few more bucks to your already bulging pockets."

"Listen to me. Please listen—"

"No. I listened to you once. There were lots of things you didn't bother to tell. Didn't tell me about sores on my gums or having to swallow food whole or that the bone would deteriorate and muscles collapse dropping my nose to my goddamn chin. Or that every four or five years I'd have to come back and drop a few more dollars in your greedy hands for new dentures. Hard earned dollars. Break your back for fifteen hours a day behind a plow in suffocating heat, bitter cold and drenching rain is how I come by those dollars. No skin off your teeth, was it? Had you a nice climate-controlled office."

"You're wrong. I helped you."

"Helped me, my ass. You lined your pockets, is what you did.

Bone grafts and implants. Any idea what that's costing me?"

Alan shook his head.

"Fifty thousand big ones. Specialist in Dallas tells me he can give me back a part of what nature intended to last for a lifetime, the teeth you took from me."

"Okay, maybe I made a mistake. I'm sorry. I'll make it up to you, pay for the implants. The entire fifty thousand."

"Hell, Alan, fifty thousand is small change to me since oil was discovered on my land. Only thing that seems fair to me is that you face what I've had to go through. Yep, losing every one of your white pearlies is the only way I can think of to even the score."

"You're crazy. Can't get away with it. You'll go to prison."

"Maybe or maybe not. Off the top of my head I can think of five or six upstanding citizens who'd testify that I was with them this entire evening at a poker game. Now if you feel strong that the truth must be told, there's a little something you ought to take into consideration. Think about your pretty daughter who flits around town in that blue Mercedes convertible and flashes that twenty thousand dollar smile. One word about me and your spoiled little princess will end up sporting a six hundred dollar smile just like mine."

"Don't you touch her. You son of a bitch, you better not touch her."

"Depends on you. If I happen to end up behind bars or even if an accusation is made, she will get a visit from someone who is not near as nice as I am. I'm sure he'd take more liberties than just pulling her teeth. Doubt she's a virgin anyway, the way I've seen her hang on some of the local yokels."

"HELP ME! FOR GOD'S SAKE, SOMEBODY—"

Fred stuffed a white rag from the shopping bag it into Alan's mouth, cutting off his screams. He removed a coil of rope and squatted in front of the dental chair. "Don't think about kicking me, you'd end up with a busted leg."

Alan sat quietly as his ankles were bound to the chair.

Fred held up a brown pint bottle. "This is ether."

Beads of sweat popped out on Alan's forehead.

"Understand, I don't have any qualms about the pain you'll suffer, but extracting those pearlies without some kind of anesthetic would rip gawd-awful screams out of you. Wouldn't do to have someone come to investigate. Don't have an inkling of how much of this stuff to use. Too much, and you might not wake up. That would be a shame, spoil our fun. You can take your chances with ether or Novocain. Nod once for ether, twice for Novocain."

Two slow nods.

"Excellent choice. I'm going to remove the gag. One peep and you'll be doused with a heavy dose of ether, the consequences be damned. Understand?"

Another nod.

Fred freed the gag. "Where do you keep the Novocain and syringes?"

Alan slumped over, his chin resting on his chest. "Top drawer of my desk there's a small gold key. It unlocks the cabinet there against the wall."

Fred smiled. It was going better than he had expected. The stupid ass even agreed to Novocain. Oh yes, Mr. Big Dentist would remain awake through the entire grueling process.

At the sight of the first bloody tooth Alan Payne wept. Heavy sobs accompanied the next three. The fourth, a lower left molar, brought with it heavy splinters of bone and a heartrending wail of agony. He then slipped into a state of shock. No more tears, no more moans, groans or wails. He simply stared glassy-eyed at a safe haven somewhere far away. He opened wide when ordered, rinsed and spit when told.

Seconds from midnight Fred slipped from the back door of the dental office. A plastic baggie containing twenty-eight perfect but bloody teeth had been added to the brown shopping bag. Sedated by ether, Dr. Payne dosed peacefully with his head tilted forward to insure against choking.

CHAPTER 57

Jeremy Ferrell drove through the yawning gates of Caddo Cemetery. Headstones standing guard over their dead flickered in the headlights, then dissolved into phantoms as the car advanced. A family mausoleum blinked by with its wrought iron gate standing open.

"Hope it was somebody coming instead of going," Jeremy said in a shot to calm his jittery nerves.

An alabaster angel shimmered to life. Its stoic stone eyes seemed to meet Jeremy's nervous gaze.

Using a dim glow in the northwest area as a beacon, he turned left onto a narrow lane. His brother's maroon Ford pickup at last stabbed into view and then a gray Buick. Relaxing his death grip on the steering wheel, he eased to the shoulder.

Karl Hargrove dropped an armload of tools from the pickup bed into Mark's waiting hands. In the radiance of a Coleman lantern, Wayne Waterfield squatted beneath a gigantic oak with a large sheet of paper—a map?—spread across his knees.

"Shut off those damn headlights before somebody sees them!" his brother shouted.

Dousing the lights, Jeremy stepped out of the car. "What's all this stuff?"

Mark turned around and grinned. "This is a shovel and this is another shovel and this is—"

"Damn you, Mark, what are they for?"

"Lighten up, bro. Come on, I'll show you." He led Jeremy to the oak tree. "You're going to love it." He jerked the paper from Wayne's hands and turned it for Jeremy to view. "This is a plan of the cemetery, tells where everybody is buried." He pulled a sheet of paper from his shirt pocket. "This is a list of every single person we had to pay money to."

"Pay money to?"

"I'll swear, sometimes you're so dense. *High school*, remember, our Halloween prank?" He tapped Jeremy on the head. "Hello, are you in there?"

"I remember. So?"

"Payback time, bro. Tonight we're going to see that each and everyone of them gets a visit from a dear departed loved one."

"You're not serious. Joking, right?" He studied each face in turn, sure that at any second one of them would burst out laughing. No one laughed. No one slapped him on the back saying, "Really got you this time, Jeremy. If only you could see your face. Come on, sport, beer's on me."

Oh yes, they were serious all right; Cheshire grins made it all too clear just how serious.

He took several backward steps, his hands out. "No way. Can't let you desecrate graves. Go home, all of you, and I'll forget this ever happened."

"No, Jeremy, you're the one who doesn't understand. You see, we made plans." Mark brandished a shovel like a baseball bat. His arm muscles rippled as he advanced to striking distance.

Jeremy had seen these intimidating displays too many times to take this one seriously. Knowing it was not within his brother to strike him, he turned and headed toward his car. His head exploded and knees buckled.

"Son of a bitch." Karl said, hovering over Jeremy's prone form. "Look at that gash. Bleeding like a stuck pig. Killed him, Mark. Sure 'nough killed him."

"Hell, he ain't dead, look at his chest. Can hear him breathing, too." A flash of headlights drew Mark's attention away from his brother. "Shit, the idiot didn't close the goddamn gates. Somebody's turning in." He leaned over and grasped Jeremy's limp legs. "Come on, let's get him out of sight."

CHAPTER 58

Cy Weinberg was proud of himself. Four beers over the course of the evening had been enough to fold him into a warm cocoon of well being. Spillover from his headlights created flickering grey and black artwork of trees and foliage lining the roadway. The occasional reflection of animal eyes added pinpoints of color to the surreal exhibit.

The cards were yours tonight, old man. Forty dollars and fifty cents. Quarter poker at that. Four Kings. Unbelievable. Jimbo nearly shit when you laid out those four royals. Outclassed them all. Yep, really kicked ass.

Cy Weinberg, First Lieutenant, US Marine Corps, had done it all. Married his high school sweetheart and sired three children, transplanted his family countless times to exotic and some not so exotic sites in different parts of the world. Deciding after thirty-five years that he had exhausted his usefulness to the Corps and them to him, he retired. To escape the roles of built-in babysitters to grandchildren, he and Beth moved to Caddo, a small town seventy or so miles northeast of Dallas. The close-knit community proved to be a dream come true. A respectable savings account and a generous military pension allowed them to settle in comfortably. They spent their time enjoying the simple life, browsing quaint antique shops, lazy afternoons on the veranda, leisurely walks, bird watching, and when the mood struck, entertaining their quite spoiled grandchildren—never for longer than a day or two, though. Five years into this idealistic lifestyle, Beth went to bed one night, and never woke up—the victim of a silent killer, a cerebral aneurysm.

Finding it impossible to fill the long, lonely days and nights, Cy accepted the position of caretaker for Caddo Cemetery. The new responsibilities proved to be a panacea for his grief. He demanded and received absolute perfection from the two-man crew; the grounds were meticulously maintained, trees and shrubbery precision trimmed. Graves were dug and the sites prepared for arriving guests. Not that Cy was a slave driver. He had no qualms about getting his own hands dirty or crawling on the earsplitting backhoe to dig graves.

From years of disciplining his body, at age sixty-four Cy was as strong and agile as most men half his age. The lined face and thinning gray hair were the only telltale signs of his true age. He maintained his military-straight stance and so far had evaded the rounded shoulders and thickened middle so prominent in the majority of men from his era. Cy Weinberg remained a man to be reckoned with.

While zipping past the cemetery he caught a glimmer of light and slammed the brake. The soft glow emitting from the northwest corner of the graveyard stood out starkly in the thick blackness.

"Damn kids. Always, they pick the cemetery." He knew what he would find: three or four boys, no more than twelve years old, relieved but unwilling to admit it, when he arrived to put an end to their see-how-brave-I-am game. Cy understood, even identified with the boys. During his youth he had been known to raid cemeteries a time or two.

This one time, what say you let them play their game out. Leave them to their fun—part of growing up. Builds character.

Cy was tempted, but decided their game was too risky, he would never forgive himself if someone turned up injured. Snakes and all kinds of wild critters were roaming at night. Bowing to his better judgement, he backed up and nosed into the entrance. The gates were standing open.

"Son of a bitch, little bastards broke the lock." They would damn well pay every last dime it'd take to get old Charlie out to fix it. He'd see that their parents administered well-earned ass-kickings, too. Every dad burn one of them. He was blowing off steam. No parents would be notified, and more likely than not, the repair fee would come out of his own pocket. After all, boys will be boys and thank heaven for that.

He made out a line of parked cars. Teenage beer bust? Why

the cemetery? Two lakes with picnic tables and restrooms were within a stone's throw.

He pulled in behind the last car, shifted to park and glanced about in confusion. It appeared to be deserted. Several shovels and a pickax stood out in the glow of a Coleman lantern.

"What the hell?"

His neck prickled.

"Something sick going on here. Gonna need help on this one."

As he shifted to reverse, a figure stepped up to the window, a double-barrel shotgun leveled on his head. Metal clinked against glass.

"Out of the car, old man."

He considered jamming the accelerator to the floor, but abandoned the idea. Backing down the narrow lane with a shotgun trained on him would be suicide. It was hard to face, but he had allowed himself to be caught in a trap like some inexperienced grunt. Disgusted, he opened the door and stepped out, his hands in the air.

He recognized the sandy-haired young man, Mark Ferrell from the supermarket. Two more men materialized from behind the trunk of a massive oak. The tall gangly man had a face that belonged on an Old West wanted poster. His small, piggish eyes had the distinct look of mild retardation. His thin lips appeared to be permanently fixed in a sadistic sneer. His ruddy pocked complexion had been ravaged by acute acne.

The second guy would have passed for a frat-man from some Ivy League college. A generous mouth revealed perfect teeth and his dark hair was thick and healthy looking. His square jaw, meticulous good looks no doubt opened many a door for him. A mother's dream of her daughter's perfect catch.

Cy saw something different in his cold eyes. He had seen his type before and knew him for what he was. College boy was capable of slaughter with no more feeling that a snake has for its prey. Oh yes, that handsome face could prove deadly in a society that put heavy emphasis on appearance.

Jeremy raised his head to twin circles of light. He blinked to clear fog clouding his vision.

Headlights?

A car door opened and he heard voices.

A rescuer?

He struggled to hands and knees. His head lolled forward. "Help me," came out pitifully weak.

He inched forward, a hand, a knee, a hand. He reached out and touched rough bark. Hand over hand he pulled himself up. Swallowing hard against nausea, he forced his head up.

"Please help me."

"Oh shit, look who's back among the living."

Mark's voice reached him from a deep well as he tumbled into an abyss of nothingness.

The injured boy was covered in blood and his skin as white as new snow. Cy recognized shock, and knew the kid could die without medical attention. He cursed himself. He let himself be taken prisoner by a bunch of amateur sickos. A sick game had not been expected in this ideal little town and his guard had been down. His stupidity would likely result in that young man's death.

"Come on, Mark, let's shoot 'em both," Karl said, dancing about in excitement. "Ain't got all night to fuck around."

"Leave Jeremy be. Got plans for him. What about you, old man, want to turn around or would you prefer to see it coming?"

Cy did not fear death. He had lived an exemplary life with a deep belief in God and country and saw no need for last minute pleas to his Creator. His only emotion was anger, anger that his life would be wantonly snatched from him by scum who didn't deserve to walk the face of the earth. Two wars. His skills, his honed senses, training and pure dumb luck had brought him unscathed through glaring mortar fire, steamy jungles and elusive sniper bullets. He had survived deadly night patrols, becoming one with rotting vegetation, his muscles tense and nerves screaming, ears tuned for a breath of noise. He had inflicted silent death on faceless phantoms. He survived it all only to stumble with the obliviousness of a bumbling, untrained recruit into a foreseeable trap. So be it. He stood proud, ready to meet his Maker face on with no apologies. Defiantly, he stared into the eyes of death.

"Not so fast," Wayne said. "Don't you know who he is?"

Mark stared hard at Cy's lined face. "Well, hell, the goddamn caretaker. Checked him out at least a dozen times at the store. Ain't that right, Mr. Weinberg, do your grocery shopping at Ferrells?"

"So what," Karl said.

"Shut up," Mark snarled. "You're too stupid to see the potential of our guest." He grinned at Wayne. "I'll swear, you're a smart one."

Karl glared hotly at both of them

"Looks like you just might live a little longer," Mark said. "That's if you got keys to the storage shed. Need us a backhoe to do some digging."

Play along. You'll get your chance.

"There's a set of keys in the glove box."

The noise from the backhoe might attract attention.

Won't matter. This is farming country. Tractor noise isn't unusual, even at night.

Coming from the cemetery?

Grave needs digging for early morning burial. Nobody would give it a second thought.

Cy arrived at the conclusion that he could not count on outside help. He was strictly on his own.

Mark waved toward his car with the shotgun. "Come on, let's get those keys and go to work."

Cy backed the roaring backhoe out of the shed. With the shotgun and a .357 Magnum trained on him, he dug where directed. He cringed at the creak of coffin lids being pried open. Sickened to his soul, he watched as corpses—in every stage of decay—were tugged from graves. The stenches that hung heavy in the air and drew gorge to his throat had no effect on the three captors.

At the fourth plot, the corpse seemed to contest its defilement and appeared to leap back into its grave. Wayne snatched at the decomposed arm and missed. He fumbled the .357 revolver and it followed the corpse into yawning blackness.

"Shit."

Karl held the flashlight while Wayne and Mark dropped into the hole.

Cy jumped from the backhoe, his legs pumping when they hit the ground. In that first burst of speed, his feet seemed to develop wings.

"Stop, you son of a bitch," Karl screamed, and took pursuit.

Cy maintained a healthy lead on the man who was thirty years his junior. The jostled flashlight beam danced about in bizarre patterns.

"Get your ass down and keep the light on him," Mark shouted.

Karl dropped to his stomach and aimed the flashlight with dead accuracy.

Evading the bright beam, Cy fell into an zigzag pattern. Bullets slammed to the ground within inches, plowing dirt. The shooter was obviously no stranger to guns.

Thank God it wasn't a high-powered rifle in those skilled hands.

A stray shot ricocheted from a headstone and zinged close enough to part his hair.

Kaboom!

Cy found himself face down munching dirt, his left thigh afire.

"Hot damn, you got him," Karl howled, lowering the flashlight.

Breathing hard through gritted teeth, Cy flexed the injured leg. It hurt like hell but moved freely. A flesh wound. He rolled, and was on his feet and back in the zigzag pattern. His injured leg stayed with him like a champion racehorse. Trees and heavy undergrowth loomed ahead. Giddy with relief, he dove headfirst into a thicket and skittered deeper into the woods like a frightened deer.

Cy Weinberg, First Lieutenant, US Marine Corps, was now in his element. The tables had turned decisively in his favor. Becoming one with the night, he maneuvered through the darkness, his hearing tuned for the slightest sound.

For a long forty-five minutes he listened to shouts, laughter and the reverberations of the backhoe. Then doors slammed and a motor rumbled to life. He listened to the vehicle accelerate and then fade in the distance.

Mere moments elapsed before a flashlight beam cut the darkness and twigs snapped underfoot. One of them had stayed behind to dispatch him.

Cy smiled.

CHAPTER 59

The rum-induced high was nothing like Naomi had ever experienced in her life. Her car seemed to float inches above the roadway like an alien craft. She expected at any moment to be swept upward into the night sky to play a celestial game of tag with the brilliant stars. Tonight she had been Cinderella, the most beautiful woman at the ball. The handsome prince had eyes for only her. With their bodies fused, they had swayed to soft, unfamiliar tunes drifting from the jukebox. The hypnotic songs had enfolded her, flowed through her veins like hot sweet oil. The words, so stirring and romantic, seemed to have been written just for her. *No one knows the troubles I've seen.*

Cliff Thorne's Dodge pickup followed into her driveway.

There had been an awkward moment or two when they had decided to leave the bar. Cliff had insisted she go to his place. Not that she hadn't been tempted, but that scenario didn't fall into her plan. She knew that the presence of a man in her bed would prove more agonizing for her father than a stake through the heart, and revenge was foremost. It took very little cajoling to bring him around.

"Oh, Cliff, I can't possibly leave my poor old father unattended for an entire night. Alzheimer victims live in an entirely different world, he won't even realize you're there. If something happened to him, I'd never forgive myself."

By the time she doused her lights, Cliff was out of his truck and opening her door. He drew her out of the car and hard against him.

She pulled away from a deep impassioned kiss. "Come on, let's take this into the house."

"That you, Naomi?" greeted them as they stepped through the front door. "It hurts. I need to talk to you."

"Poor guy," Naomi said, leading Cliff to her bedroom. "Asleep when I left. I was hoping he wouldn't wake up. Always panics when he finds me gone. Make yourself comfortable while I go check on him. Shouldn't take a minute."

"Hurry back," he said, giving her an affectionate pat on the rear.

She caught her breath as she stepped into her father's bedroom and flipped the light switch. The stink had worsened. "Are we still in pain?"

Tom blinked against the sudden glare. "Call the doctor. Please. I won't tell him anything. I'll protect you. You gotta to know I love you. How precious you are to me. Let me—"

"I have company, and you best be quiet."

A flicker of hope crossed his features. "Who's here?"

"A new friend. He's waiting in my bedroom."

"Naomi—"

"Shut up. Don't try to attract his attention. If I have to come in here again you'll be begging to die. Understand."

He nodded, tears leaking from his tortured eyes.

She turned, leaving her weeping prisoner in a tangle of fouled sheets.

Cliff, clad only in blue bikini briefs, was stretched out on the bed when she stepped through the doorway. His clothes were folded over his boots in a corner of the room.

She stopped dead to stare at his impressive physique. The steely body was every bit as beautiful as Don Miller's had been. Her scars popped to mind.

My body is so ugly. How could I have ever thought to attract someone like him?

He motioned with an index finger. "Come here, I have something for you."

She crossed the room—slow steps, her stomach churning and sunk to the side of the bed. He attempted to pull her against him.

"No, please," she said, her hands against his chest holding him back. "I have to tell you something about me. It's hard to put into words."

He sat back with his arms crossed, the epitome of patience, and studied her pained face as if expecting an I'm-not-really-that-kind-of-girl speech.

She looked down, unable to meet his eyes. "Something happened to me about ten years ago." She held out her hands. "Look at my Palms."

He moved them into the lamplight for close examination. "What in the world? Burns?"

She swallowed hard and blinked back tears. "Yes. Ten years ago a crazy man, a pervert, did this to me."

"We don't have to talk about this now, it can wait. There's plenty of time."

"You don't understand, I have to tell you now. He killed the man I was engaged to, the man I loved. With no more feeling than a stone, he took a shotgun and cut him down like a rabid dog."

He pulled her close. "How terrible for you, but it's over now."

She pulled back to make eye contact. "I stayed in mourning for a lot of years. My only involvements were in my church and helping my father on this big farm. That's the reason I didn't know anything about drinks or the popular songs we danced to."

"Like I said earlier tonight, lady luck must be with me. I was there when you decided to come out of your shell. Did they catch the bastard that did it?"

"Yes. He's paying dearly for his crimes. But there's more than the burns on my hands. He hurt me bad."

Cliff's mouth dropped. "How bad?"

"I can't explain, I'll have to show you."

She stood and began to disrobe. When her clothes were at last a crumpled heap at her feet, she stared at the floor awaiting his reaction.

"Holy Jesus. That son of bitch should have his balls cut off."

And then he was up and she was in his arms. He kissed one scarred nipple, then the other. "Doesn't matter. You're still beautiful."

His mouth closed hungrily over hers and his tongue slipped between her open lips.

Tom Duncan stared in wide-eyed terror at his mother standing at the foot of the bed. The hardened features, hateful narrow eyes, thin-lipped scowl remembered from childhood still claimed the cruel face.

"I see you're still a gutless wonder," she hissed. "Hear them? Hear what's going on right under your roof?"

"I'm hurt, Mama. Can't get out of bed."

"Wimp. Once a wimp, always a wimp. Laying there like a fat lazy slug while your daughter's screwing some stranger. I swear. Maybe the razor strop will give you some backbone."

Ghost pain from the deep lash scars covering his back flickered to life. "No, no, please, don't whip me, Mama."

She leaned close, their faces inches apart. "Maybe two or three days in the cellar is what you need."

Nine years old again, he cowered in the dank hole, strop lashes gnawing at his back and shoulders. Anemic light bleeding through the heavy door's weathered planks made the confinement bearable. When night fell and the room plunged into absolute blackness, the cellar became a torture chamber filled with phantoms and demons.

The night arrived when the monsters finally won.

His younger brother had dared to defy their mother. Nothing big, really; maybe a sassy tone or balking at an unsavory food. To Sybil Duncan, disrespect, regardless of how minor, demanded harsh punishment. The beating had been brutal.

That night in the cellar the youngster lay in Tom's arms writhing in agony, his breath coming in deep rasps. Following a spasm and a shallow gasp, he went limp. Tom sat for hours, clinging to the tiny body, the silence bearing down on him like a heavy metal shroud. When gray daylight began to filter through the darkness he began to cry.

At the age of seventeen, in a fit of rage, he killed his mother and buried her remains deep in the haunted cellar where he hoped she would be forced to fight demons and phantoms for eternity.

And now, spurred by her scorn, he sat up on the side of the bed and rose to his feet.

CHAPTER 60

Penney Sneider moaned and pulled the light blanket tight under her chin. She rolled over, fighting to escape the demon pursuing her through a dark and barren shadow world. She ascended toward consciousness like slowly rising though murky water,

Her eyes opened, and she shivered. It was so cold.

George turn down the thermostat?

She sat up, rubbing her arms against the frigid air, and reached for her robe. She stiffened and her heart skipped a beat.

A sandy-haired boy, three or maybe four years old, stood at the foot of the bed, his large dark eyes locked on her.

Jonathan?

Two words sounded in her head: *Jenni, danger,* and then he was gone.

She shot from the bedroom, down the hallway and into Jenni's room, flipping the light switch as she entered.

Lauri sat atop Jenni, a pillow pressed to the younger girl's face. Jenni's arms flailed and her heels plowed mattress.

"Lauri!" Penney jerked her backwards by the hair. She tumbled from the bed, the pillow still grasped in her hands and crawled to a corner where she drew her knees to her chest and began to sob.

Jenni continued to thrash about, still in battle with her attacker. Penney sat down and lifted her onto her lap. "It's okay. Mommy's here, sweetheart."

Jenni calmed although her eyes remained wide saucers. She gulped air and the blue tinge about her mouth began to fade. "I couldn't breathe. I couldn't breathe." Tears rolled down her cheeks.

Penney smoothed back her hair and kissed her forehead. "I know, I know."

"What the hell is going on?"

George stood in the doorway, his hands fisted at his sides and face dark with anger.

"Lauri tried to smother Jenni with that pillow. I got here just in time."

"I didn't, Daddy. I didn't. She was having a bad dream and I was trying to wake her up. Mommy pulled my hair."

"Lauri, you're lying, damn it. I saw what you were doing."

"Mommy doesn't like me." A river of tears spilled from her eyes. She raised a hand. The fingertips glistened with blood. "Mommy hurt me."

"You bitch!" George bellowed. "You've always favored Jenni. Always." Spittle spewed from his whitened lips. "She's a spoiled brat." His fist slammed into Penney's face, knocking her backwards and sending Jenni sprawling.

He picked up Lauri and stomped from the room. "Daddy'll take care of you, sweetheart." Lauri threw Penney a satisfied smirk over his shoulder.

Unable to control her trembles, Penney pulled Jenni tight against her.

"Mommy, Lauri try to hurt me and—"

"We'll talk about it later. Let's just be quiet a while, okay?"

Jenni nodded and cocooned deeper into her embrace. Soon her breathing became steady as she was claimed by sleep.

She realized Jenni had been lucky this time. Another minute or two and they would have been planning her funeral.

Next time? Maybe the bathtub, her head held under water? A hard shove in front of a moving car? A serious fall?

Penney shuddered.

Lauri, my sweet child, what has gone wrong inside that pretty head of yours? Always, you mothered your sister.

She accepted that Jenni would probably die by some freak accident if they remained in the house. There was no logical explanation for Lauri's alienation, and only one solution. They had to leave—without Lauri.

A real mother does not leave a child behind.

She pushed the hurtful thought aside. Right now her primary concern had to be for her youngest daughter's welfare. Everything would work out somehow. It had to.

She hurriedly packed clothes for Jenni in an overnight case. As an afterthought, crammed a favorite baby doll and a stuffed dog into the already bulging case. She picked up Jenni and crept down the hallway to Lauri's open doorway. George and Lauri were sound asleep on the small bed, Lauri curled in a tight ball against him. Penney eased the door shut and then hurried to the master bedroom where she deposited Jenni on the king-size bed. The child mumbled something unintelligible, but did not wake. Penney slipped into jeans, a dark cotton shirt and white tennis shoes and then tossed clean underwear, socks and a change of clothes into a nylon bag.

She hurried out to the minivan, deposited the makeshift luggage and her purse in the front seat, then laid Jenni in the back seat. Jenni sat up, rubbing sleep from her eyes with tiny fists. She glanced about in befuddlement. "Mommy."

"I'm right here, baby."

"Where we going?"

"To see Grandma and Grandpa Wilson. What you think about that?"

"Houston? Lauri and Daddy, too?"

"No, sweetheart, they'll come later. Maybe in a day or two."

"Okay."

She lifted Jenni into the car seat and buckled it, and then hurried around to the driver's door and climbed behind the steering wheel.

The engine rumbled to life loud enough to wake everyone within a country block, or so it sounded to her. When no lights blinked on in the house, she exhaled a deep sight.

So far, so good.

As she shifted to reverse, something clinked against the window. She nearly jumped out of her skin.

Millicent Forbes, wearing a frilly pink housecoat and a matching comical nightcap stared in at her. Nothing was comical about the shotgun resting against the window. Priscilla stood behind her in an identical blue robe, minus the nightcap. They both grinned.

"Roll it down, honey," Millicent said, cranking her hand.

Penney lowered the window.

"This was our Daddy's gun," Millicent said. "Keep it shined up like a new penny, don't we, Priscilla?"

Priscilla nodded.

"We heard gawd-awful yelling at your house earlier, and took Daddy's gun out and loaded it. When your lights went out we figured everything was okay. Kept watch just in case. Sure 'nough, here you come sneaking out like some kind of cat burglar."

Penney shook her head. "This is crazy. What do you think you're doing?"

"Got to know George real well. Nice man, ain't he, Priscilla?"

"Ain't? Really, Millicent."

Millicent threw her a brief sneer. "Ain't fitting that you slip off in the middle of the night. Promised that nice husband of yours we'd keep an eye on you. Now come out of the car. You too, love," she told Jenni. "Going inside to see your daddy."

Penney stared hard at the old woman.

Feeble. Maybe too arthritic to even pull the trigger.

She jammed the accelerator to the floor, and the van shot backwards, knocking the barrel of the shotgun up in the air. Contrary to her speculation, the old woman had no problem pulling the trigger, but the shot scattered benignly in the sky.

"I'll swear, Millicent. Had to do it your way, didn't you? I told you not to let her get in the van. I told you this would happen. Wouldn't let me handle the gun, like I wanted. You never listen."

I told you. I told you. I told you, clicked in Millicent's head like a stuck record.

Criticize. Criticize. All that dried up old prune knows how to do. Criticize.

Bracing the shotgun between her knees, she snapped it open, replaced the spent shell and closed it. "You make me crazy, Priscilla." She pointed the barrel at her sister's still complaining mouth and pulled the trigger. The side of Priscilla's head disappeared in a splattering of gore and bone.

Two blocks away, Penney flinched at the second report of the shotgun.

She encountered fairly heavy traffic in the downtown area; Caddo should have been rolled up tighter than a drum at the late hour. A squad car wailed past, then a blaring fire truck. A bright glow on the horizon told her something big was afire. Drifting smoke obscured buildings and muted street lights bringing to mind the fog-shrouded streets of London where Jack the Ripper stalked hapless victims. She pictured a caped figure closing in on the minivan. She shuddered, and engaged the door locks.

Too many horror movies.

Leaving the abnormal hubbub of downtown behind, she headed into the country. Ten minutes or so down the road, Jenni hollered, "Here, Mommy. Stop here!"

"What's wrong?" Penney braked toward the earthen shoulder. By the time the car had rolled to a full stop, Jenni had vacated her car seat and was working at the door handle. "Back there."

"Whoa, hold on." Penney searched for what had Jenni so excited. The only thing to catch her eye was the entrance to narrow dirt road.

"Go there, Mommy. Go there."

A sense of rightness flowed through her. Without questioning the impulse, she backed up and nosed onto the rutted lane.

CHAPTER 61

Sandra Barnes's nose crinkled in distaste at the stench of vomit and excrement. Her husband lay on the bathroom floor with the plastic shower curtain clutched in his hands and flowing across his body like a brightly colored shroud. He had jerked the flowery curtain from its rings during his last death throes. It had not been an easy death, but no less than he deserved. After all, marriage to him had not been an easy life for her.

She dumped the remainder of the rat poison from the bright yellow box into the commode and then crumbled in the eleven uneaten cookies baked exclusively for Ed.

"Thirteen, Ed," she snickered. "I baked two dozen cookies and you hogged down thirteen. Must be your unlucky number, huh? Yep, had to be that last one, cookie number thirteen that done you in."

She flushed the toilet three times before the water ran clear. Unsure if her skin could absorb the poison from handling the cookies, she lathered and then rinsed.

Humming under her breath, she hurried to the garage. Performing her own version of a jig, she removed the canvas cover from the classic 1957 Ford. Unlike her experience that morning, the car sailed backward through the opening with inches to spare on either side. It coasted to a stop within a foot of the back steps. After popping the trunk lid, she returned to the bathroom.

With a foot planted under each arm, she drug Ed's corpse through the house and out the kitchen door to the back porch. One arduous shove, and the body tumbled down the steps, the head plunking on the concrete and giving her the willies. Lifting the corpse's deadweight into the trunk proved more difficult than anticipated. She finally managed to slump the head and shoulders into the opening, then elevated the legs until the body somersaulted like an inebriated gymnast into the well. "So much for that." She slammed the lid.

She returned to the house for one last check on Jason. The boy would have to be left alone for a while, but that couldn't be helped. She smoothed his silky hair and planted a gentle kiss on his forehead. "Sleep well, little one."

The car pulled onto a secluded bluff some four miles east of Caddo. The headlights could not penetrate the expanse of inky water below her. With a bare measure of tugging and pulling, Ed's limp remains tumbled out of the trunk and onto the ground. In ten minutes time, the body was slumped over the steering wheel of the idling car where it could easily have been mistaken for an exhausted traveler snatching a few precious minutes of sleep. She reached in and slipped the gear from Park to Drive and slammed the door. The car began a slow roll down the decline, picking up speed as it traveled. It soared from the embankment as if it had sprouted wings. The beautiful old car seemed to hang in midair for several seconds as if pausing to take one last look at the world before plummeting to its final resting place. Appropriately, the classic Ford Ed had loved so much would now serve as his coffin.

Once the car had disappeared into the lake's murky depths, she began the long trek home. One hour and twenty minutes later, breathing hard and soaked with sweat, she stepped into her son's bedroom. Still asleep.

CHAPTER 62

Jeremy Ferrell opened his eyes to blackness. Sure he was immersed in another of his strange dreams, he blinked. He could feel his eyelids move. His legs and arms tingled. He ran his tongue over dry, cracked lips and tasted blood.

Not a dream.

His eyes clamped shut. Better, much better. At least there was the company of colored dots dancing through his vision. Lost in the dull ache pounding at his head, he groped about exploring his surroundings.

Smooth. Satin? What?

Memories of the night's events flooded his Head. The graveyard. Pickaxes. Mark brandishing a shovel. A list of names.

Reality ascended.

"God in heaven, I'm in a coffin."

His hands and feet strained hard against the lid. Not the slightest give. He flipped over and put his back into the effort. The lid still refused to move. He collapsed and lay quietly, fighting hysteria, chewing on his horrifying predicament.

What can I do?

Mama always said change the things you can and have the sense to recognize the things you can't change.

"No, it goes—

What the hell difference does it make. I'm sealed in a coffin and supposed to remember the exact words to some goddamn adage.

You're right, doesn't matter. What does matter is this sticky situation here. Fact is—wait a minute. Another of Mark's sick jokes. He's standing over this box laughing his ass off. Karl and Wayne, too.

A flicker of hope flashed through is mind and then blinked out. Gut level, he knew that his first impulse had been on target. He was in a coffin six feet down.

I'm going to die. A simple truth. Screaming, kicking and

attempting to claw my way out will only waste precious air.

With a conscious decision to remain calm; he opted to go for those few extra breaths of life. No words would come to offer to his Maker. As it stood, God knew his situation and last minute attempts to gain His favor wouldn't matter, anyway. The little time left would be better spent with loved ones. He closed his eyes and drifted to a world far away from his coffin prison. The son he would never see, the child growing in his wife's belly, giggled and laughed as they roughhoused in bright sunshine. His beautiful Liz, above all, was the hardest to leave behind. They made gentle love as he whispered his last goodbyes. The imagined farewell to his parents proved touching and tearful; their declining years would be disheartening without his company.

CHAPTER 63

Not bothering to proceed with stealth, Wayne Waterfield tromped through tangles of undergrowth and eons of rotting leaves. After all, he was armed, and what was there to fear from a wounded old codger who had most likely bled half to death anyway. Yep, he'd make short work of that old Jew, then hurry into town for the real fun. Distribution of their grisly harvest would be the hoot of a lifetime. Keep tongues wagging for years. He chuckled with anticipation.

He pushed deeper and deeper into the timberland, playing the flashlight about and maneuvering through limbs and branches intent on snagging his clothes and inflicting stinging scratches on his exposed arms. Caught up in the deadly game of hide-and-seek, he sang out, "Come out, come out, wherever you are." Behind him, a twig snapped. He jerked about and fired. Something dropped with an audible thud.

"Got'cha, you son of a bitch."

To his surprise, it was not Cy Weinberg lying on the forest floor with blood pumping from a gaping hole in the chest. He played the flashlight beam over a huge buck.

"Fuck a bantam rooster. Fourteen-pointer." He whistled appreciatively.

"Fourteen fucking points. Record-holder. Gotta be." He danced about, unable to contain his excitement. "Alleluia, sweet Jeeee-sus!"

In a lifetime of hunting, he never dreamed of bringing down a beast like this, and by accident, no less. And no one here to share the big moment.

He wanted that deer. Bad. Gutting it and leaving the carcass on the spot would draw predators. In this heat, it would go bad in three hours' time, anyway.

" I'll drag it to the car and—"

Wayne. What the hell are you thinking? You're supposed to kill that nosy old Jew man, not deer hunt. He's probably gotten clean away while you've been fiddle-farting around. Get on with real business, huh?

He stifled the voice. No way could he leave that awesome rack behind. No sir. In twenty minutes he could have the head off and hauled to the car. Then back to the business of the Jew man.

Decision made, he knelt, unsheathed the hunting knife strapped to his belt and went to work. His heart sang.

Cy was surprised to discover that Wanted Poster rather than College Boy had remained behind to dispatch him. Slaughtering an old man would have been right up College Boy's alley. From the time Wanted Poster stepped into the woods, Cy stayed on his heels waiting for an opportunity to take him down. The deer episode was not only amusing, but had taken the man's mind off of business at hand.

No time like the present. In three quick strides Cy crossed the clearing and had the man's head in a paralyzing chokehold. His eyes bulged and mouth widened in a silent scream.

"Goodbye, asshole." He twisted the head sharply to the right and heard the spine snap. The corpse slumped to the ground.

Breathing hard—*getting too old for this shit*—Cy cleaned the bloody blade on the dead man's shirt and then picked up the flashlight and pistol and made his way back to the cemetery. The silence told him he was alone except for maybe a restless spirit or two. Tonight's ghoulish escapade had been enough to raise any number of outraged spirits from their graves. He shivered and rubbed his arms to wipe away gooseflesh.

He groaned as he played the flashlight over his Blazer. Wires protruded haphazardly from the motor, hoses had been ripped from their moorings and the radiator cap was missing. The tires had been slashed.

"Bastards."

A red Toyota Camry had four flattened tires. The third car, an older model gray Buick, was open and untouched, obviously awaiting Wanted Poster's return. No key in the ignition or over the sun visors.

Getting careless in your old age. Should've expected something like this and searched the body. Long walk back to where you left it. Think your leg will hold up?

The wound pained him to the point of distraction. The thought of trudging back into the woods all but brought tears to his eyes. He played with the idea of hot-wiring the car, but hell, with his limited knowledge he'd probably cross the wrong wires and disable the engine.

Then what, walk to town? Just ain't your night.

Cursing his carelessness, he moved about the Buick groping the undersides of the fenders. His hand closed on a magnetized metal key case.

"God bless the rubes."

The engine turned over easy enough, but it knocked so loud he feared a rod would slam through the block at any given second. Clattering through the narrow lanes leading back to the entrance, he cringed at the sight of open graves and tossed aside coffins. The backhoe stabbed into view and loomed for a moment like an ominous steel specter before being swallowed by velvety shadows as the headlights left it behind.

He slammed the brakes and cut the motor. After dousing the lights, he stepped from the car and stood in utter blackness. Gripped by indecision, he searched his brain for what had compelled him to stop. Something was out of sync. With absolute trust in his instincts, he switched on the flashlight and began to walk back the direction he had come. The beam cut a bright path to the backhoe and the site where the exhumed corpse had slipped back into the grave. A mound of turned soil stood where there should have been a gaping hole.

He scratched his head in confusion. "What the hell?"

Words spoken by Mark Ferrell fluttered through his head: *Leave Jeremy be, I've got plans for him.*

"No." *Leave Jeremy be, got plans for him.* "No." Even they weren't monsters enough to do what he was thinking.

Bet you a dollar to a donut on this one, old man. Fact is, I'd be willing to lay my life savings on the line on this little wager. They buried that kid, all right. Six feet down. Now whether he was dead or not, is another matter. But don't kid yourself, those soulless Neanderthals are capable of burying a newborn babe alive. Wouldn't put anything past that trio of monsters.

Finding the key still in the ignition of the backhoe, he climbed aboard. A deafening roar once again claimed the uneasy hush of the cemetery. In bare minutes a metal surface glistened beneath the teeth of the mechanical shovel. He climbed down, dropped into the yawning hole and clawed loose soil from around the coffin. He raised the lid. The young man reclining on yellowed satin was the very embodiment of early manhood.

Cy pressed his fingers to the carotid artery. No pulse.

"Too goddamned late. Sorry I wasn't here sooner. If it's any consolation, I sent one of them on his way to meet the Maker. And I promise, those other two pimples on the butt of humanity will get their just due."

Heart heavy, he patted the corpse on the cheek and began to lower the lid. A barely audible gasp brought him to attention. He hurled back the lid. The corpse's eyes fluttered, popped open, then snapped shut against the bright glare of the flashlight.

Cy grasped a frail hand. "Lord, boy, you're as close to dead as I've ever seen. Can you hear me?" brought a feeble nod.

"Gonna get you out of here and to a hospital, you hear?

CHAPTER 64

His arms held stiffly before him and his glassy eyes fixed straight ahead like a zombie from a nineteen-forties' horror movie, Tom Duncan made his way out of the bedroom and down the dark hallway.

Clap-swish-clap-swish-clap-swish.

He moved along, his bare foot slapping the hardwood floor and his swollen leg dragging behind like a dead appendage. Lost somewhere in the past, he was immune to the pain that had held him prisoner in bed for some days now.

Clap-swish-clap-swish-clap-swish.

He stopped at the gun cabinet and popped the door open. His hands closed on the shotgun that so many years before had taken the life of Don Miller. One after another, the hungry chamber gobbled the large red shells.

Clap-swish-clap-swish-clap-swish.

The lovers, lost in ardor, did not see the phantom looming in the doorway.

Kaboom!

In a blinding flash, a section of wall above the bed disappeared.

The impact of the shotgun slammed Tom backwards into the wall. Now he could feel his torturous leg, but pushed the pain aside. His daughter needed a lesson.

With Naomi wrapped in his arms, Cliff Thorne rolled from the bed. Another earsplitting explosion tore into the mattress where they had been lying seconds ago. Cotton stuffing and footboard fragments rained on them.

Cliff tore a length of wood from the damaged footboard and skittered on hand and knees across the room. Not daring to breathe, he flattened against the inside wall of the doorway.

The shotgun erupted again. The nightstand splintered. He heard Naomi shriek as needle-sharp shards of the ceramic lamp bit into her bare back.

He eased his head around the door and watched as the attacker rocked unsteadily and then fell backwards, his head connecting with a thud on the hardwood floor. He was out and on the man, pummeling him in the face with the makeshift club. A gash on the forehead spurted blood like water from a burst hose.

With the strength of an angered bull, the man slammed the shotgun butt into Cliff's chest. He rolled to the floor, drawing into a tight ball and gasping for air. Each sharp breath was like sucking in the fiery air of a flaming forest. A rib moved about freely under his touch.

The intruder struggled to his feet and aimed the shotgun at Cliff's head. Through a milky haze of pain, he stared up the long barrel positioned inches from his face. He tensed, waiting for the killing blast. And then the sweetest sound in the world reached his ears: a benign click.

The man snapped open the shotgun and began to feed shells from his pocket into the empty chamber.

Cliff's eyes locked on the large man's festering leg. Drawing his knees to his chest, he kicked out with every ounce of strength his tortured body could muster. His bare feet sank into rotting flesh. Bloody pus shot from the corrupt wound. The man fell backwards, the gun swirling from his hands like a child's top. Shells clattered about the wooden floor. The man's agonized scream seemed to shake the very foundation of the house.

Cliff snatched up the length of wooden footboard, and grasping it with both hands, drove the sharp end into the chest of the wailing man. Blood gushed from the victem's mouth and his cries ceased. The stake had found a clear path through a lung and into his heart.

Cliff staggered into the bedroom on rubbery legs. "Who?" he said, pointing with a trembling hand at the dead man.

"My father."

CHAPTER 65

Nelda Crowley jerked awake at the sound of laughter. She sat up and pulled the sheet tight under her chin. An unnatural radiance flickered on the far wall of the hallway. She heard a man's voice. More laughter. After about thirty seconds in an open-mouth stupor, realization cut into her sleep-shrouded mind.

The television.

She touched the base of the bedside lamp, and a soft yellow glow illuminated the bedroom. She slipped on house shoes and a robe and hurried toward the den. The television's high volume reverberated down the hallway. It reminded her of young hooligans with car stereos tuned so loud anyone within a block got a full blast of their distasteful music.

"Lord, it's a wonder the neighbors haven't called the police."

From the den doorway a clear view of the oversized screen revealed a cast of characters seated in a semicircle. They all were chattering as one, appealing to some unseen audience.

A trashy talk show.

Not only was the television blaring full blast, but a lamp burned as well. Although advanced in age, her memory remained as sharp as a thirty-year-old. She did not leave that lamp burning. A high-tech TV capable of almost anything short of a soft shoe across the den might slip a cog and turn itself on, but lamps could not.

Her instincts ordered her back to the bedroom to call the police.

For Pete's sake, it's only a television and a lamp. Wasn't like there's some sicko with a knife lurking in a dark corner and waiting to ravish her pruned old body. In her entire affluent life she had never cowered from anybody or anything and be damned if she'd start now. Sucking up innate courage, she stomped into the large den. When she saw what awaited her, she wished with her heart and soul she had followed her first impulse to retreat to the bedroom.

Her husband was sprawled in his favorite leather recliner, the remote control in one hand and a can of Budweiser in the other. He was still wearing the dark blue suit she had selected as his burial attire. He had been dead more than ten years.

Flies had found their way into the meticulous house and were working the decaying corpse. They buzzed in seeming ecstasy over their sudden windfall.

A loathsome grin claimed the skeletal mouth. Empty black sockets stared at the television screen. Sparse wisps of gray hair clung to flaps of moldy scalp. Ribs peeked through a wide rent in the rotted jacket.

Unable to eject a scream through her tightened throat muscles, she whimpered and fled back to the bedroom, slammed and locked the door. Her head reeling, she stumbled toward the bed, gasping, unable to suck air down her constricted windpipe. Her heart raced and stomach churned. Sharp pain coursed through her aged joints as she slammed to her hands and knees beside the bed. She snatched the cord dangling from the nightstand and jerked the telephone to the floor. Sucking hard in an attempt to force breath into her starving lungs, she depressed 9-1-1. Her heart, pacing beyond endurance, seemed to explode in her chest and her head dropped to the carpet. The receiver, clutched in her dead hand, emitted ring after ring after ring.

CHAPTER 66

Dottie Hodges cowered in the shadows of a trash-strewn alley waiting for taillights to fade before sprinting to a darkened doorway. She pressed into the hidey-hole, listening for the sounds of footfalls. Blood dribbled from her nose and the corner of her mouth. Her torn bra hung loosely under her ripped blouse. One foot was bare. Her mind spun, reliving the inconceivable attack by Dean Calder, her supposed friend and longtime associate.

Twenty minutes ago she had been manning the police switchboard, finding it nearly impossible to contend with the overload of calls from a town that had gone crazy. She glanced about as Dean stepped into the cramped room, leaned against the doorjamb and crossed his arms as if bored and looking for something of interest to fill his time.

"Hey, fellow, what'cha you doing here? You're needed on the streets."

He tossed her an amused smirk.

She answered another call, jotted a name and address, and then turned to hand the information to Dean. "Woman says there's an intruder—"

He was now standing close, leering and massaging his groin. "Forget the bitch." He slapped her hard. She felt her nose collapse under the impact. Her cheek stung as if it had been set on by a swarm of killer bees.

She sprang to her feet and attempted to charge past him.

"No you don't, Cunt." He hurled her backwards onto the dispatch desk. "Time you experienced a real man. Yeah, going to loosen up that tight ass of yours." He ripped her blouse open, and with a brisk tug, snapped her flimsy bra. Her breasts spilled out under his probing hands. One quick swoop and her skirt was up around her waist. Then off came her silk panties, torn in half.

Too stunned at first to react, she lay there while he worked at his zipper. Her leg shot out, the full force of her foot catching him in the groin.

Clutching himself, he wailed and he dropped to his knees.

Instantly off the desk and running, she lost a shoe to his grasping hand.

"I'll get you, bitch!"

The threat followed her out the front door and into the moonless night. Something was wrong in Caddo. Seriously wrong. After this episode with Dean, she had qualms about trusting anyone. To make matters worse, her car keys were in her purse and her purse was tucked under the dispatch desk. She stepped from the shrouded doorway and began to make her way to—?

Where?

Instinct was tugging her in a specific direction. Giving in to the impulse, she began to walk in a crooked one-shoe gait.

CHAPTER 67

Dr. Harry Stein reclined his head and closed his eyes. "Damndest night I've ever seen."

Jeff Chambers sat across from him, his hands cupped around a mug of black coffee. The small hospital lounge with its nondescript, pale green walls and disinfectant smell was cluttered with an array of trash left behind by the harried staff. A stale, partially eaten tuna salad sandwich lay in the center of the table amid crumpled paper napkins, scattered potato chips and an untouched carton of orange juice. The owner of the uneaten meal and juice had been pulled away by another of tonight's endless emergencies.

This was Jeff's fourth trip to the hospital. It had started early evening with one of Caddo's good citizens slashed from stem to sternum during a barroom brawl, and from there, the chaos continued nonstop. The night's bloody and sometimes fatal events were all mind-boggling, but for Jeff, the most bizarre incidents involved Dr. Alan Payne and Cy Weinberg and Jeremy Ferrell.

Around two in the morning Hilda Payne awoke to find her husband had not been to bed. Following a quick check of the house, and unable to get a response on his cell, she drove to his office where she found him cuffed to a dental chair, his gums toothless and mouth drooling bloody saliva. He told Jeff that he had been assaulted by a hulking man wearing a John Kennedy mask—had no clue to his assailant's identity.

Before Jeff had finished with the dentist, a wounded Cy Weinberg staggered into the emergency room carrying the inert Jeremy Ferrell. While attempting to deal with that bizarre situation, a call came in from a hysterical neighbor of the Forbes reporting that Priscilla had been shot. Shot dead.

Jeff took a generous gulp of the coffee. The bitter brew, stout enough to dissolve a metal spoon, burned its way down his throat. "Can't figure what's got tempers so flared up. Everybody's going crazy. Seems so, anyway. Hell, it can't be the heat, we've had hotter temperatures than this."

Dr. Stein's eyes opened and he straightened his back. "I'm with you on that. Law-abiding citizens don't turn brutal over a little discomfort, at least not in numbers like tonight. Drinking water, maybe? Lead leeching into the system or terrorist introducing a hallucinogen at the water treatment plant. Whatever the cause, if we don't get to the bottom of it soon, I suspect there's not going to be much of a town left to worry about."

"Yeah, you're right. Something's been brewing for days. First Ditcher attacking January, then rattlesnakes. But hell, sure didn't expect an upheaval like tonight."

"Like I said, could be something as simple as contaminated water. Already tonight, three fires, stabbings and shootings and four deaths. Poor old Priscilla was might near decapitated. That's one I don't understand at all. Those old women were like peas in a pod, inseparable. What could have possessed Millicent to blow her sister away?"

Jeff shrugged. "Your guess is as good as mine."

"What you going to do with her?"

"She'll be charged with murder, of course. I don't think she's even aware that Pricilla is dead. She carries on one-sided conversations with her, like she can see her. Sent her to Parkland Hospital where they agreed to hold her in a mental ward for seventy-two hours."

Jeff rose stiffly to his feet. "Better get over to old lady Crowley's, let her know about her husband's corpse."

"Set your ass back down. Hell, if you leave I'll be forced to go back to that madhouse out there. I'm at my wits' end, and need a friendly face and few minutes of respite."

"Mrs. Crowley carries a lot of clout and dumps loads of greenbacks into the town. If I don't deal with her now, she'll be on my ass for months. Get her out of the way, and maybe I can figure out what's happening to Caddo and piece it back together again."

"Everybody jumps if old moneybags so much as sneezes.

Guaran-damn-tee, if you wake her with that kind of news, she'll have your balls for breakfast served on her favorite china. Remember how she reacted when that monstrosity of a statue was hauled to the courthouse lawn. Wanted those boys tethered and publicly horsewhipped."

"You mean the twenty thousand dah-lar awk-angel imported from Frawnce." Jeff's voice was a passable imitation of Nelda Crowley.

Dr. Stein snickered. "Yeah, that's the gaudy piece of crap I'm referring to." He mimicked the now toothless Dr. Payne. "Yon Ken-e-ee fulled my teef." He giggled at the unlikely picture of President Kennedy flashing a dazzling smile and standing over the cowering dentist brandishing a gleaming pair of pliers

Jeff caught the infectious giggle. "Ask not what your teef can do for you, ask what you can do for your teef."

Howls of laughter echoed through the hallways.

Jeff sleeved away tears. "I needed that. But I gotta go, much as I hate to. No choice."

"Me too, I guess. Whole new crop of wounded probably waiting for my attention."

"See ya."

Cy Weinberg, buckshot extracted from his thigh and a strong dose of antibiotics flowing through his system, spotted Jeff hurrying through the lobby. "Chief."

Jeff turned and waited for the old man to hobble over to him.

"Damn, feels like a whole nest of hornets zeroed in on my ass."

Jeff offered him a sympathetic grimace.

"Since I'm stuck without a car, reckon there'd be any problems if I drove that old Buick home?"

"Nope. Wayne Waterfield doesn't have any use for it now. Far as I'm concerned, drive it as long as you want."

"Considering who it belonged to, the sooner I get rid of it the better. After a few hours shuteye, I'll line up a rental car."

"Take your time. Like I said, there's no hurry. Cy, thanks again. What you did took a lot of guts."

"Pure damn luck. Just wasn't that boy's time to go."

"Apparently not."

After a quick handshake, Jeff hurried out the front door and Cy headed for the exit where the Buick was parked.

"Mr. Weinberg."

Cy turned to look into the troubled face of a pretty young woman, a very pregnant young woman. Her nose was lightly sprinkled with freckles and coppery hair hung in natural ringlets to her shoulders. Red and puffy sea green eyes with sweeping lashes blinked up at him.

"I'm Liz Ferrell, Jeremy's wife, and—" Her mouth quivered.

"Now, sweetheart, no need for all this bawling, your husband's going to be fine." He removed a wadded handkerchief from his back pocket, lifted her chin and dotted away tears spilling down her cheeks.

"But—"

"Dry the tears. That man of yours would have done the same for me. Isn't good for the baby or Jeremy either for you to be so upset. Now, let's see a smile on that pretty face."

Liz rewarded him with what could be loosely interpreted as a smile, but nonetheless an honest attempt at one.

"Come on, walk me to the door." He draped a large arm across her shoulders, and they strolled along like old friends. "Tell me about your baby."

Her features brightened. "A boy. Julian Aaron Ferrell. Spent months picking it out."

"Strong name. Kind of aristocratic."

"Mr. Weinberg, we owe you so much. Don't know how we'll ever repay you."

"It's Cy, not Mr. Weinberg. It's been a long time since I had a good home cooked meal. When you get Jeremy home and settled, you can fix me a feast. That'll make us even. Then we'll talk about everything that happened, okay?"

She nodded, her mouth trembling.

"Like I said, no more tears. Promise?"

"I promise."

After a fatherly hug, he turned and walked out the door. Feeling good for the first time since that fateful turn into the cemetery, he climbed into the late Wayne Waterfield's car.

The car idling at the parking lot exit, he sat for a long moment wrestling with an impulse. His instincts rarely failed him. He turned right, the opposite direction from his house. Much needed sleep would just have to wait.

CHAPTER 68

Jeff stood at his squad car with his hand resting on the door handle, his mind racing through unending duties. Despite Dr. Stein's objection, he decided his first stop would be at Nelda Crowley's. Unpleasant but necessary. Then the cemetery? Yeah, best to make sure there had been no problems locating Waterfield's remains.

Mind set, he opened the door. It took him a moment to recognize his passenger.

"No."

In the dim glow of overhead light his wife's decaying corpse reclined with her left arm draped across the back of the seat, her legs crossed and face turned toward the driver's door. Obviously, pains had been taken to pose the body for the greatest effect.

He grit his teeth against welling anger. "I'll kill the bastards. Hunt them down and ring their goddamn necks with my bare hands."

He stood rubbing his temples against a throbbing headache, unsure of what to do next. His first inclination had been to place the body in the trunk for transportation to the funeral home. No, he could not subject the woman he would always love to the degradation of a car trunk. Mollie died attempting to bear him a son and deserved better. He laid the corpse in the backseat, arms folded across the chest.

The windows were down and a handkerchief pressed to his nose to block the stench. Two blocks from Prather Funeral Home he felt a cool touch on his neck. He slammed the brake and jerked about.

"Jeff, sweetheart, please don't put me back in the cold, dark ground." Molly's full lips were puckered in a familiar pout. Her large expressive eyes pleaded.

"Molly. How—"

"It's so cold down there and I'm all by myself. You have no idea how lonely it is."

"I—"

"Why don't I move up there with you? We can take a drive and talk."

Lost in the joy of having his darling Molly back, all thoughts of the reeking corpse vanished. Giddy with elation, he scrambled from the car and assisted her from the backseat. He pulled her against him and kissed her, his tongue exploring the sweetness of her mouth.

She pulled free. "Now, Chief, wouldn't do for us to get caught making love in the middle of the street. Let's drive to the country where we can be alone."

Settled in the front seat, she took his hand and kissed each fingertip, one after another. He had forgotten this wonderful ritual.

Like a teenager in the first intense stages of puppy love, she nestled into the crook of his arm and rested her hand on his lap, her fingers kneading his inner thigh. "It's been so long. I've missed you. Let's go, shall we?"

Jeff headed into the secluded countryside, leaving the lights of Caddo behind. Unable to control his desire to look at her, he whipped to the shoulder of the road, cut off the ignition, and clicked on the overhead light. His lips explored her eyelids, the tip of her nose, lips, neck. He ran his hands through her golden hair, fingering the silky texture.

"Stop it. Please stop." She backed away, making eye contact, her mouth twisted in anguish. "I can't stay here. I have to go soon."

Her words ripped at his heart like the blade of a chainsaw. "I won't let you go. I can't let you go."

"Oh my love, my precious love. There's only one way we can be together."

"Tell me. How?"

"You can come with me."

He understood. He would have to die. His mind scanned the desolate years ahead. Nothing. His life had nothing to offer except loneliness and despair.

"Yes, I will."

"Start the car."

He turned on the ignition and pulled onto the roadway.

"Faster," she prodded.

His foot closed on the accelerator. The speedometer crept upward. Fifty. Sixty. Seventy.

"Faster."

The accelerator strained against the floor.

Eighty-five. Ninety. Ninety-Five.

Trees, bushes, foliage lining the roadway flashed by in a blur. A steel-girded concrete bridge loomed ahead.

"The abutment, my love. Then you and me together for eternity."

He adjusted the wheel. At one hundred miles an hour the car hurled toward the massive concrete barrier. Animated, he glanced at her. Next to him sat a decayed corpse. The empty sockets radiated with malevolence, and if a skull could sneer, this skull sneered with triumph.

Too late now, Jeff. Got you.

He jerked the steering wheel and jammed the brake. A screech sliced the air. Smoke and the acrid stench of burning rubber erupted from tortured tires. The car careened sideways, intent on finding a home with the death-dealing abutment. A deafening crash and grating sounds of rumpling, rending steel and shattering glass ripped the air. The car flipped, and sliding on its top, decorated the night with arcs of brilliant sparks. Fiery reds, blues and golds billowed from the asphalt. Discovering the soft shoulder, the car rolled down an embankment and splashed upright in water coursing under the bridge.

The nose dipped downward and the car submerged. Fighting the deflating air bag, Jeff groped about until finding the door handle and yanked. The door held firmly as if welded to the frame. Chilling water seeped above his head. He buoyed upwards and sucked on a pocket of trapped air. A skeletal hand encircle his throat.

"No!" He jerked away. The rotted limb ripped from the shoulder socket. He shoved it aside. His heart battering at his chest, he submerged and probed the blackness for the driver's window. The glass was webbed with tiny cracks. He slammed it with his fists. It stayed firm. His shoulder attacked it. Once, twice. The glass crumbled. His lungs threatening to explode, he again rose and sucked deep on trapped, pungent air. And then he was under water again, working his broad shoulders through the shattered window. As his hips slipped through, icy fingers closed on his ankle. He kicked, his shoe sinking into something soft and pliable.

And then he was free, scissoring toward the surface. His head broke water. The fresh air was the sweetest thing he had ever tasted. He dogpaddled through the blackness, praying he was moving toward shore. His feet finally settled in mud. Breathing hard and wading blindly, he stumbled onto dry, hard ground.

"Don't leave me, Jeff," Molly's voice beseeched from the water. "I'm cold. Please come back."

He scrambled on hands and knees up an embankment and crawled onto the roadway. There he sat, rocking back and forth with his face in his hands and tears leaking from his eyes. Molly's sweet voice continued to taunt, plead, cajole. Little by little, his will weakened; he fought a compulsion to return to the lake and join her in the watery grave.

CHAPTER 69

At the sight of a figure huddled in the middle of the road, Atrell Jones stomped the brake pedal. Despite his heavy foot, the battered Ford pickup creaked to a slow stop. The man squinted in the bright headlights.

Atrell emerged from the truck and hurried as quick his aged limbs could carry him. He remembered the state in which he had found January Rainwater. "Lord, not again."

"Precious Jesus, Chief, what you doing out here in the middle of nowhere?"

Jeff did not respond.

Atrell's stiff joints complained as he squatted to examine a bloody gash on Jeff's forehead. The cut appeared to be superficial. A goose egg-sized knot bulged on the back of the head, but the skull felt intact. A fair hunk had been bitten from the lower lip. Unlike January Rainwater, none of the injuries were life-threatening.

Jeff clutched his arm. "Atrell, listen. Do you hear her? Molly's down there waiting for me. Under the water."

"No, Chief, she ain't. Molly's dead, son. Been dead a mighty long time now."

"It is Molly. Listen."

"No, Chief. Ain't no sounds 'cept night callers. Not saying there ain't something down there, but it sure 'nough ain't your sweet Molly. Whatever is lurking in that black water is evil, can feel it in my achy old bones. Push the voice away. Tell it to go away. You hear me? Say it loud. Go away!"

Jeff explored old memories. Molly had had a genuine love for life. Any life. Not that she wasn't capable of dispatching a cockroach or housefly, but crickets, june bugs or even spiders that found their way into the house were captured in a jar and given their freedom out-of-doors.

The snake.

He smiled at the memory. Alone in the house, Molly had discovered a small black snake coiled on the den floor. She hurried to the garage and snatched a shovel. Terrified but determined, she had swept the snake into the shovel with a broom and held it in place. Shovel, broom and snake flew through the air and onto the front lawn.

Atrell was right. Even in death, Molly would never take a life, especially not his life.

"Go away!" he shouted. "Leave me alone." As if a switch had been flipped, Molly's voice was replaced by a chorus of crickets, cicadas and frogs.

"She's gone, Atrell."

Standing up stiffly, the old black man offered a hand. "Come on, Chief, let's get out of here."

Settled in the pickup, shivering from a chill that had found a home in the marrow of his bones, Jeff wondered how Atrell had appeared at precisely the right moment to save his life. He had been on the verge of following that beseeching voice back into the lake.

"Atrell, what are you doing out here?" Jeff clamped his teeth to control them from chattering. He was so cold.

Ignoring Jeff's question, he tugged a wool blanket from behind the seat. "You shaking like you got pneumonia (pneumonia coming out *ne-mon-ee*). Let's get you warmed up before anything else. Get that wet shirt off and wrap this around you."

Once Jeff was cocooned in the blanket, Atrell climbed into the driver's seat and started the truck. As he maneuvered curves and modest rises through the darkness, he began to talk.

"In a dream, the Lord told me, 'Atrell, get your lazy bones outta bed. Good people are waiting for you'. I did as He told me. Crawled outta bed, put on my clothes, climbed in my pickup and started driving. Nary a notion of where I was headed. When I seen you in the middle of the road, figured I'd arrived where He was leading me. Should've knowed better, though. Can't outguess the Lord. He was just kinda taking me on a little side trip."

"Seems you've developed a knack for pulling people from the

brink of death. First January, then me. Far as I'm concerned, that's too much of a coincidence. No doubt, you were guided, whether by God or not, I don't know."

"It was the Lord all right. He sure 'nough works in mysterious ways."

"Atrell, let me ask you a question. A serious one. And please don't think I've gone a little soft in the head. Have you felt a heaviness, a dark shadow of some kind hanging over Caddo? Something unnatural?"

"For a fact, I have, for some time now. Can't rightly say what it is I feel, but it's almost as if the air has been poisoned with some kind of gas that makes people ill-tempered, hard to get along with."

"Paranoid, defensive?"

"Plain down hateful. Some getting meaner by the day."

"My conclusion exactly. Can't pinpoint why, but it feels right being here with you. It's where I'm supposed to be. Wherever you're headed, I'm thankful to be your passenger." Jeff laid his head back, reveling in the warm wind blustering through the open window. His eyelids grew heavy and he soon dozed off.

Jarring ruts and potholes jostled him awake. He was sweaty, the chill having dissipated during the impromptu nap. He tossed the blanket aside and stretched. "How long have I been asleep?"

"Thirty minutes or so. Think we're almost there."

CHAPTER 70

Anemic light bleeding over the eastern horizon proclaimed the coming of dawn. The pickup churned to a stop amid rusted car hulls, old appliances—washing machines, refrigerators, dryers—a variety of outdated discards. The silhouette of a dilapidated building stood out in the murky gray light.

Atrell opened the door and eased out of the truck. Three men stepped from shadows. Jeff sat frozen by two rifles and a shotgun leveled on him and Atrell. A high-beam light blazed to life, first exploring the old man's sweat-shiny face and then settling on Jeff's pallid features. His hands clenched in tight fists and his gut coiled in a knot as he waited for the explosion that would rip the life from him. He grimaced at an image of Priscilla Forbes's destroyed face. Atrell's supposedly unerring senses had led him from one death trap straight into another.

"They're okay." The blinding light blinked out. Larkin Ballard and Michael Rainwater laughed and slapped Atrell on the back. January Rainwater opened Jeff's door.

"Sorry about that, Jeff. Had to check you out. About to give you up, you stubborn old rooster."

Realizing he had forgotten to breathe, Jeff sucked in deep. January's brief apology for the unorthodox welcome did little to assuage his indignation.

"What do you mean, give me up?"

"Come on in, we'll explain everything."

As Atrell and Jeff followed January and Larkin into the house, Michael moved the battered pickup behind the modest dwelling where several other cars had been concealed.

Jeff looked about in dismay at the people squeezed into every nook and cranny of the cramped room. Dottie Hodges, who at the moment should have been busy with dispatching duties at the police station, was stretched out fast asleep on an air mattress.

Huddled next to her was that striking Penney Sneider with one of her daughters cuddled against her. Hunkered in a shadowy corner with her ample legs tucked beneath her, Pearl Turner snored. It was a cinch her popular café would not be open today.

Red Meyers, hair askew, sat on the side of a cot, absently scratching and yawning.

Doug Parcell, still in uniform, leaned against a wall with his arms crossed. The grinning, sandy-haired, boyish-looking officer said, "How do, Chief?"

Slack-jawed, Jeff nodded an acknowledgment.

Cy Weinberg sat at a small scarred table across from Sharon Saunders. It seemed an eternity since the man had stumbled into the emergency room carrying the unconscious Jeremy Ferrell.

Most surprising was Dr. Stein with his lanky form sprawled in a wooden chair tilted against the wall. "Hot damn. Bad penny always seems to turn up in the dangdest places. Looks like you got in a tussle with a bobcat and lost."

"You ain't seen the bobcat," Jeff shot back.

Dr. Stein stood up. "Get your ass over here and let me check for permanent damages."

Cy Weinberg rose, and with an embellished sweep of his hands, offered his chair to Jeff.

Stitching the gash in Jeff's forehead, Dr. Stein said, "A night for miracles it seems. First Jeremy, then you. From the description of your car crash, it's amazing you survived to tell about it. Plainly not your time to go, Jeff my friend."

January told Jeff and Atrell about his dream in which the Chosen had been revealed. He talked of an evil being and of unholy plants germinated with human blood. The more the old man babbled, the more Jeff was convinced some sort of mass hysteria had taken hold. The so-called Chosen had been duped by the ravings of a psychotic who had slipped into his own little fantasy world.

Unholy flowers? Get real.

It was beyond him how intelligent people had bought into the ridiculous tale. Dr. Stein, of all people, should have been above foolish superstitions.

No explaining fools.

Jeff felt smug about his objectivity, his ability to separate reality from myth, that is until Michael Rainwater rolled out a tale that set his hair on end. He told of a visitation from his dead mother.

Red Meyers told of a similar experience involving his deceased wife. Even Dr. Stein had been visited by a love lost during his youth. He said he shrugged the brief episode off to overwork.

The sound of a throat clearing turned all eyes toward the door. A middle-aged woman stood at the entrance, shuffling from foot to foot.

"I'm Ellie Vaughan—" Her mouth dropped and she stared in astonishment at January. "It's you. It's actually you." She hurried toward him with her hands splayed. "Look." She flexed her fingers as if performing some kind of incredible feat.

Who in the hell is supposed to be standing guard? January thought, and then a picture of a group seated around a campfire formed in his head. He rose to his feet and grinned. Another of the fold had arrived.

Ellie's excited chatter finished what the table discussion had started; everyone was awake. Within minutes, the room came alive with laughter and friendly banter as air mattresses were deflated, blankets, sheets and makeshift pallets folded and stored in corners. Three ice chests brimming with juices, milk and food appeared in the middle of the room. On the front porch, January fired up an ancient, rust-pitted Coleman stove and brewed coffee in a chipped but serviceable one gallon enamel pot.

Man cannot live without caffeine. A morning without coffee would be like a car without tires. You might start the car okay, but steering it would prove sluggish and difficult. January's philosophy, anyway.

The bounty of edibles had come from the amply stocked larders of Pearl's Café. Unlike Nelda Crowley, Pearl Turner had not been the least intimidated at the sight of her husband's corpse. She had simply been saddened that his eternal sleep had been disrupted by sadistic pranksters. And unlike Molly Chambers's corpse, Tyler Turner had not sprung to life infused with malevolent intentions. While Pearl had stood looking sadly at his remains, his unassuming drawl had played through her head.

Her instructions clear, she had hurriedly dressed, and drove to the café. While gathering supplies, Sharon Saunders had appeared at the front door, shouting and pounding the glass. She insisted her mother's corpse was pursuing her. After several minutes of hard talking, Pearl had managed to calm the hysterical woman. Sharon finally accepted that she had been the victim of a sick practical joke. With Pearl's station wagon loaded with enough foodstuff to feed a small army for several days, the two women had driven to Red Meyers's secluded shack.

Breakfast finished and several people still sipping January's stout coffee, everyone gathered in the cramped room to discuss plans for destruction of the satanic plants.

CHAPTER 71

Nightmares visited on the townspeople during the bleak night had been vivid and brutal. Although an uneasy peace settled over the town, a few families decided time was ripe for unplanned vacations. After all, school would soon start, and then the whirlwind of homework, PTA meetings and a thousand other parental duties would cut into quality family time. Other citizens, as if under siege, dug in, peeking from closed blinds or drawn drapes. Some people, refusing to submit to gnawing fear, continued daily routines as if everything were normal. The animated sounds of children's laughter and frivolity normally commonplace on a fine summer day were not present.

During the dark hours of night, many individuals, drawn by the power of the unholy plants, drifted to John Wilkerson's farm. Sandra Barnes and her son were among those to arrive. Three barroom brawlers slated to be booked into jail by Dean Calder were instead escorted to the farm. Fred Zimmermann showed up, as did Mark Ferrell and Karl Hargrove.

With the arrival of dawn, apostles of the evil being, unable to resist a silent summons, converged on the remote location. The demon, growing in power, touched the black hearts of predators––thieves, murderers, child molesters, rapists—and they came from hundreds of miles away like metal drawn to a magnet. The road leading to John Wilkerson's farm was burdened with a constant flow of heavy traffic. Jockeying for position on the narrow country road strained nerves and fueled tempers. Horns blared and profanity flew. Road rage would be a mild description of what took hold of some drivers. Fist fights erupted, knives flashed and gunshots could be heard. A few unlucky individuals, having proven to be the weaker in confrontations, lay dead or dying on the side of the road. In this new world, still in the infant stages of evolution, only the fittest would survive.

CHAPTER 72

Thelma Knoll feigned contrite tears and gushed with apologies for last night's unpalatable tuna casserole. His ego inflated, Homer strutted from the house like a barnyard rooster. Thelma felt certain he would show up after work, hungry for dinner and another big helping of tears and kowtowing. She knew him well.

Her role as a contrite, groveling inferior would be well worth the effort if things worked as planned. She was a woman with a mission.

Midmorning, she drove to Baily's liquor store on the outskirts of town where she purchased a case of Budweiser beer, a bottle of Johnnie Walker Black scotch and two costly bottles of red table wine. Next was a stop at Shear Talent Beauty Salon.

Three hours later she emerged from the beveled glass doors of the expensive shop. The dowdy, middle-aged woman that had been Thelma Knoll had somehow been left behind in that miracle-working establishment. Although she could not be classified as a bona fide beauty, the complete make over had created enough allure to turn several heads. The matronly dress and practical black pumps were the only flaws in her new look.

Feeling chic and a new bounce to her step, she entered the Westside Bank and Trust. She depleted both the checking and savings accounts. Indifferent to the sputtering objections of a stone-faced vice president, she strolled from the bank swinging her imitation leather handbag bulging with Fifty-eight thousand dollars.

Following stops at the hardware store, a trendy boutique she had always considered beyond her means and Ferrell's Supermarket, she headed home to prepare a special dinner for her philandering husband. Tonight's bill of fare would not include tuna casserole.

CHAPTER 73

John Wilkerson rested his elbows on a wooden fence and studied his growing army of recruits. People brought an ever-expanding arsenal of firepower. Caches from individual collections as well as robberies and thefts provided a sterling array of weaponry. A number of people carried automatic weapons capable of firing hundreds of rounds in seconds. He counted at least a dozen Uzis, three AR15's and five or so Russian-made AK47's. Handguns ranging from .22 pistols to .44 magnums hung in holsters or protruded from waistbands. One creative army sergeant managed to pilfer a bazooka and four rockets from his home base. But for the most part, hunting rifles and shotguns were the mainstay.

He watched an Army Hummer mounted with an M60 machine gun and manned by an ape of a man clad in green fatigues rumble into camp. He did not waste brainpower attempting to figure out how the soldier managed to smuggle the formidable weapon from some military base; he simply accepted that the weapon was here as it should be. There was enough firepower on premises to do honor to the most zealous militia.

Campsites had been erected all about the farm. The more affluent nested in travel trailers and motor homes, while the less fortunate roughed it in tents or makeshift shelters. Drugs and alcohol flowed and tempers ran high. During the long night, conflicts had erupted that resulted in the wanton slaughter of six people.

Jerky Jensen had proven to be an apt general. With the aid of his companions, he had been able to whip the untrained rabble into a formidable fighting force. How clever he had been in putting a stop to the needless killings. Following a predawn outbreak of loud accusations and flying fists—not bothering to determine fault—Jerky lined the offenders against a fence and ordered them shot. The bullet-riddled bodies of three men and one woman lay where they had fallen as reminders of the consequences of future squabbles. The effect proved to be sobering.

Not that John minded the violent flare-ups, the brutal deaths. He enjoyed the raw, bloody battles and hated to see them terminated. But the barbaric conflicts would have to wait for a later time. At present, every man, woman and child was needed to protect the master's flowers.

The enemies were gathering, readying to do battle, he could feel it in his gut. Considering the impressive number of healthy-bodied individuals growing his ranks, he wasn't too worried. In another few days his adversaries would find it impossible to stop the spread of the master's influence. Three tractors were toiling at plowing under cotton fields, preparing the soil for new seed. It had been necessary to harvest a fair score of flowers to draw in converts. The remaining blooms would soon begin to seed, producing a number well beyond the paltry few discovered in the leather pouch. Their bounty would prove plentiful enough for gainful distribution to other parts of the state.

First Texas, then the United States. And finally, the world.

He turned his attention to a group of cavorting children entrenched in a game of tag. His icy gaze settled for a moment on Lauri Sneider and Jason Barnes. Yes, those two would do. His eyes continued to move about the group in search of a third victim.

Would the parents object? Possibly. If they didn't hold their tongues, they would become part of the sacrifice. It really didn't matter.

CHAPTER 74

"I'm telling you, it would be suicide to attempt to run their lines in pickups and cars. Even if we had a fucking hundred of them!" Frustration and anger colored Cy Weinberg's face a deep maroon. "You heard what Thumb said. Read my lips, people. They are well armed. Get it through your heads, this is war."

"And how do we know Thumb is telling the truth?" Jeff Chambers said. "What's to say they didn't send her here to spy on us. Hell, demoralize us. After all, she's been running with a gang of lowlife bikers."

Thumb's eyes widened and her mouth trembled. "I'm not lying. Just like the rest of you, something led me here."

Jeff scowled. "How did you end up with bikers?"

"I don't know. My dad was my entire world, called me Thumbelina because I only weighed four pounds when I was born. I was fourteen when he died. Six months later my mom remarried. Couldn't stand her anymore. Ran away from home. Somehow fell in with the Vipers. Tears flooded her eyes. "I—"

January wrapped a protective arm around her and glared at Jeff. "You slimy tip of a toad's pecker! How dare you. Every person in this room was called for a purpose. She risked her life bringing us information, you stupid piece of bat dung. If one, just one of those unholy assholes on Wilkerson's farm had suspected her, they'd have cut her throat and let her bleed out like a slaughtered hog."

Heavy silence hung in the room.

"Mommy, what's a toad pecker?" three-year-old Jenni asked.

Dr. Stein pointed at Jeff. "There, honey, take a good look. That is a toad pecker."

The room vibrated with laughter. Red Meyers fell backwards on his cot with his legs churning air and howled with gusto.

Jeff's looked miserable. "I'm sorry, Thumb, January's right. I'm stupid. No, more than stupid. I am a toad pecker. Please forgive me."

She blinked back tears.

"Please?"

"Forgiven, I guess."

"Okay, folks, fun's over," Cy said. "Let's get back to our rat killing, huh?"

Larkin Ballard slapped his forehead. "Damn. Don't know why I didn't think of this hours ago. Cy, you are absolutely right, cars and pickups ain't going to get it. We'd be asking for a slaughter. What about eighteen-wheelers? Those big mothers could plow through anything those bastards have to offer."

Cy gave a sharp clap. "Yes, of course. Now we're cooking with gas. Eighteen-wheelers."

"Know what else?" Atrell Jones said. "Seems to me there's always one or two of them gasoline tankers parked at Schilling. Ain't that right, Larkin?"

"Damn right. If we could get our hands on a couple of eighteen wheelers, you know, run interference for a gas tanker, we could blow those demon plants straight back to hell."

"I think you fellows have hit on the answer," January said. "But how in God's name are we going to lay our hands on semis?"

Larkin performed a shoulder jig. "Easy. Before you sits Schilling's transportation manager. I could go in with some cock-and-bull story about a couple of wrecked trucks and needing wheels to rescue the cargo. They wouldn't blink an eye. You know, tell them a couple of drivers got a little carried away with a road game. Happens. And believe me, when there's a truck wreck, thieves converge on the site like locust. Yep, reckon the higher-ups would be pleased to see I'm on top of it."

"The tanker?"

"That one's a little tougher. Off the top of my head, can't think of any plausible reason for taking one out." He rubbed his jaw in concentration. "Guess we'll have to steal the fucker. Sandwich it between the big rigs and drive out the gate. We'll be long gone before they figure what to do about it."

Amid a rising chatter of excitement, Cy said, "Sounds good to me."

"That's settled then," Larkin said, raising his hands for quiet. "I'll drive one of the trucks. Who else?" His eyes moved from person to person, seeking a volunteer.

"I can handle the tanker, but not one of those big 'uns," Atrell said

"I know how to drive one," Doug Parcell said.

"Do you?" Jeff asked.

"Yep. My Daddy's a long-hauler out of Dallas. Used to travel with him summers as a helper. Taught me all there is to know about those babies. Can back one into a space with a two-inch clearance on either side."

"Knew you were a pro with a squad car, but never suspected why. Three years you've been working for me. How come you never mentioned it before?"

"No need to. Never figured on driving a truck for a living."

Penney gasped.

Grinning ear to ear, Jenni held out an elaborate red bloom. "Brought you a flower, Mommy."

Penney slapped it from her hand.

Jenni's face puckered and she let out a wail.

"No, no, it's okay," Red said, rushing over to rescue the flower from the floor. He made a show of blowing dust from the bruised petals, and pressed it back into Jenni's hand. "Hibiscus. No scent to it. Three bushes out back, and it's beyond me how they've survived, never water them or nothing. They come back year after year, and this year there's a bumper crop."

"Honey child, you come on over here to Atrell and let me see your pretty flower."

Jenni wandered over to the old man, the flower held out for his inspection.

He lifted her onto his lap. "Uh-huh, about the prettiest flower I ever did see. Might near as pretty as that sweet smile of yours," he said, tweaking her nose.

Jenni giggled.

"Know what you gone and done?" His tone was low and mysterious.

"No."

"You brung us something that's gonna help us whip up on the old devil himself. That's what you done, little miss blue eyes."

"What a great idea, Atrell," January said. "Fight fire with fire."

"As I always say, the good Lord works in mysterious ways."

Michael stepped close to examine it.

"You can have it," Jennie told him, dropping it into his hand. She squirmed from Atrell's lap and headed for the back door. "I'll get you another one."

"Wait a minute, honey," Penney said. "I'll go with you."

Flashing a bright smile, she waited at the door for her mother.

"Red, you've seen the real thing up close," Michael said. "What do you think?"

"Pretty realistic clone, I'd say. Fooled Penney. She had a whole bouquet in her house."

Phyllis Mason walked over and fingered a petal. "Red's right, except for the texture and bruising, I can't tell the difference. What about the lack of odor, wouldn't that be a dead giveaway?"

"Don't think so," January said, "unless someone put their nose right up to it. Nope, I believe these sweethearts are going to be our pass into Wilkerson's farm."

Following a late lunch the Chosen got down to the serious business of finalizing their strategies. Two hours later, glancing through penciled notes, Cy said, "Everybody clear on their jobs, where you're supposed to be at what time?"

No one spoke, simply nodded.

"Remember, don't drive away from here without hibiscus blooms displayed on your dashboards. No way of knowing who's been converted to the other side. Those big red flowers may save your life. Keep a close eye on people's reactions, could give a fair idea of who is friend or foe."

Red stepped into the room and pivoted like a model displaying the latest designer fashion. "Ta dah." He then teetered about the room. "Shumbody got an extra buck or two for a fellow a little down on his luck." He smelled of cheap whiskey. His greasy, unkempt hair looked as if it had been used by sparrows to raise a brood of nestlings. A growth of grizzled whiskers added an easy ten years to his age. A length of rope had been unevenly knotted about his waist to hold up a pair of worn, two sizes too large pants. The old Red Meyers, it seemed, had returned in the flesh.

Mouths dropped.

"Makes me want to dig in my pockets for spare change," January snickered.

"Pulled it off, huh?"

"Sure did that," Cy said, glancing at his watch. "It's two-oh-five, you ready to head to town?"

"Ready as I'll ever be."

"Ellie?"

She held up car keys. "Yep. Already have hibiscus blooms in the car. I'll drop Red off then head on over to the Wilkerson's farm. Like we discussed, couldn't anybody know me there. Should be no problem getting in."

"Pistol?" Cy questioned.

She patted the side of her large black handbag. "In here."

"Don't have to do this, you know?" January said.

"Yes, I do. I don't want my granddaughters to grow up in a godless world where they could expect to be raped by the age of four. I really have no choice."

"Just be careful. From all of us, be careful."

"I will." She turned and headed for the door, Red on her heels.

"Okay, people, let's get started?" Cy glanced at Jenni who was tugging her mother's hand. "Mommy, can I go—"

"Oh, by the way, Jenni," he said, "almost forgot."

She looked up.

"Got a job for you, too. An important one."

"For me?" She released her mother's hand.

"Mrs. Mason needs some help taking care of Lonnie."

"I sure do," Phyllis said. "That boy can be a handful."

"Can I baby sit, Mommy?"

"Well, if you really want to."

"Yes, yes." Jenni's chest expanded.

"Wait a minute," Cy told her. "That's not your only job. Ms.

Turner and Dr. Stein are staying here, too. Be needing some help fixing supper."

"I can cook. Help Mommy all the time, don't I?"

"Sure do. Don't know how I could ever get along without you."

Again, her chest swelled.

"Good girl. Knew we could count on you." Cy turned his attention to Larkin Ballard. "You really don't foresee any problems hijacking three trucks from the center?"

"No I don't. All this worry's for nothing. I'm trusted at Schilling. No one would suspect me of double-dealing. And Atrell's been out there for years and is above reproach."

Cy shrugged. "Too late to worry about it now. The die is cast and whatever happens, happens."

"War is hell, ain't it?" Michael snickered.

"Yep," Cy said. "Never seen one yet that went as planned." Then added with a chuckle, "Except maybe Israel's six day war."

"Only for the Jews," Dr. Stein said. "Don't think the Arabs would see it that way at all."

Cy grinned. "That's a mouthful, Doc. It's time we get on the road. God willing, everything will go as planned and we'll all be back here no later than five. Anybody think of anything we missed?"

"I know something very important." Reverend Billy Gladstone, his stern expression belying an uncompromising man of God, stood in the doorway, his worn Bible tucked under his arm.

January smiled warmly. "Why you old Satan ass-kicker, about time you got here. Just what in hell did we overlook?"

"Prayer. Got to mingle in prayer if we expect to achieve victory."

CHAPTER 75

Larkin Ballard gave the guard a flick of his hand as he drove through the entry gate of Schilling Glass Company. Doug Parcell and Atrell Jones waited in the car while Larkin hurried into the trucking office. After scanning the dispatch schedule, Larkin selected the names of two drivers scheduled on like routes, both with reputations as cowboys, the term used in trucking circles to identify aggressive, daredevil types. He notified the superintendent of an accident on old Highway 80 involving the two men. Both trucks were down, and two trailers were needed to rescue the loads. Following a few questions, the situation, as expected, was placed in Larkin's capable hands. He left the office and handed a set of keys to Doug. He pointed to two eighteen-wheelers. "Those are the ones we're taking."

Only one gasoline tanker was on premises, its contents being pumped into an underground fuel tank. Larkin approached the attendant and ordered him to shut down the pump. Giving him a confused look, he did as told. Larkin turned to the driver and demanded the keys to the tanker.

"I'm responsible for this vehicle. You ain't gettin' shit."

Larkin did not have time to argue. He fisted the driver's flabby gut, and when the man folded with a loud grunt, he cold-cocked him on the back of the head. The man dropped unconscious to the ground. As Larkin dug in a pocket for the tanker keys, the white-faced attendant backed away

"Ain't going to hurt you, not as long as you do what I say. Get your ass over here and help me get him out of sight."

The attendant looked about to flee, but Doug and Atrell stood with arms crossed ready to take him down. He walked over and picked up the disabled man's feet.

Once the driver had been tucked away in a corner office of the fueling station, Larkin ordered the attendant to follow him. "Like I said, ain't nothing bad going to happen to you. Just can't have you raising an alarm."

"I'll keep quiet. Won't tell nobody."

"Can't chance it. And quit you're fretting, I'll turn you loose a piece down the road."

As ordered, the attendant climbed into the passenger seat of the eighteen-wheeler.

As Larkin eased the massive truck through the guard gate, Atrell behind him in the tanker and Doug bringing up the rear, the attendant screamed, "Help me. He's stealing—"

Larkin punched the accelerator, and the semi lurched through the opening.

The guard jerked up the telephone receiver. Within minutes a security man dashed from an office, jumped in a car, and with tires screeching, pursued the three trucks.

CHAPTER 76

About the time Larkin Ballard entered the dispatch office, Jeff Chambers guided Atrell's rattling pickup onto a graveled road leading to a highway storage facility. Amid a cloud of dust, he pulled to a stop beside a white Ford Taurus parked in front of a cinderblock building. The Texas Highway Department shield stood out on the driver's door.

"So much for scooting in undetected," Jeff said.

Michael was wedged in the seat between Jeff and January. "Can't be helped. Now please, let me out of here, you're crushing me to death. Damn, no air conditioner. Should be a law."

"Not everyone has had your advantages," January scolded. "Lots of people have never had the luxury of air-conditioning, car or home. So, stop your bitching and let's get this done."

As they opened the doors and slid out of the seat, a tall, gaunt man clad in Levi's, a blue work shirt and a baseball cap with the bill turned backwards stepped from the door of the squat building. He was red-faced and dripping sweat. "Whew, hotter than blazes in there." He removed his hat and sleeved sweat from his forehead. "Thought I heard someone pull up. Bartley, Raymond Bartley, friends call me Ray," he said, offering a hand. "What can I do for you fellows?"

Jeff reached out and shook the offered hand as January put a gun to the man's ribs.

"What the hell?"

"Ain't going to hurt you, mister. Need some supplies is all."

"Bullshit!" the man bellowed, knocking away January's gun hand with an elbow. In the blink of an eye, he disappeared through the building's open doorway. He was fast, you had to give him that, and almost had the steel door clamped shut before Jeff shoulder-slammed into it. Michael joined in to wrestle it open. "God in Heaven, that bastard is strong."

The door unexpectedly gave way, sending the two men

stumbling into the room. Michael managed to maintain his balance, but Jeff slammed to the floor on hands and knees. Ray Bartley had made it halfway through another doorway.

Not a man to be taken by surprise a second time, Jeff was up and with a spectacular running leap of Bob Lily caliber, tackled the guy.

Ray Bartley seemed to have lost all fight as Jeff bound his ankles and hands. He sat glaring as he watched his captors cart cases of dynamite from the room.

"Goddamn terrorists. Gonna blow up a school, maybe kill a few kids? And for what? Some sick cause that doesn't mean shit anyway."

"Stop your caterwauling," January said. "Ain't out to kill nobody."

"Sure, sure. Just like Timothy McVey didn't intend to kill all those nursery school kids."

"Don't make us gag you. You'd never believe me if I attempted to explain. So, shut your trap, and we'll be out of your hair in the next few minutes."

"That's when you'll kill me, huh?"

"Look, asshole, wouldn't have bothered to tie you up if—"

"Gran, leave the man alone. Let him think what he wants. Get that box of flairs."

Half an hour later, Jeff eased the pickup onto the roadway. Although he knew it was impossible for the dynamite to detonate, a tiny voice insisted he make the ride as gentle and smooth as possible. He had loosened Bartley's restraints enough to allow escape in an hour's time, but good old Ray had proven to be an innovative man, and he wasn't confident that the guy wouldn't make short work of the ropes. As an insurance policy, he had relieved the prisoner of his cell phone and removed the distributor cap from the Ford Taurus.

CHAPTER 77

From two blocks away, Cy Weinberg spotted the flashing blue lights of the security car in hot pursuit of the trucks. He revved the Buick's motor, and as soon as the two semis and tanker were clear, he shot from the service station driveway into the intersection slamming into the rear fender of the pursuit car. The small white Ford went into a spin and skidded to a stop against a curb. Both passenger side tires burst on impact.

Despite the seatbelt, Cy was thrown hard against the doorframe, striking his head and opening a three-inch gash in his scalp. While Dottie Hodges and Thumb rushed over to assist him from the car, Penney Sneider hurried to check on the other driver.

She needn't have bothered. The man shot from the car and stormed toward the Buick. "You crazy old man!"

Knocked somewhat senseless, Cy attempted to stand, then slumped back into the seat. Blood poured from the head wound.

"Man hurt here," Dottie shouted. "Need to get him to the hospital."

"He's not going anywhere," the security guy bellowed.

"You idiot. You can talk to him at the hospital. Now, get out of our way."

While Penney and Thumb tended Cy in the backseat, Dottie wheeled Michael's rental car away from the scene. The red-faced security man shook his fist in the air and shouted something about a lawsuit. The late Wayne Wakefield's old gray Buick remained catercorner in the middle of the street.

CHAPTER 78

At the sound of her husband's car pulling into the driveway, Thelma Knoll patted her hair and then picked up an icy can of Budweiser and a two-ounce tumbler brimming with Johnnie Walker Black. She reached the front door as it opened.

Homer hesitated in the doorway, shocked speechless by the sight greeting him. First he looked at the sweating can of beer, then the glass; he knew without a doubt that the caramel-colored liquid was not tea.

In the past, Thelma had grudgingly allowed him his beer, but hard liquor had always been a no-no, at least in the house. The generous offerings of alcohol shocked him, but what really laid a slammer between his eyes was the woman posed seductively and flashing a welcome-home-big-boy smile. He blinked twice to assure himself he was not hallucinating. Nope, the creature that was for sure his wife but not really his wife was still there.

Thelma's hair, silky and glistening with highlights, had been clipped shoulder length and formed an auburn frame around her face. He had seen the same stylish cut on tight-ass secretaries with icy stares that had a way of denying your existence. Those conceited bitches didn't have a thing over the woman standing in front of him. Subtle makeup had transformed her eyes to large mahogany pools. Somehow, her lips were fuller and imparted a sensuousness that he had never before noticed. Her skin had a velvety sheen to it. And her clothes, or let's say her lack of clothes, revealed a figure normally concealed by loose-fitting garments. Royal blue shorts clung to her sumptuous hips and enough cleavage spilled from the matching low cut blouse to tantalize the imagination.

Shaking his head in dismay, he finally found his tongue. "Sweet Jesus, I don't know what you've done to yourself, but I like it. Why, you're prettier than the day I married you. What say we go to Cross Lake Inn for dinner so I can show you off?"

"No, we eat in tonight. Got a special evening planned just for the two of us." She held out the tumbler of scotch.

Accepting the I-can't-believe-this-is-my-wife-doing-this present, he downed the liquor in one gulp. He stood there a moment savoring the delicious sensation burning a path down his throat. Smooth. He knew his scotch, and this was an expensive blend, the kind purchased to impress.

Where in the hell did she get it?

She held forth the Budweiser. "Ain't you supposed to wash it down with this?"

He started to say, "No, not this stuff you don't", but held his tongue. She had obviously put a lot of thought into this new game, and he damn well wasn't about to spoil it.

"You betcha." He was hot and thirsty and the icy brew tasted wonderful. The can close to empty, he came up for air. A belch spilled from his mouth. "Oops."

What began as a pleasant tingling in his groin escalated to a zealous throb. He set the can on a hall stand and reached for her, groping the low-cut blouse. The soft, stretchy material gave easily and her bare breasts spilled from the bodice. Unable to contain a moan, he cupped a breast in his hands and closed his mouth over the nipple. The taste of salt and the musty scent of perfume added to his fervor.

She lifted his head away and backed up a step. "Sweetheart, let's not get carried away too soon, huh? Got lots of pleasant surprises planned, and believe me, you'll enjoy the evening more if we save the best for later."

"Oh, darlin', please."

"Later. I promise, you're in for quite the evening, so go take a shower and get real comfy?"

He swallowed hard against the aching need. "All right, we'll do it your way."

I'll give that sweet thing a little taste of what she's in for later, he told himself, and pulled her close; devouring her mouth, his hardness pressed against her.

She drew away and gave him an affectionate tap on the nose.

"Enough for now. Look for another treat on your way to the bedroom."

On a small table in the hallway he discovered yet another beer and a somewhat larger glass of scotch, and even more delightful, a bowl of iced-shrimp daubed with a generous portion of cocktail sauce. Oh yes, he definitely liked this new game. Grinning, he dug into the appetizer. The booze and shrimp consumed, he ventured into the bedroom. On the bed lay clean underwear, beige shorts and a grass green pullover. Best of all, a serving-size skillet of stuffed mushrooms swimming in butter sauce had been left on the nightstand, and of course, the now expected scotch and beer. Once again, Thelma had seen fit to increase the size of the scotch glass. He shook his head in amazement.

"Yessireebob, that woman knows how to please a man when she puts her mind to it."

He sat down on the edge of the bed and dove into his wife's specialty. Gina Wilms popped to mind. Yeah, she tended to spoil him too, was always ready for a quick roll in the sack and never failed to maintain a perpetual stock of tasty snick-snacks. Today Thelma had outclassed anything Gina was capable of doing. The other woman, with her bleached hair, heavy makeup, barn-sized hips and coarse voice, was trashy compared to the new Thelma.

But, oh man, her tits.

They were a sight to behold. But even those beauties could not make up for the class difference in the two women. Besides, he had been thinking for sometime now about ending the affair. The nesting instinct was inherent in all women. Never had one failed to start the moping, the hinting at a permanent relationship. That had always been his cue to move on down the road. Gina had lasted longer than most, but even she was beginning to succumb to this basic female instinct.

He was no fool. Savings accounts well over fifty thousand, a practically new, paid for car and a nice home that had appreciated thirty thousand dollars. Divorce in a community property state and a nonworking wife? Not a chance. His ass would get kicked all the way to the poorhouse. Nope, he wasn't about to throw it all away for a piece of ass he'd soon tire of anyway.

The scotch and beer were performing their magic. Alcohol always zeroed in on his jovial, humorous side. He never failed to evolve as the proverbial happy drunk in love with everyone and everything.

He made his way on unsteady legs to the bathroom and giggled at the sight of the more than half-empty scotch bottle and an ice-filled glass waiting for him on the marble vanity top. He picked up the bottle, and swaying a bit, studied the label. "Johnnie Walker, my friend, you are about to put me on my ass."

"So what, that's what I'm here for," he answered for the bottle.

"Touché." He saluted sharply and then poured a generous portion into the glass.

Following a sizeable gulp, he stared at his reflection in the mirror. The five o'clock shadow that never failed to make its scraggly appearance by mid-afternoon stood out. "If you're going to eat pussy tonight, Homer old boy, you damn well better shave these whiskers off."

"Good idea."

After the luxury of a long tepid shower, he applied frothy shaving cream to his face and went to work with a razor.

"Ouch."

A stream of blood from a nick on his right cheek cut a crimson path through white foam. He held the razor in front of his eyes and scowled. "Look, sharpy my pal, no more of that shit, you hear?"

Clean shaven with only one additional nick, he removed a bottle of Aramis aftershave from the medicine cabinet, poured a generous portion into his palm and patted onto his face.

"Holy shit."

He danced about, gritting his teeth and fanning the stinging nicks. The Aramis bottle slipped into the sink and shattered.

Studying the shards of glass, he grinned. "Wonder where Aramises go when they die." A picture formed in his head of thousands of winged cologne bottles flitting from cloud to cloud.

"Nah." Solemn-faced, he placed his right hand over his heart. "Mr. Aramis, wherever you are, may you rest in peace."

Staggering out of the bedroom, his arms out to slow the spinning, his eyes settled on the bed. "Just for a minute."

When Homer failed to show in the dining room within the hour, Thelma went to the bedroom to check on him. She found him sprawled on the bed, naked as a new born baby and snoring with the gusto of a freight train. Her nose wrinkled at the overpowering smell of cologne.

A glance in the bathroom told the story. The splintery remains of the Aramis bottle glistened in the sink. A wet washcloth and damp towel lay rumpled on the floor. On the vanity rested the glass containing the watery remains of his last cocktail. The empty scotch bottle stood beside the glass.

She lifted his left arm and then let it drop. It plopped to the mattress.

"Out like a light."

He had passed out like this many times in the past, and she knew a drum and bugle corps marching through the bedroom and playing their hearts out could not rouse him.

Even though he was where she had intended for him to end up, she was disappointed. Hours had been spent preparing his favorite foods, and he was now unable to partake of his last meal. Despite having developed a genuine loathing for the man, she had been looking forward to his forthcoming praise.

"Oh well, chicken one day, feathers the next." She shrugged, accepting she would be dining alone.

After pushing and tugging him to and fro to strip the bed linens, he rested on bare mattress. She then dumped the contents of a brown paper bag retrieved from the top shelf of the closet on a corner of the bed. A white tube read Super Adhesive. Avoid contact with skin. Bonds in seconds.

Within minutes his arms were tethered to the massive headboard, and then the legs to the footboard. A generous line of glue was applied to his bottom teeth. After twenty seconds or so, she clamped his jaws together. His only complaint was a snort.

Next the lips.

Eight tubes of glue later, she returned to the dining room. The aromas emanating from the table made her salivate. Her stomach growled. She sat down and stabbed a large slab of rare rib roast and placed it on her plate. Normally a teetotaler, she picked up a stemmed glass and sampled the expensive red wine. The rich liquid rolled about her tongue. "Not too bad."

Had the scotch and beer failed to knock her husband out cold, the wine had been her standby to push him over the edge.

A shame, a real shame Homer had to miss this part of his surprise. She was disappointed she wouldn't see his reaction to this wonderful dinner. Too bad. Oh well, by the time he awoke, she'd be way down the road. "Be driving your almost new, paid for car, Homer. The one you never let me drive." She giggled. "Don't worry, darling, I won't scratch it. Besides, I'm leaving my old Ford for you, not that you'll have a need for it." She stuffed a large bite of meat into her mouth and began to chew.

CHAPTER 79

In predawn darkness, Red Meyers, Cy Weinberg and January Rainwater sat on the rickety front porch steps sipping steaming coffee and watching the eastern sky lighten as the sun climbed toward the horizon.

"Easy to identify John Wilkerson's recruits, huh?" January said to Red.

"Easy? Hell, it was a snap. Soon as one of them spotted that hibiscus bloom peeking from my pocket, they'd light up. I'd get this look, you know, like we were allies in some kind of conspiracy. Damndest thing I ever saw. Reminded me of Pavlov's dog, sight of red made them salivate. Not one of them took exception to my filthy clothes and the stink of alcohol. No one the least bit suspect of the flower. Course I didn't let anyone get close enough for a good whiff of it."

January glanced at Cy. "Appears there won't be a problem getting the trucks through their lines. As you put so aptly, Red, should be a snap."

"Don't get too confident," Cy cautioned. "This thing we're up against is ancient and clever. It draws on eons of experience in dealing with the human race. Don't think we can fool it that easily. Can't see it letting us drive unchallenged into the farm to destroy its precious plants. No, I think we may be in for one hell of a bloody battle." He glanced at his watch. "About time to rouse everybody, don't you think? Have a long day ahead of us. Red, you and the other volunteers need to get on the road to Wilkerson's farm in the next hour or two. Hate sending you into the viper's nest, but don't see any other choice."

"Long as we keep hibiscus blooms close, I think we'll be safe. But damn, I hate the thought of getting near those foul flowers. Churns my belly just to think about it." As if to prove his point, Red's stomach let out a robust rumble.

The three men chuckled.

CHAPTER 80

Homer Knoll awoke, confused and unsure of where he was. Weak morning light bled through cracked mini-blinds. He lay limp as a dishrag in the twilight between consciousness and sleep. He recognized the dull throb behind his eyes as a forewarning of a bad hangover. Memories began to drift through the fog clouding his mind: Thelma—sexy, hot. Smoooth scotch. Cold beer. Mushrooms and shrimp.

He remembered being a little tipsy while heading for the bathroom to take a shower. Beyond that, his mind came up blank.

Laid on a real doozy this time. Think hard about the evening. Thelma had plans, remember? Special plans, as she put it. No doubt, you screwed them up. Must be pissed as hell. Yep, big boy, you're going to pay for this one. Big time.

Who gives a shit. Right now I need to piss Niagara Falls.

He attempted to sit up, but found he couldn't move. With— What the hell?—clinging to his tongue, he discovered his jaws were locked. He could not open his mouth to loose a yawn. His tongue explored his teeth. They felt rough.

Glued? No way. I'm dreaming, Yep, smack dab in the middle of another of those horrific nightmares. Deep down, he knew better. This felt much too real to be a dream.

All remnants of sleep slipped away. Fully awake, his eyes widened in astonishment as he struggled against his bizarre imprisonment. As nude as the day he was born, he lay on bare mattress, his feet and arms tethered. He wiggled his fingers to be hit with tingling numbness. Sharp pain awakened his wrists. The pain, once stimulated, shot down his arms with the intensity of a biting electrical current, invading his shoulders and stiff back. He jerked both arms down with the strength of panic. The cords refused to give an inch.

He was well acquainted with his wife's stubborn streak. Not that she dared to defy him often, but occasionally, when something really bothersome stuck in her craw, she could be as contrary and ornery as an overworked country mule. Yep, like a wild boar mired in a swampy bog, he was stuck in this uncomfortable and degrading position until Thelma saw fit to free him.

Must've really pissed her off this time.

His penis stood at strict attention in a command from his raging bladder to provide relief.

"Mmmmaaaa!" ("Thelma!")

No answer.

Then a spine tingling thought ran through his mind: *Thelma couldn't have done this. Not enough guts.*

Who then? A burglar?

Must be.

He came close to convincing himself that some lowlife scum too lazy to earn a living had disabled him and was at this very moment ransacking the house. His ears were tuned for telltale noises.

The drone of a passing car and a faint cicada chorus bled from the outside. Inside, creaks and groans of the house settling were the only sounds. His heartbeat quickened at a click. Then recognizing the whir of the air conditioner kicking on, he relaxed.

He gave up the idea that some stranger was prowling the house in search of nonexistent jewels. No, a burglar wouldn't have gone to all this trouble. As bad as he hated to admit it, this little charade had to be his wife's handy work.

But what ever possessed her to do something like this?

Hell hath no fury like a woman scorned, the stinging voice of his conscience chided. *Maybe you pushed her a little too far with this last affair. Didn't even bother to hide it from her. A bit of payback, you think?*

He had heard of wives sewing abusive husbands in sheets and beating the hell out of them with frying pans or baseball bats. At least Thelma hadn't gone that far. He could thank the Lord for that much, anyway.

For the barest moment, he saw the humor in his situation, that was until his throbbing bladder began to tug at his temper. The tiny spot of humor dissolved into anger—the anger escalated to fury.

The stupid bitch. I'll ring her goddamn neck. You can bet your sweet ass, Thelma, you'll be fucking sorry you ever started this little game. Gotta know that nobody, absolutely nobody, fucks with Homer Knoll and gets by with it.

Okay, settle down before you burst a blood vessel. You can worry about settling up with Thelma later. First things first. Got to pee real bad, right?

Damn right. And how in the hell am I supposed to go to the pot if I can't get out of this fucking bed?

That's a problem all right. Can't be done. Your only option?

God in heaven, a golden shower? Over my dead body. Fucking mattress set cost over a thousand bucks. Ain't no way I'd piss on it.

"Mmmmaaa, ooo ooorrr!" ("Thelma, you whore!")

Silence lay heavy in the room. The house rang of emptiness.

He squirmed as much as his confinement would allow. Beads of sweat popped out on his forehead.

"Aammm ik, ooh inck, mm ooonaaas err loootin. ("Damn it, you bitch, my toenails are floating.")

You stubborn old fool, his discerning side scolded. *What you going to do, lay here gritting your teeth until your bladder bursts?*

Can't. I cannot pee in bed.

The way I see it, my miserable friend, you really have no choice. Like I said, your bladder can hold only so much. It could be hours before the bitch decides you've learned your lesson.

No longer able to stand the pressure ballooning his groin, he relaxed to allow his bladder to release. It took him a second or two to realize the needed relief, the dreaded warm drenching, was not happening. He strained, but could not pee.

What the hell has the whore done to my cock? Glued it shut too?

The reality of his situation made a chilling odyssey into his mind. Thelma would not have gone this far if she'd had any intention of freeing him. Too many times she had been the brunt of his hot temper. Too many harsh words, stinging slaps, swollen lips and blackened eyes had been meted out for him to consider that she would be willing to face his wrath after this little fiasco.

For the first time since he had opened his eyes, he was scared. Terror might be a better term for the emotion gripping him. Color drained from his face, leaving his complexion a ghostly white.

His jackhammer heartbeat and runaway pulse glutted his brain with blood, leaving him lightheaded. His stomach churned as if the shrimp he had eaten the night before were doing backstrokes through the rich butter sauce. He belched greasy gorge.

His stomach rumbled. He shuddered against a wave of nausea. Stinging sweat burned his eyes.

He tossed to and fro in an effort to free his cemented body from the mattress. His back and buttocks tore free, leaving behind several layers of bloody skin on the satiny material. Unable to loose a scream lodged in his throat, he moaned against the scalding pain.

A wave of nausea claimed his stomach's contents. Vomit gushed into his mouth, and finding no exit, followed paths to his sinus cavities and down his windpipe. The pain was more than he thought possible. Unconsciousness ended his torture and silent death descended.

Before leaving her husband to his fate, Thelma updated the message on the answering machine: "Knoll residence. Homer and I are out of town on a family emergency. Please leave a message and we will call on our return."

On her way out of town, feeling like a prom queen driving Homer's practically new, paid for Chrysler, she stopped by Schilling Glass Company and presented Homer's boss with a handwritten note. It read:

Harry,

Sorry for the short notice, but need two weeks off. Family illness. Please code me on vacation. Thanks a bunch. The note was signed "Homer."

During their long and difficult years of marriage, Thelma had become proficient in duplicating her husband's handwriting. As expected, good old Harry didn't blink an eye at granting Homer's request. After all, the two men had been lifetime buddies.

CHAPTER 81

The Chosen gathered about Red Meyers's weathered table where Cy Weinberg sat at the end with several pages of notes spread before him. Cy's intense gaze moved from face to face as if he were reading the soul of each person. "I'm going to present a serious subject. Some of you may find it uncomfortable, but it has to be discussed. Who here has ever killed another human being?"

Some shook their heads, others stared in astonishment at the thought provoking question.

"I have," Jeff Chambers admitted, breaking the heavy silence.

"So have I," Cy said. "A good number in fact. Let me tell you, friends, it isn't an easy thing to do or an easy thing to live with. It's a burden that remains with you the rest of your life. The memory will fade over time, but never completely dies. What we're facing tonight may very well come down to any one of you having to kill. Any doubts about your ability to do so, speak up now. Nothing to be ashamed of. Sometimes I wish I could turn the clock back to that innocent time of youth, to the time when I still had the option of taking a different path than the one chosen by an immature, idealistic kid. Unfortunately, I can't do that, nor will you be able to undo the act of snuffing out another's life. Think about what I'm telling you. Think hard. Are you capable of killing another person?"

Larkin Ballard answered with a decisive, "Yes."

Doug Parcell nodded. "That's a decision I made when I decided to go into police work. Without a doubt, I could."

Penney Sneider locked eyes with Cy. "When I fled the house, my husband had been in such a rage that I had no doubt he would have hurt me bad, maybe even killed me. Before the flowers he was a gentle loving man. I caught Lauri, my precious five-year-old, attempting to smother Jenni with a pillow. In mere minutes I would have been too late, we would have been planning her funeral. This demon or whatever it is took control of both my husband and daughter, turned them into people I hardly recognize. No way can this unspeakable evil be allowed to take control of this world, turn innocent children into killers. Destroying it is my only hope of getting my husband and child back. If I find it necessary to kill to rid mankind of this mind-controlling beast, then so be it." She cleared her throat. "Count me in to the death."

Cy nodded. "You summed it up in a nutshell."

From about the room, "I can." "Yes." "I think so," spilled from one mouth after another.

Cy raised his brows. "Didn't hear your reply, Red."

Red looked down at his hands and shifted in his chair, his face colored with embarrassment. "I don't think it's in me to do it."

"In self-defense?"

"I've never been faced with that situation, but even under those circumstances, I doubt I would be able to."

"Appreciate your honesty. No shame to being a gentle soul. Anyone else? I'm sure Doc Stein would welcome extra hands with the children or would be willing to trade out with one of you."

"I'm not staying here, if that's what you're thinking," Red said. "Don't need more than one adult here tonight. Each of us has an assignment. Doc was stationed here to be available for the injured. And thanks to hibiscus blooms, a number of people at Wilkerson's farm have identified me as one of their own. The farm is where I'm needed, and by God, that's where I intend to be, just like planned. I'm not afraid of death. Hell, everybody has to face the grave, and as far as I'm concerned, today is as good a day to die as any."

"All right, then," Cy said.

"God's on our side." Billy Gladstone said. "He'll look after you. We are all under His divine protection."

"Reverend, I respect your beliefs," Cy said. "But please don't try to instill these people with a false sense of security. We are at war and headed into battle. Believe me, divine protection or whatever, bullets are not particular. Any one of us may die today. And if anybody's not up to making that ultimate sacrifice, now is the time to back out. No one will think less of you."

CHAPTER 82

At the very moment of Cy's portent speech, Ellie Vaughan walked into the arms of an unkempt giant.

Yesterday morning hibiscus blooms had gained her entry into Wilkerson's farm without so much as a suspicious glance from the guards. After selecting a secluded campsite, she spent the remainder of the day and this morning tromping wooded areas in search of suitable locations to plant dynamite. Several more of the Chosen were due to arrive within the hour in Atrell Jones's old pickup, the bed loaded with explosives. The hidden caches of dynamite would be detonated to draw attention when the two eighteen-wheelers and gas tanker entered the farm. At least that was the plan.

Proceeding down an overgrown animal trail not ten feet from Myrtie Wilkerson's concealed grave, she had not detected the man's presence until caught in his rib-crushing grasp. He clamped a large hand over her mouth and warned, "Scream, bitch, and they'll shoot us both."

She struggled until he pinched her nostrils shut. In a short time her lungs seemed to fold in on themselves and her knees buckled.

"That's better. I'll let you breathe, but one peep, and I'll kill you. I don't really want to fuck a dead body, won't be near as much fun, but a man's gotta do what a man's gotta do. Understand?"

She nodded.

He removed his smothering hand. She collapsed, gasping for air. He slammed her to her back and dropped astraddle of her. "Ever been fucked in the ass, lady?" he rasped, frantically working at his zipper. His whisky-breath was almost as sickening as the foul aroma emanating from the crop of red flowers. He leered down at her, exposing scummy, nicotine stained teeth. "You cunt. Gonna fuck you in the ass, then the mouth."

She had come too far for this, and slipped a knife with a two inch blade given her by January from the miniature sheath on her belt.

"Careful handling this," he had cautioned, "sharp as a razorblade."

Her assailant chuckled at the toy-like weapon. "Who the fuck you think you're going to hurt with that?"

Hurt him she did. With the agility of a sleight of hand artist, she plunged the blade into his neck and slashed from left to right. His throat gapped open as if he had acquired a second mouth. He grappled at the wound as if attempting to close it, then collapsed. As with Homer Knoll, silent death claimed him.

Drenched in her would-be rapist's blood, she dragged the heavy body into a thicket and concealed it with dry leaves and branches. She made her way to a stream she had stumbled across the day before, and stripped. The blood washed from her body, but the stains would not so much as lighten on her white blouse. The unsightly blotches on her denim jeans would be hard to identify as blood. The blouse would generate questions, maybe even place her life in danger. For that matter, that simple piece of clothing could put their entire mission in jeopardy.

What to do? What? She thought about some of the women flaunting their bare breasts for anyone who cared to look. The fact was, some of the more brazen wore no more than thong panties and sandals. Her face reddened at the appalling idea taking shape in her mind. The thought of exposing her breasts to total strangers ranked right up there with slitting a man's throat.

I can't.

You can.

No. I'd die of humiliation.

Bull. Ain't no one ever died from humiliation. Besides, won't take long to get back to the car and another shirt.

Unless someone stole my things. Been gone all morning, and in case you haven't noticed, we're not mixing with the most desirable elements of the human race here.

Hey, you're already a killer and about to become a full-fledged exhibitionist. So what's the big deal if you have to filch a shirt somewhere.

Her belly rolling with apprehension, she concealed her bra and telltale blouse under a rotted log. Her head high, shoulders back and bare breasts bouncing in the breeze, she headed back to her campsite.

Her resolve slipped under outright ogling and crude comments accompanied with suggestive hip movements.

"Hey, hoooneee, come over here and see what I got for you." "Wanna do the nasty with me?" "Gotta have some milk."

It took every ounce of fortitude to keep her arms swinging nonchalantly at her sides.

Easy does it, almost there.

A frightening thought hit her. *The Chosen will see me, assume I've converted to the other side. Lord, help me.*

Instinct took over, giving her arms free reign to conceal her breasts. She broke into an open run.

Ellie need not have worried. Three of the Chosen had arrived in Atrell's pickup and were tracking her approach. Even at a distance, her pained expression and red face broadcast her mortification at parading au natural.

"Stop your snickering, Red," Sharon Saunders scolded, giving him a swat on the arm.

Thumb giggled. "What I wouldn't give for my cell, so I could video this. Look at those tits bounce.

"You two are impossible."

By the time a winded and sweat-drenched Ellie padded into the campsite, the three of them were laughing uncontrollably. Glowering, Ellie blustered, "Just wait, your turn is coming. See if you get any sympathy from me." The comment pushed them deeper into hysterics. The riotous laughter drew curious stares from neighboring campsites.

Ellie stomped to her car, opened the trunk and plucked the first shirt she spotted from a canvas carryall bag. Working the shirt over her head, she too joined in the laughter.

Four hours later, Pearl Turner, Penney Sneider and Reverend Gladstone showed up. Dottie Hodges and Phyllis Mason arrived in the next few minutes. The newcomers established campsites in close proximity of Sharon, Red, Thumb and Ellie. Ellie had already assisted her three companions in planting dynamite in strategic sites she had scoped out earlier. The Chosen now sat back with their eyes and ears open, and waited for nightfall before moving to designated posts.

Two hours before sunset, the body of Duane Martin was discovered in a wooded area. The giant's throat had been slashed from ear to ear. Bloody footprints led to a secluded stream where the assailant had attempted to wash away telltale signs of the murder. A damp, bloodstained white blouse and bra were found stuffed under a rotted log located twenty or so yards from the stream.

Jerky found it difficult to believe a woman could have gotten the best of Duane. The man was as strong as a bull and twice as ill-tempered. He possessed no fear and had been known to plow headfirst into brawls where his odds of coming out alive were no better than two to one. But somehow, he had always managed to emerge bruised and battered but otherwise unscathed. If a woman had managed to do in the Big D, it was a cinch she had help, a lot of help.

Jerky had a knack for getting to the truth. He harbored no doubts that the culprits would be ferreted out before an owl could hoot twice. Already his mind was munching on ideas for creative and painful punishments. Oh yes, it was turning out to be a glorious day.

CHAPTER 83

Red heard a shout as he stepped from behind a large oak where he had retreated to relieve his bladder.

"That's him. The one right there." A man pointed him out to a troop of armed men. Sharon and Ellie were face down on the ground with guns leveled at their heads. Thumb struggled with a tall, brawny man. "Let go of me," she screeched.

"On the ground, asshole," one of the men ordered, bringing a rifle to bear on Red.

Cy's words fluttered through his head: *Bullets aren't particular.*

"Don't shoot," he said, his hands in the air. As deliberate as an arthritic old man, he eased to his knees, but instead of going flat, he dove behind the oak. A stream of bullets slammed into the tree. Wood fragments bit into his back. He scrambled through a dense thicket leaving shreds of clothing and skin on the thorny branches. Then he was running with bullets buzzing about him like angry hornets. As the woods thickened, his pursuers gave up the chase. His clothes sweat-soaked and his heart threatening to explode, he dropped to his hands and knees and sucked in humid air. He lay on a soft bed of decaying leaves in dappled shade and mulled over the situation. Someone had given them away.

Who?

Couldn't have been one of the Chosen. Or could it? Thumb? Maybe Jeff had been right about her after all. No, January would have known. She couldn't have fooled him.

Then who?

It hit him.

The body. They found that creep's body. Must not have been concealed as well as Ellie thought. The way she came marching through camp wearing nothing but a pair of wet jeans and glowing from embarrassment had to have raised brows. Anyone with half a brain would have picked up that something was amiss. A few questions here and there, and presto, they were at our campsite.

"Crap." The three women were in deep trouble, and what did

he do? Run like a scared rabbit. He jerked upright, ready for hand-to-hand combat to rescue them.

Just hold on a minute. So you ran. The only sensible thing to do. Any one of them would have done the same. If you storm back in there and get yourself captured or killed, who in hell will detonate the dynamite? You four are the only ones who know where it's planted. Accept it. Those gals are incapacitated for the duration of this thing.

Can't just leave them there, maybe to die.

Yes you can. They knew the risks when they signed on for this mission. Remember, there are five other Chosen camped close who had to see what was happening. Maybe they'll think of something, but that's neither here nor there. Right now the only concern has to be getting those trucks through safely. If those demonic flowers take over, it'll be like a replay of Invasion of the Body Snatchers, only this time for real. Remember what you said to Cy? 'Today is as good a day to die as any.' That pretty well sums it up for any one of you.

Crestfallen and miserable, he accepted that he was helpless to rescue his friends. He glanced at the Timex Michael had insisted he wear. A little less than five hours until the trucks were due to arrive, the longest five hours he would ever spend.

CHAPTER 84

John Wilkerson sat slumped in a porch swing listening to revelry spilling from campsites. About midnight, after two hours of fitful tossing and turning, he had given up any hope of sleep. He brushed away mosquitoes intent on making him a banquet. A gentle breeze coaxed a lazy sway from the swing. He studied his people illuminated by campfires. His people—the term he had taken to calling the multitudes migrating to the farm. A number of naked, sweat-shiny bodies moved about the fires.

Modesty had proven to be an easy victim of the force possessing the farm. Open sex, often with multiple partners, had become a common sight. A fair number of heretofore-professed heterosexuals had discovered the carnal delights of same-sex partners.

Any man or woman on the farm would deem it an honor to have their body used in any manner by him, but he was not interested. Their erotic behavior did nothing to stir his interest in pleasures of the flesh. He was exhausted and often found it difficult to place one foot in front of the other. His eyelids hung at half-mast. His joints ached and his stomach remained in a constant state of roil. His mind could never find a stopping point; it darted from one demanding task to another. Sleep was all but impossible.

A distant rumble drew his attention to the frontage road. Running lights outlined the trailers of two advancing eighteen-wheelers and a smaller truck.

"More disciples."

That morning he had arranged for transports to be brought to the farm for delivery of forthcoming plants. Anytime now, the flowers would seed, and then the sacrifices. The taste of blood would produce a new crop of flowers. Ah yes, Houston, Austin and Dallas would soon fall under his master's control.

The lead truck maneuvered into the drive and stopped. Several mock soldiers, weapons on alert, moved to offensive positions around the cab. Uneasiness settled on him as he watched Jerky Jensen climb onto the high running board to converse with the driver.

He felt a twinge. Something wrong.

Staring hard at the three trucks, he rose to his feet.

The enemy, John. The enemy, his master bellowed in his head.

The color drained from his face.

CHAPTER 85

As Larkin Ballard maneuvered the wide right turn into the graveled drive of Wilkerson's farm, a delegation of rugged, unkempt men positioned themselves about the cab. The hibiscus blooms that had earlier provided such a strong sense of security now seemed an inept ploy against the array of firepower leveled on him. Beads of sweat popped out on his forehead.

A bearded, unkempt gorilla of a man grasped the door handle and pulled himself up to the window. He spotted the red flowers displayed on the dash, and nodded for his companions to lower their weapons.

Larkin noted the disappointment on their faces. They reminded him of a pack of hungry hyenas anxious to move in and tear their prey to bloody shreds.

"Man, we weren't expecting you until sometime tomorrow," said the gorilla, his ugly grin exposing nicotine-stained teeth. His formidable size, gapped smile and a red and blue viper coiling down his muscular arm told Larkin this was the infamous Jerky Jensen. Thumb had given an apt description.

With no idea who Jerky might have been expecting, he said, "Me and my buddies behind me decided we couldn't wait until tomorrow and miss all the fun. Any problem?"

"Hell no. Seeds should be popping anytime. Been a damn shame if you'd missed the sacrifices."

"Sacrifices?"

"Yeah. You know, slicing the kids. Using their blood."

Larkin swore the man's eyes brightened with anticipation. "Nope, hadn't heard about that."

"That's what's happening. To top that off, having us a tractor-pull. Gonna teach three bitches how painful it can be to mess with us."

"Tractor-pull?"

"Yep, one of my men got himself killed today. Hell, all Duane wanted was a little pussy, and this crazy cunt cuts his throat. Ain't a woman here who wouldn't have spread her legs for him, and she goes and does him in."

"You said three bitches?"

"One of them used to be my main squeeze. But hell, ain't got no use for a main squeeze with all the free pussy around here. I went to work with a pair of pliers on the one who done it. Have to say she was a tough old gal. Even with a broken wrist and five of her teeth yanked out of her head, she kept insisting she was the only one involved. Them camping together and all, I decided the other two were guilty by association."

Damn. Couldn't be nobody but Ellie, Thumb and Sharon. What about Red? Dead?

"The natives are getting restless, needing a little excitement. Figured a tractor-pull would be the ticket. Gonna let the boys take turns tearing those bitches into about a dozen different pieces. Yep, that'd be enough excitement to last them a while."

Jerky's words tugged at Larkin's Irish temper. He itched to slam the maggot's head into the steering wheel, beat that ugly face to a bloody pulp; show the bastard how Larkin Ballard deals with people who slash little kids and torture women. Instead he said, "Sounds like there's going to be high old times around here. Glad we decided to come on out."

Holy Jesus, another day and we'd have been too late.

"Yep, tomorrow's going to be something all right. Look out there, see them flickering lights? That's lanterns and flashlights. People out in the field watching for those red beauties to start dropping their loads. Glad you're here. My name's Jacky Jensen, Jerky to my friends. Welcome aboard."

Larkin thought he had understood what they were driving into. Thumb had attempted to explain the violent atmosphere of the camp, but he now understood that words could not relate the brutality he was seeing in the faces of these men.

Slash the children. Tear the bitches into a dozen different pieces.

"Name's Larkin. Glad to be here."

Win or lose, that sleazy son of a bitch will not live to see daylight.

Jerky jumped down from his perch and waved an arm. "Pull on in, Larkin. Park those big babies anywhere you can find spots. Plenty of food, booze and lots of good pussy."

As Larkin shifted the metal monster into gear and urged it forward, a figure waving a shotgun and shouting darted from the porch of a large farmhouse. Picking up speed, Larkin watched Jerky through the side mirror turn toward the man, his ears cupped in an attempt to make out what he was hollering.

The world lit up and the ground quaked. In a matter of seconds, another explosion flowered the night sky. Then a third.

Jeff Chambers dropped into the front seat from his hidey-hole in the sleeper compartment.

"Looks like Red's on the job. Proud the way you kept your cool back there."

"Hell, it was all I could do to keep from bashing the bastard's face. Reckon you better put on your seatbelt, be a bumpy ride from here on out. A man I suspect was John Wilkerson ran out of that farmhouse like the devil was on his tail. Bet he somehow knows we're up to something. They'll be on us damn quick."

CHAPTER 86

Lonnie Mason stepped through the front door of Red Meyers's shack. Dr. Stein, hunched over in a straight-back chair and reading the *Cat in the Hat* to his two rapt charges looked up in surprise. Two-year-old Lon, Jr. let out a squeal of delight.

"Daddy."

The cry died at the sight of a blood-stained machete grasped in his father's right hand. Fear flickered across that innocent face.

"Get over here, boy."

Dr. Stein rose to his feet. "Just a minute there."

"Fuck with me, old man, and you'll die. That brat's mother took off in the middle of the night, no note, no nothing. She didn't cut no big fat hog in the ass. Ain't no woman alive can get the best of me and ain't no woman can walk away with my son. I spotted the slut in town the other day in some car she knew I wouldn't recognize. Been keeping an eye on this place for a day or two now. Don't know what you all are up to, but seen a lot of cars drive off today. When them trucks pulled out, knew I had my chance. I've come for my boy."

Dr. Stein recognized the man had been contaminated by the flowers; corruption emanated from him like a pulsing black aura. He would no doubt prove harder to reason with than an LSD user in the throes of a full-blown psychotic episode. Any child in his hands would have little chance of survival—son or no son.

He had been ordered by both January and Cy to keep his .45 pistol within easy reach. Had he done that? Certainly not. Not with two curious children on hand. As soon as the others had vacated the house, he tucked the pistol out of sight behind canned goods stacked on the rickety shelf over the rusted-out kitchen sink. And now, literally, he would give his right leg for that pistol.

"You heard me, boy. Get over here."

Lon Jr. rose to his feet, his teary eyes pinned on the Doctor

Stein.

He reached out and halted the child. "No, you can't take him. Wait until his mother gets back and we'll work this thing out like adults. Won't be long."

"Wait for Phyllis?" Lonnie snorted. "Mister, you don't understand. I don't intend for that bitch to ever lay eyes on this kid again. She ain't no kind of mother. Boy's out of control. Time he learned some manners, and I'm the man to teach him."

In a try for intimidation, Dr. Stein stretched to his full height, back rigid, hands fisted and brow drawn in determination. "You'll have to go through me first."

Lonnie grinned and swept the machete in a whistling arc. "Ain't no problem for me, you stupid old fool." He advanced into the room.

Dr. Stein attempted to dodge the descending blade, but his old body could not muster the speed to avoid a blow. Instead of burying in his neck as aimed, the sharp blade sliced into his shoulder. He looked down in astonishment at blood pouring from the gaping wound.

"I warned you."

With a hand pressed to the cut, he sagged to his knees.

Jenni scurried toward the kitchen. Lon Jr. let out a wail and dropped to his butt.

And Dog? What a sight that forty pound mongrel made with teeth bared and a deep warning rumble issuing from his throat. As Lonnie raised the machete for a deathblow, Dog charged like an enraged pit bull. His teeth sank into the Lonnie's arm. The machete clattered to the floor.

KABOOM! The back of Lonnie Mason's head disappeared in a grisly shower of flesh and bone.

Jenni sat on the kitchen floor where the recoil of the .45 revolver had deposited her. With a quivering hand, she pointed at the dead man and stuttered. "He-he hurt you." She burst into tears.

"Jenni, sweetheart, you did right fine. You're a brave little girl. Saved my life."

She looked up, her face a mask of distress. *Are you sure I'm not in trouble?* her expression read.

His heart melted at such a dire look on so young a face. *Poor thing, what an awful burden for a child to carry—the taking of a life.* "What you did was good, Jenni. Your mother's going to be real proud of you. Everyone is."

Dog padded over to Jenni and began to lick away tears.

"See there, he knows you saved his life too."

This brought a tentative smile.

"Sweetie, I'm hurt, and there are some things I need you to do for me."

"What?"

"First, the gun. Bring it to me."

She gripped the handle with both hands, the nozzle pointing straight ahead.

"No, sweetheart, point it down and keep your fingers away from the trigger. Good girl. Now, stand up. Easy."

Jenni tossed him a perturbed look as if to say, *What's the big deal? I shot the bad guy all by myself, didn't I?*

"Walk over to me, real slow. Good girl."

A smirk told him that she had had enough of his encouragement, thank you very much. When she at last handed him the pistol, he dared to exhale trapped air from his lungs.

Lon Jr. wandered over and stared down at his father's body.

"Now take the sheet off Red's cot and cover Mr. Mason all the way to the top of his head."

With a nod, she rushed through the chore, and then took the toddler's hand. "Come on, I think Dog wants to play with you." Once she had him settled in the kitchen with the dog lapping at his face, she returned for further instructions.

"You are quite the clever young lady. Now, if you'll fetch my black bag, I need you to help doctor my shoulder."

Looking animated by the prospect of doing doctor work, she bounded off for the bag.

CHAPTER 87

With January riding shotgun, Atrell pulled the tanker up on Larkin's right. Partnered with Michael Rainwater, Doug Parcell maneuvered the unwieldy semi even with his companions. Following the path of flairs ignited by Penney, Pearl and Preacher Gladstone, they closed in on the field of red flowers like three avenging angels.

The six men were feeling jubilant about their progress when all hell broke loose. Larkin's windshield shattered, showering him and Jeff in fragments of glass. A bullet grazed Larkin's scalp leaving behind a crimson part every bit as straight as a barber's comb. As Jeff worked to remove a thick splinter of glass buried deep in his left forearm, a man with his face twisted in hate and an Uzi spitting fire, darted in front of the truck. They ducked as low as their seatbelts would allow, and Larkin increased the pressure on the accelerator. A hale of bullets shattered the remaining windows before the attacker was plowed under the massive wheels.

Jeff sucked in hard at the site of a Hummer mounted with an M60 machine gun closing in from the left. "Lean forward, Larkin, got to set my site from your window."

Leaning across Larkin's back, Jeff took aim through the scope of the AR15 rifle, targeting the forehead of the soldier manning the Hummer's machine gun. A rear truck tire exploded, and the semi veered close to the tanker.

"Shit," Jeff said, and pulled the trigger. His aim was off but deadly; the soldier fell backwards, his throat a bloody gaping hole. Another man took his place, jerking the pin from a hand grenade as he rose. Jeff fired. The bullet struck the man's throwing-hand. The grenade bounced to the floor. Under other circumstances the man's dismayed expression would have been comical. His mouth set in a perfect O, he jumped from the deathtrap a fraction too late. The blast lifted him in the air, tearing away both legs at the knees. He tumbled to earth in a crimson shower of blood. The driver arced several feet in the air as if being fired from a cannon, leaving behind his right arm and half his face.

The men in the tanker were not faring as well as Jeff and Larkin. A bullet had slammed into Atrell's right shoulder and January had lost all but the lobe of his left ear. Unmindful of the zings flying about the cab, January worked at stanching the heavy blood flow from Atrell's wound. Despite his plight, Atrell maintained the tanker even keel with the two semis.

Doug Parcell and Michael Rainwater had avoided the slightest scratch. Bullets pierced metal, imbedded in the dashboard, the ceiling and wide bench seat, but none found flesh and bone. Doug glanced in his side mirror. "Hold on," he said, and jerked the wheel to the right. A pursuing Jeep slammed into the side of the semi and spewed men in every direction as it tumbled end over end, trailing a dense plume of dust.

CHAPTER 88

Disheveled and blanketed in a sooty layer of grime from the dynamite blasts, Red looked as if black greasepaint had been applied over every inch of his body. He tromped through heavy woods guided by a weak flashlight glow that flickered and was near useless in displaying a passable walkway. After dark, he had slipped into the encampment and rummaged through a deserted lean-to, coming up with the piss-poor flashlight, two cans of Vienna Sausage, a package of saltine crackers, a bottle of water and a rusty .22 pistol—a Saturday night special. He suspected it would explode if fired.

With each stumble and pitfall, he cursed himself for not filching the six-pack of D-cell batteries that had been there for the taking.

Shouts and gunfire drew him toward the encampment. As he stepped from behind the large oak that had served as his toilet, his mouth dropped in disbelief. People rushed about in panic, some seeking cover while others fired with abandon at the invading trucks.

He cringed as a man clad in army fatigues, his face streaked red and black like a character from an action film, launched a rocket from some kind of pipe balanced on his shoulder. Red had no idea what the weapon might be, but was given a quick lesson. The shell exploded close enough to Doug Parcell's truck to contract Red's bowels into a tight ball. The semi swerved out of control, and when it finally regained stability, he felt like dropping to his knees and giving thanks to the Almighty for His mercy.

He watched in horror as the quasi-soldier loaded another shell, then knelt and positioned the pipe for a second firing. This time he knew the shot would be on target and the truck would go down. His heart thumping with the cadence of a snare drum solo, he charged the man. The surprised soldier tumbled backwards, and the shell detonated high in the sky like a Fourth of July spectacular. The soldier had youth on his side and was on his feet in seconds, a knife unsheathed and ready for the kill. A look of sadistic pleasure claimed the man's face.

Red knew he would not have a prayer of surviving hand-to-hand combat, and decided on a surprise tactic; like a forty-five-year-old virgin intent on defending her honor from a rapist, he drew back and kicked the man in the balls. The guy managed to get in a fair swipe, slicing a shallow, four-inch gap in his left arm before collapsing to the ground and sheltering his testicles.

Red was pissed, and not giving the barbarian a breath of time to recover, he pointed the .22 Saturday night special and fired. He intended to wound rather than kill, but the low-caliber bullet chose a straight path into the heart. The young man's wide-eyed look of disbelief would haunt Red until his dying day.

CHAPTER 89

Cy Weinberg slipped into the enemy camp. Like a fox in a henhouse, he moved from site to site, disabling shooters intent on incapacitating the trucks. He heard a ruthless utterance from a nearby tent: "Go ahead, bitch, scream all you want. Nobody gives a shit."

He recognized that voice. Oh yes, this was more than he had hoped for, a chance at College Boy.

Karl Hargrove drove an ice pick into Sandra Barnes's left breast, the sharp tip positioned at the center of an ugly cigarette burn, one of many marking her torso. Four-year-old Jason, as pale as a bleached sheet, huddled in a fetal-like ball within touching distance of his mother and her tormentor. "He's not real, only a nightmare. He's not real, only a nightmare," he chanted.

Engrossed in his sadistic work, Karl did not detect Cy slip into the private party. Sandra stared up at Cy in desperation, her mouth working in a hushed plea.

College Boy heard a soft whisper in his ear: "Hey, fellow, remember me?" He started so hard the ice pick flipped in the air and somersaulted twice before sticking in the dirt floor. Steely hands jerked him upright. A bare second before his neck snapped, he glimpsed the grinning face of the old Jew from the cemetery.

CHAPTER 90

Still abreast, the trucks plowed into the field. Both eighteen-wheelers buried axle-deep in soft earth. The tanker teetered left, then right, flirting with gravity for several seconds before toppling to its side with a loud whomp. Fuel bled from the ruptured tank like the toxic juices of a disemboweled dragon.

As the men emerged from the disabled vehicles, their luck ran out. A bullet tore into Doug Parcell's hip, dumping him in a moaning heap to the ground. Michael took bullets in his right calf and his abdomen. Atrell sacrificed his left pinkie to someone's stray shot. Jeff took a hit in the right kneecap, and Larkin Ballard toppled over with a head wound.

January was the only one immune to new injuries. He took a quick headcount and shook his head in amazement at finding all of them alive. "Crawl if you have to, but get the hell out of here. I'm fixing to turn this place into an inferno."

"No, Gran," Michael said. "I'll—"

"Listen, you bunch of turkey butts. I'm the only one here not seriously wounded, and I ain't lighting no fuse until I see some ass-ends making beelines out of here."

"Your fucking macho pride is going to get you killed," Michael said.

"Bullshit. In the name of humanity, I came here to do a job. You're about to fuck it up with that goddamned lip of yours. Now get out. ALL OF YOU!"

January had been the man with the visions, the first to recognize the evil, the original Chosen. And yes, he should be the man to strike the final blow.

"Okay, Gran, whatever you say." Certain this would be the last time he would ever see his grandfather alive, he hugged him. "I love you."

"Love you, too. Now, go."

Michael hauled Larkin Ballard to his feet, and with the man

heavy on his shoulder, staggered from the field and hobbled toward a copse of trees. Atrell and Doug, supporting Jeff between them, reeled into the open as if coming off of a three-day drunk.

January hunkered beneath the tanker for a long minute. Offering a prayer that the others had been given sufficient time to escape, Michael above all, he flicked a cheap plastic lighter. As sparks flowered from a fuse leading to a bundle of dynamite, he ran like a rabbit under the breath of a coyote.

Penney Sneider saw her husband dash into the field of flowers, Lauri not far behind, her legs pumping for all they were worth. "No, Lauri." With a flying leap she brought her to the ground.

"Daddy! Daddy!" Lauri shrieked, kicking and twisting.

John Wilkerson observed January barrel from the field, and brought his shotgun to his shoulder. He zeroed in on the moving target. "Say goodbye, you dirty Injun. For you, Ditcher."

The world exploded. Night became day. Flames flared hundreds of feet into the air. Fiery tentacles swept through the field of unholy flowers. Heavy, black smoke coiled from the inferno. The air echoed with the screams of victims being devoured by the greedy fire. Living torches, wailing in agony, erupted from the firestorm.

A deafening howl of rage, as people would later describe, shrilled from the conflagration.

The raging fire, consumed by its own intensity, lived but a short time.

People stopped in their tracks and looked about in confusion. Some were dismayed to find weapons in their hands, others appalled by their lack of clothes. Some wandered about, looking like shell shock victims.

Memories emerged.

Lauri Sneider pictured herself pressing a pillow hard, hard, hard to her sister's face. She threw her arms around her mother's neck and burst into tears.

Fred Zimmerman saw himself standing over Dr. Alan Payne and

working at a jaw tooth with a pair of pliers. He groaned.

An image of Ed lying dead on the bathroom floor with a flowery shower curtain draped across his body formed in Sandra Barnes head. Although she was filled with sadness that she had murdered him, she could not push away a nagging feeling of relief that he was gone.

Mark Farrell looked down in a grave at the coffin that contained his brother. He leaned over and vomited.

People wailed and lamented at the memories flowing through their heads. The most vivid of all recollections belonged to John Wilkerson; Myrtie lay on the floor, her hip twisted at an impossible angle, the blue dress that set off her eyes so well mired in garbage and blood. *You're a real tart Myrtie. Ain't never going to fool a man again.* Thick black pain welled in his chest. "Myrtie," he groaned, and slumped to the ground. His heart refused one more beat.

One last shot rang out. Jerky Jensen dropped to his knees and was dead before his head hit the ground. Larkin Ballard collapsed into unconsciousness with a smile on his face.

January lay on his back, John Wilkerson's bullet deep in his chest and leaching his life away. Michael knelt beside him.

"Did we do it, Michael?"

"Yes, Gran, we did. The field burned to the ground."

January smiled as his eyes closed and his head slumped to the side.

"Gran, no. Please don't leave me."

January could not hear his grandson's plea, he was flying through a tunnel of brilliant light. Ahead his beloved Catherine stood with her arms wide.

CHAPTER 91

Thelma Knoll slowed the car and eased to the shoulder. She flipped on the overhead light to have a better look at the red flowers resting on the seat beside her. No, it wasn't her imagination; the flowers were drying up. The blooms shriveled into crumbling, brown refuse.

"Damn. Never seen nothing like this before."

She lowered the window and tossed out the dead bouquet. Brushing minute particles from the seat she discovered two small red seeds, perfect orbs and warm to the touch. "Ain't never claimed to have a green thumb, but maybe I can make these babies grow."

She zipped the seeds into a side pocket of her purse and turned off the light. The car pulled back onto the roadway. "Look out Vegas, here comes Thelma."

Epilogue

Six months later

Jeff Chambers sat in his squad car on a bluff overlooking Caddo and mulling the appalling events that had befallen his town. With the same human spirit of any other American town recovering from a disaster, Caddo residents put the past behind them and went about rebuilding their lives. Eight people were still missing, and the final death count, including the untimely discovery of Homer Knoll's macabre remains, topped out at forty-eight. The largest number of bodies had been concentrated at the Wilkerson farm. A few Caddo citizens had been among the death toll, but the majority proved to be outsiders.

Stories concerning mind-controlling flowers surfaced from time to time, and possibly those tales might have been believed had the blooms been ingested or dried and smoked like marijuana. Unfortunately, no plants survived to be tested, and the stories were subsequently chalked up to mass hysteria. The ill-fated happenings had obviously been the work of a survival cult much like the ones that had given the federal government such headaches over the past several years. In the final analysis, the locals simply took matters into their own hands and wiped out the nest of armed radicals that had sprung up in their community. The theory proved out. The majority of outsiders who had taken root on that rural farm possessed felony records as long as the Texas coastline, everything from child-molestation to armed robbery to attempted murder. And of course, the use and sale of illegal drugs had topped nearly every conviction sheet. Once all the facts were in and sorted, the people of Caddo became the new unsung heroes of the American public. Yes sir, those with the grit to handle their own unsavory affairs without federal interference had to be admired.

Jeff missed January, the only Chosen killed during that ugly conflict. He stayed in close contact with the others and was saddened that some still faced long recuperation periods. His beloved friend, Dr. Stein, had lost the use of his right arm and retired. His affliction did not affect his ability to down a few scotches and kick Jeff's ass once a week at chess.

Dean Calder, his second in command, had not survived. Jeff sorely missed him, but young Doug Parcell was proving to be well worth his salt as Dean's successor. The criminal element continued to maintain a wide berth around Caddo.

The Sixteen-year-old run away, Thumb Riley, who for a time had been Jerky's main squeeze, had returned home to rebuild a relationship with her mother and stepfather. Jeff could not hold back a chuckle at the thought of the moniker she had hung on him. TP: Toad Pecker.

Tom Duncan was among the missing. Jeff had been surprised at his estate. The farm and a well-heeled bank account along with stocks and bonds had accumulated into a small fortune. His daughter had been set up as co-owner. Most speculated that he had perished in that terrible fire. After all, the man was well known for his fanaticism and radical views. It wouldn't have been beyond him to join that extremist group.

Even more surprising was the change in Naomi Duncan. She resigned from the church that had been her and Tom's affiliation for years. Jeff grinned. Not that those Bible thumpers would consider taking her back now that she wears makeup, formfitting clothes and gaudy jewelry. Turned into a real looker. She and Cliff Thorne married and are now traveling the world working hard to spend the money her skin-flint father left behind.

Pretty Penney Sneider. Now living in Houston close to her parent's home and attending the University of Houston where Michael Rainwater now teaches. The two of them deserve a break after the horror they suffered. Jeff expected to gear up for their wedding sometime in the near future. He glanced up at the sky. "A match made in heaven, wouldn't you say, January?"

Jeff's stomach growled. Maybe he'd wangle an invitation to join Cy Weinberg at Jeremy Ferrell's for a home cooked meal this evening. Yep, the food was always good and it'd be fun to watch Cy dote on his new namesake, Cy Joshua Ferrell.

Jeff was glad poor Millicent Forbes was declared mentally

incompetent to stand trial for murder. She appears content in her new surroundings at the mental institution. Most of her time is spent in conversations with her dead sister.

Ed Barnes and his classic Ford has not returned home. It was beyond Jeff how he could abandon that sweet wife and adorable little boy. But Sandra was doing well at a real estate agent and certainly didn't need a wife beater underfoot. Good riddance to bad rubbish.

The radio blared to life. "Chief, Doug Parcell here, ready for lunch?"

"Roger that. I'm starving. Meet you at Pearl's in fifteen minutes. Out."

Thelma Knoll would really have gotten a kick out of Caddo's theory concerning her disappearance. Henry Jackson, Vice President of the Westside Bank and Trust had given an ample description of the woman who emptied the Knoll's accounts. He admitted being suspicious at the time, but the woman did strikingly resemble Thelma and her signature matched. But now, considering all, he would swear in a court of law that the lady had been an imposter. Without a doubt, the Knolls had been victims of a sinister plot to rid of them of their money. Most likely, Thelma's remains lie in a shallow grave in some remote spot in East Texas.

Thelma, alias Kim Marie Moore, now lives in Las Vegas. She managed to parlay her fifty thousand dollars into more than seven hundred thousand at the gambling tables. A few nips and tucks by a plastic surgeon, an expensive wardrobe and a chic new hairdo in a striking blonde shade physically transformed her into a distinctly different woman—a Kim rather than a Thelma. Even her closest friends would be hard put to see any part of Thelma in the new woman.

Thelma-Kim was beginning to tire of the lights and tinsel of Vegas. Los Angeles, perhaps? New York City? Deep in thought, she fingered the locket containing two red seeds on a gold chain around her neck. After several long minutes, she absently murmured, "Boston, that's where I want to go. Boston."

Won't that snooty sister be surprised when the new and improved Thelma shows up on the doorstep of her big fine house? And those two spoiled brats, mustn't forget them. The twisted but nonetheless delightful thoughts racing through Thelma's head brought a smile to her face.

THANK YOU FOR READING

If you enjoyed this book by M.K.Sherlock. Please feel free to leave a review on Goodreads.com, your own Facebook, and Amazon.com Then, check out "Amy" available through Amazon, and Kindle.

A child is abducted from a day school and a learning disabled man is prosecuted for the abduction. Detective Darby Penner is certain that the man is not guilty and goes on a journey to find the perpetrator.

Stay in contact with M.K. Sherlock on Facebook at M.K.Sherlock or on Twitter @mksherlock.2 or mksherlock.com or you can email her at m.ksherlock@yahoo.com